5.1

THE UNTEACHABLES

ALSO BY GORDON KORMAN

THE UNTEACHABLES

GORDON KORMAN

BALZER + BRAY
An Imprint of HarperCollins*Publishers*

Library of Congress Control Number: 2018938414
ISBN 978-0-06-256388-0 (trade bdg.)
ISBN 978-0-06-256389-7 (lib. bdg.)

Typography by Erin Fitzsimmons
20 21 22   CG/LSCH   10 9 8 7
❖
First Edition

For all the teachers who soldier on

One

Kiana Roubini

I t's no fun riding to school with Stepmonster—not with Chauncey screaming his lungs out in the back seat.

Don't get me wrong. I'd cry too if I'd just figured out that Stepmonster is my mother. But at seven months old, I don't think he's processed that yet. He just cries. He cries when he's hungry; he cries when he's full; he cries when he's tired; he cries when he wakes up after a long nap. Basically, any day that ends in a *y*, Chauncey cries.

There also seems to be a connection between his volume control and the gas pedal of the SUV. The louder he howls, the faster Stepmonster drives.

"Who's a happy baby?" she coos over her shoulder into the back seat, where the rear-facing car seat is anchored. "Who's a happy big boy?"

"Not Chauncey, that's for sure," I tell her. "Hey— school zone. You better slow down."

She speeds up. "Motion is soothing to a baby."

Maybe so. But as we slalom up the driveway, swerving around parked parents dropping off their kids, and screech to a halt by the entrance, it turns out to be one motion too many. Chauncey throws up his breakfast. Suddenly, there's cereal on the ceiling and dripping down the windows. That's another thing about Chauncey. His stomach is a food expander. It goes in a teaspoon and comes out five gallons.

"Get out of the car!" Stepmonster orders frantically.

"You have to come in with me," I protest. "They won't let me register without an adult."

She looks frazzled, and I guess I don't blame her. That much baby puke must be hard to face. "I'll run home, change him, and wipe down the car. Wait for

2

me. Ten minutes—fifteen at the most."

What can I do? I haul my backpack out of the SUV, and she zooms off around the circular drive. I don't even have the chance to make my usual Parmesan cheese joke—that's what it smells like when Chauncey barfs. When I first came from California to stay with Dad and Stepmonster, I thought they ate a lot of Italian food. That was a disappointment—one of many.

So there I am in front of Greenwich Middle School, watching swarms of kids arriving for the first day of classes. A few of them glance in my direction, but not many. New girl; who cares? Actually, the new girl doesn't much care either. I'm a short-timer—I'm only in Greenwich for a couple of months while Mom is off in Utah shooting a movie. She's not a star or anything like that, but this could be her big break. After years of paying the bills with bit parts in sitcoms and TV commercials, she finally landed an independent film. Well, no way could I go with her for eight weeks— not that I was invited.

Eventually, a bell rings and the crowd melts into the school. No Stepmonster. I'm officially late, which isn't the best way to start my career in Greenwich. But short-timers don't stress over things like that.

Long before it could come back to haunt me on a report card, I'll be ancient history.

I check on my phone. It's been twenty minutes since "ten minutes—fifteen at the most." That's SST—Stepmonster Standard Time. I try calling, but she doesn't pick up. Maybe that means she's on her way and will be here any second.

But a lot of seconds tick by. No barf-encrusted SUV.

With a sigh, I sit myself down on the bench at student drop-off and prop my backpack up on the armrest beside me. Stepmonster—her real name is Louise—isn't all that monstrous when you think about it. She's way less out of touch than Dad, which might be because she's closer to my age than his. She isn't exactly thrilled with the idea of having an eighth grader dropped in her lap right when she's getting the hang of being a new mom. She's trying to be nice to me—she just isn't succeeding. Like when she strands me in front of a strange school when she's supposed to be here to get me registered.

The roar of an engine jolts me back to myself. For a second I think it must be her. But no—a rusty old pickup truck comes sailing up the roadway, going much faster than even Stepmonster would dare. As it reaches the bend in the circular drive, the front tire climbs the curb, and the pickup is coming right at me. Acting on instinct alone, I hurl myself over the back of the bench and out of the way.

The truck misses the bench by about a centimeter. The side mirror knocks my book bag off the armrest, sending it airborne. The contents—binders, papers, pencil case, gym shorts, sneakers, lunch—are scattered to the four winds, raining down on the pavement.

The pickup screeches to a halt. The driver jumps out and starts rushing after my fluttering stuff. As he runs, papers fly out of his shirt pocket, and he's chasing his own things, not just mine.

I join the hunt, and that's when I get my first look at the guy. He's a kid—like, around my age! "Why are you driving?" I gasp, still in shock from the near miss.

"I have a license," he replies, like it's the most normal thing in the world.

"No way!" I shoot back. "You're no older than I am!"

"I'm fourteen." He digs around in his front pocket and pulls out a laminated card. It's got a picture of his stupid face over the name Parker Elias. At the top it says: PROVISIONAL LICENSE.

"Provisional?" I ask.

"I'm allowed to drive for the family business," he explains.

"Which is what—a funeral parlor? You almost killed me."

"Our farm," he replies. "I take produce to the market. Plus, I take my grams to the senior center. She's super old and doesn't drive anymore."

I've never met a farmer before. There aren't a lot of them in LA. I knew Greenwich was kind of the boonies, but I never expected to be going to school with Old MacDonald.

He hands me my book bag with my stuff crammed in every which way. There's a gaping hole where the mirror blasted through the vinyl.

"I'm running late," he stammers. "Sorry about the backpack." He jumps in the pickup, wheels it into a parking space, and races into the building, studiously avoiding my glare.

Still no sign of Stepmonster on the horizon. I call again. Straight to voice mail.

I decide to tackle the school on my own. Maybe I can get a head start filling out forms or something.

The office is a madhouse. It's packed with kids who a) lost their schedules, b) don't understand their schedules, or c) are trying to get their schedules changed. When I tell the harassed secretary that I'm waiting for my parent and/or guardian so I can register, she just points to a chair and ignores me.

Even though I have nothing against Greenwich Middle School, I decide to hate it. Who can blame me? It's mostly Chauncey's fault, but let's not forget Parker McFarmer and his provisional license.

My phone pings. A text from Stepmonster: *Taking Chauncey to pediatrician. Do your best without me. Will get there ASAP.*

The secretary comes out from behind the counter and stands before me, frowning. "We don't use our phones in school. You'll have to turn that off and leave it in your locker."

"I don't have a locker," I tell her. "I just moved here. I have no idea where I'm supposed to be."

She plucks a paper from the sheaf sticking out of the hole in my backpack. "It's right here on your schedule."

"Schedule?" Where would I get a schedule? I don't even officially go to school here yet.

"You're supposed to be in room 117." She rattles off a complicated series of directions. "Now, off you go."

And off I go. I'm so frazzled that I'm halfway down the main hall before I glance at the paper that's supposed to be a schedule. It's a schedule, all right—just not mine.

At the top, it says: ELIAS, PARKER. GRADE: 8.

This is Parker McFarmer's schedule! It must have gotten mixed up with my papers when we were gathering up all my stuff.

I take three steps back in the direction of the office and freeze. I don't want to face that secretary again. There's no way she's going to register me without Stepmonster. And if there's a backlog at the pediatrician's, I'm going to be sitting in that dumb chair all day. No, thanks.

I weigh my options. It's only a fifteen-minute walk home. But home isn't really home, and I don't want to be there any more than I want to be here. If I went to all the trouble of waking up and getting ready for school, then school is where I might as well be.

My eyes return to Parker's schedule. Room 117. Okay, it's not *my* class, but it's *a* class. And really, who cares? It's not like I'm going to learn anything in the next two months—at least nothing I can't pick up when I get back to civilization. I'm a pretty good student. And when Stepmonster finally gets here, they can page me and send me to the right place—not that I'll learn anything there either. I've already learned the one lesson Greenwich Middle School has to teach me: fourteen-year-olds shouldn't drive.

That's when I learn lesson number two: this place is a maze. My school in LA is all outdoors—you step out of class and you're in glorious sunshine. You know where you're going next because you can see it across the quad. And the numbers make sense. Here, 109 is next to 111, but the room next to that is labeled STORAGE CLOSET E61-B2. Go figure.

I ask a couple of kids, who actually try to tell me that there's no such room as 117.

"There has to be," I tell the second guy. "I'm in it." I show him the schedule, careful to cover the name with my thumb.

"Wait." His brow furrows. "What's"—he points to the class description—"SCS-8?"

I blink. Instead of a normal schedule, where you go to a different class every period, this says Parker stays in room 117 all day. Not only that, but under SUBJECT, it repeats the code SCS-8 for every hour except LUNCH at 12:08.

"Oh, here it is." I skip to the bottom, where there's a key explaining what the codes mean. "SCS-8—Self-Contained Special Eighth-Grade Class."

He stares at me. "The *Unteachables*?"

"Unteachables?" I echo.

He reddens. "You know, like the Untouchables.

Only—uh"—babbling now—"these kids aren't un-touchable. They're—well—unteachable. Bye!" He rushes off down the hall.

And I just know. I could read it in his face, but I didn't even need that much information. Where would you stick a guy who could annihilate a back-pack with a half-ton pickup truck? The Unteachables are the dummy class. We have a couple of groups like that in my middle school in California too. We call them the Disoriented Express, but it's the same thing. Probably every school has that.

I almost march back to the office to complain when I remember I've got nothing to complain about. Nobody put *me* in the Unteachables—just Parker. From what I've seen, he's in the right place.

I picture myself, sitting in the office all day, waiting for Stepmonster to arrive. *If* she arrives. Chauncey's health scares—which happen roughly every eight minutes—stress her out to the point where she can't focus on anything else. To quote Dad, "Jeez, Louise." He really says that—an example of the sense of humor of the non-California branch of my family.

So I go to room 117—turns out, it's in the far corner of the school, over by the metal shop, the home and careers room, and the custodian's office. You have to walk past the gym, and the whole hallway smells like old sweat socks mixed with a faint barbecue scent. It's only temporary, I remind myself. And since my whole time in Greenwich is temporary anyway, it's more like temporary squared.

Besides—dummy class, Disoriented Express, Unteachables—so what? Okay, maybe they're not academic superstars, but they're just kids, no different from anybody else. Even Parker—he's a menace to society behind the wheel of that truck, but besides that he's a normal eighth grader, like the rest of us.

Seriously, how unteachable can these Unteachables be?

I push open the door and walk into room 117.

A plume of smoke is pouring out the single open window. It's coming from the fire roaring in the wastebasket in the center of the room. A handful of kids are gathered around it, toasting marshmallows skewered on the end of number two pencils. Parker is one of them, his own marshmallow blackened like a charcoal briquette.

An annoyed voice barks, "Hey, shut the door! You want to set off the smoke detector in the hall?"

Oh my God, I'm with the Unteachables.

Two

Mr. Kermit

The first day of school.

I remember the excitement. New students to teach. New minds to fill with knowledge. New futures to shape.

The key word is *remember*. That was thirty years ago. I was so young—not much older than the kids, really. Being a teacher was more than a job. It was a calling, a mission. True, mission: impossible, but I didn't know that back then. I wanted to be Teacher of the Year. I actually achieved that goal.

That was when the trouble started.

Anyway, I don't get excited by the first day anymore. The things that still get my fifty-five-year-old motor running are the smaller pleasures: the last tick of the clock before the three-thirty bell sounds; waking up in the morning and realizing it's Saturday; the glorious voice of the weather forecaster: *Due to the snowstorm, all schools are closed down . . .*

And the most beautiful word of all: *retirement*. The first day of school means it's only ten months away. My younger self never could have imagined I'd turn into the kind of teacher who'd be crunching numbers, manipulating formulas, and counting the nanoseconds until I can kiss the classroom and everybody in it goodbye. Yet here I am.

I sip from my super-large coffee mug. The other teachers call it the Toilet Bowl when they think I'm not listening. They gripe that I owe extra money to the faculty coffee fund because I drink more than my fair share. Tough. The students are bad enough, but the dunderheads who teach them are even worse. Colleagues—they don't know the meaning of the word. A fat lot of support they ever offered me when it was all going wrong.

"Mr. Kermit."

Dr. Thaddeus is standing over me in the faculty room, his three-thousand-dollar suit tailored just so. Superintendent. Major dictator. A legend in his own mind.

Christina Vargas, the principal, is with him. "Nice to see you, Zachary. How was your summer?"

"Hot," I tell her, but she keeps on smiling. She's one of the good ones, which puts me on my guard. Thaddeus uses her to do his dirty work. Something is coming. I can smell it.

"There's been a change in the schedule," the superintendent announces. "Christina will fill you in on the details."

"As you know, Mary Angeletto has left the district," the principal says. "So we're moving you into her spot with the Self-Contained Special Eighth-Grade Class."

I stare at her. "You mean the *Unteachables*?"

Dr. Thaddeus bristles. "We don't use that term."

"Every teacher in this building knows what they are," I fire back. "They're the kids you've given up on. They had their chance in sixth and seventh grade, and now you're just warehousing them until they can be the high school's problem."

"They're a challenging group," Christina concedes.

"Which is why we've chosen a teacher with a great deal of experience."

"Of course," the superintendent goes on pleasantly, "if you don't feel you're *up* to the job—"

Light dawns. So *that's* what this is really about. Thaddeus figured out that I qualify for early retirement after this year. He doesn't want the school district on the hook supporting me forever. The Kermit men live till ninety-five, minimum. My grandfather, at 106, is still president of the shuffleboard club at Shady Pines. That's why they're giving me the Unteachables. They aren't interested in my experience. They want my resignation.

I look the superintendent right in his snake eyes. "You're just trying to make me quit before I qualify for early retirement."

His response is all innocence. "You're up for retirement already? I think of you as so young. It still seems quite recent—that horrible Terranova incident. The media attention. The public outcry. The scandal."

Well, there it is. Jake Terranova. Thaddeus is never going to forgive and forget, even though it wasn't my fault. Or maybe it was. They were my students, after all, and it happened on my watch.

What a hypocrite. Thaddeus wasn't superintendent

then. He had Christina's job—principal. And did he ever take the credit when a class at his school scored number one in the country on the National Aptitude Test. He squeezed every ounce of glory out of that—interviews, profiles in magazines. When there was traffic in the driveway, you could bet it was because of a TV station mobile unit on its way to interview the high-exalted lord of all principals.

Until the truth came out. A kid named Jake Terranova had gotten hold of the test and charged his classmates ten bucks a pop for a copy of it. That's why they aced it—they were cheating. And when the whole thing blew up, was Thaddeus there to take the heat the way he'd taken the acclaim? Not on your life. The teacher was to blame. That's who I've been ever since. The guy who . . . The teacher whose class gave the entire Greenwich School District a black eye.

Officially, life went on after that. No one revoked my teaching certificate or docked my pay or kicked me out of the union. But everything was different. When I stepped into the faculty room, people stopped talking. Colleagues wouldn't look me in the eye. Administration kept changing my department. One year it was English, then math, French, social studies, even phys ed—me with my two left feet.

I went into a blue funk. Okay, that wasn't the school's fault, but it began to affect my personal life. My engagement to Fiona Bertelsman fell apart. That was on me. I was lost in my own misery.

Worst of all, the one thing that was most important to me—teaching—became a bad joke. The students didn't want to learn? Fine. I didn't particularly want to teach them. All I needed to do for my paycheck was show up.

Until next June, when early retirement would carry me away from all of this.

And now Thaddeus thinks he can make me throw that away too, just to avoid a year with the Unteachables. Obviously, the superintendent doesn't have the faintest idea who he's messing with. I would happily go into room 117 with a pack of angry wildcats before I'd give him the satisfaction of forcing me out.

I look from the superintendent to the principal and back to the superintendent again. "I enjoy a good challenge." I pick up the Toilet Bowl and walk out of there, careful to keep the big mug steady. Can't risk spilling coffee all over myself. It would spoil the dramatic exit.

Three decades in this school, and never once have I set foot inside room 117. I know where it is, though, from the stint in phys ed. Somebody has to be in the remotest classroom of the entire building, but I decide to be offended by it. It's just another part of the conspiracy to force me out.

Well, it won't work. After all, how bad can these Unteachables really be? Behavior issues, learning problems, juvenile delinquents? Does Thaddeus honestly think I've never crossed paths with students like that throughout thirty years in the classroom? Bad attitudes? The kid hasn't been born with an attitude that's half as bad as mine at this point. Face it, the Unteachables can only hurt you if you try to teach them. I gave up on teaching anybody anything decades ago. Since then, my relationship with my classes has been one of uncomfortable roommates. We don't much like each other, but everybody knows that if we just hold our noses and keep our mouths shut, we'll eventually get what we want. For me, that means early retirement. For the SCS-8 students, it means being promoted to ninth grade.

That part's a slam dunk, because surely the middle school is dying to get rid of them. What would they have to do to get held back—burn the whole place to the ground?

I walk into my new classroom.

A roaring fire in a wastebasket. Smoke pouring through the open windows. Kids toasting marshmallows on the end of pencils. Pencils catching fire. One pyromaniac-in-training seeing if he can get his eraser to burn. An escapee standing outside in the bushes, gazing in, eyes wide with fear. A boy draped over a desk, fast asleep, oblivious to it all.

Most kids would scramble to look innocent and be sitting up straight with their arms folded in front of them once the teacher puts in an appearance. Not this crew. If I came in with a platoon of ski marine paratroopers, it wouldn't make any more of an impression.

I stroll over to the flaming wastebasket and empty the giant cup of coffee onto the bonfire, which goes out with a sizzle. Silence falls in room 117.

"Good morning," I announce, surveying the room. "I'm your teacher, Mr. Kermit."

Only ten months until June.

Three

Parker Elias

I love the sound the pickup truck makes when the motor roars to life. It's even cooler now, with that little muffler problem, but that'll only last until Mom and Dad save up the money to get it fixed. Even without the extra noise, though, it's still awesome.

I look down at the start button:

That's what I saw the first time, anyway. Now I know that it really says:

ENGINE
START/STOP

That's what reading is for me. I *see* all the letters, but they're kind of a mishmash. Like my class at school, which is SCS-8, although it looks like SS8-C or S8-SC or even C-S8S. It messes me up at first a little until I figure out where I have to go, and then it doesn't matter what order the letters and numbers are in.

The pickup jounces over the packed dirt of the driveway before bumping onto the paved road where our property ends. Our farm is right outside town, so I haven't gone very far when a police car pulls up beside me. The cop gives me a thorough once-over with his eyes. I'm used to it. I'm kind of small for my age, so I look like a twelve-year-old out for a joyride. I thought that new girl's eyes would pop out of her head when I jumped down from the pickup on the first day of school. Or maybe that's the expression she gives everybody who knocks her book bag halfway to the moon.

Let's set the record straight: I'm fourteen. They

don't let you drive any younger than that no matter what your special situation is.

It's okay, though. The police around here all know me. The cop rolls down his window and peers into the flatbed of the pickup, taking note of several bushel baskets of fresh tomatoes.

"You're just taking those over to the farmers' market, right, Parker?" he calls.

"Right, Officer."

"And straight to school after that?"

I shake my head. "First I have to pick up Grams."

The cop frowns. "Grams?"

"My grandmother," I explain. "I have to take her to the senior center. Then school."

That's why I have a driver's license in eighth grade. It's a *provisional* license—although, to me, it usually looks more like RIVALSNOOPI ICELENS. I'm allowed to drive the pickup, so long as it's for farm business or for Grams, who's pretty old and sometimes kind of confused, no offense. My folks both work crazy hours on the farm, so I'm the only one who's free to pick her up at her apartment and take her to the center, where she hangs out all day. Then I drive to school, and after school, I pick her up and take her back to our house for dinner. She doesn't live with us, though. She refuses to give up her own place. "My independence," she calls it.

The law says I can do all this because running a farm is considered a "hardship." That's pretty stupid because we actually prefer living outside the city and having tons of open space when everybody else is stuck on a little postage stamp of grass. Plus, we don't have livestock, so we don't have to do any of the really gross farm things, like sticking your arm up the butt of a sick cow. (I've only seen that on TV, but—hard pass.)

I drop off the tomatoes at the market, watching the clock impatiently while Mr. Sardo weighs everything to the millionth of an ounce. Then straight to Grams. She's waiting for me in the lobby of her apartment building, but she's wearing a winter coat, and it's like eighty degrees out. So I have to park and we go upstairs to put away the coat, and by the time I return from the closet, she's in the kitchen, warming up leftover meatloaf for me.

"But Grams, I'm going to be late for school."

"Breakfast is the most important meal of the day, kiddo."

I used to like it when she called me kiddo—but now I'm pretty sure it's because she can't remember my name. It bums me out. To be fair, she called me kiddo before she forgot my name too. The difference is now it's the *only* thing she calls me.

"I already *had* breakfast," I tell her.

"You want mashed potatoes with that?" she asks. "It won't take long."

"No, thanks. This is fine."

Obviously, I eat the meatloaf. It's actually pretty good. Grams can still cook, even though she's forgotten most other things. She's been knitting me a sweater for the past three years that she can't seem to finish. I've gotten a lot bigger in that time, but it's okay, because so has the sweater. It's draped over the back of the couch, a mass of dropped stitches, hanging strands, and random colors. It looks like a giant psychedelic wool amoeba.

I gulp down the food as fast as I can, but it still throws off the schedule. By the time I drop Grams at the senior center, I can already hear the bell ringing at school. With my grandmother, there's always something to slow you down—if isn't meatloaf, then she's buttoned her blouse wrong, or she's wearing slippers instead of shoes, or she's waiting for Grandpa to come home, even though he died a long time ago. I'm used to being late—Grams is worth it. But it's my fourth time already, and it's only the first week of school.

I barrel around the streets, busting the speed limit by

a lot, and blowing at least one stop sign. I screech into the school parking lot, leaving a small mark on the side of Mr. Sarcassian's BMW. Not good. Carefully, I back out and find another spot, this one on the opposite side of the lot. I pull my trusty can of scratch guard out of the glove compartment and rub the evidence off my front bumper. Then I work on the Beemer a little. Not perfect, but it should keep Mr. S. from noticing the damage long enough for him to have absolutely no idea where it might have come from.

This is usually the part where my day starts to go downhill. I love getting to school—the driving and all that. But once I'm here—not so much. There's no problem with the building, and the teachers are okay, I guess. It just happens to be a place where I'm bad at everything that's considered important.

It's a long walk to room 117. I take it slow, because who wants to rush to somewhere you hate? I'm already late, though, so I open the door and walk inside.

Before I know it, my feet slide out from under me, and *wham!* I'm flat on my back on the floor.

It gets a big laugh and scattered applause from the six kids who are already there. The only person who doesn't react is our teacher, Mr. Kermit. He never lifts his face from the *New York Times* crossword puzzle, except occasionally to take a sip from a humongous coffee cup. And that's not just today. He's like that all the time. Yesterday, when Barnstorm chucked one of his crutches and shattered the globe, the teacher didn't so much as flinch, not even when the Horn of Africa bounced off the side of his head. You could probably set off an atomic bomb on his desk, and he'd never notice.

I scramble up. But when I turn back to the doorway to see what tripped me, I go down again, on my face this time. I can smell the floor, and taste it a little. There's butter all over it!

"Who greased the floor?" I howl.

The kids laugh louder—enough to penetrate the cone of silence and capture Mr. Kermit's attention. He glances up, sees me flopping like a fish out of water, and quickly goes back to his puzzle. If he's not the worst teacher in the world, he's definitely bottom five.

Most embarrassing of all, Kiana has to rescue me— she's the girl whose backpack I hit with the truck. She hauls me far enough from the buttered area that I can stand upright again. My shoes are still a little slippery, but at least I can walk to my desk.

Kiana turns to the rest of the class. "Who did that?"

Rahim, who's fast asleep, lifts his head off the desk and looks around like a deer in headlights. "Did what?"

"Let it go," I murmur, red-faced.

"Why should you?" she demands. "Somebody buttered the doorway. Mr. Kermit's not going to stand for that."

An absentminded "Mmmm" comes from the direction of the teacher's desk.

"Shhh!" I drag my broken body into my chair. Who's the mystery prankster who almost put me in intensive care? Plenty of possibilities in this class. Barnstorm, the injured sports star. He gets away with everything— at least he did until they put him in SCS-8. Aldo, the jerk who flies off the handle every time the wind blows. Elaine—I sneak a look over my shoulder at the scariest girl in the eighth grade. Oh, please don't let it be her. Elaine rhymes with pain.

I'll probably never find out who buttered the floor. If it was Elaine, I don't want to.

When I glance up, Mr. Kermit is standing in front of me. At first I'm flattered that he's come over to make sure I don't have a concussion. But no. He places a worksheet on my desk and wordlessly returns to his crossword puzzle.

That's what we do in the Special Self-Contained Eighth-Grade Class. At the beginning of each period, Mr. Kermit hands us each a worksheet. No one does them.

At least that's how it was at the beginning. There were a lot of paper airplanes sailing around the room for the first few days. I figured Mr. Kermit would get mad, but he never made a peep about them. So the airplanes stopped. What was the point of making them if you couldn't get a rise out of the teacher? Eventually, it got so boring that the only possible thing to do was the worksheet.

It's kind of hard for me, though, because the letters get all jumbled up. Even if it's math, they never just ask what's five plus three. They have to make it into a story about five brown rabbits and three white rabbits having a rabbit cotillion. That's where I get lost. *Cotillion* looks like *licit loon* to me.

I'm hunched over my paper, trying to make heads or tails of what seems to be unbreakable code, when, at the desk beside me, Kiana sets down her pen and peers at my paper, which is as untouched as the minute I got it.

"You haven't started yet?" she hisses.

"Sure I have," I reply defensively.

She isn't sold. "What question are you on?"

"One," I shoot back. "I'm taking it slow, okay?" I return to work, staring at the letters, willing them to arrange themselves into a form that makes sense to me.

I guess I look like a scientist peering into a microscope, because she blurts, "You can't read!"

"Yes I can!" I say defensively. "I'm just—pacing myself."

She reaches over and plants a finger on question one. "What does that say?"

"There's no talking in class," I tell her. "You want to get us in trouble?"

Mr. Kermit takes a long, loud slurp of his giant coffee.

"Read it!" she orders.

And I don't. It's not that I can't. But it would take time. "I don't feel like it," I mumble.

"Parker," she urges, "this is stupid. You can get help with this. You just have to tell the teacher. But nobody can help you if they don't know there's a problem!"

My eyes find Mr. Kermit. His attention never wavers from his crossword puzzle, even though Rahim and Barnstorm are sword fighting with rulers, and Aldo leaves the room altogether. If I have to depend on Mr. Kermit for help, I'm going to be older than he is before I get any.

Four

Aldo Braff

The first time I saw Kiana, I knew she was going to be a pain in my neck.

It was the first day of school—the marshmallow roast. She was the new girl, so I was nice. I took a pencil, speared a marshmallow, and made room for her around the fire. Talk about rude! She refused to take it because it was "unsanitary."

That's the last time I try to be a gentleman.

You know those bossy types who think they know everything? That's Kiana. One time I'm in the cafeteria when she comes up to me and tells me to stop kicking the candy machine.

If I'm kicking the candy machine, I'm doing it for a very good reason! Who put her in charge of the world?

She grabs my arm and hauls me away from the machine. "What's wrong?"

"I wanted a Zagnut!" I tell her in fury. "It gave me a Mounds!"

"So?"

Man, she really isn't from around here. At Greenwich Middle School, everybody knows two things about me: 1) when I want something, nothing stands in my way, and 2) I don't like coconut.

I look around. There's dead silence in the cafeteria, but nobody's eyes are on me. They know better than to get between me and a Zagnut bar. All except Kiana. Maybe all Californians are like that. They can't mind their own business.

She asks, "And if you keep on kicking it, will the Zagnut come out?"

"Maybe," I say stubbornly.

She shrugs. "Then go ahead."

But here's the thing: I don't want to kick it anymore. She's ruined it for me!

The worst part is, she's in SCS-8, so I can never get away from her. We spend the whole day in room 117, except for lunch in the cafeteria and phys ed, which is in the gym with a couple of other classes. The only surefire place to avoid her is the boys' room. She hasn't followed me in there. So far.

Our teacher, Mr. Kermit, is probably in his fifties, but he looks about nine hundred. Actually, he looks like he's dead already, hunched over his desk, his eyes half-closed. He never moves a muscle. It's hard to tell if he's even breathing. I'm amazed he isn't swinging from the light fixture, for all the coffee the guy drinks. Mostly, he's working on a really complicated crossword puzzle. He hates my guts—at least I think he does. All the teachers in this dump have it out for me, so why should he be any different?

He's dumb too. He doesn't even realize that we all call him Ribbit. There's this nut job in our class, Mateo Hendrickson—he pointed out that the only Kermit he ever heard of was Kermit the Frog. Turns out Mateo's a fan of the Muppets, not just *Star Trek*,

Star Wars, *Harry Potter*, *Halo*, and every comic book ever printed.

Anyway, a nickname was born. Every morning when the teacher walks in, late as usual, we start ribbiting.

"Ribbit . . . Ribbit . . . Ribbit . . ."

Mr. Kermit doesn't even notice. Either that or he thinks it's a compliment.

As a teacher, he stinks—not that I've had any good ones. He never gives lessons. In fact, he hardly ever speaks out loud. He just passes around these stupid worksheets all day long. Boring doesn't even begin to describe it.

With a normal teacher, if you don't do the work, you get in trouble. Not Ribbit. He acts like he couldn't care less if we do his worksheets or not.

"I've turned in every assignment and he's never graded a single one or handed it back," Kiana complains. "What's he doing with them?"

"Maybe he's eating them," I suggest. "He's weird enough."

She rolls her eyes at me.

She's annoying, but it's not like the other kids in SCS-8 are any better. There's Parker Elias, who has to be the dumbest person in the whole school. Remember the kid in first grade who, when he got picked to read aloud, everybody else wanted to drink bleach? Well, Parker still reads that way today—one word at a time, at the speed of molasses, sounding out every letter. This is the idiot they give a special driver's license to. No one is safe.

There's Barnstorm Anderson, super jock. Super jerk would be more like it, but I guess he's both. He's an unstoppable running back, an amazing point guard, and a lights-out pitcher, which is why the school gives him an automatic get-out-of-jail-free card. That makes me mad—why should scoring touchdowns mean you get special treatment? But here's the thing: last spring, Barnstorm blew out his knee. He's on crutches now, banned from sports for a whole year, and by that time, he won't be in middle school anymore. So all the teachers have suddenly started to notice that the last time he turned in a homework assignment was never.

That's the kind of person who lands in our class. Like Elaine Ostrover, who sits in the back row. She has to be six foot two and is solid as an oak tree. She hardly ever opens her mouth, but when she does, her voice comes out a low rumble, like a subwoofer.

Kiana asks me about her.

"That's Elaine," I reply. "Rhymes with pain."

She frowns. "Everybody says that—'rhymes with pain.' What does it mean?"

"You don't want to mess with Elaine," I advise her seriously. "Last year she head-butted this kid down the stairs because he was looking at her funny. Wiped out, like, fifteen people. The line outside the nurse's office stretched halfway to the cafeteria. If that's not pain, I don't know what is."

Kiana checks out Elaine's head, which looks like one of those giant statues on that island from the cover of our world geography textbook.

"She has to register her head as a deadly weapon with the FBI," I put in.

Kiana skewers me with a sharp glance, so I say, "Well, not really. But she definitely tore the door off one of the bathroom stalls and used it to crush the laminating machine." I add, "I mean, I wasn't *there*, but everybody knows it."

"You're scared of her," Kiana decides.

"I'm not scared! I can handle Elaine—rhymes with pain." If you don't say the full name, it increases your chances of being the next victim. "I just—don't want to get in trouble for fighting, that's all."

She nods. "Because you're the big expert at not getting in trouble."

By the time I realize that I'm mad at her for saying that, she's on the other side of the room, and the chance to yell at her is lost forever.

Rahim Barclay is supposed to be this amazing artist, although all I've ever seen him do is doodle. I guess his doodles are pretty good, if you're into that kind of thing. He drew one of Ribbit that's a dead ringer for our teacher—the sunken cheeks and dark circles around the eyes. Just the right amount of gray in the thinning hair. Rahim blew one part of it—he drew the coffee mug too big, almost the size of a trash barrel. Maybe that's how he ended up in SCS-8, which isn't exactly for geniuses. It doesn't help that Rahim's stepdad is in a rock band. They practice all night, so Rahim sleeps most of the day.

One day Mateo welcomes me to class with a whole story in this deep, throat-clearing gibberish that sounds a lot like he's trying to spit out a bug he swallowed by mistake.

I don't appreciate being messed with—especially when I'm not even sure *how* I'm being messed with. "What did you say?" I demand.

"It's a Klingon greeting!" Mateo explains cheerfully. "It means, 'May you die well.'"

My eyes widen. "You want me to *die?*"

"The Klingons are a warlike race!" Mateo says quickly. "Dying in battle is an honor. They love that!"

"But I don't! From now on, if you've got anything to say to me, say it in English, not some phony language—"

"Klingon is *not* phony!" Mateo cuts me off, outraged. "It may have started out on *Star Trek*, but it's turned into a legitimate language with a dictionary and an alphabet. There are even regional accents, depending on which part of the Klingon home world you come from. In the south, for example . . ."

He keeps talking—*lecturing*—clueless that my blood is boiling. And the other kids are *laughing!* Like it's a big joke that this little creep is making fun of me!

"What's the matter with you?" I shout at them. "Doesn't anybody have my back?"

Kiana steps forward, struggling to keep a straight face. She reaches for my arm. "Aldo—"

It's the last straw—that this California girl, who isn't even from around here, thinks I'm the entertainment.

A soupy fog swirls around my head, tinged with orange, until I can actually feel the heat from it. I've got to get out of here before I explode, leaving bone fragments and bits of skin all over the walls of room 117.

"I hate this class!" I pick up my backpack and hurl it through the open door—just as Mr. Kermit walks into the room. The heavy bag misses his head by about a quarter of an inch. At that point, I'm so mad I don't even care. In my white-hot haze, it would make no difference to me if the backpack knocks the teacher's block off and I get suspended, expelled, and banished from the town. I do notice, through my rage, that Ribbit doesn't flinch—not even when I storm past him, slamming the door behind me hard enough to raise the school off its foundation.

And just like that, I'm alone in the hall, barely sure how I even got there. I slam my fist into a locker. It hurts, but I hope it hurts the locker even more. The locker is attached to the wall, and the wall is part of the school. And it's the school's fault that I'm so mad. I hit it a few more times—with an open hand, because that hurts a bit less. I don't feel better, exactly. It's more like every blow lets off a little more steam, so the pressure inside my head goes down. I'm still ticked off, but I can live with it. I slump against the lockers, breathing hard.

The guidance counselors say I have anger management problems. They don't know what they're talking about. I manage to get angry better than anybody else in the whole school. No problem.

The door of room 115 opens and this lady walks up to me. At first, I think she could be another eighth grader—that's how young she looks. But no, she's definitely an adult. And the way she takes hold of my wrist—gentle but with authority—screams *teacher*. I've never seen her before, so she must be new.

"Come with me." She knocks on the door of SCS-8. "Mr. Kermit?"

I shoulder my backpack and stand behind her. We wait at the door, but there's no answer.

"He's probably in the middle of a puzzle," I offer in a subdued voice.

"Puzzle?" she echoes.

"Like a crossword. Ribbit—uh, Mr. Kermit—is really into them."

She knocks again and then opens the door. It sticks a little, and she has to put her shoulder into it. I guess I slammed it really hard. She leads me inside. Kiana is looking right at me. I feel myself starting to get mad again, but only for a second. It doesn't usually happen twice in a row.

"Mr. Kermit, I'm Emma Fountain," the woman introduces herself. "I have the class next door."

So far this year, not a single thing has gotten a reaction out of Ribbit. That streak ends here. The puzzle forgotten, he rises to his feet really slowly, never taking his eyes off her. They're practically bugging out of his head!

He blurts, "I'd know you anywhere!"

She smiles, which makes her seem even younger. "Mom said to tell you hi. But that's not why I'm here." She indicates me. "Is this your student?"

Mr. Kermit looks blank. It hits me—he doesn't have a clue, even though I nearly took his head off with my backpack ninety seconds ago! My own teacher doesn't know me from Jack the Ripper.

"Of course it's your student!" Kiana pipes up. "It's Aldo!"

"Well, he's making a lot of noise in the hall," Miss Fountain announces. "That's not being a bucket-filler."

Mr. Kermit goggles. "A what?"

"A bucket-filler is someone loving and caring, who fills other people's invisible buckets with good wishes and positive reinforcement that make them feel special." She regards Aldo disapprovingly.

40

"Someone who creates a disturbance and makes it impossible for other children to learn is not a bucket-filler. That's a bucket-*dipper*."

Suddenly, I realize what she's talking about. It's from this picture book that's supposed to teach little kids to be nice to each other. It's really big—in about first grade.

"It's an elementary school thing, Mr. Kermit," Kiana supplies helpfully.

"Just because this is middle school doesn't mean we shouldn't treat one another with *respect*," Miss Fountain says earnestly. "It worked for my kindergarten class last year, and we should have higher expectations for children who are even older. Right, Mr. Kermit?"

I wait for our teacher to give her the brush-off. Good old Ribbit could brush off World War Three. But for some reason, he doesn't. With great effort, he tears his eyes off her and swivels to me. "Were you—*dipping*?"

I stare at my sneakers. "I guess."

Mr. Kermit turns back to Miss Fountain. "You look just like your mother."

She smiles. "I'll take that as a compliment." To me, she says, "You should apologize to your classmates too. You wasted their learning time as well as your own."

"Sorry," I mumble. "You know—about the learning time."

"Relax," Rahim drawls. "Who learns?"

"Thank you, Mr. Kermit," Miss Fountain says uncertainly. "I'll give my mother your regards." She backs out of the room, shutting the door quietly behind her.

"Weird lady," Barnstorm puts in, waving a crutch dismissively. "All that bucket-filler stuff. Like we're six years old."

"Hey!" Mr. Kermit shoots him a sharp glance. "Miss Fountain is not 'weird.' She's a teacher."

"Can't she be both?" Rahim wonders out loud.

Kiana won't let it drop. She's not just bossy; she's nosy too. And the combination makes her like a bloodhound. "What gives, Mr. Kermit? What's the deal with you and Miss Fountain?"

For the first time all year, he actually looks annoyed. "Did I or did I not distribute worksheets?"

A paper airplane does a loop-the-loop in front of him. There's a chorus of *ribbits*, including one from Elaine that sounds like it came from the underworld.

Parker chimes in. "Face it, Mr. K. You've barely looked away from your puzzles since school started. But the minute she shows up, you hit the ceiling."

"She's your kryptonite," Mateo puts in.

Kiana snaps her fingers. "It's her mom, right? You and Miss Fountain's mother used to be a thing."

Mr. Kermit, who couldn't even be riled by a roaring bonfire in his wastebasket, picks up his crossword puzzle, rips it into a million pieces, stomps on them, and stalks out.

Even though I can't stand the guy, at that moment, I actually relate to him a little bit. He may be the worst teacher in the world, but we have something in common.

He has anger management problems too.

Five

Mr. Kermit

Emma Fountain! I can scarcely believe it. Of all the classrooms in all the schools, she has to walk into mine!

She's a time machine—that's what she is. The spitting image of her mother. It brings back memories I thought were buried forever.

I can still see the engagement notice in the newspaper—Fiona Bertelsman and Zachary Kermit, the photo of the happy couple cheek to cheek, eyebrows perfectly aligned. Smiling like nothing was ever going to come and rain on our parade. How innocent we were then. How blind. How foolish.

It was all over in a heartbeat. The test. The scandal. The breakup. Since then, I've only seen smiles like that twice: seven months later, when Fiona lined her eyebrows up with Gil Fountain in the engagement notices; and today, when their daughter, Emma, stepped through the doorway of room 117.

Fate has a way of sticking it to you twice, resurfacing like a bad burrito. This morning was my second shot. Every day draws me twenty-four hours closer to early retirement, but the last lap isn't going to be a cakewalk. First Thaddeus and the Unteachables, and now Fiona's clone in the room next door—a living, breathing, bucket-filling reminder of the life I missed out on.

If that poor kid tries to teach middle schoolers the way she ran her kindergarten classes, her students will have her throat open by Columbus Day. I should sit her down and explain a few things, but that would mean I *care*. Caring is where the trouble starts—hard experience taught me that. I didn't make it to the cusp of early retirement by caring. I made it by keeping my head down, regardless of whether they give me honor students or Unteachables or the zombie apocalypse. All I have to do is *endure*.

There are small satisfactions. The hiss of the air-controlled closing of the school entrance behind me as I exit the building. The crunch of my shoes on the bad pavement of the parking lot. The stab of pain in my sore shoulder as I open the ill-fitting door of my 1992 Chrysler Concorde—the one Fiona and I bought to start our new life together. Sky blue, although now it's mostly rust. I don't know why I've kept it so long. For sure it isn't the money. The repair bills alone would have bought me a Lamborghini.

I turn the key in the ignition, and the motor coughs and dies. A few minutes later, the hood is open, and I'm staring in at who knows what. Suddenly, there's a screech of tires and a pickup truck is reversing across the parking lot at top speed, hurtling toward me. My one thought is that, if I'm crushed to death here and now, Dr. Thaddeus and the school district won't ever have to pay for my early retirement.

The pickup roars to a stop with its rear bumper six inches from my legs.

Eyes blazing, I shout, "Are you crazy—?"

The door opens and the driver gets out. I blink. It's one of my *students*! I know the Unteachables are a rough crowd, but I never expected one of them to steal a truck and use it to try to kill me!

"Sorry, the gas pedal sometimes sticks a little." When my shocked expression doesn't fade, the kid adds, "It's me—Parker from class. What can I do to help?"

"To start with," I rasp, "you can stop reversing at ninety miles an hour. Why is a middle schooler driving at all?"

As he launches into a whole story about his grandmother, the family farm, and a provisional license, I conjure up a picture of him in a front-row desk, examining worksheets from point-blank range like he's staring through a jeweler's eyepiece.

"Wow, that's a pretty old car," he tells me. "I mean, *mine's* old, but yours is like—classic." He squints at the name in raised chrome letters. "It's a—Coco Nerd."

"Concorde," I correct impatiently. Didn't anyone ever teach this boy to read? "Never mind that. Any idea how I can get it started up again?"

Give Parker credit—he's better with cars than he is with words. He tinkers around under the hood, and pretty soon the motor is running again, although it's belching gray smoke all over the parking lot.

"Stop it!"

A silver Prius pulls alongside. The window is open,

and through the billowing clouds, we can just make out Miss Emma Fountain.

"Turn it off! Turn it off!"

Parker rushes behind the wheel and kills the engine.

She gets out of the Prius, waving her arms to clear the air. "Do you have any idea how much carbon is in that smoke?"

"Mrs. Vardalos is the chemistry teacher," I reply, deliberately misunderstanding the point she's trying to make. "I'm in charge of—well, you know which class I'm in charge of." I indicate Parker with a slight nod.

"I'm bucket-filling," Parker tells her proudly. "You know, helping Mr. Ribbit—I mean Kermit—"

"Mr. Kermit," she asks, "how *old* is this car?"

"Your mother picked it out," I inform her with an oddly defiant smile.

Her eyes widen. "Oh, wow, that's old. It's just that people didn't understand emissions back then. It was before everyone started putting the environment first— recycling, composting, installing solar panels . . ."

A long speech forms in my mind—about how this is a free country, and it's none of her business what anybody drives, or how old it is, or what it spews into the atmosphere. But for some reason I can't say it. Not to *her*; not to that face that looks so much like Fiona's.

She softens. "Well, maybe you can keep it. But you definitely have to put in a catalytic converter."

"It's on my list," I assure her. "Right after a new floor for the back seat, just in case I ever have passengers."

Parker peers into the back. "Whoa, is that the *ground*?"

"Air-conditioning," I supply, tight-lipped. "Old-school."

Emma regards me with pity.

On the plus side, she and Parker manage to get the motor running again—minus the smoke this time.

"Wow, Miss Fountain," Parker raves. "You're really good with cars."

"I learned from my mom," she explains. "She took a course in auto mechanics because she bought a real lemon once and . . ." Her voice trails off as she frowns at the old Concorde, connecting the dots.

I swallow what's left of my pride. "Thanks for your help." I'm positive that her first act after getting home will be to call her mother and say, *Ma—guess what? He's still got that car. . . .*

The calendar appears in my mind, that magical date in June circled in gold Sharpie.

Only 172 more school days to go.

Six

Mateo Hendrickson

When I get really bored—which is every day—I match people I know with characters from TV and movies. For example, my sister Lauren is like Venom from *Spider-Man* because she's evil and she spits poison. Well, not literally, but since I invented the classification system, I get to choose who's what. Just don't tell my mom, because she's like Professor McGonagall from *Harry Potter*. Smart and usually fair, but she can be nasty when something ticks her off—like me comparing Lauren to a *Spider-Man* villain.

It works for the kids at school too. Parker is like Lightning McQueen because he's the only kid who drives. Barnstorm is the Flash since he was such a great athlete before he wound up on crutches. Rahim is a little tricky, but I think of him as Birdman, because he has really big ears that could easily expand to wings if he gets bitten by a radioactive canary. Crazy, I know, but in comics, that kind of thing happens all the time. Anyway, I can always switch him to Sleeping Beauty. He's not that beautiful, but he is that sleeping.

Elaine is a cross between Chewbacca from *Star Wars* and Lois Lane, who also rhymes with pain. I try not to get too close to her. She once picked a kid up by the belt and used his head to poke at a fluorescent light that was buzzing.

Kiana is Blonde Phantom, since they're both from California, even though Kiana's hair is closer to light brown. And Aldo? That's easy. Dr. Bruce Banner, who turns into the Incredible Hulk when he gets mad.

As for me, I'm part hobbit and part Vulcan—Bilbo and Spock. Big logic in a small package.

That leaves just our teacher, Mr. Kermit. He's tough to characterize. I'm leaning toward Squidward because when he comes to class in the morning, he reminds me of Squidward coming to work at the Krusty Krab—bored and bummed out. And he treats us the way Squidward treats the customers. He doesn't hate us exactly, but he definitely wishes we were someplace else. He's even a little grumpier than Squidward because he doesn't have a hobby like playing the clarinet—unless you count crossword puzzles and consuming mass quantities of coffee.

For someone who's supposed to be a teacher, he sure doesn't do too much teaching. He mostly just hands out worksheets. The only time he talks is when somebody asks a question. That usually ends up being me.

"Mr. Kermit, why do the magnetic poles reverse?"

With effort, the teacher tears his attention away from his puzzle. "Excuse me?"

"Every two hundred and fifty thousand years, Earth's magnetic poles reverse," I explain. "I was just wondering why that happens."

"Yes, but what does it have to do with"—reluctantly, he glances from his *New York Times* to the worksheet on his desk beside it—"using vocabulary words in a sentence?"

"I want to do a sentence on Magneto," I reason. "But since his superpower is magnetism and electric charge, he'd be affected by that."

That's another thing about Mr. Kermit. He isn't very helpful when one of his students is curious about something.

The only other time there are questions is when Parker is trying to figure out what a word is. That turns into kind of a game in SCS-8—figuring out what he means by *tramgulley* when the word is really *metallurgy*. Sometimes the whole class gets in on guessing. It's the only fun we have during school. It can get pretty loud when people start laughing at Parker. Mr. Kermit's usually okay with it, unless Miss Fountain comes over to complain that we're disturbing her class. Then he chews us out. He doesn't get mad at us, but he can't stand it when *she* does.

This one time, Barnstorm makes a big stink, pounding his desk with both crutches, because the football team is holding its first pep rally and he isn't going to be up there with the players. "It's not fair, man!" he roars. "Just because I'm injured doesn't mean I'm not a Golden Eagle!"

Mr. Kermit's curiosity is suddenly piqued. "If you were in the pep rally, you'd have to leave now, right? You'd be somewhere else for the rest of the day?"

Barnstorm nods. "The team gets the whole afternoon

off to prepare for it, and I'm stuck here working."

That might be pushing it a little. I've seldom seen Barnstorm pick up a pencil.

"That sounds reasonable to me," Mr. Kermit agrees. "It isn't your fault you got injured. Why should you have to suffer for it?"

I get the feeling that Mr. Kermit doesn't care that much about justice for Barnstorm. What he really wants is to get this disturber of the peace out of room 117 before he puts one of those crutches through a wall. Miss Fountain would definitely notice that.

So he goes on the intercom and demands to have Barnstorm included in the rally. He argues his way through three secretaries and the assistant principal, and he won't take no for an answer. We're blown away. It's a whole new side to our teacher none of us has seen before. He's actually fighting for one of us, when we would have bet money that he barely even noticed we were here.

"Put me through to Coach Slattery," Mr. Kermit insists.

"He's in class right now" comes the reply from the speaker.

"Well, get him *out* of class," our teacher retorts. "Justice and fairness aren't just part of the social studies curriculum, you know. They're the building blocks of our entire society."

No one is more amazed than Barnstorm himself. "That's what I'm talking about," he approves in a satisfied tone.

By the time Mr. Kermit gets on with the athletic office, he's really worked up. "You ought to be ashamed of yourself!" he accuses Coach Slattery. "You send these kids out there to be tackled and elbowed and hit with hockey sticks. And when they get injured, you abandon them?"

When the coach finally breaks down and says, "Okay, whatever. Send him down," our whole class breaks into applause.

"You were awesome, Mr. Kermit!" Kiana exclaims.

"You should be in the Justice League," I add.

He looks startled, as if he didn't realize anybody was listening. He turns to Barnstorm. "Well, off you go. Enjoy your . . ." His voice trails off.

"Pep rally," I supply helpfully.

Barnstorm is already thump-swinging toward the door. "Thanks, Mr. Kermit."

Throughout the afternoon, our teacher keeps looking at Barnstorm's empty desk and smiling—another first for him. And at the end of the day, when we're called down to the pep rally, he smiles all the way to the auditorium—even though our class is always terrible marching through the hallways. Aldo karate-kicks lockers, and Rahim stakes out a water fountain so he can spray people. This seventh grader gives Elaine a hard time about blocking the stairs but only till he realizes who he's talking to. Better to be blocked on the stairs than to take a one-way trip down them or to have a classroom door slammed on your head or any of the other things Elaine does to people who annoy her. The kid apologizes and gets out of there so fast that he slams into Parker, and they both end up blocking the stairs for real.

Not even that spoils Mr. Kermit's mood. It's a problem. He's much too happy to be Squidward now.

Until we reach the auditorium. We're standing there waiting for our turn to file in when an earsplitting honk goes off right behind us. Mr. Kermit practically hits the ceiling. He wheels around to see this kid with a bright green vuvuzela—one of those noisemakers that look like a long plastic trumpet. They're kind of a tradition for Golden Eagle sports, because one of our school board members is from South Africa, where they were invented.

Without a word, Mr. Kermit snatches the thing out

of the kid's hand, throws it to the floor, and stomps it flat.

The boy looks up at him, lip quivering. "But it's a pep rally."

"Who says pep can't be quiet?" The teacher's furious eyes fix on a girl, who's holding a purple one. "Don't even think about it."

Nervously, she whisks the instrument behind her back.

Mr. Kermit nods. "That's the spirit."

Problem solved; he's Squidward again. When it comes to vuvuzelas, he might even be Lex Luthor.

At the pep rally, they make us sit in the back, just in case we have to be kicked out. Our class always sits in the back, even in the cafeteria. The teachers don't want us anywhere near the soda machine. They think giving us sugar is like sprinkling water on the Gremlins.

I cheer when Barnstorm is introduced. I've never known anybody on a team before. He waves a crutch in our direction, and a few of the other kids clap too.

Then Rahim falls asleep. His head slumps over and conks the girl sitting next to him.

We get kicked out.

Seven

Kiana Roubini

'm still in SCS-8.

Well, technically I'm in nothing, since I never officially enrolled in school. Back on the first day, Chauncey turned out to have stomach flu. That's why he barfed—like there needs to be a reason for him to paint the town. So Stepmonster never showed up to register me.

That night, eating takeout pizza for dinner, while feeding Chauncey medicine out of an eyedropper, she asked me, "Kiana, did you get everything straight-ened out with the office?"

"Jeez, Louise!" my father exclaimed. "You were supposed to take care of that."

"Chauncey got sick—" she began defensively.

"It's okay," I interrupted. "It's all taken care of."

I'm still not sure why I said that. Nothing is taken care of. There's no such student as Kiana Roubini at Greenwich Middle School. If I had any teacher besides Mr. Kermit, I would have been busted on day one.

What's more, I'm in the Unteachables. Oh, sure, they call it the Self-Contained Special yada, yada, yada. But that's just code for burnouts, nitwits, rejects, and behavior problems. Plus one displaced Californian.

It goes without saying that I don't belong. I've kind of boxed myself into a corner, though. It wouldn't be hard to switch out, since I was never really switched in. But then I'd need Stepmonster to register me for real. *And* I'd have to explain what I've been doing for the past two weeks.

It's not worth it. I'm a short-timer anyway. I never changed my address from Los Angeles, so no one will ever find out there's a girl living here who isn't enrolled in school. And believe me, Mr. Kermit isn't going to notice he's got an extra kid in his class. Most of the time, he doesn't even notice he's got a class.

I'm not learning anything. But even if I was in genius classes, I don't think there's much this one-horse town can teach me in two months. Could be even less—Mom says her movie is going really well, which means I could be back in California even sooner than expected. Fingers and toes crossed.

In spite of all that, I have to admit I'm fascinated by SCS-8. It's not a good class—not even close. It's kind of an interesting one, though. I always assumed that kids who end up in programs like that are just plain dumb. Not this bunch. They have quirks, sure. But unteachable? I don't see what's so terrible about them that they can't be with everybody else. Well, maybe Aldo. Anybody who can get that mad at a locker, and all that. Still, when I look into Aldo's eyes—which are green, by the way—I see a person who doesn't want to be so angry.

Anyway, if the kids are a little strange, they're not half as strange as their teacher. I use the word *teacher* very loosely. That's another problem I have about calling them the Unteachables. How can the school know they're unteachable if nobody ever tries to teach them?

It's been two weeks and Mr. Kermit hasn't taught anything yet. He barely even speaks. He doesn't like kids, and he doesn't seem too fond of other adults either. Yet there's something cool about him too. Nothing throws him, except maybe vuvuzelas. Anybody who could put out a trash can bonfire with a cup of coffee and never mention it must have ice water in his veins—even by LA standards.

And just when you think you've got him figured out, something new about him comes out. Like his secret past with Miss Fountain's mother. Or when he fought like a tiger to get Barnstorm included in the pep rally. Now Barnstorm is fully reinstated to the Golden Eagles. He even stands on the sidelines at football games, leaning on his crutches and dispensing advice to the players. He has Mr. Kermit to thank for that.

One day, Barnstorm is off at a team meeting when Miss Fountain pokes her head into the room.

"Mr. Kermit," she calls, "my group is about to have Circle Time, and we were wondering if you and your students might like to join us."

"Circle Time?" he repeats, mystified.

I stare at our teacher. How could anybody in the school business never have heard about Circle Time? "You know," I explain, "like the little kids do."

"It's not just for little kids," Miss Fountain corrects.

"It's for everybody. Positive reinforcement is something you never outgrow. Think of how much better our world would be if national leaders would only sit in a circle and be kind and civil to one another."

So we all troop over to room 115, and let me tell you, that class doesn't look too thrilled to see us coming in the door. They're seventh graders—only a year younger than us—but it's a major year for growth spurts, so they seem a lot punier. Plus, we have a reputation—that was obvious from the VIP seats they gave us at the pep rally, and how quickly we got thrown out at the first sign of trouble.

Miss Fountain's students are intimidated by all of us, so you can imagine how they feel about Elaine, the subject of school legends about force-feeding people pages of their own textbooks and pounding them with uprooted ficus trees. Plus, she covers literally thirty degrees of the whole circle. There really is a circle, marked off with yellow tape on the floor. In the middle is a smiley face, also in yellow tape. If my friends in LA could see me now. On second thought, God forbid. Kid drivers, Unteachables, and now this. Greenwich sure is some town.

Mr. Kermit doesn't want to sit on the floor with the kids, but Miss Fountain does it, so he has to do it too.

There's a lot of groaning as he lowers himself down, and a crack that might be from a hip joint. He balances the bucket of coffee precariously on his lap.

The room is like an overgrown kindergarten class. Bright colors blaze from every wall. There are class lists with multicolored stars awarded. Every single piece of information comes in a voice bubble emerging from the mouth of a happy cartoon animal—Suzy the Science Snake and Harvey the Hall Pass Hippo. I'd probably like it—if I was about Chauncey's age. Mateo *does* like it. He lives his life through fictional characters anyway. He lingers in front of the big posters, drinking in the details of the vibrant caricatures. Mr. Kermit has to order him to take a seat on the circle.

Miss Fountain even has a *real* animal. In a glass terrarium in the corner of the room, under a sign proclaiming him to be VLADIMIR, is some kind of lizard about eight inches long.

"A miniature Gorn!" Mateo blurts.

"He's a gecko," a seventh grader corrects.

Parker snaps his fingers. "Like that lizard from the TV commercials."

"He's a gold dust day gecko," Miss Fountain explains. "You can tell by the flecks of yellow in his scales."

"Gorns are from *Star Trek*," Mateo supplies, although nobody asked for an explanation. "They're a reptilian race from Tau Lacertae 9, advanced enough to have mastered space travel."

A loud snicker comes from one of the seventh graders.

"Class, let's welcome our new friends to the circle," Miss Fountain announces. "Who has a compliment to offer?"

"Somebody's feet stink," Aldo complains.

Mr. Kermit glares at him. "That's not a compliment!"

"Yeah, I know," Aldo concedes, "but something smells pretty ripe around here."

"Maybe it's the Gorn cage," Mateo puts in.

"A compliment," Miss Fountain goes on as if no one else has spoken, "is a positive comment, a 'well done!' to make people feel good about themselves. Try again, Aldo."

Aldo is thinking so hard that his face screws up, like Chauncey's when he's going to the bathroom in his diaper. He looks all around the circle and comes up empty.

I know I'm just a short-timer and it's pointless to care about people I'll never have to see again once

Mom finishes shooting her movie. But my heart goes out to Aldo, who has this red, red hair that just won't stay combed. How must it feel inside when the closest you can get to saying something nice involves foot odor?

From the opposite side of the room, a low voice announces, "That's a nice color."

We all crane our necks to see who's speaking. To my amazement, it's *Elaine*!

"I beg your pardon," says the young teacher, distracted.

"Your shirt," Elaine tells Miss Fountain. "It's a nice look for you."

"What a lovely thing to say! Thank you—" Miss Fountain frowns at Elaine. "I don't think I know your name."

"I don't think so either," Elaine rumbles back.

Miss Fountain turns questioningly to Mr. Kermit, who gives her a blank shrug.

"That's Elaine!" I exclaim. We've been in class with him for two weeks. Doesn't he know any of us?

A few whispered murmurs of "rhymes with pain" come from our class and the seventh graders.

A voice sounds in the hall. "Where'd everybody go?" A moment later, Barnstorm swings into the doorway on his crutches, fresh from his meeting with the football team. "I was wondering where you guys—hey, check it out! Circle Time!"

"Join our circle," Miss Fountain invites. "Why don't you share how you hurt your leg? I'm guessing it was a football injury."

"No way," Barnstorm scoffs. "The tackler isn't born who can catch me. I was changing a lightbulb in the bathroom and I slipped off the toilet seat."

I can see it coming, but I'm powerless to stop it. As Barnstorm plops himself down on the floor next to Aldo, one of his crutches whacks the red-haired boy in the side of the head.

"Ow!" Enraged, Aldo sweeps the offending crutch aside, knocking it into the corner. The rubber tip clips the cover on the lizard terrarium, sending it skittering across the floor.

"The Gorn!" Mateo exclaims.

"Vladimir!" cry several of the seventh graders.

The gecko is out of his home like a shot. He does a quick loop of the room and finds the door, posthaste.

Mateo frowns. "Gorns are slow and plodding in *Star Trek*."

"I guess *Star Trek* isn't that much like real life," Parker observes.

You can say that again. There's nothing slow or lazy about Vladimir. By the time the first seventh graders reach the hall, their class pet is long gone.

I'm kind of impressed by how calm Miss Fountain stays. She's all business on the intercom with the office describing the escaped lizard.

"Thank you for a very enjoyable—uh, Circle Time," Mr. Kermit says formally. "We should probably say our goodbyes, though."

I doubt she even hears him.

Back in room 117, I'm thinking now we're really going to get it. But our teacher silently returns to his crossword puzzle, leaving us to the worksheets on our desks.

Eight
Mr. Kermit

When breakfast is mustard on toast, that's a sure sign that it's time to go back to the grocery store. It means I've run out of butter and cream cheese and jam, and I'm digging into the condiment packs left over from my last McDonald's run. Come to think of it, this is my last slice of bread too, and stale doesn't begin to describe it.

The apartment is a dump—clean enough, but definitely from a bygone era. I can afford much better, but I'm too disinterested to redecorate and too lazy to move. It's the perfect place for a meal of mustard on toast—the breakfast of the disinterested and lazy. Not for the first time, I picture Fiona's house, with its picket fence and oh-so-green lawn. It's more vivid now, since I can imagine Emma growing up there, playing on the swings, riding her tricycle on the driveway, and playing with her first lizard. I don't want to think about her *last* lizard, thanks to the Unteachables. God only knows what happened to Vladimir. He's probably trapped in the walls of the school somewhere, starving to death. If he made it out of the building, he's roadkill for sure.

Eventually, I go down to the Coco Nerd and start it up in a cloud of burnt oil. I'm actually calling it that, thanks to Parker. For some reason, I can't get it out of my head. Something else to lay at the feet of the Unteachables.

June has never looked farther away.

I'm not even a third of the way to school when the billboard looms up:

COME SEE THE LARGEST INVENTORY OF
NEW AND USED
VEHICLES IN THE TRI-COUNTY AREA

And there's his face, grinning out through a flaming hoop like he's some kind of circus performer and not the sleazy used-car dealer he was always meant to be. Jumping Jake Terranova, who will jump through hoops to get you a great deal on the perfect new or used car.

Even though I pass this billboard every day, it's always somehow a blow to see him up there. He doesn't look much different than he did as a seventh grader. Always grinning, like he's got it all figured out. And he's still selling—cars and SUVs now, instead of stolen copies of the National Aptitude Test. He's good at it too. Terranova Motors is the third-largest auto dealership in the state. That's quite an accomplishment. Jumping Jake has come a long way since seventh grade, when his biggest accomplishment was ruining his teacher's life.

No, I remind myself, Dr. Thaddeus did that. Sure, the cheating thing was an ugly scandal, but it's not as if I was in on the scam. All I was guilty of was trusting my students—and believing that their best-in-the-nation test score was an honest achievement.

My *real* crime—the one I'll never be forgiven for—was making Thaddeus *look bad*. The principal-turned-superintendent has been taking his revenge ever since. Jake Terranova was just the first tile that started the dominoes tumbling.

The giant dealership looms up on the left. I can't help it—I count how long it takes to pass the vast lots and showrooms. Fourteen full seconds at the speed of traffic. It isn't enough that the Terranova kid got away with his seventh-grade shenanigans; obviously, they gave him the formula for getting rich. He's rolling in money while the teacher he took down is living on bread and mustard and driving a Coco Nerd—although the main reason I haven't replaced the car is that I blame all auto dealerships for Jake Terranova.

I turn into the school lot where Parker's pickup truck is sprawled across the last two open spaces. Sure, give a middle school kid a driver's license. What could go wrong? Annoyed, I block the pickup in, making a mental note to keep the kid after school just long enough to beat him out here.

I didn't pack a lunch, but I remember buying a falafel a couple of days ago that I never got around to eating. It isn't on the passenger seat, so I try the glove compartment. No luck. It must have fallen on the floor and rolled under the seat when the car went over a bump. The Coco Nerd doesn't have much in the way of suspension.

Bending over double, I reach around and pat the floor on the passenger side. Sure enough, I find the paper sack. But when I pull it out, there's a hole in the bag, and the falafel is half-eaten and torn to shreds.

I get on all fours and peer under the seat. It looks like somebody lost a leather wallet down there. Then it shifts, and two beady eyes peer out at me.

I recoil in shock, slamming the back of my head against the dashboard. With a squeak of fear, the creature begins to scramble away, but I jam my hand in and grab it before it can escape through the hole in the floor.

Breathing hard, I draw the little guy out and hold him against my chest. "Vladimir, I presume."

In answer, the gecko poops on my shirt. I sigh, unable to muster up any anger or even surprise. Vladimir is merely continuing a pattern of treatment that's been going on for twenty-seven years. I brush the tiny pellets away.

So the fugitive lizard *did* make it out of the building. Not only that, but he managed to find the one car in the parking lot with a hole in the floor and a falafel just waiting to be feasted on. And he's been here for the past eighteen hours, safe and sound while the custodians scoured the school, listening to every wall with stethoscopes.

Still toting the little beast, I get out of the car. I hold on pretty tight at first, but relax when I realize Vladimir isn't going anywhere. Why should he? He's eating the rest of my lunch as we enter the school.

I'm actually looking forward to restoring Vladimir to his rightful owner. True, that's dangerously close to caring. But Emma is almost like my daughter from an alternate universe, her being Fiona's kid. The young teacher already thinks my class is a horde of barbarians—mostly because they are. This might get her to consider the possibility that I'm not to blame for it.

As I approach room 115, her voice stops me in my tracks.

"I know teachers get burned-out, Mom, but this is different. He's barely even alive! I teach right next door to him. He doesn't open his mouth all day! Those poor kids are going to learn nothing because nobody's there to teach them! It's such a shame . . ."

I back up a step. She's stalking around the room, updating her bulletin boards with gold stars, holding her phone to her ear with one hunched shoulder. What she's saying hurts all the more because of who she's saying it to.

A surge of resentment. What does Emma Fountain

know about being burned-out? She's barely older than the students. She thinks giving middle schoolers gold stars and class pets and lecturing them about being bucket-fillers is education. How long has she been teaching—ten minutes? The first time she tried to take on the Unteachables, they laid waste to her circle and released her lizard to the four winds.

But Fiona's never going to hear *that* side of the story.

Emma adjusts a drooping nostril on Harvey the Hall Pass Hippo. "Okay, fine, he used to be a great teacher once. It's *now* that counts! Honestly, I can't believe you were actually *engaged* to that—"

I tense up, giving the gecko a squeeze. A short, sharp squeak is torn from his little mouth.

She wheels, and the phone drops from her ear.

"Vladimir!" She grabs the lost pet from my arms and rains kisses down on his scaly head. "Where did you find him?"

"Around," I reply stiffly. I'm not in the mood for a conversation about the hole in the back of my car.

She's red in the face now. "How long have you been standing there, Mr. Kermit?"

I'm tempted to say, "Long enough," or something else to make her feel bad, because she of all people should know that wasn't a very bucket-filling conversation. But I hold my tongue.

This used to be my favorite part of the day—when the students haven't come yet to ruin it. It's usually downhill from there.

My dramatic exit is spoiled by a small mustard burp as breakfast climbs a little higher up the back of my throat.

I need coffee. I cheer myself by picturing the Toilet Bowl on the shelf in the faculty lounge, dwarfing all the lesser mugs.

Nine

Parker Elias

Back when Grandpa was alive, he and Grams ran the lunch counter at the bus station. I can still picture the LUNCHEONETTE sign, which always looked like ELECT THE NOUN to me. I don't remember much about Grandpa except that he used to tell me it was a "ten-dollar word" and I'd be able to read it just fine when I got older. (We know how that worked out.)

Grams would stand me up in front of the candy

counter, which seemed like it was a mile high—although that was just because I was small. She'd say, "What'll it be, kiddo?" and I could pick out whatever I wanted.

In those days, I didn't mind being "kiddo," because she definitely knew my real name. "This handsome fellow is my grandson, Parker!" she'd announce whenever the regulars came by. You could just tell by the way she boomed it out that she was totally thrilled by the idea.

I wonder if she knows that the guy who drives her every morning is the same little kid she used to brag about to her customers. It's not her fault—when Grandpa died, she started forgetting a lot of stuff. But you'd think a grandson could be an exception to that—especially a grandson who's supposed to be her favorite person in the whole world.

Grams insists that the reason she can't get her act together is she isn't a morning person. This from a lady who gets up at four a.m. So we'll be halfway to the senior center before I look down and notice that her shoes don't match, or that instead of her purse, she brought a half loaf of Wonder bread. There are those red, yellow, and blue polka dots smiling up at me, along with the name, which looks like DOWNER.

Today Mom's driving because Grams has her

semiannual conference with the social worker at the senior center. Mom calls it Meet the Teacher, since I guess it's a lot like a parent conference at school.

"Speaking of which," she says to me, "how's eighth grade going? I understand you're in a different kind of program this year."

I almost reply, "Yeah, the Unteachables." But that wouldn't be a good idea. The minute she got through with *Grams's* Meet the Teacher, she'd be stalking the middle school looking to meet *my* teacher. I picture my folks trying to hold a conversation with Ribbit, who never glances up from his crossword puzzle. Dad, especially, would have no patience for that. Fall is our busiest season on the farm, with so much harvesting still to do.

So I tell her, "It's going fine, like always."

She casts me a doubtful look. *Like always* might not have been the best choice of words. Mom signs my report cards. She knows better than anyone what *like always* probably means.

I add, "Our teacher has a lot of experience." He started out teaching stegosauruses and pterodactyls before moving on to Unteachables. Dinosaurs had no problem being in class with a guy who did crossword puzzles all day.

Mom looks like she has more questions, but luckily, Grams is waiting outside her building—no mismatched clothes or missing socks, no rubber gasket from the coffeemaker on her wrist instead of her medical-alert bracelet. She's thrown a little to see me in the passenger seat instead of behind the wheel, so it takes some coaxing to get her into the truck. She has to sit on the hump between Mom and me, since the pickup has no back seat.

"Of all the cars, you picked this one?" she asks Mom. "You're crazy."

"It's just for a couple of minutes," my mother promises. "Once we drop Parker at school, you'll have plenty of room."

"*I'm* Parker," I put in quickly, since Grams is looking around the car in confusion.

She beams at me. "Hiya, kiddo! Want breakfast?"

"No time. We're coming up on my stop."

Mom pulls up in front of the school and I get out. She waves. "Have fun."

Yeah, right. *Fun*—that's the last word that comes to mind when I think of SCS-8. On the other hand, a sit-down with Grams and a social worker won't be a party either. I'm probably getting the better deal.

As the pickup roars off, I hear a crunching sound.

A crushed vuvuzela lies on the pavement, the plastic busted by the weight of the truck. It seems like there are more of them around every day as we get closer to Spirit Week. And these are just leftovers from last year. The word is that Principal Vargas just placed this giant order of new ones for 2019. They're going to be bright yellow—our school color—and say *Go, Go, Golden Eagles* on the side. It doesn't make much sense to me that you can get a detention for chewing gum, but blasting away on a horn as loud as an air raid siren is considered school spirit.

Instead of being late like most other mornings, I've got the opposite problem. I'm early. The buses haven't started arriving yet. I wander down to room 117, but nobody's there. The kids of SCS-8 dribble in ten seconds before the late bell, and at that, we're usually ahead of Mr. Kermit. The only signs of life are coming from the room next door: 115.

Miss Fountain is in her classroom, rearranging the Velcro smiley faces on her job boards. There's already a Hershey's Kiss sitting in the middle of each desk. You know what Mr. Kermit gives us every morning? Nothing—if you don't count the dirty looks.

She spots me standing there in the doorway. "Good

morning, Parker. You're early today. Come have a kiss."

I stare at her for a long time before I realize she's talking about the candy. "Uh—thanks." The chocolate is sweet in my mouth. When you spend all your time in SCS-8, you almost forget there's another way to live.

My eyes find the lizard terrarium. "Hey," I say suddenly. "Vladimir's back!"

She beams. "Mr. Kermit found him for me."

"Really?" That doesn't sound like the Ribbit I know—the one who wouldn't give anybody the skin off a grape.

Suddenly, I experience an almost irresistible desire to drop to the floor and sit cross-legged on the taped circle. I know Miss Fountain's teaching style is too babyish for our age, but Circle Time that day might have been the most comfortable I've ever felt in middle school. When you're in that circle, nobody's going to ask you to read something that's written in Unbreakable Code. Maybe Aldo can't come up with any nice things to say, but I'm willing to go with it. If it means no reading, I'll even say nice things about Elaine.

A couple of the seventh graders show up, and there's an emotional reunion with Vladimir. I join in for a while, but eventually one of them notices I'm there.

"*You're* not in this class," he comments meaningfully.

That's right, I reflect with a sigh. I'm not. I shoulder my backpack and head next door, even though it's still early.

Kiana crouches in the hall outside SCS-8, a look of intense concentration on her face.

"What's going on?" I ask.

"Shhh!" She presses a finger to her lips and points inside the classroom.

Mr. Kermit is talking, and at first I think he's chewing someone out. His voice is a lot sharper than his usual half-sleepy drone. Then I hear the reply—tinny and very close. It's coming from the intercom, right on the other side of the door. Principal Vargas.

"I'd think you'd be happy about this, Zachary," the principal is saying. "It's no secret that the sound of those vuvuzelas drives you over the edge."

Zachary. Mr. Kermit's name is Zachary.

"That's not the point," our teacher replies. "You've already separated my class from everybody else in the building. Maybe you have your reasons for that. But you can't exclude them from the activities for Spirit Week. That's punishing them for something they haven't done yet."

"You loathe Spirit Week," Mrs. Vargas accuses.

"We're not talking about me. We're talking about my students. As happy as I'd be to ignore the whole thing, I'm their only teacher. Who's going to stick up for them if I don't?"

Beside me, Kiana pumps a fist and whispers, "Go, Ribbit!"

"Think of who we're talking about here," the principal insists. "Think of the disruption they're capable of. Now picture them with vuvuzelas in their hands."

"Let that be my problem," Mr. Kermit says stubbornly.

"It's not going to be anybody's problem," Mrs. Vargas insists. "It's a done deal, Zachary. Your kids are out."

We hear a click as the office breaks the connection. On the other side of the door, Mr. Kermit mutters something I can't make out.

"Did you hear that?" Kiana breathes. "Mr. Kermit cares about us!"

"I didn't hear anything about caring," I retort.

"That was all about vuvuzelas—which we're not getting anyway."

"Weren't you paying attention? He *fought* for us!"

"I can't figure him out," I complain. "He hates vuvuzelas. Why would he want us to have them? So he can kill whoever blows one?"

She throws up her hands in exasperation. "Don't you see? It's not about the noisemakers. It's about *fairness*!"

That doesn't make much sense to me. If life was fair, there would be no such thing as the Unteachables in the first place.

Ten

Kiana Roubini

Bad news from Utah—the equipment trailer got struck by lightning, so production on my mom's movie has to be shut down for a couple of weeks.

"Can't I come back home while you guys are waiting to start up again?" I ask Mom over Skype.

"That wouldn't work," she tells me. "What about school? How can we pull you out of Greenwich when you just got started? And then re-enroll you once shooting resumes here? That would be too disruptive."

I have to hold myself back from screaming: *There's nothing to disrupt! I don't really go here! Jeez-Louise never registered me! I'm not even in a real class!*

Forget it. Mom would be on the phone to Dad in seconds flat—never a pleasant convo. I'd be back in that office fast enough to make my head spin, registering for eight classes instead of just one. Eight new teachers to get used to—who give real assignments and real homework.

No. My life here isn't perfect, but it's designed for maximum bearableness. Why get complicated? I'm a short-timer—just not quite as short as I thought.

Two extra weeks in Greenwich. Of Dad and Stepmonster. Of Chauncey's sniffles and fevers and rashes and barfs.

Two more weeks in the Parmesan House. Two more weeks of the Unteachables.

Fine. I can handle it. I can do two more weeks standing on my head.

"Speaking of school," Mom goes on, "how are you fitting in? I went there, you know—back when it was the old Greenwich High."

"Great," I tell her. "I've already gotten picked for this special program."

Mom beams. "Special?" I knew she wouldn't be

able to resist the idea of me being exceptional.

I plow forward. "It's called SCS-8. Really hard to get into." I should know. I'm not even really in it. "The teacher is fantastic. He's super hands-off because he wants us to learn to work independently. Mr. Kermit believes—"

"Kermit?" she interrupts. "You mean from the cheating scandal?"

"Cheating scandal?"

Mom's brow furrows. "It was an awfully long time ago—the early nineties. I remember I was away at college when it happened. But it must be the same person. Kermit isn't a very common name."

I'm intrigued. "What did Mr. Kermit do?"

"I don't remember the details. But the whole town was up in arms about it. I'm surprised he's still teaching. It was a horrible black mark against him."

Wow—Mr. Kermit has a *past*. The plot thickens.

Mom adds, "Do you want me to call the school and get to the bottom of it?"

"No!" I blurt. "I mean, Mr. Kermit's an awesome teacher *now*, and that's the main thing, right? Who cares what happened in the nineties?"

"But, Kiana—it was a *cheating* scandal! I don't want you mixed up in something like that."

"Relax, Mom," I assure her. "I guarantee that there isn't any cheating going on in SCS-8." I can say that with total confidence because there isn't anything going on, period. Why would we bother to cheat when Mr. Kermit never even looks at the few papers he gets?

Eventually, she agrees to let the subject drop. I end the Skype call, my mind racing. Suddenly, I've cracked a mystery that's been nagging at me from the very first moment I followed Parker's schedule into room 117: Why would Mr. Kermit want to teach a class like the Unteachables?

Answer: he doesn't. He gets a bad class every year because of what happened way back in the nineties. Seems a little crazy that he's still paying for a mistake from so long ago. But if Mom remembers, other people do too.

Turns out SCS-8 isn't just a dumping ground for the rejects of the school. The reject teachers wind up there too.

So Mr. Kermit is famous. If Mom still remembers what he did way back when, that counts as fame. Okay, it was a bad thing, but so what? On reality TV shows, the biggest stars are always the jerks.

Besides, cheating scandal or not, I can't forget how he spoke up for our class to Mrs. Vargas. And how he fought for Barnstorm's right to stay with the football team. He may not be much of a teacher, but I'm more convinced than ever that he's one of the good guys.

I'm almost anxious to get to school the next day, and it isn't just because Chauncey is barking the house down with whooping cough. When I get to room 117, though, Mr. Kermit is absent. We have a substitute, Mrs. Landsman.

Mr. Kermit's not exactly a young guy, but Mrs. Landsman is really old. Rahim does a quick sketch of her, rising from the grave as part of a zombie apocalypse—the kid is really talented. The picture makes the rounds of the class by paper airplane.

"Dawn of the Dead!" hisses Mateo when the portrait lands on his desk.

"No talking!" Mrs. Landsman orders.

Too late. A nickname is born. She's Dawn of the Dead—Dawn for short.

She's grouchy, but we should be used to that by now, our regular teacher being a gold medalist at the Grouch Olympics. It feels different, though. Dawn crabs *at* us, while Mr. Kermit just crabs because crabbing is his natural state. So when some of it lands on us, we don't take it personally. We just happen to be in the same room.

Dawn is yammering on about the Battle of Gettysburg when I hear a power hum, low but growing in volume. At first, I'm afraid the school is about to blow up. Then I realize the sound is coming from the desk next to me—Aldo. His face is almost as red as his hair as he devotes all his breath to maintaining the sound.

Now the hum is coming from behind me, at a slightly different pitch. I risk a glance over my shoulder. Barnstorm's doing it too, a look of unholy glee on his face. Next, the noise drops at least an octave—Elaine, buzzing like a bassoon.

Well, we Californians know how to prank a sub as well as anybody. So I jump right in. Pretty soon, SCS-8 is vibrating.

Alarmed, Dawn of the Dead puts in a call to the custodian. As soon as Mr. Carstairs comes in, we stop humming.

"It was happening just a second ago," the substitute teacher insists. "It sounded like a problem with the wiring."

The custodian rakes us with a rueful look. "It's the kids, ma'am. They're messing with you. They do it to all the subs."

Dawn doesn't like that. For a minute there, I'm afraid we're going to have a real zombie apocalypse on our hands. But in the end, what can she do besides yell? She does a whole lot of that. It's pretty jarring when you're used to Mr. Kermit, who barely speaks at all.

We fight back. We do the old drop-a-textbook trick at least twenty times. Barnstorm drums with his crutches on the floor. Elaine pretends to be asleep, which is odd because Rahim stays awake and alert. Mateo speaks to the substitute in Dothraki and does all his written work in Elven Runes.

That's right, I said work. Dawn of the Dead is trying to run this like an actual *class*. Who does she think she is?

"Take out your math books," she announces.

"What math books?" Barnstorm returns.

"Surely, there are math books." Her frustration is growing. "How do you study math?"

"We do worksheets," Mateo supplies.

"*What* worksheets? I don't see any worksheets! There should be lesson plans—"

Of course there should—*if* we had a normal teacher. But Dawn of the Dead doesn't know Mr. Kermit. Maybe she thinks we ransacked the classroom before she arrived and threw out all the notes on how she was supposed to run the day. Whatever the reason, she's getting madder and madder.

With no lesson plans to go by, Dawn finds a language arts paragraph in some random book. But then she chooses Parker to read it aloud. So obviously, he takes forever to sound out the first word. And because we've been giving her a hard time all day, she picks now to decide that somebody's yanking her chain— when Parker's the only one who isn't. So she sends him to the principal's office. Sixty seconds later, we hear a pickup truck with a broken muffler start up and peel out of the parking lot.

"You know, he didn't do that on purpose," I tell Dawn. "He has a reading problem and he's sensitive about it."

Miss Fountain comes over and tries to calm everybody down by inviting us for another Circle Time.

"Circle Time?" Dawn is outraged. "These students are too old for Circle Time—and so are yours."

Miss Fountain seems to be about to launch into her speech on how no one is too old for positive reinforcement. But then she takes a good look at Dawn of the Dead, who actually might be. She beats a hasty retreat to her own class.

When the bell finally rings at three-thirty, Dawn

of the Dead tells us we're the most disrespectful class she's ever met in her long teaching career, and we should all be ashamed of ourselves. "My son went to this school. He's a successful journalist today, and he'd be appalled to see what's become of the place that gave him his education. You students are a new low. I don't think you'd ever behave for Mr. Kermit the way you behaved today."

As we listen to her sensible heels clicking down the hall, a strange quiet descends in room 117.

"Yeah, well, maybe Mr. Kermit isn't a cranky old bag, like you," Aldo tosses after her when she's too far away to hear it.

"The thing is, she's right," Rahim muses, brow furrowed. "We *wouldn't* behave that way for Ribbit. I wonder why."

I could have answered that. Because even though Mr. Kermit kind of ignores us, he knows we're his class and he sticks up for us when we need it. He *likes* us—in his way. And I'd never be able to explain it to the others, but I think—in our way—we might be starting to like him too.

When Mr. Kermit enters room 117 the next morning, he's greeted by a sight he's never seen before—the seven of us, quiet and attentive, seated at our desks, hands folded, eyes front. Let's face it, there's no way Dawn of the Dead said anything good about us yesterday. This, then, is Payback Time, and none of us are looking forward to it. You can feel the tension in the air as we wait for our teacher to let us have it.

Mr. Kermit sets his newspaper and his coffee down on his desk and looks from face to face. "What?"

Nobody answers, so he starts handing out the first worksheet of the day. The instant the papers hit our desks, there's a pen in every hand and all heads are down.

Out of the corner of my eye, I see the teacher pull up short, frowning. This is another first—the entire class hard at work, no airplanes circling overhead, no talking. He shrugs and returns to his desk, peering down at the crossword puzzle.

I turn my attention to the assignment, which is about current events, and I think hard about what I've seen lately in the news, on the Internet, and in social media.

The intercom buzzes to life. "Mr. Kermit," comes the voice of the secretary, "Principal Vargas is available this morning if you'd like to discuss Mrs. Landsman's report on your students from yesterday."

You can almost hear the jarring sound of a needle scratching across a vinyl record. We all freeze, staring up at our teacher. If Dawn of the Dead filed a report, you can bet she gave us a Z-minus-minus.

"No," Mr. Kermit replies. "Thanks anyway."

That gets our attention. Is Mr. Kermit so detached from reality that he doesn't think anything that happened yesterday was bad? Or is it that he never read Dawn's report, just like he never reads any of our work? The mood in room 117 lightens a little. Whatever the reason, it looks as if we might be off the hook.

It occurs to me that maybe Mr. Kermit never reads our stuff because none of the Unteachables ever hand in anything worth reading. That's an easy fix. There's an essay question on the back of today's worksheet, and I make up my mind to knock it out of the park. The prompt is about mass transit—subways, buses, and light-rail trains. I believe in that kind of thing anyway—I'm from LA, where our transit systems are a joke, and what do we get for it? Traffic jams and pollution. Pretty soon the entire page is full, and I'm only getting started.

I approach Mr. Kermit's desk. Ribbit has pushed his puzzle aside. He's examining a memo from the office. I catch the heading—REPORT OF SUBSTITUTE

TEACHER—across the top. He notices me and I search his eyes for any reaction to what has to be a horrible rundown of her day with a class of unteachable barbarians.

"Are you really mad at us?" I ask in a small voice.

He looks like the question never occurred to him. "There are two sides to every story," he says finally. He reaches down and slides the report into the trash can.

"Is there something I can do for you?" he adds, obviously wishing I would go away.

"Can I have more paper?"

His brow furrows. "For what?"

"My essay. I ran out of space."

That causes kind of a stir in our class. In SCS-8, kids do too little work, never too much.

Mr. Kermit's back into his puzzle now. It's almost as if he's hoping I'll forget what I asked for and leave him alone.

"So can I have it?" I persist.

He looks blank.

"The paper."

"Yes—fine."

"Well, where is it?"

He gets up from his desk and surveys the room, and

it's like he's suddenly found himself in some strange and exotic location—a place he's never seen before. He leads me to a storage closet and opens the door. Empty, except for the cobwebs.

He turns to me, completely helpless.

"Maybe Miss Fountain has extra paper," I suggest.

"I'm on it!" Parker bolts for the door so suddenly that he knocks over his desk and goes flying. He face-plants on the floor, springs right back up, and disappears into the hall.

The next thing we hear is Miss Fountain's voice from the next room: "Parker—you're bleeding!"

"He has a *driver's* license?" Barnstorm sneers. "The kid can barely *walk*."

Parker's back a few minutes later, holding a wad of pink-stained paper towels to his bloody nose. He hands me a sheaf of lined paper, also pink-stained.

I fill four full pages before I'm done with my essay, and I'm pretty satisfied with it. I know I'm just a short-timer, but I can't let my work habits go totally down the drain while I'm here. I'm going to have to be ready to hit the ground running when I get back to my real school in California.

I march up to the front to hand my paper in to Mr. Kermit. He looks at me like I've just presented him with a plate of baby scorpions.

"It's my essay," I reply to the question he probably won't ask. "I can't wait to hear what you think."

He accepts the papers, places them on the corner of the desk, and goes back to his crossword.

"Aren't you going to read it?" I press.

"Of course," he assures me without looking up.

Three days later, the pages still sit on the corner of the desk, untouched.

Parker's blood spots are turning brown.

Eleven

Barnstorm Anderson

Thanks to Ribbit, I'm still on the Golden Eagles. It's the nicest thing any teacher ever did for me. Not that I love teachers so much. It's their fault I'm in SCS-8.

I'm not unteachable and I'm definitely not stupid. I'm like any other kid—I can learn, but if you give me the choice not to, I'll pick that. They were totally cool with letting me slide so long as the trophies kept coming. But now that I can't play anymore, all of a sudden my grades aren't up to scratch. Funny how that wasn't a problem last year, when I beasted in three sports.

I load up my tray in the food line and hobble out to the cafeteria—it's not easy to balance a big lunch when you're on crutches. As I scan the tables, this seventh-grade girl I don't know—real cute—smiles and waves at me. This happens to athletes a lot. We're kind of celebrities around school.

I'm trying to figure out how to wave back without dropping either my tray or a crutch, when her gaze veers off to my left. She's not looking at me at all! She's waving to *Karnosky*, one of my teammates on the Golden Eagles, who's coming up beside me!

It's like a gut punch. Karnosky the scrub, who never even got off the bench before I landed on the injured list! Now he's somebody and I'm somebody you look right through.

"'Sup, Anderson," he mumbles, stepping in front of me. He and the girl connect and take the last two spots at the front table—the best location. Last year, half a dozen people would have scrambled to make room for Barnstorm Anderson. Not anymore.

I can take a hint. I'm a Golden Eagle, but not really. What have I done for them lately? If I can't put points on the board today, I'm dead to them.

Not even Ribbit can change *that*.

I keep on hobbling, head held high. I'll die before I let them see I care. It stinks that just moving across the cafeteria has to be a major operation. The way I could *move* used to be what made me who I am. I guess that means I'm nobody—at least till next year.

Another problem: I've hung out with jocks for so long, I've got nowhere else to go. I set my lunch down next to Aldo and Rahim. As I lean my crutches against the side of the table, one of them tips over and whacks Aldo in the shoulder.

"Hey!" he barks angrily.

"Chill out! It was an accident."

It wasn't an accident.

In my athlete days, my mind was always on the field or on the court, juking and cutting, faking imaginary defenders out of their jockstraps. Now that I'm off sports, I don't do that anymore, and my poor mind has nothing to focus on. So I spend my time thinking of ways to get a rise out of Aldo. It's almost too easy.

Aldo is halfheartedly eating a bowl of split pea soup while gazing over at Kiana, who's a few tables away, sitting with Mateo and Parker. That's the rest of SCS-8 except for Elaine, who eats alone, surrounded by a buffer zone of empty tables. People have been keeping their distance from her ever since she chucked this kid into the salad bar. Even in the lunchroom, Elaine rhymes with pain.

While Aldo's staring at Kiana, I reach over and dump half a shaker of black pepper into his soup. I can't help it. It's almost not my fault.

Rahim snickers and doodles a napkin sketch of Aldo with smoke coming out of his ears.

Meanwhile, Kiana catches Aldo looking at her. Embarrassed, he picks up his soup bowl and guzzles what's left of it, pepper and all. A split second later, a green geyser of pea soup sprays across the room, propelled by a scream.

"What did you do that for?" he rasps.

I can't answer because I'm laughing too hard. So is Rahim. When Aldo sees the napkin sketch, he stabs it with his spoon, which snaps in half.

That gets us a caution from the lunchroom monitor, who raises the quiet alert level from green to amber on the traffic signal at the front of the cafeteria.

"You've got to tone it down, man," I manage, fighting to control my laughter. "Everything makes you fly off the handle."

"Not true!" he bellows in my face, and the traffic signal goes to red.

Now nobody's allowed to talk for the rest of lunch, and it's all Aldo's fault. Rahim and I exchange a fist-bump under the table.

Afterward, when we're walking back to room 117—I mean everybody else is walking; I'm thumping on my crutches—I can't resist rubbing a little more salt in Aldo's wounds. "Kiana was watching you the whole time," I assure him. "She probably thinks you're nuts or something."

"Did I ask you to put a pound of pepper in my soup?" he demands.

"Okay, but you don't have to get so mad about it. You're mad at me; you're mad at Rahim; you're mad at the cafeteria for changing the chicken nugget recipe; you're mad at Ribbit—"

"I'm not mad at Ribbit," he mutters.

"You said you were before."

"Yeah, well, I changed my mind."

"Fine," I agree. "Everything makes you mad *except* Ribbit." And I stop bugging him because I keep thinking about Mr. Kermit, fighting with the office to get me in the pep rally.

Back in room 117 with the rest of the class, we can't help noticing a bright green vuvuzela, bent double, sticking out of our teacher's trash can.

"If Ribbit thinks he can get rid of all those things one at a time," puts in Rahim, "he's in for a really rough Spirit Week."

"I can't understand what makes him tick," puts in Kiana. "Most of the time, he never opens his mouth, but blow a vuvuzela and he'll scream you an opera."

"They make him mad," I say, with a wink at Aldo.

"He's the Grinch!" Mateo pipes up suddenly.

"I thought he was Squidward," Parker reminds him.

Mateo shakes his head. "The Grinch—definitely. The Grinch hates Christmas because he can't stand the noise. Well, Mr. Kermit hates Spirit Week because he can't stand the vuvuzelas."

"Everybody hates something," I retort. "I don't like lima beans—am I the Grinch too?"

"It's not just what you hate; it's why you hate it," Mateo replies seriously. "Indiana Jones hates snakes because he's afraid of them. Superman hates kryptonite because it's his weakness. The Wicked Witch of the West hates water because it makes her melt. But Mr. Kermit and the Grinch are both haters for the same reason—noise."

Ribbit comes in, and the first thing he sees is all of us staring into his wastebasket at the broken vuvuzela. He seems annoyed at first, but then his expression changes to one of sympathy. "I have some bad news about Spirit Week—"

"It's okay, Mr. Kermit," Kiana interrupts. "We know you tried your best to talk the principal into letting us be a part of it."

"Let me tell you about spirit." The teacher comes alive, making eye contact with each of us as he speaks. "No one can command you to have spirit—not principals, governors, presidents, or even kings. There's no spirit switch in your brain that can be flipped on or off. Spirit isn't a week you can put on your calendar. It doesn't come from posters, or streamers, or rallies, or funny hat days. And it definitely doesn't come from making an ungodly racket with a cheap plastic instrument of torture that was invented purely for disturbing the peace!"

It's the most he's said to us all year. I can't explain it, but it feels like a kind of breakthrough—although what we're breaking through to, I have no clue.

Maybe it's this: in all my years in school, I've never heard a teacher say something that was so completely, totally honest.

Twelve
Parker Elias

I kick off Spirit Week by getting arrested.

I'm on my way to pick up Grams on Monday morning when this cop pulls me over because my taillight is out. The problem is this guy is new, and when I show him my provisional license, he thinks it's a fake ID. So he takes me into the police station, and by the time the desk sergeant straightens him out, I'm late for picking up Grams.

She's not waiting outside her apartment building,

but when I run upstairs and knock at the door, nobody answers. I drive around the neighborhood, and sure enough, there she is, walking along the main drag.

I pull up alongside her and lower the window. "Grams, where are you going? Get in the truck!"

She keeps on walking and never even glances in my direction. Way back when she was growing up in Israel a million years ago, her mother taught her never to get into a strange car. She forgot most of everything else—including the grandson who's supposedly her favorite person—but that stuck. I have to drive half a block ahead, park, get out, and "accidentally" run into her on the sidewalk. She recognizes me now; in fact, she's really glad to see me—but not half as glad as I am that I found her. (She could have gotten on a bus somewhere and be really lost.)

She still can't come up with my name, though. "You look skinny, kiddo. Have you been eating?"

Sigh. Why can't she just say: "You look skinny, *Parker*"?

"Hey, here's the pickup," I announce in surprise. "Hop in. I'll give you a lift."

By the time I drop her off at the senior center, I'm way late. To make things worse, I get stuck behind this giant truck in the driveway of the school. I squint at the sign on the back. At first, it looks sort of like ALIEN ROT ANT GRID, but that can't be right. Then I recognize the logo from the internet. It's Oriental Trading, that website where you can order bulk amounts of things like joke glasses and light-up necklaces and party stuff.

I honk for them to let me pass, but they're already out of the truck—two big guys. They open the back and start hauling these giant cartons onto the loading bay of the school. There's no writing on the boxes, but there's a picture, so I know exactly what's inside. Vuvuzelas for Spirit Week. Hundreds of them. If they really ordered for every class but us, a thousand.

My grip tightens on the wheel. What do I care? If SCS-8 is being left out, it makes no difference to me if they've ordered noisemakers for every man, woman, and child on the planet.

Then I think of Mr. Kermit—the way he tried to make the principal change her mind, even though he hates vuvuzelas. Man, the sound of just one drives him bananas. In all these boxes, there must be enough noise power to bring down a herd of elephants.

I pull around the truck, thumping over the curb and driving across some of the front lawn to the parking lot. (That's against the rules of my license too, but this is an emergency.) I roar into a spot, putting only a tiny scrape on the side mirror of Mrs. Oneonta's Mini Cooper. I jump out and head for the school without even using my bottle of scratch guard. By the time I hit the entrance foyer, I'm flying.

I sprint clear across the school, past the gym to room 117. What luck—the other kids are there, but Mr. Kermit hasn't arrived yet. Considering he's a teacher, he sure doesn't seem to have a problem with tardiness—his own, anyway. If they gave late slips to staff members, Ribbit would spend his whole life in detention. (Maybe that wouldn't be a bad thing for someone who loves crossword puzzles so much.)

"The vuvuzelas are coming!" I gasp.

"One if by land, or two if by sea?" Barnstorm snorts.

"This is serious," I insist. "Oriental Trading is parked out front right now, unloading them."

Kiana clues in. "Mr. Kermit's going to lose it."

"And it's going to be hard to get any rest," adds Rahim with a yawn.

"It's no fair that everybody gets them but us," Aldo complains. "I mean, I don't want a stupid vuvuzela anyway. But it's still annoying."

"Ribbit's right," says Barnstorm. "It's fine to have spirit if you really *do*—like if your team is winning the championship or something. But to have spirit because your principal tells you to—because of what *week* it is? That's just dumb."

"What does school spirit have to do with vuvuzelas anyway?" I complain. "Because they're loud? So are car accidents." I actually think about that a lot.

"Poor Mr. Kermit," Kiana adds. "This is going to be rough for him. I wish there was something we could do to make it better."

"Maybe there is," Mateo muses.

Aldo rolls his eyes. "What—we send him on vacation to the Death Star until Spirit Week is over?"

"Of course not," he dismisses this. "The Death Star is *Star Wars*. Mr. Kermit is the Grinch."

"The Grinch isn't real," Kiana explains patiently.

"But what the Grinch *did* can be real," Mateo insists. "He didn't like Christmas, so he stole it. All of it—all the Christmas stuff in Whoville. Even the Who pudding and the roast beast."

Barnstorm's eyes widen. "*Steal* the vuvuzelas? There are, like, seven of us, and I'm on crutches. How are we supposed to carry that many vuvuzelas?"

"They're in boxes," I put in. "Big ones, but I don't think they're super heavy. At least, the Oriental Trading guys are having no trouble unloading them."

"Where do we put them?" Aldo demands. "In our lockers?"

Mateo is stuck on the holiday TV special. "The Grinch loaded the Whos' Christmas stuff on a sled to dump off the top of Mount Crumpit . . ."

"Too bad there aren't any ten-thousand-foot cliffs around here—" That's when it hits me. "Guys—what about the river?" If you follow the school property straight on past the athletic fields, you'll eventually come to the banks of the Greenwich River, which divides our town in two.

Kiana shakes her head sadly. "It's just not practical. There's no way we could move giant boxes all that way."

"I'll drive them," I say suddenly. "We just have to load them into my truck." I can't quite describe how I feel. It's not that I'm so anxious to *do* it, but suddenly it just seems so *doable*. And knowing it's possible, it feels like we have to try.

Rahim looks up from his doodles. "We'll get in trouble."

No kidding. If we get caught, it's hard to imagine the school will go easy on the kids who hijacked a thousand vuvuzelas.

The answer comes from, of all people, Elaine.

"We're already in trouble," she rumbles from her spot at the back of the room. "This class *is* trouble. What can they do to us—put us in here twice?"

"Let's do it." Kiana reaches a hand into the center of our group. "For Mr. Kermit."

Barnstorm places a crutch over it. "I'll show them where they can stick their spirit."

Aldo tries to lay his hand over Kiana's, but the crutch is in the way. "Nobody tells me what to get worked up about."

"To the universe and beyond!" Mateo exclaims.

We all sign on, even Rahim, who is as close to wide awake as I've ever seen him.

"We have to hurry," I urge. "Once the custodians start unpacking those cartons, it's all over."

We head for the loading bay, taking the long way to avoid passing the faculty lounge. The last thing we need is to run into Mr. Kermit heading for room 117—not that he'd ask us where we're going.

Luckily, the halls are busy, so nobody takes much notice of us as we loop around the main foyer and backtrack to the storage rooms that connect to the loading bay.

Kiana peers around the door frame. "Uh-oh."

Following her lead, I peek into the storeroom. The

loading bay door is still open to the driveway, but the truck is gone. Just inside stand the big boxes. I count—seven of them, stacked three, two, and two. Mr. Carstairs stands next to them, the packing slip in one hand, a half-finished bagel in the other.

"Why hasn't he started unloading yet?" I murmur.

"He's probably waiting for help," Kiana whispers back. "That means the other custodians could be here soon."

Aldo curses under his breath. "How are we supposed to get the boxes with Carstairs right there?"

Mateo has an idea. "We need to create a distraction."

"What distraction?" Kiana asks.

"I can talk to him about *The Silmarillion*," Mateo volunteers. "That's the creation story for the entire mythology of *The Hobbit* and *The Lord of the Rings*. And I'll try to get him to walk away."

"That's the stupidest thing I've ever heard in my life," Barnstorm hisses. "We're going to need a better distraction than that."

"Definitely," deadpans Elaine. She rears up a heavy black boot and brings it down full force on Barnstorm's sneakered foot.

The scream could probably drown out all those

vuvuzelas put together. It causes a major freak-out in the hall. Mr. Carstairs comes running. What he sees is the school's injured sports hero, on crutches, howling in agony. The custodian gets his shoulder under Barnstorm's arm, and the two of them begin hobbling in the direction of the nurse's office.

Kiana turns accusing eyes on Elaine. "You didn't have to do that! He could have just faked it."

Aldo chortles. "Not as good as that."

We race into the loading bay.

"Oh, gross," Rahim complains.

"What's gross?" I ask.

He points. "It says it on the boxes. They're gross."

Kiana throws up her hands in exasperation. "That's not gross; that's *one gross*. It means there's a hundred and forty-four vuvuzelas in each carton."

"That makes"—Mateo does the calculation in his head—"a thousand and eight. I thought we were only getting a thousand." It really seems to bother him.

"Never mind that! I'll go for the truck!" I scramble out of the loading bay and jump the three feet down to the pavement. I sprint for the parking lot and leap into the pickup. It takes all the restraint I can muster to keep from stomping on the gas. The last thing we need is for my squealing tires to attract the attention of every adult in the school. Suddenly, my perforated muffler doesn't seem like such a great asset either. It may sound cool, but we're trying for stealth here.

I get out and scramble onto the platform to help with the loading. You know all that stuff about vuvuzelas being light? Well, that goes out the window when you're lifting a box with a hundred and forty-four of them. On the plus side, we've got Elaine, who could lift the load and the loading bay with it—and maybe the truck too.

Kiana and Mateo pile in beside me, but Aldo, Rahim, and Elaine have to jog alongside the pickup. I pull around the side of the school and then jump over the curb and start driving slowly along the grass. I glance at the rearview mirror, and see Elaine flashing me a thumbs-up. I normally try to have as little interaction with her as possible, but right now the gesture gives me heart—because I'm pretty scared at this point.

Are we crazy? Probably, but that's not the part that bothers me. My main worry is that none of this is covered by my provisional license. And if it gets revoked, who's going to pick up Grams every morning and drive her to the senior center?

Thirteen

Mr. Kermit

No one can stop the passage of time.

I've tried. It can't be done.

Case in point—every year in early October, Spirit Week comes along. It's like death and taxes. Actually, my 106-year-old grandfather is doing a better job at putting off death than I am at avoiding Spirit Week. There's only one word for it: *inevitable*.

At the sight of the truck from Oriental Trading, I head for the faculty lounge, fill the Toilet Bowl with coffee, and sit in a dark corner, steeling myself for what's ahead. My fellow teachers cast sympathetic glances in my general direction, but no one approaches me directly. They know there's nothing they can say. Already, those South African air horns from Hades have begun to sound in the halls. Once the mother lode is passed out, the noise will be beyond imagination.

When the cacophony starts, I resolve to close my eyes and dream of June—of early retirement, of another life beyond these walls. I'll unwind, relax, maybe travel—avoiding South Africa, of course, and any other countries where vuvuzelas are part of the local culture. That's the only thing with half a chance of getting me through this—the thought that this Spirit Week, awful as it is, will be my last.

I arrive at room 117 to find it empty. For a fleeting instant, I toy with the possibility that my dreams have come true, and every single one of the students is absent on the same day. Maybe they all gave each other mono. That would mean I could miss Spirit Week altogether!

The intercom interrupts that pleasant thought. "Mr. Kermit? It's Bonnie Fox in the nurse's office. I've got Bernard Anderson here with me."

The name doesn't ring a bell. "Bernard?"

"You know, the boy they call Barnstorm. Someone stepped on his foot, but when I asked for a name, he clammed up. I'm worried that there might be some kind of bullying involved."

I almost ask if the others are there with him, but I keep my mouth shut. On the off chance that it's true, she might send them back.

"He's already got crutches, but that seems to be unrelated," the nurse goes on. "I've iced the foot, but Bernard refuses to let me call his parents. He says he doesn't want to miss anything."

"Spirit Week," I mutter. Even students who are deliberately excluded still find something irresistible about this three-ring circus. Into the intercom, I add, "Well, thanks for letting me know. Please don't feel you have to send him back to class anytime soon. Take your time. We don't want to risk reinjury."

I break the connection. One mystery solved; six to go. Except is it really a mystery if you don't care? Just the fact that they're absent is enough for me.

At that moment, the PA system crackles to life. "Your attention, please. It's Principal Vargas." Her voice seems higher-pitched than usual, and a little shrill, like she's under stress. "Seven large cartons are missing from the loading bay. That's all the vuvu-zelas for Spirit Week. Perhaps somebody thinks this is a joke. I assure you that it isn't. This is stealing, pure and simple. If the school doesn't get its property back immediately, we'll turn the matter over to the police."

I sit down at my desk and open the paper to the crossword puzzle. Who would have believed that Spirit Week could start out on such a hopeful note? First, no students. Next, no vuvuzelas. How could it be better—Superintendent Thaddeus being abducted by aliens?

I frown. Missing students . . . missing vuvuzelas . . .

Miss Fountain bursts in from next door. At the sight of the empty desks, she exclaims, "Mr. Kermit—where are your students?"

I shoot her a coy look. "Shhh. You'll jinx it."

"But—but—" Totally flustered, she rushes across the room and yanks up the Venetian blinds.

An appalling sight meets my eyes. A pickup truck is jouncing across the schoolyard—not just any truck; *Parker's* truck. The payload is piled high with boxes. Parker is at the wheel, his face and shoulder crowded up against the driver's-side window by the rest of the missing Unteachables. Three more jog alongside the pickup.

"They hate me!" I exclaim.

"Of course they don't hate you," Miss Fountain shoots back. "Why would you say such a thing?"

"They know how much I can't stand vuvuzelas. They're cornering the market so they can torture me forever."

"Come on!" She grabs my arm and literally drags me to the nearest exit. "We've got to stop them before this becomes a police matter and the children end up in trouble!"

Out on the lawn, she runs after them, so I run too. I haven't run in fifteen years, and I'm not good at it. Six steps in, I'm out of breath. Gasping and wheezing, struggling to keep up, I reflect once again how much Emma Fountain is like her mother. In the middle of a crisis, her number one concern is that the "children" shouldn't get in trouble. Why not? Trouble was invented for juvenile delinquents who do things like this! Fiona was the same way. And her onetime fiancé used to be just as naïve—until a certain seventh grader named Jake Terranova showed me how the real world worked.

A glance over my shoulder reveals that Emma and I aren't the only ones chasing the runaway Unteachables. It looks like half the faculty is racing across the grass, running full tilt. Christina Vargas is in the lead. But wait—who's that inching ahead of her? Oh no, it's Dr. Thaddeus! The superintendent's face is bright red, and he's sweating all over his hand-tailored silk suit. Not far behind the leaders is Barnstorm, thump-swinging skillfully on his crutches. The kid really is a great athlete. He's having no problem keeping ahead of Nurse Fox and the custodial staff. Even a couple of the lunch ladies have joined the stampede.

Up ahead, the pickup stops in a spray of dirt and grass. The Unteachables set about unloading the big boxes, yanking them out of the payload.

"What's that noise?" Emma tosses over her shoulder.

I hear it too—a low, hissing rumble. The Greenwich River. The students have the boxes ripped open and lined up along the riverbank, as if they're planning to—

The truth hits me like a cannonball to the stomach, knocking the wind out of me. Or maybe it just feels that way because I have so little wind left.

They're not *stealing* the vuvuzelas; they're going to dump them!

I resolved long ago never again to waste any brain activity wondering what makes a bunch of rotten kids do what they do. But this is something that can't be ignored. Hijack a shipment of vuvuzelas only to throw them away? *Why?*

Aldo's voice reaches me from the riverbank. "It's Ribbit!"

What happens next might be the strangest part of an already bizarre episode. The Unteachables—caught red-handed in the middle of a ridiculous crime—all start *cheering.*

What choice do I have but to try to get to the bottom of this?

I charge up to the group. "Has everybody gone crazy?" I demand, panting from the long sprint. "What could possibly be the point of—" That's all the breath I have left. I double over, clutching my thighs, gasping.

"We did it, Mr. K!" Parker crows. "We got the vuvuzelas! All one thousand of them!"

"One thousand and eight!" Mateo corrects.

At this point it's just babble.

"I saw the shipment in the loading bay—"

"Elaine created a distraction on Barnstorm's foot—"

"We got the idea from the Grinch—"

I throw my arms around a carton and pick it up, nearly rupturing a disc in the process. Who knew that a box of light plastic horns could be so *heavy*?

It's a titanic struggle to get it up onto my shoulder. "We're taking these back to school right now!" I exclaim, voice strained. "Honestly, what were you kids thinking?"

Kiana regards me earnestly. "We know how you feel about Spirit Week, Mr. Kermit. We took the vuvuzelas because you hate them so much."

The bulky carton freezes on its unsteady perch on my shoulder. The thought knifes through my oxygen-starved brain. They're doing this—for *me*!

"Kermit!" roars an enraged Dr. Thaddeus. *"Control your students!"*

I barely hear him. The flood of emotions brings me back decades—to a time before Jake Terranova and the cheating scandal. Back when I was Emma's age, and I'd step into the classroom every morning with high hopes of shaping young minds.

The mere memory of the teacher I used to be causes my posture to straighten—and that might explain why the giant box of vuvuzelas overbalances. I cry in alarm as the carton tips over, taking me with it. As I fall, a hundred and forty-four *Go, Go, Golden Eagles* vuvuzelas drop out of the container into the water. I'm only a split second behind them, plunging headfirst into the river in a not-too-graceful reverse swan dive.

The cold water delivers a shock to my central nervous system, starting my heart beating triple time. Shivering, I break the surface just in time to see my students scrambling, tumbling, jumping, and belly flopping to my rescue. Even Barnstorm joins the mission, flinging aside his crutches and hurling himself into the drink. In the process, the kids manage to overturn the other boxes and kick most of the remainder of the shipment into the river with them.

It's a moment that's definitely not covered in teacher's college—standing with your entire class in chest-high water while a thousand and eight bobbing vuvuzelas drift off downstream. Elaine has Mateo by the collar to keep him from sailing away with the noisemakers.

Of all the miserable things that have happened to me during Spirit Week over the years, this ranks about sixth.

Fourteen

Dr. Thaddeus

HIJACKED HORNS SCUTTLE SPIRIT CELEBRATION

The Greenwich Telegraph, Local News

By Martin Landsman, Staff Reporter

Greenwich Middle School's annual Spirit Week was a disappointment this year after a prank gone awry dropped a shipment of the traditional vuvuzelas into the river. Although more than half the noisemakers were eventually recovered, there was little enthusiasm at the school for blowing them. "I'm not putting my mouth on those things," one student commented. "You know, fish go to the bathroom in that water."

District officials are not revealing the names of the perpetrators of the prank, saying only that they have been "appropriately reprimanded," and that their teacher is a "veteran educator." But the *Telegraph* has learned that the teacher in question is Mr. Zachary Kermit, who is still remembered for his involvement in a 1992 cheating scandal that remains a serious black eye for the Greenwich schools. . . .

Christina Vargas finishes reading the article and slides it back across my desk. "Surely you're not still angry at Zachary Kermit for what happened twenty-seven years ago."

"Why shouldn't I be?" I ask irritably. "The whole town remembers the scandal. The fact that it came up in this story proves that."

The principal shrugs. "You know as well as I do that the real culprit was Jake Terranova. He's the one who got his hands on a stolen exam and went into business selling it to his classmates. He may have been only twelve at the time, but he was the same wheeler-dealer that he is today with his car business. All Zachary was guilty of was being fooled like everybody else. Like me, for one. And you."

I grimace. Superintendent is a powerful job, but a lonely one as well. When big decisions have to be made, there's no higher authority to appeal to. You are the law. Christina's right that in 1992, Zachary Kermit knew nothing about what the Terranova kid was up to. But when you're the big boss, you don't have the luxury of considering things like that. All that matters is *optics*. How does it *look*?

In 1992, it looked very bad. And if the mere mention of Zachary Kermit's name reopens that old wound in a newspaper article written by a reporter who probably wasn't even *born* in 1992, then the optics haven't gotten any better. An elephant never forgets; the people of Greenwich have memories that are longer still.

"The district wasn't exactly supportive when the cheating scandal was going on," the principal adds. "You can't fault Zachary for feeling abandoned. No wonder he got so burned-out."

"And what about this latest incident?" I probe.

"That wasn't Zachary's fault either," she offers. "We gave him the Unteachables. What did you expect?"

"I expect him to control seven kids. Is that so unreasonable? I knew he wasn't going to turn them into future presidents, or even into solid citizens. But to keep them from Grand Theft Vuvuzela—is that too much to ask?"

I have her there. Not even the most sympathetic principal can condone the kind of stealing, disruption, and destruction of property that transpired on Monday.

"And look what happened when he tried to stop them," I go on, pressing my advantage. "They all ended up in the river. I just got off the phone with our insurance company. They had a few choice words to say about that, let me assure you."

She sighs wanly. "I like Zachary. We started out in teaching together. He was brilliant and dedicated. What happened in 1992 destroyed his confidence. We should have stepped up to make sure he didn't blame himself. Instead, all we cared about was making sure we were covered when the newspapers got hold of the story. It ruined Zachary's career."

Another difference between principals and superintendents: principals can be nice. "He ruined his own career. He might have been a good teacher once, but he isn't anymore. I agree—we gave him the most difficult kids in the district. And he made them worse."

"He'll be out of our hair soon enough," she offers. "We both know he's planning to take early retirement."

I wince. In the education business, you don't reach the level of superintendent without knowing how to do a little homework. The health and longevity in the Kermit family are appalling. Zachary Senior celebrated his eightieth birthday by going skydiving. The grandfather just turned 106. If the youngest Mr. Kermit has the same genes, he'll be collecting a pension from the school district for more than fifty years!

"The taxpayers of Greenwich shouldn't be on the hook for a bad teacher," I tell her. "If he's fired for cause, he'll get no pension at all."

She doesn't like that. "You have no cause. Not for a few lost noisemakers and something that happened twenty-seven years ago."

"Not yet," I concede. "But I'll find cause. Zachary Kermit is untrustworthy and incompetent. I know he's your friend, but as his boss, can you really defend him?"

She doesn't answer. A principal always knows when there's deadwood on staff that needs to be cleared away.

I don't gloat. That would be unbecoming of a super-intendent. But privately, I enjoy watching her squirm as she struggles to come up with an answer to that.

"I wonder," she muses finally. "When Zachary fell in the river—"

"No defense of a teacher should include a sentence that ends with 'fell in the river,'" I cut her off.

"The students didn't fall," she persists. "They jumped in because they thought they had to rescue Zachary. Remember the kids we're talking about—some of the most difficult and antisocial we've ever seen. But they're loyal to him. Why?"

Twelve hours later, as I lie in bed, trying to sleep, that *why?* is still reverberating inside my skull.

Fifteen

Mateo Hendrickson

The whole class gets suspended for the rest of Spirit Week. If that doesn't sound like a bad punishment, remember that your parents need to rearrange their work schedules so you're not left completely alone. I can't speak for the others, but my folks are pretty mad.

"It's no big deal," I tell my father. "Syfy is running a *Battlestar Galactica* marathon this week. That should keep me busy until at least Thursday."

Dad is like Zeus from *Percy Jackson*. No thunderbolts, but when he's in a bad mood you definitely want to stay clear of Olympus. "If you think this is a vacation, mister, you're sadly mistaken. You're going to sit in your room and reflect on how it's wrong to steal."

"It wasn't stealing," I insist. "Stealing is *The Great Train Robbery*. This is the Grinch. Better than the Grinch. The Grinch tried to steal Christmas, but he couldn't. We really did steal Spirit Week."

"You stole it from *yourselves*," he retorts. "Everyone else gets to enjoy it."

"We were already banned before we were suspended. Besides, Mr. Kermit's right. It's dumb to have spirit because it's on the calendar, or because people are blowing horns in your ear."

He frowns. "Mr. Kermit. I don't like what I'm hearing about that guy."

"Mr. Kermit's a good teacher," I argue. At least, he could be if he ever teaches anything. Look at Yoda. He may be a puppet with bad grammar, but he's also the greatest teacher in the galaxy. In fact, I might have to switch Mr. Kermit from the Grinch to Yoda, just like I'm going to have to switch Barnstorm from the Flash to Aquaman, because he's an amazing swimmer, even with a bad knee and a foot that's been stomped on by Elaine.

Come to think of it, if we're all suspended, does Mr. Kermit still have to go to school? There's nobody there for him to teach. Actually, I think he might like that. But it's possible that he's suspended too. Dr. Thaddeus seems really mad at him.

"Nah, Ribbit's not suspended," Parker tells me when I run into him on a delivery to the farmers' market. "His car's been in the parking lot all week."

"How would you know that?" I ask.

"Whenever I'm near the school on business, I look around a little."

"Business?" I echo.

"Farm business. I've got potatoes for Foodland, cantaloupes for the truck stop, and rutabagas for Local Table—Dad says they pay the most because they can't bring in produce from more than twenty miles away."

By the time we get back to school the next Monday, Spirit Week is over, and there isn't a vuvuzela in sight. Otherwise everything is the same—except for room 117. In fact, the place looks so different that, when I walk in, I actually step back into the hall to check the number on the door. No—it's 117 all right, and the other SCS-8 kids are taking their seats as usual. But we're all looking around in wonder.

There's a huge map of the world on the back wall, next to star charts from the northern and southern hemispheres. At the front, there are bulletin boards for math, science, English, and social studies. There's a rolling cart of laptop computers. There are books on the bookshelves. The empty supply closet isn't empty anymore. Through the open door we can see stacks of paper, pencils, scissors, and art supplies.

Another thing that's different: Mr. Kermit is already here. He's at the science board, pinning up a large periodic table of elements. It throws some of us because when the teacher makes his usual entrance ten minutes after the bell, that's our signal to start *ribbit*ing. Sure, there are a few *ribbit*s, but they seem random and halfhearted.

Kiana speaks up. "Mr. Kermit?"

"Oh!" He turns away from the board, as if noticing us for the first time. "Good. Everybody's here. Before we get started, I want to say something about last Monday down at the river. I know you were only trying to help, so let's chalk it up to temporary insanity. And— uh—thanks. But next time—not that there will be a next time—well, please find somebody else to help."

"But, Mr. K—" Parker interjects, waving his arms to take in the transformed classroom. "What gives?"

Mr. Kermit looks uncomfortable. "Well, last week I had some spare time since all my students were—uh—absent. So I did some redecorating."

An uneasy murmur buzzes through room 117. It's hard to put my finger on it, but it comes from the fact that this "redecoration" smells an awful lot like school. It isn't a big problem for me. I'm okay with the *school* side of things. But I don't like change. And for sure, this isn't the Ribbit we're used to. Where did all this come from?

At that moment, the door is flung open, and Miss Fountain breezes in, beaming. "What do you think, everybody? Isn't it *awesome?*"

"I forgot to mention," Mr. Kermit adds. "Miss Fountain helped a lot, so we owe her a big thank-you."

Nobody utters a sound.

Our teacher shuffles uncomfortably. "Well, Miss Fountain, I'm sure you're in a rush to get back to your students—"

Miss Fountain is looking around in growing concern. "But—where is it?"

Mr. Kermit seems flustered. "Well, there wasn't much space, and—" In resignation, he walks to the storage closet and opens the door the rest of the way. On the inside is a chart with all our names in a column. At the top is written: GOODBUNNIES.

Miss Fountain's brow furrows. "This isn't going to work. It has to hang in a place where everybody can see it." She pulls the poster from the door and rehangs it on the front wall right behind the teacher's desk. "Much better."

I raise my hand. "What are Goodbunnies?"

"You are," she explains. "You're the Goodbunnies. Every time you're a helpful hare—like when you do a good deed or get a good grade—you earn one puffy-tail. When your line of puffy-tails reaches the basket of carrots, you get a reward."

"I don't like carrots," Barnstorm complains.

"It could be a treat, or maybe even a pizza party with a cake—"

"A carrot cake?" Barnstorm asks suspiciously.

"The carrots are just a symbol. Here, I'll get you started." From a baggie attached to the bottom of the poster, she removes seven Velcro-tipped cotton balls and pins one to the first slot beside each of our names.

For some reason, I feel like I've accomplished

something, even though the week has barely started.

Aldo lets out a loud raspberry. "This is stupid! What are we—five? I'm not wasting my time collecting rabbit butts."

Mr. Kermit is annoyed. "All right, smart guy. You just cost yourself one"—his face twists—"puffy-tail." He pulls off the Velcro sticker and puts it back in the bag.

"No fair," grumbles Aldo.

Miss Fountain is just about to go back to her own class when there's a knock at the door, and this new guy walks in. He's an adult, but not one of the teachers, and he looks really familiar, although I can't place where I've seen him before. Mr. Kermit knows him—that's for sure. Our teacher has gone white to the ears, like he's staring into the Great Pit of Carkoon from *Return of the Jedi*.

The newcomer says, "I don't know if you remember me, Mr. Kermit—"

As soon as I hear the voice, I recognize him.

Barnstorm beats me to the punch. "Dude—you're Jake Terranova!"

Sixteen
Parker Elias

Jake Terranova!

Everybody knows Jumping Jake Terranova, who will jump through hoops to get you a great deal on a new or used vehicle. The billboards are all over town (although to me, TERRANOVA MOTORS looks more like AROMAVENT ROTORS). Anyway, there's no mistaking the face. This guy's famous! What's he doing in room 117?

Mr. Kermit has an expression on his face as if he

smells something really bad. It's the way he looks when there's a vuvuzela blaring. And since the vuvuzelas are all gone, it can only mean one thing: he hates Jake Terranova's guts.

Miss Fountain steps forward. "I really should explain, Mr. Kermit. I ran into Jake—that is, Mr. Terranova—at my parents' country club. I wanted to see if he remembered me. He sold me my Prius last year."

Mr. Terranova smiles with all thirty-two teeth. "Great car. Are you in the market for a new vehicle, Mr. Kermit? Emma loves hers."

"It makes me feel good to know I'm helping the environment every time I drive," Miss Fountain says with a meaningful look over her shoulder at Ribbit.

Our teacher's eyes get so narrow that they're barely slits.

"Anyway," Miss Fountain goes on, "we got to talking, and your name came up, Mr. Kermit. I told him about that story in the *Telegraph*—"

The car dealer cuts her off. "This should come from me." He turns to Mr. Kermit. "I read the article about the vuvuzelas. They mentioned something from the past—something I was involved in."

Our teacher has his teeth clenched until his lips have practically disappeared. "Mr. Terranova used to be one of my students," he explains, his speech clipped, "some years back."

"That's not enough. They should hear the whole truth." He addresses us. "You might have heard about a cheating scandal. Well, Mr. Kermit had nothing to do with it. It was me. I can't believe the newspaper dredged up that old story."

"Don't worry about it, Mr. Terranova," I assure him. "None of us read newspapers."

"I do," Mateo puts in. "*Middle Earth Weekly*. Of course, it's more fanfic than news."

The car dealer gives him a strange look. "The point is I don't want you kids to think that Mr. Kermit did anything wrong. It was my fault. I got caught and I got suspended for it."

"No kidding," Aldo pipes up. "We just got back from being suspended. But I didn't think it would happen to a big-shot rich dude."

Barnstorm snorts a laugh. "He wasn't a big shot when he got suspended, dummy. He was a kid like us."

Aldo and Barnstorm wheel around in their seats, turning belligerent expressions on each other. But Mr. Terranova quickly steps between them. "Guys, I was in middle school once too. If you two want to throw hands, there's nothing I can do to stop it. But not here and not now."

Aldo and Barnstorm back down.

The car dealer faces Mr. Kermit again. "So I came here to apologize, which I should have done years ago. And if there's anything I can ever do to help out—you know, with the class—all you have to do is say the word."

"Thanks for your generous offer," our teacher says stiffly. "But that won't be necessary—"

"Of course we want your help!" Miss Fountain exclaims, and it's pretty obvious this was her plan all along.

Mr. Kermit's sour expression gets worse. "I'm sure Mr. Terranova wouldn't appreciate it if you and I went to his lot and tried to sell cars. And he would be just as unsuccessful trying to teach our students."

"Be reasonable," she pleads. "He's built a business. He could give a math unit on earnings versus expenses, or how to amortize a loan. He could let us tour his repair shop and maybe teach us about basic auto mechanics."

"He could let me take out a Dodge Viper for a test drive." I add, "I have a license."

Mr. Terranova doesn't answer. He's beaming at Miss Fountain, and at that moment he looks exactly like his picture on the billboards (without the flaming hoops, obviously). "It's a date," he says, and Miss Fountain's cheeks get all red, even though it isn't really hot in the classroom.

"Well, maybe," Mr. Kermit concedes. "If the curriculum allows."

"We don't have a curriculum," Mateo points out. "We just get worksheets while you do crossword puzzles."

That costs him a puffy-tail.

Seventeen

Mr. Kermit

The Goodbunnies chart is mocking me.

No matter where I am in the room, my eyes are drawn to the bright pink poster board with its white puffy-tails. Even at my desk—when I can't see it—I sense it behind me. Knowing it's there is almost as bad as looking at it.

As great as the temptation may be, I can't bring myself to throw it out. Emma keeps finding excuses to come over and check on it. She's frustrated that no one is earning any puffy-tails. She's determined to stick with the teaching style that worked with her kinder-garten class last year. Her mother was like that—100 percent headstrong when she believed she was right. Middle schoolers won't excel for that kind of infantile reward system. And these particular middle schoolers wouldn't excel if you put ten thousand volts to the soles of their feet. The only thing that motivates them, apparently, is the prospect of dumping mass quantities of vuvuzelas into the river.

But that's another story—and a much more bizarre one. I don't like to think about that. There are some questions that should never be answered.

My new habit is to get to class before the kids. That way, I can be finished with the *New York Times* cross-word puzzle by the time they arrive. Just because the school saddled me with the worst class in the district doesn't mean I have to pass that disrespect on to the students. They deserve better—some of them. One or two. And anyway, all of them jumped into the river when they thought their teacher was drowning. That says something.

I'm still not sure what.

As I spread the newspaper out, I have to push the Toilet Bowl to the edge of the desk, which sends some papers skittering to the floor. A couple of weeks ago, I would barely have noticed. But now that this place looks sort of like a real classroom, it's worth a little effort to keep things neat. If not, one of these days Emma might show up with a CLEANBUNNIES poster board, and this one will have the name ZACHARY on it.

I'm about to toss the papers when I recognize the first page. It's one of my old worksheets, accompanied by four additional pages of neat handwriting. *Kiana Roubini*, reads the name at the top. I remember her handing in something like this. And come to think of it, she's always been a little less out to lunch than the rest of them.

I scan a few lines. It's an *essay* of all things, and it seems to be pretty well written. I read on, drawn in by her compelling sentences and well-constructed arguments about mass transit. She's really enthused about the subject, and she expresses herself beautifully. What's she doing in SCS-8? This is brilliant work!

Any teacher would be delighted to receive an essay like this. Why, back when I was first starting out—

My vision clouds. That was a long time ago, when teaching was more than a job; it was a sacred mission. I was young and stupid then, and I've vowed never again to make the mistake of caring about the students. I cared about Jake Terranova once. Look where that got me.

On the other hand, it isn't Kiana's fault that Terranova went into business selling exams. It won't be breaking the promise I made to myself to give her the feedback she deserves for a fantastic piece of work.

So later, when the students arrive, I return her paper. Written across the top is: *A+ Excellent.*

She's surprised at first, then thrilled. It triggers more long-suppressed memories: well-deserved praise, pride, and satisfaction. Motivated teacher, motivated student.

Then she asks the question I expect the least: "Do I get a puffy-tail?"

Why would Goodbunnies even be on the radar screen of someone capable of writing such a top-notch essay? But I reply, "Sure, why not?"

As I attach the Velcro puffy-tail next to her name on the chart, I have the undivided attention of every soul in that classroom. If I'd taken out a sword and knighted the girl, it couldn't have been a bigger event.

Barnstorm raises a crutch. "How come she gets one of those things? What about the rest of us?"

"She wrote an essay," I explain. "If you want a

puffy-tail, you have to work for it."

"Not necessarily," Parker pipes up. "Miss Fountain says you can also get one for being a helpful hare. I drive my Grams to the senior center every day. If that's not helpful, what is?"

So he gets a puffy-tail too. That opens the flood-gates:

"I loaded the dishwasher after dinner last night!"

"I did blue face paint at the *Avatar* convention!"

"I broke scoring records in three sports!"

"I took out the garbage!"

I award puffy-tails like it's going out of style. True, most of these "accomplishments" aren't very impressive. But puffy-tails themselves are so meaningless that it would be hypocritical to raise the standard to earn them.

Rahim gets one for staying awake long enough to receive it.

Only Aldo can't come up with anything better than "On the bus today, this kid tripped over my book bag and landed in gum."

I sigh. "That doesn't sound very—uh—helpful to me."

Aldo tries again. "Well, now it's in his hair and he can't get rid of it. He looks like a doofus!"

"Dude, you could have moved your bag out of his way," Barnstorm pronounces. "That's the helpful hare way. Otherwise, you should *lose* a puffy-tail."

"He's already at zero," Mateo puts in.

"Zero is *better*!" Aldo explodes. "Because rabbit butts are stupid!"

"Easy to say when you don't have any," Barnstorm needles.

"Come on, Aldo," Kiana whispers. "You must have done something nice!"

The boy's still stumped. He sulks for the rest of the day.

Just before lunch, Emma looks in, catches sight of the poster board with so many new puffy-tails, and beams with pleasure.

When I submit the official request for a school bus, Principal Vargas regards me with deep suspicion. She's probably thinking about how many vuvuzelas you can cram into a whole bus. A lot more than a thousand, for sure.

I elaborate. "It's for a field trip."

"Field trip?" She's amazed. "For *your* kids? Where?"

"We're going to Terranova Motors." Speaking those words is even harder than I thought it would be.

"We've been invited to tour the repair shop . . ." I regurgitate Emma's reasons why this is a good idea.

"Back up, Zachary. I've known you for a long time. Why would you go anywhere near Jake Terranova?"

I sigh. "Emma found him at some country club shindig. She's a serious busybody, that one. She told him about the Spirit Week kerfuffle, and how it dredged up what happened. Now he wants to make amends."

The principal folds her arms in front of her. "And you want to give him an opportunity to clear his conscience?"

"It's not me," I admit. "It's the kids. They came alive when he walked into the room. They consider him some kind of celebrity. Listen, Christina, I know they're awful, but what we did to them is just as awful. Are we really going to keep them cooped up like prisoners until they can be the high school's headache? If there's a chance for them to have a real education, we have to take it. And if that means Jake Terranova, then so be it."

She looks at me for an uncomfortably long moment. "The last time I heard words like that, they came from a young teacher I used to work with. A teacher named Zachary Kermit."

"That person is gone forever," I assure her. "And he's

never coming back, which is a good thing because he was an idiot."

"All right, you've got your bus." The principal scribbles a signature on the requisition form and leans back in her chair, her expression sober. "One more thing, Zachary. You've probably already noticed that Dr. Thaddeus isn't exactly your biggest fan. Well, the vuvuzelas didn't do anything to change that."

"I don't lose sleep over what *he* thinks." That's mostly because I have such terrible insomnia that there isn't much sleep for me to lose. But I don't mention that to Christina.

"You didn't hear this from me," she persists, "but I think he's going to try to go after your early retirement."

I shrug. "He's done it already. I know why I got saddled with the Unteachables. He wants me to quit. He'll see his own ears first."

"There's another way," she reminds me grimly. "One wrong step and he'll fire you. Don't give him cause. I'll protect you as much as I can, but I'm not the superintendent. He is. And never underestimate how much power that gives him."

I nod, take the bus authorization, and get out of

there. It's the cheating scandal, still haunting me after all these years. Thaddeus will never forgive me for it.

I thought Jake Terranova was back. Correction: he never left.

Eighteen

Kiana Roubini

TOP 4 REASONS WHY MY HALF BROTHER, CHAUNCEY, IS LIKE VLADIMIR:

1. The smell. Dirty diapers and baby puke. Enough said. Vladimir's terrarium after the weekend is no perfume factory either.
2. The noise. Chauncey's howling has the edge in volume, but Vladimir's high-pitched squeaks are even more piercing. It goes

without saying that both of them are spoiled by too much attention. That's Stepmonster's fault in Chauncey's case. For Vladimir, it's Miss Fountain's seventh graders, and, lately, us. When he wants somebody to feed him a dead cricket—which is all the time—the cheeping and chirping are at a frequency that feel like a miniature blender at the center of your brain.

3. The teeth. They both have zero. Okay, Vladimir probably has more than that, but you don't know they're there until he nips you. And to be fair, Chauncey does have a couple of chompers breaking through, bottom front. It's pretty cute, actually.

4. The time-suck. That's the biggest similarity between them. Dealing with Chauncey is a twenty-five-hour-per-day job, mostly for Stepmonster, but also for Dad and me. If you leave him alone for ten seconds, he'll find a way to stick his drool-covered finger into an electric outlet, light himself on fire, and roll down at least one flight of stairs. Vladimir is every bit as impossible to ignore. When he starts squeaking, you go running. And he's

not satisfied with just anybody. These days, the attention he craves is from Aldo. Leave it to Vladimir to love the least lovable person in the whole school, except maybe Elaine. Maybe it's the red hair. It's hard to ignore.

Anyway, I shouldn't really complain that Stepmonster is so distracted. If it wasn't for Chauncey, she might call up the school to ask how I'm doing and get told, "Kiana who?" The last thing I need is to get put in regular classes and have to break in eight new teachers, just when I'm starting to get the hang of Mr. Kermit.

Now that Ribbit's doing real teaching, I don't even have to make things up when Dad and Stepmonster ask, "How's school?" I have something to tell them. There are things going on in room 117—things beyond worksheets and crossword puzzles.

"Hang on a sec. Back up." My father stops me at dinner. "What are these puffy-tails you keep talking about? Some kind of science unit?"

"Right," I stammer. "Animal anatomy."

"If you're going to be dissecting some poor little bunny, I don't want to hear about it," Stepmonster puts in, shoveling strained bananas into Chauncey's waiting mouth.

"And we're going on that field trip tomorrow, remember?" I move on quickly.

"To a rabbit laboratory?" Dad asks.

"No, this is different."

We're going to Terranova Motors as Jake Terranova's personal guests. I don't know what we're supposed to learn there, but the class is actually pretty psyched about it. One of the downsides of being in SCS-8—besides the obvious—is that you're stuck in the same room all day. So the change of scenery will do us good.

Our two chaperones are Mr. Kermit and Miss Fountain. Mr. Kermit has no choice, but it's really nice of Miss Fountain to volunteer, since her own classes have to have a sub today. As it turns out, they get Mrs. Landsman—aka Dawn of the Dead. Poor Vladimir. If he squeaks too loud, she'll probably gut him with a protractor and barbecue him on a rotating spit in the home and careers room.

The bus is just a minibus, and it's pretty uncomfortable with the whole class packed into one side and Elaine all by herself on the other. Aldo is getting mad because Barnstorm keeps thumping the back of his seat with one of the crutches. It doesn't bother Rahim, though. He falls asleep as soon as we make the right turn out of the school driveway. Mateo stands in the aisle, knees bent, working on his balance, just like the Silver Surfer from *Spider-Man*.

Miss Fountain seems pretty uncomfortable with the bad behavior—and especially the fact that Mr. Kermit isn't saying anything. So she tries to change the subject by talking about how SCS-8 should participate in the district science fair. She's always coming up with suggestions for our class, like the Goodbunnies thing, or inviting us for Circle Time or to help out with Vladimir.

Sometimes, Mr. Kermit lets her push him around a little, but not today. "No," he says simply. I think this field trip has put him in a bad mood. It's pretty obvious that Jake Terranova isn't his favorite person.

"But it's a fantastic competition," Miss Fountain persists. "Teams enter from every school in the district. There are prizes. And the first-place winners get an extra ten percent added to their grades on the state science assessment. It's a win-win."

"Not for us," Mr. Kermit replies firmly.

His expression says it all: *Do these really look like the kind of kids who will come in first place at anything?*

It bugs me a little. Not that I'm dying to get mixed

up in any science fair, me being a short-timer. But I'm used to Mr. Kermit sticking up for us, not writing us off. Maybe it's part of his bad mood.

The other kids talk about Jake Terranova like he's some kind of superstar. As we pull up to Terranova Motors, I finally understand why. It has to be the biggest car dealership I've ever seen—and that includes LA, where everything is kind of supersized. Mr. Kermit's ex-student owns all this? That's pretty cool—especially when Mr. Terranova himself comes out to welcome us.

"Hey, guys! Glad you could make it! Come on inside!" Like we're longtime friends, not random middle schoolers getting our moment with the big boss.

We tour the showroom first, which, I have to admit, is pretty fun. All the vehicles are shiny, new, and top-of-the-line. We try out every seat in every car—front, back, and third row—and even climb into the payloads of the pickups. For the first time since blundering into SCS-8, I feel like I could be with any class of kids in the country, not Greenwich Middle School's dreaded Unteachables. Ribbit sees it too—his bloodshot eyes are half-open, instead of the usual 25 percent. Or maybe he's just on the alert because Mr. Terranova is here, and this is enemy territory.

Miss Fountain, the Prius driver, is looking disapprovingly at the giant SUVs and light trucks that dominate the showroom when Mr. Terranova walks up to her.

I'm wondering if she's going to lecture him on the environment. Instead, she says, "This is a wonderful thing you're doing. I don't know if you can tell, but some of these kids have—special issues."

"You think?" His grin is irresistible. "My floor manager just pulled a sleeper out of the trunk of that Cadillac."

"That's Rahim," Miss Fountain explains. "He doesn't get enough sleep at home. But he's a talented artist, sensitive and observant. They've got their quirks. They're good kids, though. Okay, maybe *good* is too strong a word—"

"Gotcha." He's watching Barnstorm poking tires with his crutches.

"Hey, Mr. Terranova." Parker approaches. "I want to take the red Mustang out for a test drive."

"Right. Very funny, kid."

"No, really. I have a license." Parker digs a mangled ID out of the pocket of his jeans.

"It's a provisional license, Parker," Miss Fountain reminds him gently.

"This is a hundred percent farm business," Parker promises. "I just remembered I've got to swing home and pick up a load of turnips for the Safeway."

Looking for a lifeline, she calls out, "Mr. Kermit, I think it's time for lunch!"

It's hard to get a handle on what Ribbit thinks of all this. On one hand, it's obvious that he can't stand his former student because of what happened in the past. On the other, that must have been forever ago. Mr. Terranova was a seventh grader, even younger than we are. He's an adult now, running a big business, and he's trying to make amends. Why can't Mr. Kermit see that?

We brought bag lunches, but Mr. Terranova ordered pizza for everybody in the dealership dining room. Only Ribbit turns him down—like anything from his old nemesis would turn to poison as soon as it enters his mouth.

The employees are really friendly, and we get to ask them questions. I want to know about fuel-efficiency standards. Barnstorm wants to know: "When you sell a car, do you get to keep the money?" Aldo asks the lease specialist, "How long did it take to grow that mustache?"

Elaine gets into the cookie platter set aside for

customer appreciation week.

After lunch, we tour the service department. That's where the field trip starts to get really good. Motor vehicles are such a huge part of life, especially in a place like LA, where you have to drive pretty much everywhere. People take it for granted that their cars will work, like they're powered by some kind of magic. How often do we ever take a peek under the hood at the machinery that makes it happen?

Mr. Terranova leads us onto a raised catwalk, and we can look down on at least a dozen vehicles on lifts in various stages of being taken apart and put back together again. The noise is a cacophony of revving engines, pneumatic tools, and the clang of metal on metal. The smell is a mix of oil and grease, with a little bit of exhaust, whatever the ventilation fans miss. Yet there's almost a kind of grace to it, and a rhythm that's hard to resist. It feels *productive*, like necessary work is being done.

Parker is practically drooling, and even Aldo is leaning over the railing, fascinated. It's the first time I've ever seen him interested in something, and he looks older and more mature. Mateo is babbling about how the shop reminds him of the engine room of the USS *Enterprise* on *Star Trek*. Rahim is sketching furiously on a napkin from the lunchroom. Elaine is watching in rapt attention while double-fisting stolen cookies from her jacket pockets.

Suddenly, she clutches the rail in distress. For a second, I wonder if she's trying to hype her reputation by ripping it free from the catwalk. But no—her cheeks are pink, her eyes terrified. Sharp staccato choking sounds reach me over the clamor of the shop. Mr. Kermit pounds her on the back, but to no avail.

I run up behind Elaine and reach around her to perform the Heimlich maneuver, positioning my hands below the rib cage, like they told us in lifesaving class back in California. Once . . . twice. No good. Three times—

"Heads up!" bellows a wild voice.

I glance over my shoulder just in time to see a crutch hurtling toward me in a home run swing. I drop to the metal floor of the catwalk a split second before the wooden shaft would have taken my head off. It slams across Elaine's broad back and—with a thud that momentarily drowns out the noisy shop—splits in two.

Everybody waits for her to crumple to the catwalk, unconscious, but that's not what happens. Elaine doesn't even flinch. Instead, a chunk of cookie comes flying out of her mouth. It sails over the rail and drops into the half-disassembled motor of a vintage Corvette.

The mechanics look up in horror.

"What was that?" Mr. Terranova asks urgently.

I confirm that Elaine is no longer choking. "She's okay."

The car dealer looks at me like I'm totally missing the point. "But what did she spit in the engine?"

Elaine smacks her lips. "I think it was a gingersnap."

The word is like a panic alarm to Jake. "Guys!" he calls down to his team. "I want that engine taken apart and every piece wiped clean! *Now!*"

I'm mystified. "What's so bad about a gingersnap?"

"Sugar!" he exclaims in agony. "It's the last thing you want in a car engine. It dissolves in the gas and ends up everywhere. If word gets around that I sold a car with a sugared tank, I'm *finished* in this business."

Mr. Kermit is beaming from ear to ear. It's the first time we've ever seen him so happy, and what did it take? Problems for Jake Terranova. I actually feel a little guilty. I saw Elaine pocketing those cookies, and kept my mouth shut. I may be a short-timer, but you don't have to be at our school very long to know that Elaine rhymes with pain.

The field trip breaks up soon after that. Mr. Terranova is focused on the Corvette, so he's not playing host anymore. Plus, Barnstorm is complaining about his mobility with only one crutch.

"Then you shouldn't have busted the other one over Elaine's head," Aldo tells him.

"It was her back, not her head," Barnstorm retorts. "I saved her life, man. She'd better remember that while deciding who her next victim's going to be."

"You just cost yourself a puffy-tail, buster," Mr. Kermit snaps.

Barnstorm is bitter. "No fair! I save a life and I'm out a crutch *and* a puffy-tail? What kind of justice is that?"

"He should *earn* a puffy-tail for helping and lose it for being mean," Parker puts in. "At least then he breaks even."

"We should all get a puffy-tail except Elaine," Aldo reasons truculently. "You know, for *not* barfing a cookie into that Corvette." This seems to be his idea of fairness.

Elaine tosses a mild glance in Aldo's direction, and he decides to stand on the other side of a tall cargo van.

It's too bad that such a great field trip has to end on

a down note. But by then the minibus is waiting outside, so there's nothing to do but get on it.

Halfway back to school, Miss Fountain gets a call on her cellphone. It's the dealership. There's a middle school boy asleep on the couch in the showroom.

Mr. Kermit does a head count. "It's Rahim," he reports. "We have to go back and get him." And we turn around.

"Wait." I frown at Miss Fountain. "How come they called *you*? I mean, why does Jake Terranova have your phone number?"

She blushes the color of Chauncey's diaper rash.

Nineteen

Parker Elias

Grams has a lot of life experience, being super old and all that. For example, she tells me that when she was first dating my grandfather back in Israel, there was this other girl who was trying to steal him away while Grams was doing her military service in Haifa. So Grams challenged this girl to an arm-wrestling match, and the prize was Grandpa.

I peer over at her in the passenger seat of the pickup. "What if you lost?"

"I was loading supply trucks, kiddo. I was strong as an ox."

As much as I love Grams, I'm not so sure I believe the story. The last time she explained how she got rid of the girl who moved in on Grandpa, she said she backed over her Vespa with a jeep. Grams tells the same stories because she doesn't remember telling them last time and the time before that. Some people might find that annoying; to me it just means that we've always got something new and interesting to talk about while I'm driving her around. I just wish she could remember my name.

The reason the subject comes up—dating and boy-friends, I mean—is that there's a rumor that Miss Fountain and Jake Terranova are going out. Our class thinks this because Jake has kind of adopted SCS-8. Jake—that's what he told us to call him. Even the employees at the dealership call him Mr. Terranova, but to us, he's Jake. Except Ribbit. He always uses *Mr.* when he talks to Jake, which is almost never. (Jake may be hitting it off with Miss Fountain, but he isn't getting very far with Mr. Kermit.)

Here's how it usually goes down. Jake shows up in room 117 to invite us to Terranova Motors so the mechanics can show us how windshield wipers work, or how a battery supplies power to the starter. He has to come in person because Mr. Kermit's phone is so old that it would probably explode if it ever received a text. Meanwhile, Miss Fountain randomly walks in from 115—"Oh, what a surprise. Mr. Terranova's here." She calls him Mr. Terranova too. (We're not fooled. He calls her Emma.)

From there, something always happens to connect our two classes. Maybe Vladimir starts squeaking because he hears Aldo's voice, and won't shut up until Aldo goes over there. Or the seventh graders are just about to have Circle Time, and we get in on that. Jake loves Circle Time, and whenever it's his turn to compliment someone, he always picks Miss Fountain.

Mateo is confused. "I thought Jake chose us because he wants to make up for the cheating scandal, not because of Miss Fountain."

"That's just his excuse," Barnstorm puts in wisely.

"Do you think it's the car?" I muse. Jake rolls this really snazzy Porsche convertible that's got to be a lot of fun to drive.

"Of course it's not the car," Kiana retorts angrily. "Miss Fountain isn't that kind of person. She wants a *relationship*."

I don't understand how Kiana can know something

like that. But whatever the reason, life is definitely better since Jake started hanging around. Everybody loves him—even Aldo, and Aldo hates everybody. Jake's more like another kid than an adult—but a kid who has a dream life, with tons of money and no adults telling him what to do. He talks to me about cars, to Barnstorm about sports, and to Mateo about *Game of Thrones*. He talks to Elaine—I guess car dealers don't worry about being head-butted down stairs or tossed into garbage dumpsters. He talks to Kiana about practically everything. He asks Rahim's opinion on the art for new ads for Terranova Motors, and Rahim never so much as yawns when he's around.

The only person Jake can't schmooze is Mr. Kermit. Our teacher isn't quite mean to him. Most of the time, he just ignores Jake the way he used to ignore us. When Mr. Kermit's old car breaks down, he has it towed all the way across town, even though Jake offers to fix it for free. Ribbit would rather pay a lot of money than accept a favor from his old enemy.

Whatever the reason Jake has started hanging around, the trips to Terranova Motors are amazing. At first, the service staff aren't too thrilled to see Elaine because of what happened that time with the cookie.

But then the compressor for the pneumatic system conks out, and Elaine's the only one who can loosen a stripped bolt using a hand wrench.

All the mechanics stop what they're doing and applaud.

"Kid, that was something!" the service chief exclaims admiringly. "If the lift system loses power, can we count on you to pick up cars on your shoulders?"

It's the first time I've ever seen Elaine blush. I'll bet the kid she head-butted down the stairs wouldn't think it's so funny that an eighth-grade girl is stronger than a shop full of adult mechanics.

At first, the mechanics just talk a lot and show us stuff, but pretty soon we're doing real work. Jake guides my hand as I fit a new hose into the radiator of a Jeep Cherokee. As I set the ring to seal the connection, it just feels right. Somehow, I *know* that hose isn't going to leak.

The boss reaches in and tests my handiwork. "Perfect. Not so tight that the rubber might split. Nice job, Parker."

It's weird. I open a book, and the letters are all jumbled together into Unbreakable Code. But I look at a car engine and it all makes sense—even if the tires still say READY GOO. (That's supposed to be GOOD-YEAR.)

Mr. Kermit is watching me, and he's almost smiling. I think I can count on a puffy-tail being added to my line of the chart today.

Terranova Motors isn't the only place we're doing real work. It's happening in room 117 too. Mr. Kermit is teaching stuff—math, science, English. We have our first test of the year—social studies—and Mr. Kermit even grades it.

When we get to class the next day, our papers are facedown on our desks.

Aldo flips his over. "D? Ribbit never gave tests before, and now he's throwing Ds around?"

Barnstorm laughs in his face. "It isn't Ribbit's fault you're stupid." He examines his own paper. The word *INCOMPLETE* is written across the top.

"What?!" he complains.

"At least I *got* a grade," Aldo tells him.

"I miss the old Ribbit," Barnstorm complains.

"Yeah," Aldo agrees. "This is way too much like education."

I get an incomplete too—mostly because I finished only seven of the twenty questions. But—I blink—seven check marks parade down the page. Which means whatever I did I aced! I still got an incomplete—but not incomplete-dumb, just incomplete-*slow*.

It stinks to fail, whatever the reason. But I disagree with Aldo and Barnstorm that our class was better before. We'll be in high school next year. Will they have an SCS-9 for us? Followed by SCS-10, SCS-11, and SCS-12? And then what? Sooner or later, something has to change. It might as well start now.

As I take my seat, I catch a glimpse of the test paper on Elaine's desk. I shake my head. I must be reading it wrong. That's what I do. On the other hand, how do you scramble a single letter?

If I didn't know better, I'd swear Elaine (rhymes with pain) just pulled an A.

Twenty

Jake Terranova

As I cruise along River Street with the top down, the red brick of Greenwich Middle School heaves into view. That place used to be a bad memory. I was never much of a student, but middle school was a really rough time. I was lucky to get away with a suspension over the cheating thing. If my dad hadn't belonged to the same college fraternity as a couple of school board members, I probably would have been expelled. It was that close.

Now, though, Greenwich Middle School means Emma. She's the best thing that's ever happened to me. Just the thought that she's somewhere inside the building puts a smile on my face.

The smile disappears when I recognize the figure standing at the entrance to the driveway, glancing impatiently at his watch. Mr. Kermit, my old teacher. The man who has every reason to drink from the Haterade where I'm concerned.

Back in seventh grade, I was so happy not to be expelled that there wasn't another thought in my head. It never crossed my mind that the episode might cause problems for my teacher. Why would it? Mr. Kermit was completely innocent. Who knew that better than the guy who was completely guilty?

But that's only the half of it. According to Emma, Mr. Kermit's life crashed after that. His reputation was shot. His engagement to Emma's mom fell apart. And he got totally burned-out professionally.

Honestly, I had no clue until Emma showed me the article about the vuvuzelas. The fact that the scandal still sticks to Mr. Kermit after all these years is nuts. Not that I ever had the power to change anything. I was a middle school kid in big trouble. I followed my parents' instructions to the letter—basically, shut up and keep your nose clean.

Now that I know the extent of it, I'd do *anything* to make things right. The problem is it's too late. Sure, Mr. Kermit is letting me help with his class of Unteachables. And I'm getting along great with the kids. But as for the teacher himself, no dice.

I check the clock on my Porsche's high-tech dashboard. It's only two p.m. Why isn't Mr. Kermit in school?

I pull alongside him and wave. Mr. Kermit scowls at me with what Mateo calls the Squidward-Grinch face. That kid's pretty weird, but he's usually spot-on. He's nicknamed me Han Solo because both of us are "lovable scoundrels." Maybe I walked away from the cheating scandal with a slap on the wrist, but lately it's come back to haunt me in all sorts of ways.

"Everything okay, Mr. Kermit?" I ask.

"My taxi is late."

Right. His "car" is in the shop. I volunteered to fix it no charge, but he wasn't having any of that. To say he's stubborn as a mule is an insult to mules.

"Hop in," I invite. "I'll give you a ride wherever you need to go."

"No, thanks," he replies formally. "I've been waiting

forty minutes for this taxi. It'll be here any second."

"It's not coming," I persist. "Did you try Uber?"

He looks blank. I remember that Mr. Kermit has a flip phone that's probably as old as his car. There are smart phones and dumb phones. His is a rock.

I unlock the passenger door. "Mr. Kermit—please. Let me give you a lift."

When he reluctantly gets in and announces his destination, I nearly choke. He's going to pick up his car—from Kingston's Auto Works.

"Are you serious? You took your car fifteen miles out of town just to avoid my offer to fix it for free?"

The response is a heavy dose of the Squidward-Grinch face. "I don't want to owe you anything."

"You *wouldn't* owe me anything!" I'm practically whining. "I would have been happy to do it."

He's sarcastic. "Well, so long as *you're* happy."

"That's not what I mean and you know it. I enjoy doing favors for friends"—Mr. Kermit doesn't like that, so I adjust my word choice—"for people I know. You used to be my teacher."

"I remember."

This is it—my chance to clear the air and apologize. But as soon as the thought pops into my head, I know he won't let me. Better to shut up about it. Maybe, as the two of us spend more time together, I'll get another chance.

And maybe the moon will fall out of the sky.

When the Porsche reaches Kingston's Auto Works, Mr. Kermit takes out his wallet and tries to pay me for the gas. When I won't accept it, he stuffs a twenty-dollar bill into the glove compartment and gets out, not bothering to say thank you.

I get out too, and receive a generous helping of Squidward-Grinch face.

"I can handle it from here," he assures me.

"I'm going in with you," I insist. "I don't want you to get ripped off. These guys are all crooks."

"Including you?" Mr. Kermit inquires innocently.

I run a totally honest shop, but still I feel my cheeks flush. "An old clunker like yours—the parts probably have to come from the third world. Who knows what they'll try to charge you for them."

It must make an impression, because Mr. Kermit actually allows me to follow him inside.

The place is a dump. You could probably catch plague just standing there breathing the air.

The mechanic behind the counter instantly recognizes me. "Hey, you're Jake Terranova. What are you doing here?"

"My *very good friend* is picking up his car," I reply pointedly. "I want to make sure he gets a fair deal."

"We barely know each other." Mr. Kermit sets the record straight.

The mechanic picks up a clipboard. "Which car?"

"The Coco Nerd," the teacher tells him.

"The *what*?"

Mr. Kermit flushes. "It's a Chrysler Concorde—1992. One of my students calls it that. He's—different."

I snap my fingers. "Parker, right? What's up with that kid? He's got a lot of mechanical ability. But ask him to read the name off a part, and it comes out pure gobbledygook."

"It's not gobbledygook," he says, insulted on Parker's behalf. "The boy has a perception problem. He sees all the letters, but his mind rearranges them—*Concorde* to *Coco Nerd*."

"Like an anagram," the mechanic butts in. "You should meet my boss—he's an anagram maniac. You look at a word, and to you it's just a jumble, but he can pick it out in a heartbeat."

Poor Parker. The kid's got real potential, but how's

he ever going to pass an engineering exam if he can't read the questions? "All right, where's the car?"

"Car's not ready," the mechanic tells us. "There's a part coming from the Bahamas, and it's held up in customs."

Instead of getting mad, Mr. Kermit acts like he's in a completely different world. "Anagrams," he repeats slowly. He grabs my arm. "Let's go."

"You have to stick up for yourself," I say sternly. I turn to the mechanic. "Is this what you call service? If I ran my shop this way, I'd be out of business in a week. How's the part coming from the Bahamas—by manatee?"

"It doesn't matter," Mr. Kermit insists. "Take me to the bookstore."

"The *bookstore*? You don't need books; you need *wheels*!"

Back in the Porsche, he explains what all this is about. "Parker's mind turns text into anagrams."

"Yeah? So?"

"So anagrams are something you can get good at, like any other puzzle."

I stare at him. "Solving anagrams can teach you to read?"

Mr. Kermit shakes his head. "Of course not. Parker

needs a reading specialist. If I was half a teacher, I would have gotten him one weeks ago."

I'm confused. "So where do the anagrams fit in?"

"The kid's reading has been a disaster for so long that he looks at it like it's magic—something he'll never be able to master. But solving anagrams will show him it can be done. So when I get him the help he needs, he'll believe it can work."

"*Can* you get him the help he needs?" I ask.

"The district has reading specialists," he explains. "Nobody sends them to SCS-8 because they consider my students a lost cause. That ends now." He glares at me. "The bookstore!"

I step on the gas and the Porsche surges forward. It's amazing how Mr. Kermit's whole face changes when he's talking about the kids in his class. He becomes a totally different person—younger, more alive. He's the teacher I remember from all those years ago.

At the bookstore, he's a whirlwind, stacking up an armload of anagram puzzle books tall enough for him to hold in place with his chin. By this time, school is out, so he demands to be taken to Parker's *house*.

"Can't you just wait to see him tomorrow morning?"

"I want to strike while the iron is hot."

The Elias family lives just outside the Greenwich

city limits on a small farm that was designed to keep sports cars out. The long "driveway" is really just a pair of ruts worn into the unpaved ground by vehicles much higher and wider than the Porsche. I can actually feel the weeds brushing the low undercarriage as we jounce along. Eventually, we come to a low wood-frame home next to a shed amid fields of tall corn.

No sign of life from the house. I cut the engine. "Should I honk?"

"Let's give it a while," Mr. Kermit decides.

After about fifteen minutes, Parker comes roaring up the drive, his famous grandmother in the passenger seat of the pickup. I know a moment of agony as the kid pulls far too close behind the parked convertible.

Parker is pretty bewildered to see his teacher rushing across the front lawn toting a pile of books he can barely see over.

The grandmother spies me standing by my car. "I know you," she calls. "You're Jumping Jake Terranova."

"That's right, ma'am. Pleased to meet you."

She beams. "I see you on television. You'll jump through hoops to provide fast relief from painful athlete's foot fungus."

"That's not me," I tell her. "I get you a great deal on a new or used vehicle."

She looks at me like I'm feeble-minded. "Why would I need that? I've got my grandson to drive me around."

Mr. Kermit is having an animated conversation with Parker, holding up anagram books and talking a blue streak. They're well into it when a small tractor chugs out of the field and an older, taller version of Parker hops off and joins the group. Parker's dad is surprised that a teacher would make house calls, but as Mr. Kermit explains his plan, the man looks impressed and smiles with appreciation.

The contrast isn't lost on me—Mr. Elias's gratitude for a teacher who's willing to move heaven and earth to help a student, versus my folks all those years ago. They rescued their son—and I'm thankful. But in the process, they hung the teacher out to dry.

Mr. Kermit deserved better. I hope someday I'll get the chance to make it up to him.

Twenty-One

Kiana Roubini

NO BIKINI AURA.

That has nothing to do with bathing suits. It's an anagram of my name.

Mr. Kermit has me working with Parker on anagrams to improve his reading. Parker's getting pretty good, but for me, it's just fun. It's amazing the stuff you can come up with. For example, ZACHARY KERMIT can be scrambled into CRAZY TRAM HIKE, or ALDO BRAFF into FOLD A BARF.

Even Aldo laughs at that one, and he doesn't strike me as someone with a great sense of humor—especially about himself. He looks pretty different when he smiles—like his face is going along with all that red hair instead of fighting against it.

Or maybe Aldo decides to be mellow because he doesn't have a lot of choice. His reading partner is Elaine. It's one thing to kick a locker. A locker can't head-butt you down a flight of stairs, or any other of Elaine's Greatest Hits, like chucking a fire extinguisher at your face, or giving you a new ear piercing with a fishhook.

To everybody's surprise, Elaine turns out to be kind of a serious student, which nobody noticed before, since they were too busy being terrified of her. Mr. Kermit assigns them *Where the Red Fern Grows*, and Elaine is totally into it. So Aldo has to read it too, even though he claims the last book he finished was *Hop on Pop*.

The other reading group is Barnstorm, Mateo, and Rahim. This works because Mateo never shuts up, which keeps Rahim from falling asleep. Actually, Rahim is more awake lately anyway. Mr. Kermit talked to his stepdad, who agreed to move his rock band's nighttime rehearsals to an "alternate venue."

Guess where—an empty storage garage at Terranova Motors.

Sometimes, I join those guys because Parker goes to a reading specialist three days a week. That makes four of us, but it's usually just three, because Rahim isn't around as much these days. Mr. Kermit got him accepted as a part-time art student at the community college on the other side of the river. Since he draws all the time anyway, it makes sense to send him somewhere that's a good thing. It's complicated, but it works. On any given day, Barnstorm might have three partners, or two, or just one. It doesn't make that much difference, because the only thing he really cares about is puffy-tails.

Like any athlete, Barnstorm's competitive. But since he's sidelined from sports, all that competitive energy gets channeled into Goodbunnies. His parade of puffy-tails stretches past the basket of carrots, off the poster, and two-thirds of the way across the wall. He's miles ahead of me in second place. Mostly, that's because he won't cash them in. He's too greedy.

Whenever my line of puffy-tails reaches the carrots, I redeem them for a reward. Our class has already had two pizza parties, thanks to me. Plus, I lent Aldo a bunch so he could pay off the penalties for some late homework assignments. That was Mr. Kermit's idea. He's using puffy-tails to teach us how an economy works. We're free to trade them, spend them, sell them, or lend them—but the lenders have to charge interest. Aldo owes me 10 percent every week, and he's sinking deeper and deeper into debt.

"You're a sucker," Barnstorm tells me. "He's never going to pay you back. It's puffy-tails down a sink-hole."

"He is so," I defend Aldo. "And with interest."

"Using what?" Barnstorm retorts. "He's never earned a single puffy-tail."

Aldo leaps up. "I have too! I just spend mine on fines and stuff."

"Sit," Elaine rumbles, and Aldo plunks back down onto his chair.

Barnstorm won't let it go. "Name one thing you ever did for a puffy-tail."

Aldo thinks hard. "I—I changed the bulb in the projector."

"No, that was Rahim," Mateo puts in.

In frustration, Aldo runs his hands through his red hair, which makes it even messier. "Big deal. Who cares about a bunch of rabbit butts?"

I glare at Barnstorm. "I have faith in Aldo."

"Oh yeah?" he shoots back. "Why?"

It's a good question. Why would I put my trust in a bad-tempered redhead and a straight-D student? Well, part of it is probably because I don't care that much about puffy-tails to begin with. But I think the other part might be Vladimir. Eight classes a day make their way through room 115, and that lizard doesn't squeak his head off for any of them. He loves Aldo—only Aldo. And aren't animals supposed to have instincts about people who are good at heart?

I turn on Barnstorm. "At least Aldo's not a tight-fisted cheapskate like you. When the year's over and we're in high school, all those puffy-tails will be worthless."

"You can't take it with you," Elaine adds philosophically.

Barnstorm is smug. "At least I'll be rich."

"You're a Ferengi," Mateo tells him. "That's a race of aliens from *Star Trek*. They worship money and profit above all things."

"Settle down," Mr. Kermit says mildly. "We're free to spend—or not spend—our puffy-tails however we choose. That's how a market economy works."

As we settle back to work, I can't help thinking about what I said to Barnstorm: *When the year's over and we're in high school . . .*

I'm not going to be in high school with these kids. I'll be gone before the end of the semester. How many times can Mom's movie get struck by lightning?

But at the moment the words were coming out of my mouth, I meant them. I actually saw myself finishing out the year in this class I don't belong in, in this school I don't really go to. And in this town where my only connection is the fact that my parents grew up here.

Oh man, I've got to get back to LA—and fast.

Twenty-Two
Mrs. Vargas

In all my years in education, the greatest teacher I've ever worked with was a young man named Zachary Kermit. Oh, sure, we were all dedicated back then—fresh out of college and convinced we were destined to change the world one student at a time. Zachary was different. All teachers dream of changing lives; he really changed them. The kids had no way of knowing it, but being placed in Mr. Kermit's class was like winning the lottery. It actually got to the point where I'd look out over my own group and feel a little sorry for them because there was a much better teacher just down the hall.

That was before the Terranova incident turned him into a zombie. He went from best to worst. If I were doing my job, I'd have fired him long ago, because heaven knows he wasn't doing *his* job. Maybe I didn't see things clearly enough because he was a friend. Or maybe I was waiting for the teacher he once was to reappear. But after twenty-seven years, even I had to know that the old Zachary Kermit was gone forever.

Well, guess what: he's back. And it took the worst group of kids in the whole district to make it happen.

That's what brings me to the district offices this afternoon. The first semester progress reports are out, and I can't wait to share the big news with Dr. Thaddeus.

When it's my turn, I don't even say hello to my boss. I just march in and place the seven pages on the blotter in front of him.

"What are these?" he asks.

"Progress reports from SCS-8," I tell him. "Prepare to be amazed."

He sifts through the papers, giving a cursory scan to

each. "You're right," he says finally. "I am amazed—that an experienced administrator like yourself would be fooled so easily."

I'm shocked. "Fooled? Look at those results. Okay, they're just brief summaries, but last year these kids were all floundering. This is miraculous."

"It would be," he concedes, "if it was real."

"Why wouldn't it be real? Zachary Kermit is a fantastic teacher. Oh, sure, he was in a funk for a while—"

"I'd hardly describe twenty-seven years as a 'while,'" the superintendent puts in drily.

"But these kids and their needs have brought him back," I persist. "It's wonderful."

"It's phony," he retorts.

"Zachary would never falsify student reports."

"To keep his job long enough to finish out the year he would," he tells her. "Your Mr. Kermit has figured out what thin ice he's on. He'd do anything to make sure he qualifies for early retirement."

"Not this," I say stoutly. "I admit Zachary hasn't been the greatest teacher up until now, but his integrity has never been in question. Even at his very lowest point, he never claimed to be anything that he wasn't. There's a difference in those kids now. It's not just Zachary. The phys ed coaches see it. The lunchroom monitors see it. Emma Fountain sees it. *I* see it. They're not angels, but they're *better.* They go on field trips. A local business leader has taken them under his wing."

"What local business leader?"

"Jake Terranova," I admit. "I know it's a little odd—"

He laughs mirthlessly. "Spare me. I reject this so-called wonder of yours. In fact"—he takes out a large ring binder and begins flipping pages—"I've been reviewing the district contract. I'm sure you're familiar with Article Twelve, Subsection Nine."

"Refresh my memory," I reply warily.

He smiles. "It states that any teacher presiding over declining test grades in a core subject for three straight years can be deemed an ineffective educator and fired for cause."

I'm appalled. "You mean Zachary? He's been moved around so much that you couldn't possibly blame any class's failing grades on him."

"There's a formula," he explains. "You calculate a baseline using past performances of the individual kids. And it just so happens that Mr. Kermit's students have shown declining results on the state science exam for the past two years. If the assessment at the end of this month goes the same way, then I've got him."

I don't even watch my words. "That's so unfair!"

He raises one jet-black eyebrow. "How can you of all people say that? You just told me that he's turned this class around. If that's true, they'll ace the test, and Mr. Kermit will have nothing to worry about."

I bite my tongue. This man is my boss. He speaks for the school district, and what he says goes. He may be a stinker, but that doesn't change the fact that it's everybody's job to carry out his instructions.

Besides, he's just being sarcastic, but in this case he happens to be right. Zachary really *has* transformed that class. They don't have to "ace" the science test; they just have to beat their scores from past years. How hard can that be? Tests like this one got them placed in SCS-8 in the first place.

I leave the office feeling a lot better about Zachary's chances of making it through till June. Still, it can't hurt to pass on a suggestion that he might want to do some extra test prep for the coming science assessment. Forewarned is forearmed.

Zachary Kermit is too good a teacher to lose his retirement just because a certain cranky superintendent can't forgive him for something that was never his fault in the first place.

Twenty-Three
Kiana Roubini

"**C**ut it out, Chauncey!"

My half-pint half brother is crawling all over my notes, which are spread out around me on the floor of the den. His onesy is open, his diaper is sagging, and he's teething and drooling, an action figure of a Power Ranger or Transformer clutched in his little fist. Mateo can probably ID it—I make a mental note to Snapchat him a picture.

Chauncey's chubby knee comes down on my chart

of the atomic masses of elements, shredding the paper, and I freak out.

"Louise!" I bellow. Then, borrowing Dad's line: *"Jeez, Louise!"*

Chauncey is startled and bursts into tears. I feel bad about that. Pesky as he is, you can't help getting used to a cute little guy who seems to love you for no logical reason. On the other hand, I *need* my chart of atomic masses just like I need my periodic table, and all the other notes I have carefully organized on the floor.

I'll never understand teachers. Sure, I get it that Mr. Kermit has come back from the Lost Land of Crossword Puzzles. But now, totally out of nowhere, he's gone science crazy.

"The state science assessment is on October twenty-third," he announced last week. "This is our chance to prove that our class can do as well as any other group. Maybe even better than some."

The way he said it—how he made it sound like it was us against everybody else who calls us unteachable— got the whole class on board the Science Express.

Elaine's eyes were practically shining with excitement and purpose. Maybe she thought we were going to dissect somebody.

"We're like Frodo going up against the dark forces

of Middle Earth," Mateo declared.

Okay, that's standard Mateo. But even Aldo is sort of into it. Ribbit is framing this as a giant *in-your-face* to the whole school. No way Aldo can pass up a chance at that.

So that's why I'm in the den, up to my ears in graphs and formulas, yelling at a baby. You think I'm thrilled about it? The best thing about being a short-timer is you can slack off with no consequences. And I can't even get that right.

"What's wrong?" Stepmonster rushes in and spies her little darling laying waste to my work like Godzilla stomping Tokyo—oh man, I really am spending too much time with Mateo!

She expertly scoops him up using one arm.

I almost bark something rude like "What took you so long?" But then I spot the tall glass of iced tea in her other hand.

"I thought you could use a study break," she offers, setting the drink down on the edge of the coffee table. "Kiana, your dad and I are so proud of how hard you've been working lately."

It annoys me. Who does she think she is—my mother?

She's definitely not that. I know because she isn't on

a movie set in Utah, leaving me in exile.

Chauncey hangs off her hip, arms and legs flailing. The action figure flies from his little hand, landing with a *ker-plop* in my iced tea.

"Chauncey!" she scolds. "You ruined your sister's drink!"

Believe it or not, I actually sympathize with her then—overworked, sleep-deprived, and saddled with her husband's California kid.

"It's not ruined," I say quickly. "It's just—" I fish the Power Ranger out, watching the level of tea go down. I drop it back in again, and the level rises. My eyes widen in understanding. "Archimedes' first law of buoyancy—a floating object displaces its own weight in liquid! I've been trying to understand it all day!" I spring up and wrap my arms around Stepmonster. "Thanks for the tea!"

Chauncey sinks his newly cut tooth into his thumb and starts bawling again.

The science craze even extends to Terranova Motors. Jake buys these rolling whiteboards, and his mechanics show us how to calculate horsepower and torque. We have a contest to see who can be the quickest to label the parts of an internal combustion engine. Parker wins, even though some of his spellings are a little creative, like CRANKSHAFT = SCARFTHANK.

Jake keeps telling us how important it is to do well on the test to make Mr. Kermit look good. He says it over and over again, until his face gets flushed like he's really stressed about it. What's the big deal? If, by some miracle, we ace the exam, those good grades will be ours, not our teacher's. And if we bomb out— well, that'll be on us too. How is it Mr. Kermit's fault if his class happens to be dumb at science?

Or maybe we're not so dumb. On Friday, we take a practice test, and we do pretty well. I pull off a 92, which is amazing, considering science isn't my best subject. Elaine gets an 86, and both Barnstorm and Rahim crack 70. Even Mateo squeaks out a pass at 67, which isn't bad for someone who can't tell the difference between Earth and Middle Earth, and thinks the Force and magic are real.

Aldo brings up the rear with a 62, but Mr. Kermit steps in before he can get too worked up about it.

"Think about it, Aldo—three more points and you would have *passed*. You're a completely different student now. You're reading *Where the Red Fern Grows*, an award-winning novel. I believe in you. And on test day, I know you'll be able to scrounge up three more points."

"Yeah!" Aldo exclaims, energized. "If I can care whether Old Dan and Little Ann win the coon hunt, I can care about anything! Even stupid science!"

"Puffy-tails for everybody!" crows Barnstorm, waving a crutch in the air.

"Let's not get ahead of ourselves," our teacher tells us. "We don't want to be overconfident for the real test next week. But," he adds, "I'm proud of each and every one of you. If you put up these kinds of scores on the actual assessment, it'll say a lot about what we've accomplished together as a class."

Those words stick with me: *what we've accomplished together as a class.*

Well, okay, I'm part of the *accomplishment*—but I'm not actually part of the *class*. Technically, I'm not even part of the *school*.

It doesn't make any real difference. I'm going home to LA, but not next week. I'll be taking the science assessment alongside everybody else.

Still, I can't help wondering how the others would react if they knew the truth about me. It makes me uneasy. I can't get past the guilty feeling that I'm keeping a secret from my friends.

Twenty-Four

Barnstorm Anderson

Just when you think you've got it figured out, everything changes.

First, life's about scoring touchdowns, shooting baskets, hitting home runs—until you get injured for the rest of middle school, which might as well be five hundred years.

Then life's about having a sweet row of thirty-seven puffy-tails, three times as many as anybody else. But pretty soon, nobody cares about that either.

Now it's all science, all the time. My head is stuffed so full of facts that I can't blow my nose for fear it'll come out paradichlorobenzene. I've stopped watching TV, because any new information going in might push out something that's already there. My parents think I'm nuts; *I* think I'm nuts. I'm definitely not me anymore. But when that test happens, I'm going to be ready.

And then life changes again. On test day, I thump out of the house, swinging on my crutches, just in time to see the school bus disappearing around the corner.

"Hey—!" I'm so shocked that, for a second, I forget about my injury and try to sprint after it, landing face-first on the sidewalk. By the time I pick myself up again, the bus is out of sight.

"No!" My eyes turn back to home. Mom had to work early this morning, so there's no one to bum a ride from. I'm in agony—and not just because my nose is bleeding. You know the phrase "It's no skin off my nose"? Well, there's actual skin off my actual nose!

But the worst part is I've studied for this test more than I've studied for every other test combined, going back to kindergarten. And I'm going to miss it! The others will kill me—and that includes Elaine, who might really do it!

Out of options, I start hobbling along the sidewalk in the direction of school. There's no chance I'll make it, but what choice do I have?

I'm thumping and swinging at maximum speed when one car engine roars above the others. From our many field trips to Terranova Motors, I recognize the sound of a broken muffler. An old pickup truck is zooming along in the right lane, passing cars on the inside. To my surprise, I recognize it from vuvuzela-dumping day. It's Parker's pickup! I spot him behind the wheel, beside some old lady in the passenger seat.

Saved!

Without thinking, I step into the road, waving both crutches over my head. With a screech of brakes and burning rubber, he comes to a halt about three inches from my skinless nose.

Parker rolls down the window. "Get out of the way, Barnstorm! I'm in a hurry!"

I yank open the passenger door. "Me too! I missed the bus! You've got to give me a ride to school!"

"I can't!" he protests. "I'm not allowed. I can only drive for farm business!"

"What about her?" I demand, indicating the old lady.

"That's different! That's my grams. I have to take her to the hospital!"

Grams—who seems fine to me—shoves over and pats the seat beside her. "Hop in, kiddo!"

For some reason, that drives Parker crazy. "He's not kiddo! *I'm* kiddo!"

I climb up to the seat, pulling the crutches in after me, and shut the door. Aggravated, Parker stomps on the gas and we lurch away, sideswiping a garbage can at the curb. I guess you don't have to be a very good driver to get a provisional license, compared to a real one.

As we approach the hospital, Parker cranes his neck. "We need the entrance that says EMERGENCY—I'll probably read it wrong, but you'll see it regular."

"You might see it regular too now," I remind him. Parker has been seeing a special reading teacher, and he's supposedly making a ton of progress.

"There—emergency!" We wheel onto a driveway.

"You got it!" I congratulate him. "But what's the emergency? Your grandma looks fine."

Grams peers at me. "Your nose is bleeding. You should see a doctor about that."

"She's not fine," Parker insists. "She's walking funny. Duck!" he adds as we approach a police officer on my side.

So I bow down out of sight, and that's when I spot the old lady's white Nikes.

"You'd walk funny too," I tell Parker. "She's got her shoes on the wrong feet."

We pull over and Grams switches sneakers. Lo and behold, she walks fine.

So we drop her at the senior center, and Parker and I head to school.

"You're welcome," I tell him. "You could have been sitting in emergency all day and missed the science test."

"I shouldn't be driving you," he retorts resentfully. "If I get pulled over, I could lose my provisional license."

But we don't get pulled over. We've even got a few minutes to spare before school starts. I thank him for the ride, and he thanks me for looking at his grandmother's feet. He's not a bad kid. We've gotten to know each other pretty well since being in SCS-8.

We're on our way to room 117, when the door of the boys' room opens and out steps Mateo.

"Hey," we both greet him.

He doesn't answer, which is weird. Mateo usually talks at the speed of light—186,000 miles per second, in case it comes up on the science test. His expression is weird too—embarrassed? Upset? I look down. The kid is standing in a puddle. Water drips from his clothes and even the tips of his fingers.

I'm mystified. "Dude, why are you all wet?"

My answer comes when three big guys emerge from the bathroom, shoving each other and laughing. I know them. They're football players—my teammates, not that they want anything to do with me now that I'm on the sidelines. It doesn't take a genius to figure out they're the reason Mateo's half-drowned.

The biggest of them, Faulkner, nods in my direction. "Anderson," he mumbles, and starts away.

I stick out a crutch and stop him. "Get the others," I tell Parker. He runs off in the direction of room 117, and I turn back to my former teammates. "Real nice. Picking on a kid a tenth your size, three on one."

"Like you never did it," sneers another of the three, Karnosky.

"I did it. Once." Last year. It was stupid. I just wanted to prove my aim was better than Karnosky's. The trick is to stick your finger in the faucet and direct the stream of water with deadly accuracy at the target.

But when I saw the kid I hit, dripping and miserable, I never did it again.

Besides, I didn't know that kid. I know Mateo.

"So you've got nothing to say," Faulkner grunts. "What's this dweeb to you, anyway?"

"His name is Mateo," I say stubbornly.

I hear footsteps in the hall behind me—Parker leading the rest of SCS-8. I don't actually see them, but I know they're there. My attention stays focused on the three football players.

Faulkner looks surprised. "Wait—you're with *them*? The Unteachables?"

"They're better friends than I ever had when I hung out with you!" I spit back.

Karnosky kicks the crutch out from under my left arm, knocking me off-balance. Rahim catches me just in time to keep me from hitting the wet floor. Aldo leaps forward and shoves Karnosky back against the wall. It's a dumb move—typical Aldo. Karnosky is as mean as they come, and Aldo isn't nearly as tough against real people as he is against lockers, which don't hit back.

Sure enough, the third kid, Bellingham, takes a swing at Aldo, and I'm thinking: *Here we go* . . .

But Aldo ducks, and a big body steps into the path

of the flying fist. The heavy blow lands on Elaine's shoulder. It makes a loud smack, but she doesn't budge, solid as an oak tree.

Bellingham's eyes widen in horror as he realizes who he's hit. Faulkner and Karnosky turn pale.

I get the feeling Faulkner's tempted to snarl something like "This isn't over." But Elaine rhymes with pain. He wants it to be over.

The three football players turn tail and flee.

I bray a laugh at their receding backs. "Gee, guys, can't you run away any faster?"

Kiana starts hustling the lot of us toward room 117. "Lucky for us there weren't any teachers around."

"Lucky for *us*?" I crow. "Lucky for those jerks! Elaine was about to stomp them into hamburger."

"Me?" Elaine asks, confused.

"We should have let you wipe up the floor with them," I enthuse. "You know, like that kid you knocked unconscious and duct-taped to the flagpole."

Elaine looks totally bewildered.

"Or when you tipped the steam table over onto the lunch ladies because you didn't like crunchy peanut butter," Rahim adds.

"I love crunchy peanut butter," Elaine rumbles.

"What about the guy you head-butted down the stairs?" I demand. "You can't say that never happened! Like twenty people wound up in the nurse's office!"

"He just dropped his phone," she explains. "He bent to pick it up. I bent to help him. We bumped heads." Elaine assumes a faraway expression as she relives the moment. "The kids on the steps didn't stand a chance. He took them all out on his way down. It looked like a giant wave of people breaking over the staircase."

We end up standing there outside room 117, staring at each other in amazement.

"It's just rumors, you guys," Kiana tells us. "You know how stories spread in a school."

"The uprooted tree?" Parker persists. "The bathroom stall door? The fire extinguisher? Come on, the fire extinguisher has to be true."

Elaine shakes her head. "Sorry."

"Okay, fine," I say finally. "But it has to stay our secret. If word gets out that you aren't a doomsday machine, the entire football team's going to kick our butts."

Ribbit appears in the doorway. "What's everybody doing out here? The science test starts in three minutes."

The science test! After all the craziness of the morning, I almost forgot about it. Who knows how many important facts already leaked out of my head?

Ribbit distributes the test booklets as we take our seats.

It's game on.

Twenty-Five

Kiana Roubini

The first time the Unteachables go to Sonic is the day of the state science assessment. We don't know if we'll be able to celebrate how we did, but we can definitely celebrate the fact that it's over and we survived. Plus, Parker has his family's pickup, so we can use the drive-thru.

Of course, he's not allowed to have passengers except his grandmother, so we have to walk and meet him there. But we can drink our slushes and sodas in the

flatbed, lounging among the bushel baskets of potatoes and onions. It's pretty fun, so we go back a couple
of days later when the weather's still nice.

It's a long walk home, though. So it's pretty late in
the afternoon when I come stumbling through the
door, hyped up on sugar, to find Stepmonster in the
front hall waiting for me.

I'm instantly on my guard. I've been in Greenwich
more than a month, and she's never once waited for
me. She's always too busy chasing after Chauncey,
trying to keep him from spontaneously combusting,
or flushing himself down the toilet, or whatever.

"What?" I ask her.

"Your school called," she tells me grimly. "Or maybe
I should say *a* school called, since you don't really go
there."

My first instinct is to try to bluff through it. "Of
course it's my school. Where do you think I hang out
every day?"

"Save it, Kiana. It's all out in the open now. That
science exam you've been working so hard on—they
graded your test, but couldn't find a student to match
it to. They called us because we're the only Roubinis
in Greenwich. You're busted."

The science test! I should have known. Just because

Mr. Kermit never checks his class list doesn't mean nobody else checks theirs.

I kick off my sneakers and stomp into the living room. Wouldn't you know it—Chauncey is fast asleep in his playpen. The one time I need him awake and alert and ripping the curtains down, he fails me.

"It's not my fault," I complain. "You left me alone on the first day of school, so I found a class and stayed there."

Believe it or not, Stepmonster actually looks a little bit ashamed. "I'm sorry. I should have been a little more on top of things. But your education isn't a game, and a school is more than a drop-in center where you can come and go as you please. Why in a million years would you think you could get away with this?"

"Because nobody cares about me!" I explode. "If you did, you wouldn't have flaked off before making sure I got registered. And anyway, what difference does it make? My real school is in LA. Nobody's going to sweat what happened during the few weeks I was here. This isn't my home; it's just a place to park me until Mom gets done in Utah!"

For a split second, Stepmonster looks as if she's about to cry. But she doesn't. I'll always appreciate her for that, because I definitely would have cried too.

"Dad and I know you live with your mom," she says at last. "But this is your home too—and we're your family."

I peer over at her. She really thinks that? News to me. I mean, she's always *nice*, when she isn't too distracted by her kid—who, admittedly, is a full-time job. But *family*?

"So what happens now?" I ask in a small voice.

"I do what I should have done on day one," she decides. "I'm going to the school to get you properly registered."

"No!" I howl. "They'll put me in regular classes! They won't let me stay in SCS-8!"

"Why not?"

"Because—because"—I blurt out the only thing I can think of—"because I'm not dumb enough!"

She's blown away. "*Dumb* enough?"

I spill my guts—the Unteachables and Mr. Kermit, and how we started out a bad class, but we're turning into an amazing one, and pretty good friends besides.

Stepmonster listens to my sob story, and the longer I go on, the more stunned she seems. By the time I get to the end of it, Chauncey is awake. But instead of fussing, he's watching me through the mesh of the playpen, listening intently, like he can't wait to hear how it all turns out.

Stepmonster looks me straight in the eye. "If that's the class you want, that's the class you're going to be in, unteachable or not."

I jump up and wrap my arms around her. I don't know if she expected it, but I definitely didn't. It's a weird moment, but not totally in a bad way.

Chauncey isn't a big fan of that. He screams his head off.

I pull back. "You'd better go get him. In his mind, hugging privileges are his and his alone."

She laughs. "You're probably right. And by the way, I don't think you're very unteachable. That science test? The school says you aced it."

Twenty-Six
Mr. Kermit

I never thought it could be like this again.

Every morning, as I park the Coco Nerd—good as new; or at least good as twenty-seven years old—I can't wait to get into the classroom. There's a spring in my step; I'm practically jogging. At the coffeepot in the faculty lounge, I fill the Toilet Bowl only half-way. I don't need coffee to stay awake. I'm firing on all cylinders, as Jumping Jake Terranova might say. Even that name doesn't sour me the way it once did.

I'll never be able to forgive the cheating scandal, but there's no denying the role Jake played in turning the class around.

The class! Just the thought of them sends a jolt of electricity up my spine. Who could have guessed that the rejects of the whole district would turn out to be exactly what I needed? The Unteachables! Well, not anymore. Oh, sure, there are better students in this world—okay, there are better students in this hallway. But comparing what they've become to what they started out as, it's clear that something very special is happening. And their teacher has to believe in something I haven't believed in for a long time: myself.

It was the state science assessment that did it for me. There was a moment at the beginning—Parker in his usual pose, hunched low over his exam booklet, staring as if trying to see inside the individual molecules of paper.

"Hose hypnotists . . . ," he was mumbling, struggling to make sense of the letters on the page. "Hose hypnotists . . ." Then all those hours of reading support kicked in. "Photosynthesis!" he exclaimed triumphantly.

I had to hold myself back from cheering out loud.

Jake actually took test day off so he could be with

the class to provide "moral support." In reality, he was more stressed out than the students and putting everybody on edge. Eventually, I had to coax him into the hall and tell him to go back to his dealership.

He protested. "But what if . . . they . . . you . . ." Bereft of speech, he threw his arms around me. This was not something I ever wanted to happen.

"Go," I told him, wriggling free. "Sell cars. Jump through hoops."

"You're the best teacher ever," Jake declared emotionally. "I'm so sorry I did, you know, the *thing*."

"Goodbye, Jake."

More memories of that morning: looking out over my students and suddenly the whole room was blurry because my eyes were filled with tears. Just like they dove into the river because they thought I was drowning, they dove into this, and they did it for me. They had no way of knowing my job was on the line. That made it all the more impressive. I said this was important, and the kids took my word for it. They even *studied*! As I walked between the desks, peering over shoulders, the scratch of number 2 pencils filling in ovals made my heart swell to bursting.

I knew it then, and the feeling has only gotten stronger since: I *love* these students. Parker, Aldo, Elaine,

Barnstorm, Rahim, and Mateo. And Kiana, who, it turns out, isn't even really in the class—or any class.

That's my fault. I'm the one who never bothered to glance at my own attendance list long enough to realize that my top student wasn't on it. How blind I was! How burned-out and detached! On the other hand, who expects a kid to come to a school she isn't signed up for?

"Her stepmother straightened everything out," Christina Vargas explains at our meeting the week after the test. "Kiana's only here for a couple of months, and the registration process was too much red tape. So she blundered into your class and figured she'd be gone by the time anybody figured out she didn't belong. It's ridiculous, but almost understandable."

My cheeks get hot. "I suppose that doesn't make me look very on top of things."

"We're all at fault," the principal says kindly. "I had her progress report right in my hand. I remember struggling to put a face to the name, but I never took it any further."

"Well, I'm not sorry it happened," I go on. "She's a fantastic kid and a brilliant student. Look at her score on the exam—ninety-six. She sets a positive example for the rest of the class . . ." My voice trails off.

Christina's face has turned ashen. I take a guess at the reason. "Are you moving her? Because her science score proves she doesn't belong with my kids?"

"I'm not moving her," she replies grimly. "Her stepmother specifically asked that Kiana stay with you. Demanded, actually. But there's something else."

I sit back, waiting.

Christina takes a deep breath. "This is difficult, Zachary. I hate to be the person who has to give you the news. The truth is, you won't be a teacher here much longer."

It comes so far out of left field that I'm shocked into silence at first. Then light dawns: "Thaddeus? The science test? But the scores were *good*! Kiana's alone—"

"That's just it," she tells me. "You know Dr. Thaddeus wants you gone. As soon as he realized what was happening with the Roubini girl, he had her result disallowed."

"Even without her," I insist. "The others have made so much progress! Surely their grades are enough."

"Almost," she says sadly. "Remember, Dr. Thaddeus has access to every test these kids have taken since preschool. He can cherry-pick exactly the numbers he needs to make sure you can't win."

It reminds me of an old saying I heard somewhere: *Figures don't lie. But liars figure.*

Devastated, the principal removes an envelope from her desk drawer and hands it over. "Dr. Thaddeus dropped it off this morning. I pleaded with him, Zachary. I pointed out how close they came to making it, even though he stacked the odds against them. I raved about how absolute zero was expected of these kids, so any proficiency at all is a credit to a remarkable teacher. He couldn't have cared less. He said even if they had fallen short by one-millionth of one percent, it wouldn't have changed anything . . ."

She's still talking—weeping, practically—but I can't make out any of it. It's like I'm in a tunnel and the echoes are rattling around but not quite reaching me. Fingers numb, I fumble the letter out of the envelope.

NOTICE OF TERMINATION
ATT: Kermit, Zachary

Please be advised that, pursuant to Article 12, Subsection 9 of the Greenwich Teachers Association contract, your services will no longer be required as of December 22 of the current school year. . . .

My eyes skip down the page, bouncing off terms like "poor performance," "unacceptable results," and "ineffective educator." I can't bring myself to read it all, but the message is painfully clear. This magical semester—in which I turned my own life around as much as the students'—was nothing but a tease. It raised my hopes, only to dash them to pieces at my feet. It restored my faith in teaching and in myself purely so the taste would be all the more bitter now. I'm fired—sacked, kicked to the curb, canned, given the boot—as of December 22.

Merry Christmas.

Worst of all, my career is going to end six months too soon to qualify me for early retirement. Fade to black.

I barely hear Christina's tearful words of sympathy as I wander out of her office. Instead of heading to room 117, I stagger through the main doors and find the parking lot. I can't face the kids—not now, when I'm still so stunned. What would I say to them? How could I explain it? I don't blame them for the superintendent's malice, but how could I ever convince them that this isn't their fault? I'll have to find those words eventually, but not today.

The outside world sounds different than it usually

does—subdued, muffled. Somehow, my feet carry me to the Coco Nerd, and I climb behind the wheel—the locks haven't worked in more than a decade. The car starts in its customary cloud of burned oil. Outside, it begins to rain, and I activate the lone functioning wiper. Too bad it isn't the one on the driver's side. I squint through the water-spattered windshield. At least it's forcing me to watch the road. Otherwise, I'd probably wrap the Coco Nerd around a telephone pole.

At the entrance to the parking lot, I signal left and press the gas. There's a loud pop, followed by a clatter, and everything goes quiet. I try the key a few more times. Nothing. Not even a feeble attempt to catch. The turn signal clicks once more, and then it dies too.

I get out of the car and open the hood. To my amazement, nothing's there. On closer inspection, I spy the motor lying on the pavement next to the battery, the radiator, the transmission, and a lot of other stuff that used to be attached to the car. Over a quarter century with the Coco Nerd, and I thought I'd seen it all. Wrong again.

This is an ex–Coco Nerd.

It's raining harder and I'm getting soaked. There's probably something I should be doing, but what? Call a tow truck? Why? This heap of scrap metal isn't really a car anymore. Inform the school that their driveway is blocked? They'll figure it out sooner or later.

I flip up the collar of my jacket and start walking toward home.

Twenty-Seven
Kiana Roubini

The first day I'm officially a student in Mr. Kermit's class, Mr. Kermit doesn't even show up.

It doesn't bother us at first. It reminds me of the beginning of the year, when Ribbit was late every day. It takes a long time to fill a coffee cup the size of a bathtub.

I guess we get a little loud, but when Miss Fountain sticks her head into the room, we quiet down in a hurry.

She's frowning. "Where's Mr. Kermit?"

We stare back at her blankly. How should we know? We listen to her high heels clicking urgently down the hall.

"Do you think we're getting a sub?" asks Rahim.

"Please don't let it be Dawn of the Dead," Barnstorm groans.

Ten minutes later, we hear running footsteps in the corridor, and Jake Terranova bursts into room 117. "Hi, guys—sorry I'm late. Mr. Kermit can't make it today."

"Are you our sub?" Parker asks.

"Not exactly," he tells us. "But since you're coming to the dealership later anyway, Emma—Miss Fountain, I mean—well, why bring in a substitute for just a couple of hours?"

"Is that legal?" Mateo inquires.

"Technically, Miss Fountain is covering both classes. Think of me as an assistant. You know, a volunteer."

"Is Mr. Kermit sick?" Rahim asks.

"Nah!" Jake shrugs this off. "I mean, not *really*. He might be *upset* a little—"

I jump on that. "Upset about what?"

Jake is flustered. There's obviously something going on that we're not supposed to know about, and Jake has the kind of face that can't hide secrets. When you're the boss of a giant car dealership, you don't have to answer questions from your employees, because what you say goes. But that doesn't work with a bunch of kids.

"It's the science test, isn't it?" Aldo says belligerently. "I flunked and now Ribbit won't come to school."

Barnstorm cackles. "If that's how it went, you'd have been in an empty classroom your whole life."

"Is that it?" Elaine rumbles. "Did we fail the test?"

The babble of agitated voices grows louder until Jake waves his arms for quiet. He perches on the edge of the teacher's desk and motions us close. "Okay, I'll tell you. But you have to promise not to say anything to *her.*" He motions over his shoulder in the direction of Miss Fountain's room.

What he reveals turns our blood to ice. Dr. Thaddeus—superintendent of the whole school district—has been out to get Mr. Kermit all year. He found a way to use our scores on the state science assessment to get Ribbit declared an incompetent teacher. He'll be out of a job at the end of this term.

"I knew it!" Aldo rages. "We flunked the test!"

"You *didn't,*" Jake insists. "None of you did. It's a numbers game—if you fiddle with them enough, you can get them to say almost anything."

"It's no game," I say bitterly. "It's our teacher, and he's getting fired for no reason."

"Who does that guy Thaddeus think he is?" Barnstorm growls.

"He's like Voldemort and Darth Vader rolled into one," Mateo adds.

Miss Fountain appears in the doorway. "Since Mr. Kermit's absent, I thought it would be nice if both classes shared Circle Time today."

She picked the worst possible time for that invitation. Circle Time? When our teacher's getting shafted? A chorus of protest begins in our throats—one that Jake silences by raising one warning finger.

"Circle Time sounds great, Em—uh, Miss Fountain," Jake accepts on our behalf. "We'll be right there."

It's the last thing we're in the mood for. How can the superintendent be so mean? Why would he even want to? Maybe Mr. Kermit was a lousy teacher back in the crossword puzzle era, but now he's the greatest!

As we grumble and seethe our way next door to room 115, I sidle up to Jake. "How can this be?" I ask in distress. "I know I got a ninety-six. And if everybody else passed, that shouldn't add up to failure no matter how much you crunch the numbers."

He looks at me sympathetically. "You have to understand, Kiana. You weren't a registered student on test day, so the ninety-six doesn't count."

I stumble into Miss Fountain's classroom, my mind a pinwheel. The news of the past few minutes has been a bomb blast, but this might be even worse. Our teacher is being fired, and sure, it's the superintendent's fault. It's the school's fault for not supporting Mr. Kermit. It might even be a little bit Jake's fault for that cheating scandal so long ago.

But mostly, it's *my* fault. If I was properly registered, Dr. Thaddeus would have to count my score. But no—I was a short-timer. This hick town and hick school had nothing to teach me. I was just passing through. What difference did it make what happened here?

Well, it's making a pretty big difference now!

By the time we take our seats on the floor around the circle, I feel like my head is about to explode. A nervous murmur comes from Miss Fountain's students. They can sense the emotional upset coming from the seven of us. Vladimir is beeping like a robot in one of Mateo's sci-fi movies, but Aldo is too wound up to respond to his reptilian friend.

Miss Fountain addresses the group: "Who would like to be first to contribute to our circle?"

It comes pouring out of me. "It isn't Mr. Kermit's fault that I never registered, and now he's getting fired, and it isn't fair—"

I've got more to say—a lot more. But my words trigger Aldo, who bursts out, "I hated all teachers until Ribbit came along! And teachers hated me! But then—"

"Everyone thought I was weird before Mr. Kermit's class!" Mateo blurts over him. "Like I was an android in a human world—"

"Ribbit's the only person who notices what I'm *good* at instead of just what I'm *bad* at—" Rahim adds to the clamor.

"I used to be stupid before Mr. Kermit!" barks Parker. "Nobody ever tried to get me any help—"

"This school only cared about me when I was scoring touchdowns!" Barnstorm blusters. "But Ribbit's *better* than that—"

Even strong, silent Elaine speaks up in her deep voice. "I never had any friends until this year—"

We're all talking at the same time, hollering to make ourselves heard. The seventh graders are really nervous. Vladimir is running crazed loops in his cage because Aldo's so upset. He's yelling louder than any of us, his red hair practically defying gravity.

Miss Fountain is trying to restore order, but no one is paying any attention to her. Finally, she inserts both index fingers into her mouth and unleashes an ear-splitting whistle that threatens to have plaster raining down on us from the ceiling. It isn't very Circle Time, but it gets the job done. Silence falls and we stare at the young teacher in awe. How did such a large noise come from such a small person?

"Thank you," she says, her quiet self again. "Now, where did you kids hear that Mr. Kermit won't be back after the end of this term?"

Nobody answers, but we all look over in Jake's direction. Miss Fountain glares at him.

He shrugs helplessly. "It just slipped out."

Miss Fountain takes a deep breath. "Mr. Terranova, please stay with my group while I take Mr. Kermit's students back to their own room. We've had enough Circle Time for today."

She sweeps us back to room 117.

"This is so unfair!" I'm still shaking with anger. "How can they do this to Mr. Kermit? How can they do it to *us*?"

Miss Fountain tries to be sympathetic and reasonable

at the same time. "I agree with you, Kiana. It's very upsetting. But there's nothing we can do about it. Even Principal Vargas—this is above her level too. It comes straight from the district office."

Parker is bitter. "Mr. Kermit helped every single one of us. And what can we do to help him back? A big fat zero!"

Something stirs in the back of my head—something I heard a long time ago. Something *Miss Fountain* said!

And then I have it. "The science fair!"

"What about it?" Barnstorm groans. "Haven't we had enough science for one lifetime?"

I turn to Miss Fountain. "Remember on the bus ride to Terranova Motors? When you tried to convince Mr. Kermit to have us enter the science fair?"

She looks annoyed. "That was *supposed* to be a private conversation."

"Well, I heard it. You told him the winning team gets ten points added to all their scores on the science assessment. Would that be enough to put us over the top and save Mr. Kermit's job?"

Suddenly, all eyes are on Miss Fountain, waiting for her answer.

"I'm sure it would," she says finally. "But remember— Mr. Kermit's answer was no to the science fair."

"Yeah, but that was before he got canned," Barnstorm reasons. "That changes everything, right?"

She shakes her head. "Mr. Kermit is a very private person. He wouldn't want you to take his personal problems onto yourselves."

"What if we don't tell him about it?" Rahim muses.

"Be serious," Miss Fountain insists. "He's still your teacher until the end of the term. How can you expect to do a science fair project and keep it a secret from him?"

"Terranova Motors!" I exclaim. "I bet Jake will let us work on it there. Miss Fountain, we can *do* this. I know we can."

By now, the others are grouped around me, and we're confronting Miss Fountain as if daring her to say no.

"Entering doesn't mean you're going to win," she reminds us.

"But not entering means we lose for sure," Mateo counters.

"It'll be a long shot," the teacher warns. "You don't even have a topic yet, and the other groups have already been working for weeks."

"So it's a yes?" I prompt.

The cheer that erupts when Miss Fountain nods

is loud enough to bring Jake running from the next room. He loves the idea and pledges to do everything he can to help us, courtesy of his dealership.

Rule 1, which Mateo calls the Prime Directive: Mr. Kermit is not allowed to know about our project. If he finds out, the deal is off.

We'll up our Terranova Motors visits to three afternoons per week. Miss Fountain will come with us if Mr. Kermit will look after her class. We'll work weekends too. Whatever it takes.

After lunch, Jake acts as our chaperone on the minibus over to the dealership. As excited as we are, the ride is somber. With Mr. Kermit's job on the line, the stakes are sky-high. And we haven't even started planning yet.

"Do you really think we can pull this off?" Parker asks dubiously. "Have you seen the kind of kids who enter the science fair? They're, like, *smart*."

"There are different kind of smarts," Jake puts in positively. "School is important, but there are things you can't learn from books."

"You mean the internet?" Mateo asks.

"I mean *street* smarts," Jake explains. "I was never the greatest student, but I knew how to scratch and claw and build a business. Trust me, you guys have street smarts coming out your ears. *That's* what's going to give you the perfect project."

"What's the project going to be?" Aldo asks.

"That's what we have to figure out," I say. "It can't be too simple, because we have to blow the judges away. But we don't have much time, either. The science fair is in three weeks."

The bus pulls up to the dealership's service area and we file out onto the pavement. We're about to enter the building when Parker points. "Hey, isn't that Mr. Kermit's car?"

We all look. On a flatbed tow truck parked outside the service bay sits the rusted remains of an ancient Chrysler that might have once been blue. Parts are strewn all around it, also rusted, some broken.

Jake sighs. "Poor guy. Like he doesn't have enough hanging over his head, now he has to take taxis to school."

"When's it going to get fixed?" Mateo asks.

"You don't fix something like that," Elaine remarks. "You give it a decent burial."

Jake nods. "I only towed it here to get it out of the school's driveway."

"Seems a shame to waste a whole car," Parker muses.

"That's no car," Barnstorm retorts. "It's a pile of

garbage. It was garbage even when Ribbit was still driving it."

"Have some respect for the dead," I put in morosely.

"Respect," Jake echoes wanly. "Emma says her mom picked out that Chrysler. It's older than she is."

Mateo pipes up. "You know the part in *Harry Potter* where Mr. Weasley uses magic to enchant an old car to make it fly?"

"Not now, Mateo." I try to say it kindly. "We have to come up with a topic for our science fair project."

"Well, that's just it," he insists. "The car needs respect, and we need a project. All that's missing is a little magic."

Twenty-Eight
Mr. Kermit

The minutes blur into hours, which blur into days, which blur into weeks.

The first thing the condemned man loses is his sense of time. All I know is that it's flying by too fast.

For so long, I couldn't wait to be finished with my teaching career. Now—barreling full speed and out of control toward the finish line—all I want to do is make it last.

It's tough to tell the kids that I won't be back after

Christmas, but they take it better than I expected. Maybe they already know—the rumor mill in a middle school can be like that.

They're the ones who changed everything for me. The "Unteachables." Ha! That's what happens when you put a closed-minded bully like Thaddeus in charge—a school district where wonderful students are tossed aside like the trash.

Parker—the kid has a reading problem, nothing more. The fact that no teacher ever bothered to find that out says more against the Greenwich schools than any cheating scandal.

Barnstorm—look at what they let him get away with because he happened to be a sports star. He never learned how to work before because he never had to.

Elaine—I'm as guilty as anybody for taking so long to figure out that Elaine is smart. And she is. She's also good at hiding it. Her reputation doesn't help. But teachers are supposed to see around things like that.

Mateo—the school jumped to conclusions about the kid's quirky personality. They wrote him off. He deserves better.

Rahim was allowed to sleep and doodle through sixth and seventh grade before he was dumped into SCS-8. Today, he's an absolute star over at the community college, but what's more important is how well he's doing in eighth grade.

Aldo might be the only one who belongs in SCS-8. But he's come a long, long way. He passed that science test—and the fact that he did isn't half as amazing as the fact that he even bothered to try.

Finally Kiana. She never had any business being in the class. She just drifted in and stayed. And not a single faculty member—myself included—bothered to look into who she was and what she was doing there. True, it worked out in the end. Kiana is a huge part of what went right in room 117. But she could just as easily have fallen through the cracks, and all her potential would have been wasted.

What's going to happen to the kids on December 22 when I have to leave? Kiana will be fine. She'll be back in California, and anyway, a bright girl like that will find a way to succeed wherever she ends up. But what about the others? Will the class get a real teacher, or will the replacement be a babysitter? Or worse, a warden? It's too easy to see the progress of the past weeks being rolled back. Christina will try to do right by the students. But in the end, Dr. Thaddeus calls the shots. He might even kibosh the trips to Terranova Motors, which mean so much to the kids.

It hurts to admit it, but the transformation of SCS-8 never could have happened without Jake. Part of it's the field trips, the time away from school. For kids like Aldo and Parker, the things they learned about cars are among the first things they ever learned, period. Or at least, learned without hating it. It might have started out as Jake trying to make up for his misdeeds of twenty-seven years ago, but he's taken a real interest in those kids, and they know it. When someone cares about you, it's natural to respond.

Strange that the man who used to be twelve-year-old Jake should star in my teaching rebirth. And his costar? Even stranger—Emma Fountain, daughter of my fiancée who married someone else. Emma may be a fish out of water in middle school, with her bucket-filling and her Goodbunnies. But her energy and enthusiasm are boundless and pure. She awakened a love of teaching in me that was buried before she was even born.

Lately, I've been covering Emma's classes while she takes the SCS-8 group over to the dealership. I can't bring myself to go there anymore. I've made a kind of peace with Jake, even started to like him a little. But it doesn't change the fact that he's the reason Dr.

Thaddeus developed his grudge way back when. Better to stay here in room 115, running Circle Time and playing nursemaid to Vladimir.

Emma's students are okay. Mostly there are just too many of them. Forty-three minutes go by, a bell rings, and a new crew is sitting there, looking exactly like the old crew. I can't tell them apart—not like the Unteachables, who are so distinctive and full of personality. Nobody is likely to mistake Aldo or Elaine for any other middle schooler.

As the weeks fly past and December 22 looms closer, I savor my time with the kids the way a gourmet lingers over a fine soufflé. The class is spending so many afternoons at Terranova Motors these days that they're almost lost to me already. They leave on the minibus at eleven and barely make it back before the three-thirty bell.

I read and reread Kiana's essays, lingering over her well-reasoned arguments; I relish the discussions with Elaine and Aldo as they work their way through *Where the Red Fern Grows*; I listen for the faint sound of Parker whistling through his teeth, a surefire sign that he's reading without having to struggle over every word. I cherish these things because I know I won't have them much longer.

At this point, every puffy-tail I award may well be my last.

At home, the walls of the apartment are closing in on me.

It never bothered me before, but it's driving me crazy now. This is the future, kicking around these two and a half rooms, one bath. I was planning to cash it in at the end of this year anyway. But with early retirement, I would have been able to redecorate, maybe even move to a nicer place in a better part of town. For sure I would have traveled. I might not have the money for that now. And anyway, I'm so down that I can't think of a single spot on this green Earth that I'm interested in visiting.

Of course, I could look for a new job. There are other schools in America. But Thaddeus has pretty much taken care of that. How do you explain to a prospective employer that you were fired for cause? Any Google search of the name Zachary Kermit will eventually spit out the words *cheating scandal*, and that'll be a deal breaker. Besides, at fifty-five, I'm not exactly a spring chicken. Starting over from scratch isn't a very attractive option.

Saturday morning. I shuffle into the kitchen to investigate the prospects for breakfast. A cheese stick and a semi-stale dinner roll. I've stopped food shopping again. I was doing okay for a while, but the bad news jolted me into old ways. Oh well, with coffee, it should at least go down and stay there.

Breakfast is interrupted by a series of clicks. It's the doorbell—or what would be the doorbell if the doorbell worked. Must be a mistake. Nobody ever comes to visit, and I haven't ordered anything.

I pad barefoot to the door and peer through the peephole into the smiling face of Emma Fountain. What does she want at eight o'clock on a Saturday morning?

She says, "Don't pretend you're not home, Mr. Kermit. I can hear you walking around in there."

I open the door. "What brings you here so early?"

"I've come to give you a ride to the science fair," she replies, as if it's the most obvious thing in the world.

"I'm not going to the science fair," I tell her. "I'm not feeling very warm and fuzzy toward that school these days."

"But you can't miss it!" she pleads. "What about the kids?"

"What kids? *My* kids? They won't be there. Nobody entered."

She looks evasive. "That might not be exactly true."

The coffee is getting cold. "Of course it's true. I'm their teacher. Don't you think I would have noticed if one of them was working on a science project?"

"They did it as a group."

"I repeat: not possible."

She drops the bombshell. "They've been working on it at the dealership."

It strikes a chord. The frequent extended trips to Terranova Motors. Emma accompanying the kids so I won't see what's going on. They've been doing this behind my back. It all fits—except for one gigantic question—

"But *why*?"

"They did it for *you*," she announces.

"For *me*? Why in a million years would they think I'd want them to—"

Then I remember: that random district policy—ten points added to the science scores of all winners. That would be enough to—

"They're trying to save my job!"

She beams. "Isn't it wonderful?"

"No!" I explode. "It means the kids blame themselves

242

for what happened. How would they even know about the connection to their test results?"

She studies the threadbare carpet.

"You had no right to tell them that!" I rave. "It's a gross violation of my privacy. Worse, it made them feel pressured to enter a science fair they have no chance of winning!"

"Don't be mad at them—"

"I'm not mad at them," I exclaim. "I'm mad at *you*! They could never do this on their own. You set this up—you and that Terranova dimwit!"

"Jake loves you."

"Yeah? Well, I tremble to see what would happen if he hated me!"

She puts on an expression I remember from Fiona— the *I'm-not-taking-no-for-an-answer* face.

"Okay," Emma concedes, "so maybe we weren't totally up front with you. But your kids are at school ready to present their project. And if you're not there to support them, you're never going to forgive your-self."

She doesn't fight fair. "Pour yourself a cup of cof-fee," I say. "I'll get dressed."

Surrender. Total and unconditional. I might as well get used to it.

Jake is waiting outside in the Porsche. "Hi, Mr. Kermit. Long time no see."

I scowl at him. He's a partner in this deception, and deserves no better. Plus, with an entire car dealership at his disposal, he chose to bring this motorized roller skate.

For the students, I remind myself, squeezing into the tiny back seat.

All the way to school, Jake keeps up a steady stream of conversation, ignoring frantic signaling from Emma to keep his big mouth shut.

"How about those kids doing this project on their own?" he enthuses. "They're really something!"

I'm too angry to answer. It's also possible that I'm too contorted in the back seat to make any sound. I'm getting reacquainted with my knees, which are pressed up against my chest.

When the Porsche reaches Greenwich Middle School, it takes the two of them to drag me out of the car.

A banner over the front entrance declares:

GREENWICH PUBLIC SCHOOLS
SCIENCE FAIR
DISTRICT CHAMPIONSHIPS

The parking lot is packed. The school halls bustle with students and parents. I forgot how popular the science fair is. I knew once, back when I cared about such things.

Walking stiffly—zombie style—after the tight car ride, I lumber inside, following Emma and Jake into the gym, which is the epicenter. The large space is filled with long tables, and colorful displays stretch as far as the eye can see. Students stand like sentries in front of their projects, excited and nervous, ready to face the judges.

It's been a rotten day so far, but as soon as I spot the kids of SCS-8, I feel the corners of my mouth turning upward. Even though I'm against this science fair idea 100 percent, I couldn't be more proud. My Unteachables did this for me. Okay, I won't be their teacher for long, but I'm their teacher today, and I intend to act like it.

Seeing me, their faces light up, and I smile wider. I must be losing my mind. A real teacher would be chewing them out, not beaming at them. I beam anyway, because they look so thrilled with themselves—Kiana, Aldo, Barnstorm, Mateo, Rahim, and Elaine.

I approach the group. "Where's Parker?"

"With his grandmother," Kiana supplies. "You'll see him soon."

Ah, the famous Grams. Some things never change. "Well, let's have a look at this top secret project."

I turn my attention to the display board behind them. The title is *The Internal Combustion Engine*. Obviously, the idea came from working at Terranova Motors. There are several fantastic drawings and diagrams done by Rahim. They're so professional that I wonder if the judges will believe it's real student work.

Beyond that—my heart sinks a little—the project is pretty thin. There's an information booklet with a few pages that could have been copied from any automotive web page. That's it. No working motor in a study that's supposed to be all about them. Not even a model of one.

I picture some of the other displays on the labyrinth of tables throughout the double gym. There's a miniature wind turbine and batteries that store the electricity it generates, a Foucault pendulum, a replica of the internal gyroscope that provides telemetry guidance for a ballistic missile. Everywhere, microscopes peer down at single-celled organisms, Geiger counters click, test tubes bubble, and static electricity jumps up Jacob's ladders. These projects come from the most talented science students in the entire district, not just Greenwich Middle School. *The Internal Combustion Engine* is a nice effort, but it doesn't come close to anything else here. This is like entering a grape into competition against a two-hundred-pound watermelon at the state fair.

Anger surges inside me. Maybe Jake doesn't know any better, but surely Emma understands that *The Internal Combustion Engine* doesn't stand the chance of an ice cube in molten lava against the other projects here. I take in the proud, hopeful faces of the Unteachables. It goes without saying that they're about to finish dead last. They could very well be laughed out of the competition. The blow could destroy their confidence and undo most of the progress of the past weeks.

The judges are at the very next table, practically chortling with glee as they watch a small robot shoot baskets at a Nerf hoop built into the giant crate that is the display. Two men and a woman—the high school science teachers along with a professor from the local college. They make notes on their clipboards, but there's no mistaking the enjoyment on their faces.

Not for long, I think, as the threesome approaches *The Internal Combustion Engine.*

The kids are so amped that you can almost hear a

power hum emanating from them. I feel a little sick. I resolve then and there to make a big stink if the judges are unkind about the project. Why not? There's no downside. What can they do—complain to Thaddeus and get me fired?

To my relief, the three are respectful and professional. They're obviously not very impressed, but they go through the motions of examining the display. They even come up with a few questions to ask.

The college professor reads through the booklet and comes to the last page—I never made it that far. There are exactly two words, written in large block capitals:

LOOK OUTSIDE
→

An arrow points toward the gym's corner exit, which opens out to the parking lot.

The man frowns. "What does this mean?"

Elaine's deep baritone supplies the answer. "Maybe it means, you know, look outside."

"This way!" adds Barnstorm, thump-swinging on his crutches toward the door. The judges follow, herded like cattle by the rest of the class.

"What's going on?" I whisper to Emma.

She smiles at me, misty-eyed. "That would spoil the surprise."

Jake is grinning, which is almost worse than her kindergarten ways. I am so not in the mood.

I step out of the gym and look around, mystified. Nothing's there—nothing but parked cars.

And then an enormous roar cuts the air, an ear-splitting *vroom* so loud that you feel it under your fingernails. All attention is wrenched away from the vehicles in the lot to the single car standing in the driveway, revving its enormous engine.

It's an amazing sight. The paint job is bright red with flecks of silver that catch the sunlight and dazzle the eye. Emblazoned on the driver's door is the image of a leaping frog. Sparks fling from the animal's powerful back legs, spraying the full length of the chassis to the rear bumper. There's no hood, and the motor has been raised to full view, shiny and brand-new. Twin tailpipes, gleaming chrome, slash down both sides of the car. Multicolored LED lights flash from every wheel rim.

Stunned and speechless, all I can do is stare. Emma is clamped onto my arm, cutting off the circulation. What does this hot rod have to do with a middle school science fair entry?

The judges are pop-eyed.

"*This* is your project?" the woman from the high school breathes.

The kids nod, tickled pink with themselves.

"It's our working model," Kiana brags.

Aldo leans into the gym and bellows, *"In your face, losers!"*

"They built the engine from parts in my shop," Jake explains, his voice hoarse with pride. "My mechanics supervised, but the kids did all the work."

"They did everything," Emma confirms. "One of them is even the driver."

That's when I recognize Parker at the wheel, grinning so wide that his face is about to break.

"Why is there an elderly woman with him?" the professor wants to know.

"That's Grams," Kiana explains. "It's a long story."

"They did a lot more than just put an engine in," Jake goes on. "You're looking at new tires, rims, glass, wipers, interior. And the body work—remember, this car is twenty-seven years old."

I snap to attention. "Twenty-seven years old?"

I can't believe I didn't see it before. Sure, it's all rebuilt and fancy and souped-up, but the original shape is still there, hidden beneath the tailpipes and the chrome and the blinding paint job.

It's . . . it's . . .

God bless America, it's the Coco Nerd.

Twenty-Nine
Parker Elias

t's worth all the hard work to see Mr. Kermit's face when he recognizes his car, brand-new and so much better. Although how could it be any worse than it was when he left it, being shoveled up off the entrance to the parking lot?

I tap on the gas and listen as the roar echoes off the front of the school building. Some cars purr like a kitten; this one screams like a howler monkey—all thanks to 585 horses under the hood. (If it had a hood.)

Howler monkey. I saw that in a book a couple of days ago. At first, it looked like HOLEY WORKMEN, but I figured it out in record time. That's been happening faster and faster lately, thanks to the extra reading help Mr. Kermit has gotten for me.

And not just me. Ribbit helped every kid in our class. There's no way we could ever thank him enough for what he's done, but that doesn't mean we can't try. That's why we rebuilt his car for him. And it's why I have to use this science fair project to totally blow the judges' minds and save his job.

Grams regards the large eggplant in her lap quizzically. "I can't imagine why I bought this pocketbook," she complains. "It doesn't match anything I wear."

"Please don't squeeze it," I request. "It's the blue-plate special at Local Table tonight." If I'm driving, there had better be farm business involved.

At that moment, Kiana raises her arm and drops it. The high sign! I stomp on the gas.

Even I'm shocked by the burst of acceleration as those 585 horses hurl us forward at breakneck speed. In a heartbeat, the others are far behind me in the rearview mirror. The feeling of raw power is so awesome that, when we run out of driveway, I almost forget that I'm the one who's steering the car. At the last instant I yank on the wheel. We thump onto River Street and fly down the block, tires barely touching the pavement. According to Jake, this engine should get us from zero to sixty in 4.6 seconds. By now, we've got to be just about there.

As we pick up speed, Rahim's banner unfurls from the car's old-fashioned radio antenna. I can see it in the mirror, fluttering in the slipstream behind us—the expertly painted words of the message we need to deliver beyond any other:

FIRE RIBBIT? NO WAY!

My classmates are jumping up and down and cheering, so it must be open and readable.

The adults aren't moving at all, which might be from shock. We didn't tell Jake or Miss Fountain about the banner part. And, of course, Mr. Kermit himself didn't suspect any of this until a few seconds ago. (He might not even know he's Ribbit.)

Then everybody's gone as I screech around the corner to circle the block. That's the plan—a quick loop of the school, banner flying, and back up the driveway to stop at the judges' feet so they can examine this monster engine, every inch of it built by us.

By this time, Grams is enjoying the ride. "Where are we going, kiddo?"

"The senior center, like always," I reply, "with a short detour to impress the judges!"

"Judges?" she echoes in a strange tone. "Don't you mean firemen?"

"No, Grams, they're judges," I explain patiently. "This is a science fair project."

She frowns. "Then who's going to put out the fire?"

That's when I spot tongues of bright orange flame in the rearview mirror. I panic. "The car's on fire!"

Grams is totally calm. "No, it isn't, kiddo. It's that rag we're towing."

"The banner!" I risk a glance over my shoulder. She's right! The heat of the tailpipe set fire to the bedsheet fabric we used to make the banner. Come to think of it, Jake mentioned that he filled the gas tank with racing fuel to get maximum performance for the judges. He said it burns really hot! Yeah, no kidding!

What should I do? If I stop, then we won't win the science fair and Mr. Kermit will be gone. But how can I drive a car that's on fire? Well, technically, the car isn't burning—just the sheet attached to the radio antenna. Already, FIRE RIBBIT? NO WAY! is down to FIRE RIBBIT? NO W. It looks like we want him to get fired right now! That's the *opposite* of the message we're trying to send!

I wheel around another corner. Since I can't stop, I speed up, flooring the gas pedal again. Maybe the wind will put out the fire. Instead, it fans the flames. The banner whips from side to side, leaving glowing embers dancing in the air. The next time I look back, a honeysuckle hedge is ablaze. This is definitely not covered under my provisional license!

"Nice moves, kiddo!" Grams cheers. "I never knew you were such a good driver."

All the months I've been driving Grams, and she doesn't notice my skills until I'm laying waste to the neighborhood. As I streak back toward River Street, I leave a line of smoldering bushes in my wake. Black smoke hangs in the air. Now the banner is down to FIRE RIB, which sounds like an ad for a restaurant. All along the sidewalk, people are shouting and pointing and scrambling to get out of the way of the swirling sparks.

Breathing a silent prayer, I make the final turn onto River Street and streak up the school's driveway. Even though this is a disaster, there's only one place to go—back to the judges. Remember, our project isn't Banner Making 101; it's *The Internal Combustion*

Engine. And that part works amazing.

Suddenly, some guy in a suit steps from the parking lot right into the road in front of me. I slam on the breaks, sending the car into a skid. At the last second, the suit guy hurls himself out of the way, somersaulting through a flowerbed.

The car fishtails around and lurches to a halt right before the three judges. Mr. Carstairs runs up with a fire extinguisher and puts out the burning banner with a sea of foam. All that's left is a single word, hanging limp from the antenna: FIRE.

Like we didn't already know that.

Half the science fair is out on the lawn, gawking at me in horrified silence. I say the thing I've been rehearsing all along: "Ta-da!"

It doesn't go over as well as I expected.

Jake rushes to help Grams out of the car. The eggplant drops to the pavement and splits open. Miss Fountain comes for me.

From the direction of the flowerbed, the guy I almost hit marches up, red with fury under the layer of mud that cakes his face and expensive suit. Oh man—it's Dr. Thaddeus, the superintendent!

"Who's the driver?" he rages. "I'll have you arrested! You lunatic, how dare you . . ." His voice trails off when he realizes he's talking to a kid.

It's an awkward moment. None of the adults have the guts to say anything, because most of them are teachers, and this mud ball is their boss.

The only person who speaks up is Grams.

"Who do you think you are?" she storms at the stunned Dr. Thaddeus. "You ought to be ashamed of yourself, a lowlife who hasn't got the sense to put on a clean suit! Where do you get off yelling at my grandson—my grandson—"

Then she says it: "—my grandson, Parker!"

Parker.

She called me Parker.

A lot of crazy things happened this morning—like when our banner caught on fire and the eggplant got ruined. And I almost killed the superintendent, obviously.

But for me, today will always be the greatest day ever, because Grams remembered my name.

Thirty

Aldo Braff

Just because you've got anger management problems doesn't mean there isn't plenty to be ticked off about.

Second. *The Internal Combustion Engine* finished second in the district science fair. It would have been better to finish 150th than to come *so close* to winning only to take an L. I don't care about the trophy. You can find that plastic junk in any dollar store. But we were a *hair* away from saving Ribbit! And they gave first place to a bunch of dweebs whose teacher didn't even need saving. I barely remember their project—some windmill thingy. No one's ever going to forget ours—definitely not the fire department, who had to spray down all those bushes and trees because of "conflagration containment," whatever that means.

Miss Fountain tries to make us feel better. "You can't take this so personally," she tells us on Monday morning. "Your project was just as good as the wind turbine, but clean power is very hot these days."

"Hot?" I echo. "We set the whole street on fire! What could be hotter than that?"

She's patient. "I mean popular. People care about the environment. Your project was wonderful, but internal combustion engines are so last century."

"How do you think everybody got to the science fair?" Barnstorm challenges. "They drove internal combustion engines."

"I'll bet nobody came by wind turbine," Elaine adds in her usual rumble.

Miss Fountain just sighs. I can't be mad at her. She wanted this every bit as much as we did.

It was Ribbit who showed me that teachers aren't always the enemy, even when they make you do work, or yell, or take away your rabbit butts. If it wasn't for

Ribbit, I never would have heard of *Where the Red Fern Grows*, which I'd be done with by now if we didn't drop everything to work on the science fair. I can barely picture my life before I knew about Billy, Old Dan, and Little Ann, who feel like real people to me—except Old Dan and Little Ann, who are dogs.

"Poor Mr. Kermit," says Kiana. "I can't believe we let him down."

"I don't want any more of that kind of talk," Miss Fountain lectures sternly. "You didn't let him down. Just the opposite—he's prouder of you than he's ever been of any class. And he *loves* his new car."

"Then how come he was afraid to drive it home from the science fair?" Mateo asks.

"That was just because of the racing fuel," she explains. "Once Jake drained all that out and put in regular gas, Mr. Kermit was fine. He has the cutest nickname for it. He calls it Coco Nerd. Isn't that adorable?"

Miss Fountain thinks a lot of things are adorable. That's not my style. Maybe Vladimir, in a lizardy kind of way. And Old Dan and Little Ann, although I never met them in real life.

Anyway, Ribbit might be psyched about his car, but he isn't psyched enough to come to school today.

Even worse, our sub turns out to be Dawn of the Dead again.

To be honest, she's not as mean this time around. Some of that might be that we're so depressed about losing Ribbit that nobody has the energy to give her much of a hard time. We drop a few textbooks, but our hearts aren't into it enough to get the timing right. Who can buzz out a fake power hum when the best teacher in the world is getting shafted—and you could have helped, but you failed? We deserve Dawn of the Dead. We deserve someone even meaner than her. I can't picture who that would be. Mateo probably knows.

When she tells us to work, we don't argue with her. We don't groan and complain. We don't even goof off. I'm just as happy to get back to Old Dan and Little Ann. It might take my mind off Ribbit and how we blew it for him.

Dawn watches us a few minutes. Then she sighs and says, "All right, let's hear it."

We stare at her blankly.

"Come on," she persists. "Something's eating you— all of you. Tell me what it is."

It's like a dam breaks, and we all start jabbering at the same time.

"Our teacher's getting fired for no reason at all!"

"It's not fair!"

"That jerk Thaddeus hates Mr. Kermit!"

"He's worse than the Dementors!"

"I should have run him over when I had the chance!"

It goes on and on. We never run out of complaints about how awful and unfair it is. It's the first time I've ever been in a class where everybody else is just as mad as I am. And we can't *all* have anger management issues.

Sometimes mad is exactly what you're supposed to be.

The amazing part is Dawn of the Dead doesn't chew us out or shut us down. She *listens*, which can't be easy with all seven of us yelling over each other. Then she has a long conversation with Miss Fountain, who comes to see what the racket is about.

The two of them are in the hall talking for what seems like forever. Finally, the substitute walks back into the room and faces us.

"Well, it seems as if I misjudged you young people."

She's wrong about that. Anything bad she thought about us last time goes double. Because we had the opportunity to help Ribbit.

And we came up empty.

Thirty-One
Mr. Kermit

The Coco Nerd is back—in a manner of speaking. Not that anybody would recognize it. It bears very little resemblance to the 1992 Chrysler Concorde Fiona picked out all those years ago. It looks like exactly what it is—a mean set of wheels designed by a bunch of eighth graders who think nothing is worth driving unless everybody's staring at it. Chrome. Glitter paint. LED lights. Tailpipes the size of cruise missiles. And an engine you can barely see over.

I'm afraid to honk the horn. I know their taste in music.

Even without the racing fuel, the thing is a rocket. The first time I dare to tap the gas pedal, I nearly rear-end a cement truck. Only Dale Earnhardt Jr. could drive this car. It should be outlawed by the government.

I'm crazy about it. My kids built this for me. It's the second-greatest gift they could have given me—number one being the sight of Superintendent Thaddeus diving headfirst into a muddy flowerbed, coming up fragrant with fertilizer, a chrysanthemum behind his ear.

They're the best class any soon-to-be-ex-teacher could ever hope to have. They even put a frog logo on the door in honor of my last name. Kermit the Frog. Come to think of it, the frog theme has been in place since the beginning of the year—more proof that the so-called Unteachables have better heads on their shoulders than anyone suspected. I just never connected it with all that ribbing before.

I don't mind. It's kind of a tribute.

On day one, a cop pulls me over just to get a good look at what I'm driving. The officer writes out a ticket giving me one week to cover up the engine.

I call Jake, who promises to design a hood that complies with the law. He also agrees to raise the seat four inches so I'll be able to see the road in front of me.

"I don't want the kids working on it," I insist over the phone. "They've done more than enough for me already."

"I've loved being their sponsor," Jake replies. "They're a fantastic group." A brief pause. "Too bad not all your classes measured up to their level."

He's 1,000 percent right about that. Who'd know better than Jake, who single-handedly made the 1992 class a nightmare and messed up my life in the process?

On the other hand, 1992 was a long time ago. In 1992, the Coco Nerd was just a car. Today it's a weapon of mass destruction. The transformation of Jake Terranova has been no less dramatic. He's a businessman, an entrepreneur. A grown-up. A solid citizen who's done so much for the Unteachables. Plus, a few days ago, I spotted his Porsche parked in front of the Greenwich Diamond Exchange, and Jake himself inside, examining velvet trays of rings.

Fiona's daughter could definitely do worse.

"People change," I tell my former student. "You're—

you're a good guy, Jake."

Jake actually gets choked up on the other end of the line.

I've never ruined anyone's life, but apparently it's almost as hard on the messer as it is on the messee.

I go back to school on Wednesday. Not because I care one way or the other whether the place is still standing, but because I don't want the kids to think I blame them for not winning the science fair. In fact, the opposite is true. They exceeded my wildest expectations. They've been doing that on a daily basis ever since they dumped the vuvuzela shipment in the river.

Another thing about the new and improved Coco Nerd: it's unparkable. Those external tailpipes make it as wide as a ferryboat. But I finally get it jammed in between Emma's Prius and the pickup truck belonging to the Elias farm. The door opens and I have about four inches of clearance to squeeze myself through. Amazingly, I make it. I've been slimming down lately, thanks to the mustard-on-toast diet. Since I'm going to be out of a job soon, maybe it's time to reinvent myself as a weight-loss guru. I'll be rich. Or at least I'll be able to afford gas for the Coco

Nerd's 585-horsepower engine.

I've barely set foot inside the entrance foyer when Principal Vargas rushes up and grabs me by the arm. "Zachary, I need to talk to you."

"Later," I promise her. "I want to reassure my class—"

"Now!" And she literally drags me into her office and shuts the door.

She's obviously been staking out the front hall. It can only mean one thing. Thaddeus is using the events of the science fair to fire me effective immediately. The superintendent is so mad that he won't even let me finish out the semester.

"So," I say bitterly, "is Thaddeus planning to ax me in person, or has he got you doing his dirty work for him?"

In answer, she presses a copy of the *Greenwich Telegraph* into my hands.

I don't even glance down at it. "How do you like it, Christina?" On some level, I regret unloading my emotions on the principal, who has never been anything except supportive. But I'm just too upset to hold it inside. "How does it feel to wield the hatchet for him?"

"Read it, Zachary," she orders.

SUPERINTENDENT TO SUPER TEACHER: "YOU'RE FIRED!"

The Greenwich Telegraph, Local News
By Martin Landsman, Staff Reporter

It's the goal of every community to create a school system in which each pupil is inspired to excel. This can't be accomplished without great teachers. But an educator who can truly transform the lives of his or her students is the rarest of gems. Meet Mr. Zachary Kermit, teacher of the Self-Contained Special Eighth-Grade Class at Greenwich Middle School. By any objective measure, Mr. Kermit has performed a miracle. His students' test scores are up 87 percent this semester. SCS-8 took second place at the competitive district science fair. Disciplinary problems have virtually disappeared. Most impressive of all, the atmosphere in his classroom—formerly one of Greenwich's most difficult—has become nurturing, supportive, enthusiastic, and successful. And there's no mistaking the students' opinion of their teacher: they adore him.

I read on. The reporter calls out Dr. Thaddeus by
name and demands to know why the best teacher in
the district is being fired. He accuses the superintendent of holding a personal grudge dating back to the
cheating scandal in 1992. And he includes a quote
from a member of that 1992 class—prominent local
business owner Jake Terranova—guaranteeing that
what happened back then wasn't the teacher's fault.

The article concludes:

I look up at my principal. "Who wrote this?" I
squint at the byline. "Who's Martin Landsman, and
how did he find out about my class?"

"Beatrice Landsman is the sub who covered your group on Monday. Martin is her son. I guess the kids gave her quite an earful."

"They're something special." I have to work hard to keep my voice steady. "Every time I think I've seen the best they have to offer, they climb one rung higher. That's why I'm anxious to get to my room. We don't have very many more days together."

"That's what I've been trying to tell you!" she exclaims. "Everyone in town has seen this article. The district offices are buried in phone calls and emails. You're not fired anymore!"

I'm stunned. "Thaddeus changed his mind?"

"He didn't have much choice. You're a hero. And that means you can finish out the year and take your early retirement in June. Congratulations, Zachary. I'm so pleased for you."

A flood of relief and satisfaction washes over me. And yet . . . for some reason, I'm not as thrilled as I thought I'd be at such good news. Where's the happy? The joy? The triumph at beating back that overblown, self-important tyrant of a superintendent?

It comes to me in a moment of clarity: the problem isn't the reinstated part. It's the part about retiring in

June. Why would I fight off Thaddeus's attempt to force me out in December only to exit voluntarily a few months later?

The Unteachables have done a lot for me this semester, but their greatest gift is this: they showed me that I'm still a teacher. I have a lot to offer students—not just this class, but many classes to come.

"I'm not retiring," I tell her. "Sign me up for next year."

She stares at me uncertainly. "Zachary?"

I head for the door. "And I want SCS-8. Nobody else. If anyone has questions, I'll be with my kids."

I stride to room 117 with an energy and a sense of purpose I haven't known in decades. By the time I get there, my feet are barely touching the floor. So I'm a little shocked when I see how down the students are. Here I am, on top of the world, and they're positively drooping. Barnstorm's left crutch is the only thing keeping him from falling out of his chair. Rahim's head is on his desk again. But he isn't sleeping; he's just too depressed to sit upright. Even Aldo is missing his usual belligerent expression, making him look almost agreeable. And there isn't a single *ribbit*. Not one.

I sit down on the edge of my desk. "I have an announcement to make."

Kiana stands up. "Us first, Mr. Kermit." Her voice is thin and watery. "We're really sorry we couldn't win the science fair for you. We came so close, but in the end, it just wasn't enough. Maybe it's true what everybody says—that we're a bad class."

I leap to my feet. "Don't ever say that! You're the best class in this school, and I know, because I've been shuffled around to most of them. You've got *nothing* to be sorry for! Besides," I add, realizing I should have said this part first, "I'm not fired anymore."

Heads snap to attention, even Rahim's. Elaine jumps up, sending her chair skittering.

"You're messing with us," Barnstorm accuses.

"For real, Mr. K?" asks Parker, his eyes huge.

"For real," I confirm. "I can't explain it exactly, because I'm not sure I understand it myself. But it has a lot to do with—"

That's as far as I get. They swarm the desk, cheering and howling, almost knocking me over, battering me with high fives. Their behavior is loud, unruly, and borderline violent—completely unacceptable. I accept it. They've earned that much and more.

Emma rushes over from next door to investigate the ruckus.

"Ribbit isn't fired anymore!" Parker yells at her, and

she joins the celebration, unruly as any of the kids.

I can't help noticing that she's wearing an engagement ring—a big one. I'm not her father, but in a strange way, I feel like a proud parent.

"*Enough!* Settle down, everybody!" I glare my Unteachables back to their seats. "Just because we got some good news doesn't mean this isn't a school. Haven't you all got work to do?"

There's a shuffling sound as books, papers, and iPads are pulled out of desks. Aldo and Elaine disappear behind their copies of *Where the Red Fern Grows*.

"That's wonderful, Mr. Kermit," Emma breathes as she heads back to her own class. "We're going to have something inspiring to talk about during Circle Time."

As I sit down, I catch a flash of sunlight reflecting off the red and silver of the Coco Nerd out in the parking lot. We have a lot in common, the car and I. Just like me, it was a beat-up old wreck on the verge of falling apart at any moment. But we were refurbished—both of us—brought back to life by seven Unteachables.

"*No-o-o-o!*"

The cry from Aldo is pure agony.

I turn to him in alarm. "Aldo—what's wrong?"

His face is redder than his hair, and streaked with tears. "Old Dan and Little Ann!" he gasps, waving *Where the Red Fern Grows* in front of him. "They're dead! Both of them!"

"Heavy," Elaine agrees, her expression solemn.

"Well," I begin, choosing my words carefully, "some stories—"

Aldo cuts me off. "I read *one* book all the way through—just one! And this is what I get for it? The cover should come with a sticker: *Warning: Do not read unless you hate dogs!*"

The kid is totally inconsolable. By eighth grade, most readers have already experienced plenty of devastating sad endings. But in Aldo's case, this is the first novel he's ever finished.

I turn to the Goodbunnies chart, pluck a puffy-tail from the Ziploc baggie, and affix it next to Aldo's name.

"Well done. You showed empathy in reacting to a piece of literature. Congratulations."

Aldo seems shocked at first. Then, amid a smattering of applause, he walks to the front of the room, removes his one and only puffy-tail, and offers it to Kiana.

"Fair is fair," he says bravely. "I owe you a lot more than just this one."

"Please keep it," Kiana tells him.

He shakes his head. "It has to work like a market economy."

She looks at me. "Come on, Mr. Kermit. Do I have to take it? Even in a market economy, there's such a thing as giving someone you like a present if you want to."

Aldo's eyes widen, and his hair seems to become just a touch redder—or maybe it's a reflection of the sudden flush in his cheeks.

I issue my ruling. "Absolutely. A lender is allowed to forgive a debt."

And Aldo Braff, the toughest case in the entire Greenwich School District, throws his arms around Kiana and hugs her.

My career has taken some strange detours. Yet here I am, surrounded by the worst class I've ever had in every way but one—the fact that they're the best class I've ever had. Somehow, it feels like I'm exactly where I was meant to be, doing exactly what I was meant to do.

Teaching the Unteachables.

Thirty-Two

Kiana Roubini

My mother is going to be a movie star.

Well, not exactly. I guess she's a pretty good actress, though. As soon as her movie wraps in Utah, she gets offered a part in this other film that's shooting next month in British Columbia. This one has a big budget, so it's a great career move. It also means the studio is willing to hire me a tutor so I can go live with Mom while she's on location.

I hope she isn't too upset when I tell her thanks but no thanks.

I actually kind of surprise myself with that answer, considering how anxious I've been to blow this Popsicle stand. And believe me, it's not—repeat, *not*—because Aldo asked me to the Fall Ball, which is this big dance they throw before Thanksgiving break. I'm never going to be the kind of girl who drops everything and changes all her plans because of some guy. Stepmonster did that—she left Chicago to come to Greenwich to marry Dad, and she still regrets it. Not the marrying-Dad part; but she's always complaining that you can't get decent pizza around here.

I know this is pretty unexpected, me being temporary and all. But that's the life of a short-timer. You are one until you aren't anymore. You start putting down roots. I've got friends, and a baby brother who'll be taking his first steps in the next few months. Besides, Stepmonster finally got around to registering me at school, so I probably owe it to her to hang around for a while.

A few days later, Mom calls from the Vancouver airport to see if I've changed my mind. Shooting starts in three more days, so this is the last chance for the studio to bring in a tutor.

"That's okay," I tell her. "I've decided to finish out the year here. Besides," I add, smiling to myself, "you don't hire a tutor for an Unteachable like me."

More favorites by
GORDON KORMAN

THE MASTERMINDS SERIES

BALZER + BRAY

An Imprint of HarperCollins*Publishers*

www.harpercollinschildrens.com

DEBBIE MACOMBER

Always
DAKOTA

MIRA®

ISBN 1-55166-632-4

ALWAYS DAKOTA

Copyright © 2000 by Debbie Macomber.

Visit us at www.mirabooks.com

Printed in U.S.A.

To my
Aunt Betty Stierwalt
and
Aunt Gerty Urlacher
For gracing my life with their incredible gift for love and laughter
I love you both

Prologue

September

Bernard Clemens was dying and he knew it, despite what the doctors—all those fancy specialists—had said about his heart. He knew. He was old and tired, ready for death.

Sitting in the den of the home he'd built thirty years ago for his wife, he closed his eyes and remembered. Maggie had been his great love. His only love. Delicate and beautiful, nearly sixteen years younger, she could have had her choice of husbands, but she'd chosen *him.* An aging rancher with a craggy face and work-roughened hands. A man who had simple tastes and lacked social refinement. And yet she'd loved him.

God help him, he'd loved *her,* loved her still, although she'd been gone now for nearly twenty-seven years.

Her love had been gift enough, but she'd yearned to give him a son. Bernard, too, had hoped for an heir. He'd purchased the Circle C as a young man, buying the land adjacent to his parents' property, and eventually he'd built the combined ranches into one huge spread, an empire to pass onto his son. However, the child had been a girl and they'd named her Margaret, after her mother.

The pregnancy had drained Maggie and she was further weakened that winter by a particularly bad strain of the flu.

Pneumonia had set in soon afterward, and before anyone realized how serious it was, his Maggie was gone.

In all his life, Bernard had never known such grief. With Maggie's death, he'd lost what he valued most—the woman who'd brought him joy. When they lowered her casket into the ground, they might as well have buried him, too. From that point forward, he threw himself into ranching, buying more land, increasing his herd and consequently turning the Circle C into one of the largest and most prosperous cattle ranches in all of North Dakota.

As for being a father to young Margaret, he'd tried, but as the eldest of seven boys, he had no experience in dealing with little girls. In the years that followed, his six younger brothers had all lived and worked with him for brief periods of time, eventually moving on and getting married and starting families of their own.

They'd helped him raise her, teaching her about ranching ways—riding and roping...and cussing, he was sorry to admit.

To this day, Margaret loved her uncles. Loved riding horses, too. She was a fine horsewoman, and more knowledgeable about cattle than any man he knew. She'd grown tall and smart—not to mention smart-mouthed—but Bernard feared he'd done his only child a grave disservice. Margaret resembled him more than she did her mother. Maggie had been a fragile, dainty woman who brought out everything that was good in Bernard.

Their daughter, unfortunately, revealed very little of her mother's gentleness or charm. How could she, seeing that she'd been raised by a grief-stricken father and six bachelors? Margaret looked like Bernard, talked like him and dressed like him. It was a crying shame she hadn't been a boy, since, until recently, she was often mistaken for one. His own doing, he thought, shaking his head. Had Maggie lived, she would have seen to the proper upbringing of their daughter. Would have taught their little girl social graces and femininity, as mothers do. Bernard had given it his best shot. He loved his daughter, but he felt that he'd failed her.

To her credit, Margaret possessed a generous, loving heart and she was a fine businesswoman. Bernard couldn't help being proud of her, despite a constant sense of guilt about her unconventional upbringing.

There was a light knock. At his hoarse "Come in" the housekeeper opened the door. "Matt Eilers is here to see you," Sadie announced brusquely.

With effort, Bernard straightened, his fingers digging into the padded leather arms of his chair as he forced himself to meet this neighbor. "Send him in."

She nodded and left.

Less than a minute later, Matt Eilers appeared, Stetson in hand.

"You'll forgive me if I don't get up," Bernard said.

"Of course."

Bernard gestured toward the matching chair on the opposite side of the fireplace. "Sit down."

Matt obliged, giving Bernard his first good look at this man his daughter apparently loved. Frankly, he was disappointed. He'd seen Matt at social affairs, the occasional wedding, harvest dance or barbecue, but they'd never spoken. Somehow, he'd expected more substance, and he felt surprised that Margaret would be taken in by a pretty face and an empty heart. Over the last few years Bernard had heard plenty about his neighbor to the west, and not much of it had been flattering.

"I imagine you're wondering why I asked to meet with you."

"I am," Matt said, perching on the edge of the chair. He held his hat in both hands, his expression questioning.

"You enjoy ranching?"

"Yes, sir."

At least he was polite, and that boded well. "How long you been ranching the Stockert place?"

"Four years. I'd like to buy my own spread one day, but for now I'm leasing the land and building up my herd."

"So I understand." Bernard leaned back in his chair. His breath came slowly, painfully. "You have family in the area?"

Matt's gaze shifted to the Oriental rug. "No. My parents divorced when I was five. My father ranched in Montana and I worked summers with him, but he died when I was fifteen."

"Ranching's in your blood then, same as mine."

"It is," Matt agreed.

Bernard hesitated, waiting until he had breath enough to continue. "You know my daughter Margaret."

Matt nodded.

"What do you think of her?"

The question seemed to take him by surprise. "Think of her? How do you mean?"

Bernard waved his hand. "Your general impression."

Slumping back in the chair, Matt shrugged. "I...I don't know what you want me to say."

"Just be honest," he snapped, impatient. He didn't have the strength—or the time—for word games.

"Well..." Matt paused. "Margaret's Margaret. She's... unique."

That was true enough. As far as Bernard knew, she'd only worn a dress twice in her entire life. He'd tried to get her into one when she was ten and the attempt had damn near killed him. "Did you know she's in love with you?"

"Margaret?" Matt sprang to his feet. "I swear I haven't touched her! I swear it." The color fled from his face and he shook his head as though to emphasize his words.

"I believe you.... Sit down."

Matt did as asked, but his demeanor had changed dramatically. His posture was stiff, his face tight with apprehension and uncertainty.

"She's gotten it in her head that she's going to marry you."

Matt had the look of a caged animal. "I...I'm not sure what to say."

"You don't know my daughter, otherwise you'd realize that when she sets her mind to something, there isn't much that'll stand in her way."

"I...I..."

Bernard cut him off. He was growing weak and there was still a lot to be said. "In a few months, Margaret's going to be a very wealthy woman."

Matt stared at him.

"I'm dying. I don't have much time left." His gaze burned into Eilers. Then he closed his eyes, gathering strength. "God knows what she sees in you, but it's too late to worry about her judgment now. I raised her the best

I could, and if she loves you, there must be more to you than meets the eye.''

Matt stood and started pacing. ''What makes you think I'd marry Margaret?'' he asked.

Despite the difficulty he had in breathing, Bernard laughed. ''Because you'd be a fool not to, and we both know it. She's going to inherit this ranch. I own more land and cattle than you'll see in ten lifetimes. She'll give you everything you've ever wanted.''

It was clear from Eilers's expression that he was shocked.

''I called you here today to tell you something you need to hear.''

Matt clutched his Stetson so tightly, his knuckles whitened. ''What's that?''

Bernard leaned forward. ''You hurt my girl and I swear I'll find a way to make you pay, even if I have to come back from the grave to do it.''

Eilers swallowed hard. ''You don't have anything to worry about, Mr. Clemens. I have no intention of marrying Margaret.''

Bernard chuckled, knowing otherwise. Eilers would marry Margaret, all right, but it wouldn't be for love. He'd marry her for the land and the cattle. No man with ranching in his blood would be able to refuse what she had to offer.

Yes, Matt would marry her, but it was up to Margaret to earn Matt Eilers's affection.

One

Margaret thought she was ready, as ready as any daughter could be to face her father's death. She'd been at his side, his rough, callused hand between her own, when it happened. For hours she'd sat with him, watching the intermittent rise and fall of his chest, waiting, wondering if this breath would be his last, praying it wasn't. Clinging to what little life was left in him.

Bernard Clemens had refused to die in a hospital and at his request, she'd brought him home. The hospice people had been wonderful, assisting Bernard in maintaining his dignity to the very end. Margaret had stayed with her father almost constantly the final week of his life.

She watched him draw his last shallow breath, watched him pass peacefully, silently, from one life to the next. Margaret wasn't sure what she'd expected to feel, but certainly not this torrent of agony and grief. She'd known he was dying, known it for months, and she'd thought that knowledge would blunt the sharp rawness of her pain. It hadn't. *Her father was gone.* She'd spent every day of her life with him, here on the Circle C, and now she was alone. In time, she realized, she'd be able to look back and see the blessing her father had been, but not yet. Not when her loss hurt as much as it did now.

She'd waited until she'd composed herself and then, dry-eyed, walked out of the large bedroom and awakened the sleeping family members, who'd gathered at the ranch. She'd announced that Bernard had died and his death had been peaceful. No tears were shed. That wasn't how grief was expressed in the Clemens family.

Almost immediately, everyone had found a purpose and the house was filled with activity. More and more people arrived, and then, two days later, it was time for the funeral. Bernard Clemens's three surviving brothers stood at the grave site with Margaret; they stayed long enough to greet folks and thank them for coming. Then they left, to return to their own families, their own lives.

The reception following the funeral was well attended. Nearly everyone in Buffalo Valley came to pay their respects. Hassie Knight, who owned Knight's Pharmacy, took charge of organizing the event. She'd been a family friend for many years. At least a hundred people had gathered at the large ranch house, and there was more food than Margaret could eat in six weeks. She never had understood why people brought casseroles and desserts for a wake; the last thing she wanted to think about was eating.

"Margaret, I'm so sorry," Sarah Urlacher told her, gently taking her hand and holding it. She was sincere, and her kindness touched Margaret's heart. Sarah's husband, Dennis, stood with her. His eyes revealed genuine compassion.

Margaret nodded, wishing she knew the couple better. It was her father who was well acquainted with the folks in Buffalo Valley. He'd been doing business there for years. Dennis delivered fuel to the ranch, so Margaret at least knew him, even if their relationship was just a casual one. Sarah owned and operated Buffalo Valley Quilting Company, a growing enterprise that seemed to be attracting interest all around the country. Margaret knew Sarah only by sight; they hadn't shared more than a few perfunctory greetings.

She wanted to thank everyone for coming—she really did appreciate their expressions of sympathy and respect—and at the same time find a way to steer them out the door. Making conversation with people she hardly knew was beyond her. She was polite, cordial, but a tightness had gripped her chest, and it demanded every ounce of restraint she could muster not to rush to the barn, saddle Midnight and ride until she was too exhausted to go farther.

Bob and Merrily Carr came next, with their little boy, Axel. They owned and operated 3 OF A KIND, Buffalo Valley's bar and grill. After that, the banker, Heath Quantrill, offered his condolences. Rachel Fischer was with him, and if Margaret remembered correctly, they were a couple now.

Ranchers and farmers crowded the house. So many people. There barely seemed room to breathe.

"Do you need anything?" Maddy McKenna asked with a gentleness that nearly broke Margaret's facade. Maddy was the best friend she'd ever had. If anyone understood, it would be Maddy.

"I want everyone to leave," Margaret whispered, fighting back emotion. The lump in her throat refused to go away and she had trouble talking around it.

Maddy took Margaret by the arm and led her down the long hallway to her bedroom. The two of them had spent many an afternoon in this very room; at Margaret's entreaty, Maddy had tried to instruct her in the arts of looking and acting feminine—feminine enough to attract Matt Eilers. Not that her efforts had been noticed. Not by him, anyway.

"Sit," Maddy ordered, pointing to Margaret's bed.

Without argument, Margaret complied.

"When was the last time you had any sleep?"

Margaret blinked, unable to recall. "A while ago." The night before the funeral she'd sat up and gone through her father's papers. He had everything in order, as she'd suspected he would. He'd realized months ago that he was dying.

"Lie down," Maddy said.

"I have a house full of company," Margaret objected weakly. It went against the grain to let someone dictate what she should or shouldn't do. With anyone else, she'd have made a fuss, insisted it was her place to be with her father's friends.

"You're dead on your feet," Maddy told her.

Margaret nestled her head in her pillow, surprised by how good it felt against her face. How cool and comforting. "I...I thought I was prepared," she said, her eyes closed. "I thought I could handle this."

"No one's ever ready to lose a father," Maddy said as she covered Margaret with the afghan from the foot of the bed. The weight of it settled warmly over her shoulders.

"Sleep now. By the time you wake, everyone will be gone."

"Nothing's ever going to be the same again," Margaret whispered.

"You're right, it won't."

Maddy's voice sounded soothing, even if her words didn't. But then, Margaret could count on her friend to tell the truth. Already she could feel sleep approach, could feel the tension leave her body. "Matt didn't attend the funeral, did he?"

"No," Maddy said.

"I thought he would." She was keenly disappointed that he hadn't bothered to show up.

"I know."

Maddy was disappointed in him, too. Margaret could tell from the inflection in her voice. Few people understood why she loved Matt. If pressured to explain, Margaret wasn't sure she could justify her feelings. Matt Eilers was as handsome as sin, shallow and conceited. But she loved him and had from the moment she'd met him.

With Maddy's tutoring, Margaret had done everything possible to get Matt to recognize that she was a woman with a woman's heart. A few months back, she'd had her hair permed and donned panty hose for the first time in her life. The panty hose had nearly wrestled her to the ground and the perm had made her look like one of the Marx Brothers—in her own opinion, although Maddy said she looked like the pretty actress in the original episodes of a popular TV show, *Felicity,* which Margaret had made a point of watching in reruns. She couldn't quite see the resemblance but certainly felt flattered. The whole beautifying operation had been a unique form of torture, but she'd willingly do it all again for Matt.

"I'm sure he'll stop by later and pay his respects," Margaret whispered, confident that he would.

"He should have been here today." Maddy wasn't nearly as forgiving. "Don't worry about Matt."

"I'm not."

"Call me in the morning," Maddy said.

"I will," she promised, exhausted and grateful for Maddy's friendship. Her last thought before she drifted off to sleep was of the father she loved and how bleak her life would feel without him.

Jeb McKenna knew his wife well, and her silence worried him as he drove the short distance between the Clemens house and his ranch. Unlike the Clemenses and most other ranchers in the area, Jeb raised bison; Maddy owned the grocery store in town. Right now, though, she was staying home with their infant daughter.

"You're worried about Margaret, aren't you?" he asked as he turned down the mile-long dirt driveway leading to their home. Maddy had barely said a word after seeing Margaret to her room.

"She was ready to collapse," Maddy told him. "God only knows the last time she slept. Sadie said she'd been up for two nights straight."

"Poor thing." One didn't generally think of Margaret in those terms. She came across as tough, strong, capable. They'd been neighbors for about five years—ever since Jeb had bought the property—and he'd seen Margaret on a number of different occasions. It was some time before he'd realized Margaret was a *she* instead of a *he*. It'd startled him, but he wasn't the only person she'd inadvertently fooled. Maddy confessed that when they'd first met, she'd taken Margaret for a ranch hand.

"Bernard's death has shaken her."

Jeb understood. Joshua McKenna was in his late sixties now, and Jeb knew that sooner or later, he too would lose his father. The inevitability of it made him feel a wave of sadness…and regret. He parked the car and turned off the engine.

"I'll talk to Margaret in the morning," Maddy said absently.

The October wind beat against him as Jeb climbed out of the vehicle and reached in the back to unfasten Julianne's car seat. At three months she was showing more personality than he would've thought possible. She gurgled and smiled, waving her arms as though orchestrating life from her infant seat. She'd proved to be a good-natured baby, happy and even-tempered.

Carrying the baby seat, he covered Julianne's face with the blanket and hurried toward the house, doing his best to protect his wife and daughter from the brunt of the wind.

Maddy switched on the kitchen lights and Jeb set the baby carrier on the recliner, unfastening Julianne and cradling her in his arms.

"I liked Pastor Dawson," Maddy said casually.

The Methodist minister had recently taken up residence in town. Although John Dawson had grown up in Buffalo Valley, Jeb didn't remember him. That wasn't surprising, seeing that the pastor was near retirement age. Dawson was slight in stature, his hair—what was left of it—completely white. He hadn't been in contact with Bernard Clemens for many years, but he'd given a respectable eulogy.

"The pastor invited us to church services on Sunday," she murmured.

Although it was an offhand remark, Jeb knew Maddy was interested in becoming involved with a church community. He hesitated; the drive into Buffalo Valley took at least fifty minutes, and that was on a good day. Going to church would consume nearly all of Sunday morning. He opened his mouth, about to offer his wife a list of excuses as to why it would be inconvenient to attend. Before he could utter a word, he changed his mind. The fact that she'd mentioned the invitation at all meant this was important to her and shouldn't be taken lightly.

When he married Maddy Jeb knew there'd be a number of concessions on his part, but he loved her enough to make them. She'd certainly made concessions of her own—one of which was living so far out of town, away from her friends and the grocery she'd purchased a little more than a year ago. Church for Maddy would be a social outlet, and it would uplift her emotionally and spiritually. Women needed that.

Jeb and Maddy had met soon after she'd bought the one and only grocery store in Buffalo Valley. Her lifelong friend Lindsay Snyder had begun teaching at the high school and married Gage Sinclair the following summer. Maddy had been Lindsay's maid of honor; the very day of the wedding she'd decided to settle in Buffalo Valley herself.

Jeb would be forever grateful that she had. His life changed the day he rescued Maddy during a blizzard. She'd been trapped in her car while delivering groceries and would have frozen to death if he hadn't found her when he did. He'd brought her home with him, never suspecting that their time together would have consequences affecting both their lives. Consequences that included an unexpected pregnancy... He'd fallen in love with her in those three snowbound days. After losing his leg in a farming accident several years earlier, Jeb had thought it would never be possible for him to live a normal life again—or to feel normal emotions, normal desires. Maddy had shown him otherwise. They'd been married five months now and he was so much in love with her he had to pinch himself every once in a while to convince himself this was real.

"What do you think about us attending church services?" she pressed, studying him closely.

"I think that's a fine idea," he said. It wouldn't hurt and might even do him some good.

Her smile told him how much she appreciated his response.

A few minutes later, Maddy efficiently changed Julianne's diaper, then settled into the rocking chair. She unbuttoned her blouse and bared her breast for their baby. Fascinated, Jeb watched as his infant daughter instinctively turned toward her mother and greedily latched on.

Maddy rocked gently and hummed a lullaby. It wasn't long before his daughter had taken her fill and Maddy carried her into the nursery to prepare her for the night.

Jeb had the television on, watching a news broadcast, when Maddy joined him. They'd decided to skip dinner, since they'd eaten the equivalent of a meal at Bernard's wake that afternoon. Now, sitting at her husband's side, Maddy picked up her knitting, a recently learned skill. Leta Betts, a devout knitter and Lindsay's mother-in-law, had taught both Maddy and Lindsay how to knit while they were pregnant. "I wonder what Margaret's going to do now."

Jeb glanced away from the television long enough to recognize that Maddy needed to talk about this. He reached for the remote control and muted the sound. "It wasn't as though Bernard's death came as a shock."

"I know. It's just that...."

"What?" he urged.

"I'm worried about what'll happen to Margaret without her father there to protect her."

"How do you mean?"

"She's alone for the first time in her life—and vulnerable."

Jeb frowned. He hadn't given the matter much thought, but Maddy was right. Margaret had lived a sheltered life, protected by her father and his name.

"She's easy prey for some man. Anyone with a good line can just step in and take advantage of her. Look at all the attention she got at Bob and Merrily's wedding."

Jeb had no recollection of anything about that night except Maddy. She'd been seven months pregnant with his child. It was the night he'd asked her to marry him and she'd agreed.

"Almost every single man in Buffalo Valley invited Margaret to dance."

It went without saying that the transformation in Margaret's appearance and manner was due to Maddy's efforts.

Maddy's knitting needles clicked more rapidly, signalling her anxiety. "Margaret is about to become a very wealthy woman."

"Credit her with some sense, Maddy," Jeb said. "She's intelligent and capable. Bernard made sure of that."

"I agree with you, except for one thing."

"What's that?"

"She'd marry Matt Eilers in a heartbeat. Don't ask me why, but she's in love with the man." The knitting needles were a blur by now. "He'd take advantage of her, too."

"You don't know that," Jeb said, although he suspected she was right. He wasn't any fonder of Matt Eilers than Maddy was. They'd never had any business dealings, he and Matt, so Jeb had no concrete reason to distrust the rancher. But he did.

"I hate myself for thinking ill of him," she muttered.

Jeb shrugged. He viewed Eilers as a weak man, although he wasn't sure exactly what had shaped that opinion.

Maddy's sigh was expressive. "Last I heard, he was dating Sheryl Decker in Devils Lake."

Jeb had never heard of her. "Who?"

"Sheryl Decker. She waits tables at a truck stop outside town."

"Maybe he'll marry her, then," Jeb suggested, hoping that would be the end of the discussion.

Maddy sighed and relaxed the knitting needles in her lap. "We can always hope."

"Matt," Sheryl Decker called from the bedroom. "Bring me my cigarettes, would you?"

Matt opened the refrigerator and grabbed a cold can of beer. Sheryl knew he didn't like her smoking, but his wishes didn't dissuade her.

He returned to the bedroom and tossed the pack onto

the bed, the abruptness of his action telling her he didn't approve.

"You know how much I enjoy my smokes," she said, pulling open her nightstand drawer and reaching for a lighter. She placed the cigarette between her lips, lit up and blew a stream of smoke toward the ceiling.

Matt joined her on the bed and took a deep swallow of beer. He was upset with himself and with Sheryl. She knew he'd wanted to attend Bernard Clemens's funeral. He might not have liked the wealthy rancher, but Clemens was his neighbor and he felt honor-bound to pay his last respects. Sheryl, however, had other ideas, and like a fool he'd fallen under her spell—and not for the first time, either. Without much effort, she'd managed to lure him into bed; despite his best intentions, he'd let it happen.

"Are you still mad at me?" she asked, running her long fingernail down the length of his arm.

"No," he muttered. He couldn't blame anyone but himself.

"You know I have to work tonight, and this afternoon was the only time we could be together."

He did know. His mistake was in stopping by Sheryl's place at all. He'd come into Devils Lake for feed and had expected to get back before the funeral.

"You can still go to the reception, can't you?"

"No."

She wrapped her arm around his bare chest. "I'm really sorry," she purred like the sex kitten she was. Matt had never wanted this relationship to take the path it had. He'd started coming by once or twice a month for dinner and companionship. Occasionally he spent the night. They had an understanding, or so he'd assumed, one that provided mutual satisfaction. Lately, however, Sheryl had begun to bring up the uncomfortable subject of marriage. Matt didn't try to simply because it was easier to let her talk than to argue.

"I was thinking we should get married after the first of the year," she said, taking another deep drag of her cigarette.

Matt sighed. He didn't understand what it was with women and marriage. "Yeah, maybe. Whatever."

"Don't sound so enthusiastic," she said with heavy sarcasm.

"I can't figure out why women are always so eager to get married."

Sheryl stared at him incredulously. "Do you think I want to wait tables the rest of my life?"

To be perfectly honest, he'd never thought about it one way or the other.

"You planning to marry anyone else?" she demanded, then without asking helped herself to a long swallow of his beer.

"Margaret Clemens," he said, knowing that was sure to get a reaction.

"Margaret Clemens," Sheryl repeated with a harsh laugh. "That's a joke, right?"

"Not according to her father."

Sheryl twisted around so she could look him in the eye. "You talked to Bernard Clemens about marrying Margaret?"

"No," he said, disliking the cold tone of her voice. "He mentioned it to me."

"When did he do that?" She brushed the bleached blond curls away from her forehead.

"A few weeks back. He asked to talk to me and I went over to see him."

"And what exactly did he say?"

"He claimed Margaret's in love with me."

"Is she?"

Matt lifted both shoulders in a shrug. He hadn't told anyone about the conversation. He'd never considered Margaret in romantic terms, and it flustered him to think she held any such feelings for him. Not that he was interested. Margaret was, well...Margaret. He didn't even view her as a woman, like Sheryl, for instance, who was feminine from the top of her head to the tips of her crimson-painted toes. Although if memory served him right, Margaret had been dressed in something pretty the night of Buffalo Bob and Merrily's wedding.

"Her dad warned you off, did he?" Sheryl asked, apparently finding the question humorous.

Matt wasn't sure how to answer. "As a matter of fact, no. He seemed to think I'd marry her."

"For her money?"

Matt nodded. "According to him, Margaret's determined to have me."

"Really?" Sheryl made a low snickering sound.

"That's what he said." It wasn't something to brag about. Actually it was more of an embarrassment than anything. Ever since their conversation, Matt had gone out of his way to avoid Margaret Clemens.

"Are you going to marry her?"

"No!" His denial was swift and angry. How could Sheryl even suspect him of something like that?

She didn't say anything for several moments, then seemed to come to some conclusion that excited her. Tossing aside the blankets, she scrambled to her knees and a slow smile crept over her wide mouth. "Why *not* marry her?"

"Well, for one thing, I don't love her. For another..." He couldn't think of a second reason fast enough. "Hey, I thought you wanted me to marry *you*."

"You will, make no mistake about it. But you could marry Margaret first."

He couldn't believe his ears. "Why would I want to do that?"

"Why?" she asked as if that was the most hilarious question anyone had every posed. "Because she's *rich.*"

"So?"

"You've been hoping to buy the Stockert ranch for years."

"Yes, but—"

"You can have it."

Matt frowned, beginning to sense what Sheryl was suggesting. "I hope you're not saying what I think you are."

"Sure I am. Marry her. She's already in love with you—isn't that what her daddy said? Give her what she wants, and then after a few months file for divorce."

Matt had never heard anything more heartless. "That's cruel."

"Matt, she has more money than she knows what to do with. Think of the months you're married to Margaret as a way to help her through her grieving. She needs someone and she *wants* you. All you'd be doing is giving her what she needs *and* what she wants. You'd just be…providing a service.''

Matt's frown darkened.

''Why else do you think her daddy called you in for that little talk?'' Sheryl continued persuasively. ''He knew that Margaret was going to need you. In his own way, he was asking you to watch over his little girl. And once Margaret understands that, she'll be grateful. Grateful enough to buy you the Stockert place.''

Matt didn't like the sound of this. ''Bernard warned me not to hurt her.''

''You wouldn't be hurting her, you'd be helping her through a difficult period in her life. Think about it, Matt. Bernard practically *ordered* you to step in and take care of his little girl. Besides, she's in love with you, so she'll do whatever you ask. It's only fair that you be compensated for what you're giving her. You'll just have to convince her that a year of marriage is worth the price of the Stockert place. And then…you'd have your ranch.''

He wanted Sheryl to shut up; her plan was starting to seem plausible.

''I could quit my job and then the two of us could get married….''

Matt shook his head. ''Forget it,'' he said. ''Besides, once I married Margaret, what makes you think I'd want a divorce?''

Sheryl burst out laughing. ''Two things,'' she said. ''First of all, we're talking about Margaret Clemens here. She's got about as much sex appeal as a bag of potatoes.''

Matt couldn't really argue with that, especially when he

looked at Sheryl, with her lush body, large full breasts and long legs. What he'd seen of Margaret, and that was damn little, was no comparison.

"You said two things," he reminded her.

Sheryl's sultry smile returned. "I'd make damn sure you wanted to come back to me," she whispered. As if to prove herself, she showed him exactly what she meant.

Two

Minutes for the November meeting of the Buffalo Valley Town Council.

As recorded by Hassie Knight, Secretary and Treasurer, duly elected.

The meeting was brought to order by council president Joshua McKenna with the Pledge of Allegiance to the American flag. Council members in attendance were Joshua McKenna, Dennis Urlacher, Heath Quantrill, Robert Carr, Gage Sinclair and Hassie Knight. Reverend John Dawson was an invited guest.

1. In the matter of old business, Joshua McKenna reported that a new siren has been installed by the Volunteer Fire Department. It will be used to alert the community in the event of a fire and to summon volunteers to the station. While the alarm was being tested, there were several complaints regarding the loud, piercing sound. Mrs. Summerhill, an elderly friend visiting Leta Betts, assumed the siren was an early warning of an air attack and was upset to learn there were no bomb shelters in Buffalo Valley. Joshua McKenna suggested a sign be posted informing visitors about the meaning of the siren.

2. Also in the matter of old business, it was reported that the high school will not be putting on the annual Christmas play this December, due to the birth of Mrs. Sinclair's daughter. Gage Sinclair provided the council with the most current pictures of two-month-old Joy Leta Sinclair and reported that both mother and daughter are doing well.

3. In the matter of new business, the council officially welcomed Reverend John Dawson back to the community. Although his family has long since moved away, John has fond memories of growing up in Buffalo Valley. If all goes well, John and his wife, Joyce, plan to retire here. A buffet lunch was served following the meeting, catered by Bob Carr of 3 OF A KIND.

4. Joshua McKenna announced that the growth of Buffalo Valley has attracted the attention of the state government. He has been contacted by the governor's office, enquiring what actions the town council has undertaken to bring about the changes. Further to this subject, Dennis Urlacher reported that Sarah now has five full-time employees and has expanded the business into the building connected to the one she now occupies. Because Buffalo Valley Quilting Company is attracting not only business, but tourists, Dennis suggested a beautification program, including stone flowerpots and flags on each corner for the Fourth of July. The matter was discussed, but a vote delayed until after Christmas.

The meeting adjourned at twelve-thirty for the luncheon to welcome Reverend John Dawson.

Respectfully submitted,
Hassie Knight

"Bob! Bob!"

Merrily's cry jolted Buffalo Bob Carr out of a deep sleep. Hearing the panic in his wife's voice, he instantly threw aside the covers and bolted out of bed. She called him a second time but Bob was already staggering toward Axel's bedroom. The toddler had been fussy all night and they'd taken turns comforting him. Bob felt sure the two-year-old was coming down with another ear infection. Each bout seemed to be worse than the one before.

"What's wrong?" he asked, blinking the sleep from his eyes.

Merrily sat on the edge of the bed with Axel in her arms. "Look. He's got a rash or something. What is it?"

Bob rubbed his eyes, then stared at the child in the dim light. Axel gazed up at him, his brown eyes filled with fear. Merrily was gazing at him too, her face anxious.

Bob let out a short, abrupt laugh. "That, my dear wife, is chicken pox. Axel has chicken pox."

Merrily framed the boy's face between her hands and studied him intently. "Where did he get them?"

Bob shrugged. "Who knows? It's contagious. Every kid gets chicken pox at some time or other."

"But he's miserable!"

Bob didn't know much about childhood diseases, but he knew chicken pox was a common enough ailment. "I'll go and see Hassie in the morning. I'm sure there's something she can suggest."

"Daddy, Daddy." Axel stretched his arms toward Bob.

"I'll stay with him," Bob volunteered, knowing Merrily had been up most of the night.

"Thanks," she whispered, and kissed Axel's head before she handed him to Bob.

With regret Bob watched her return to their bedroom, wishing he could join her. Instead, he slipped beneath the covers in the narrow single bed and cradled Axel against his chest. The boy rested his head there and whimpered softly. "Hurt, Daddy, hurt."

Bob pressed his hand against Axel's forehead and noted that he didn't have a fever. Merrily had probably already given him Tylenol. "Try to sleep," Bob urged.

Axel nodded. "Sing the song about nannytucket."

Grinning, he shook his head. Merrily didn't approve of his singing off-color ditties to the boy. Especially the one that started "There once was a man from Nantucket."

Instead he hummed a nursery rhyme the two had learned from a *Barney* video. Six months ago, if anyone had told him he'd willingly sit with a two-year-old to watch a purple dinosaur, Bob would have called that person a bold-faced liar.

Trusting and small, Axel nestled in his muscular arms. In the faint light, Bob ran his hand over the youngster's head, still humming softly. He loved the boy as dearly and completely as if they shared the same blood. However, his feelings for Axel hadn't started out that way.

Nearly four years ago Bob had been riding through Buffalo Valley on his Harley when he met Dave Ertz. Dave owned the bar and grill, which was also the town's only hotel. He'd been trying to sell it, but when no buyers materialized, Dave—an inventive sort—had thrown a poker game with a thousand-dollar entry fee. The winner got the entire business, lock, stock and barrel. Bob won with three of a kind, hence the bar's new name.

Bob had been a loner and a drifter all his adult life. Because he rode a Hog, most people assumed he was part of the biker crowd. Bob enjoyed the reputation—he dressed the part, talked the talk—but he'd never been a gang member or participated in gang activities.

He'd been in business a few months, struggling to make ends meet the same way Dave had, when Merrily appeared. He'd recognized immediately that they were two of a kind. Now, with Axel, they were three of a kind. He grinned— three of a kind. Just like the bar.

Merrily had walked in one day looking for a job, and despite his lack of spare cash and customers, he'd hired her on the spot. Bob had sensed then that she was more than simply passing through his town—and his life.

They hit it off, and within weeks, Bob was entertaining thoughts of asking Merrily to move in with him, when suddenly she disappeared. That first time, the second time, too, had unsettled him. After that, he'd realized this was a pattern with her. Sometime around the third year, her visits came fast and furious and then one day, out of the blue, she showed up with Axel.

Bob knew the kid didn't belong to her. For one thing, the timing was all wrong. And whenever Bob asked her about Axel, she clammed up. Once, when he'd pressured her, she'd flippantly announced she'd won him in a poker game. Funny, real funny.

Not knowing the kid's background was worry enough,

but during those first few weeks, the boy was also a real pain in the butt. He constantly needed attention and no matter what Bob did, Axel refused to look him in the face. The toddler clung to Merrily, which proved to be downright frustrating to a man in need of his woman.

Little by little, the details came out, and Bob learned that the burn scars on Axel's thighs had come from his father. His parents had physically and mentally abused him; heaven only knew what would've happened had Merrily not been there to protect him. When it looked as though they were going to sell Axel to the highest bidder, Merrily had taken him herself. It went without saying that if the authorities were ever to find Axel, she'd be hip-deep in trouble. Him, too, seeing that he was part of all this now.

When he'd heard some of what the little boy had suffered at the hands of his parents, Bob's heart softened. He hadn't been keen on sharing Merrily, but she'd made it plain that she and Axel came as a package deal. Within a month he felt as protective toward the boy as Merrily did.

Soon Bob found himself looking forward to spending time with the child. At night, after Axel's bath, he often read to him. Merrily claimed that Bob's stories were the only thing Axel would sit still for. Bob had never felt completely responsible for another human being before; now he did. Now he had someone who needed him and loved him unconditionally. In the same way that Merrily was the only mother Axel had, Bob became his father.

After a trip to the doctor's office, when Axel developed his first ear infection, it became apparent that they were going to need a forged birth certificate. Bob had obtained one; that same day, he bought an engagement ring and asked Merrily to marry him.

She agreed, and their wedding was the best day of his life. The entire town of Buffalo Valley had celebrated with them. Bob had never known such happiness. Merrily was his wife and for all intents and purposes, Axel was his son. Life was good—and he should have known it wouldn't last. Should have realized that anything this perfect was bound to fall apart, probably sooner rather than later.

He and Merrily had been married only a few weeks when Bob learned that Axel's picture had appeared on a flyer sponsored by the Missing and Exploited Children's Center. It had circulated throughout the country.

How many had turned up in Buffalo Valley, Bob didn't know. Most folks tossed them aside without looking carefully, and anyone who might have recognized Axel wasn't saying. But the fact remained: the authorities were searching for Axel. Not knowing what to do, Bob had discussed the situation with Maddy, who until recently had been employed as a social worker. Circumstances being what they were, Bob wasn't exactly able to disguise his predicament.

Maddy gave him the name of an attorney in Georgia she said he could trust. A man who specialized in difficult cases like this one.

Yes, Merrily had stolen Axel and transported him over state lines, but in doing so she'd saved his life. Bob's greatest fear was that if he approached the lawyer, he'd be in danger of losing both Merrily and Axel. His life wouldn't be worth living without them. But the crazy part, the incredible part, was that no one seemed to have connected Axel with the boy in the flyer. Within a few weeks,

Bob began to believe they'd had a lucky escape, so he'd done nothing more. He hadn't called the lawyer. Why look for trouble? In the months since, the only people they'd allowed near Axel were town folks. No one had questioned either Merrily or him about the boy, and he trusted that the people in this town, whether they were aware of the truth or not, would protect the family as much as possible.

Axel stirred, and Bob could see that the boy had fallen asleep. Lovingly, he leaned down and kissed his forehead. No one was taking this child away. As God was his witness, he wouldn't let that happen.

"Sleep well, little man," he whispered, awake and alert.

Three weeks following the burial of Bernard Clemens, Matt Eilers decided to pay Margaret a condolence visit. Sheryl continually pestered him about it, wanting to know when he intended to see the dead rancher's daughter. She'd gone so far as to tell him what to say and how to act. The idea of marrying Margaret Clemens—or any woman—for money was repugnant to him. Sheryl tried to make it sound as though he'd be doing the poor girl a favor, but Matt wasn't naive enough to swallow that. He did, however, feel almost sorry for Margaret. She wasn't outright homely, but she wasn't pretty, either. Tall and skinny, she didn't have much of a shape. She was definitely lacking in charm and in social skills, and she seemed rather lonely.

Sheryl argued that Margaret was ripe for the picking and if Matt didn't marry her, then someone less scrupulous would. Of all the arguments she'd put forth, that one struck him as true.

Snow had fallen the week before, and his tires crunched

on the gravel drive as he pulled to a stop in the Clemens yard. No one came out to greet him, so he moved onto the back porch and with his hat in his hand, waited for someone to answer his knock.

The housekeeper appeared. Her name was Sadie, he recalled from that first and only visit. It suited her—a plain, old-fashioned name. "You're here to see Margaret?" she asked, her gruff tone devoid of welcome.

"I'd like to pay my respects."

"Seems to me you're about three weeks late."

Matt let the comment slide. He knew one thing for sure: if he did marry Margaret, the first thing he'd do was hire a different housekeeper. The thought pulled him up short. Sheryl was getting to him. He *wasn't* going to marry Margaret, no matter how many arguments Sheryl advanced.

He remembered reading advice from Ann Landers years ago, in a newspaper he'd found in a doctor's waiting room. She'd said something to the effect that the people who worked hardest for their money were those who married for it. Matt wasn't in the habit of shying away from real work, and he didn't intend to live off anyone else. When he was able to buy the Stockert ranch, it would be with money he'd earned himself.

"Margaret's in the barn," the housekeeper told him. Her gaze narrowed as if she were Bernard Clemens himself warning Matt to tread lightly around his daughter.

"How is she?"

Sadie paused. "She has good days and she has bad days."

"She was close to her father, wasn't she?"

The housekeeper nodded. "Mr. Clemens was a good

man. Margaret is a good person, too.'' With that, she slammed the door, leaving him to make his own way to the barn. Not that Matt needed anyone to draw him a map, but he would have appreciated at least the pretense of welcome.

He found Margaret inside the huge structure that put his own barn to shame. She was dressed in a heavy coat and thick boots; a knit cap covered her head. Her hair, which she'd grown over the last year, was pulled away from her face and tied at the base of her neck. He could see she'd had it curled. Working at a fast and furious pace, she pitched hay into an empty stall, her back toward him. Matt breathed in the satisfying scents of horses, straw and well-oiled leather.

''Margaret,'' Matt called softly, not wanting to frighten her.

She whirled around and when she saw him, she stood transfixed, as if she'd been waiting for exactly this moment for a very long time. ''Matt!''

''I wanted to stop by and tell you how sorry I am about your father.''

She stared at him with wide, adoring eyes, then raised her sleeve to her red nose, cheeks ruddy with exertion. So it was true, what Bernard had said—she was in love with him. But despite Sheryl's urging, he refused to do anything about it. He wouldn't lead Margaret to believe he reciprocated her feelings—or that they had any kind of future.

''I knew you'd come,'' she whispered.

He looked away, embarrassed that it'd taken him three weeks to make an appearance. ''I meant to get here before this.''

Her timid smile forgave him and he wanted to kick himself. Sheryl was right, even if her reasons were wrong; he should have come earlier.

"Your father was highly thought of around here."

Margaret nodded, and he could see by the way her lip trembled that she was fighting back emotion. "I miss him something fierce."

"I know you do." Matt remembered when his own father died. He'd been fifteen, an age when it was difficult to express grief. He'd feared that if other kids saw him cry, they'd call him a sissy, so he'd lashed out at his mother. Why, he didn't know. Probably because his parents had divorced and he'd blamed her, always blamed her. She never knew—or perhaps she did—that he'd been the person who'd slashed her tires. He'd done it in a fit of rage, and that had been the beginning of trouble for him. Before he was out of his teen years, he'd had more than one scrape with the law.

Now his mother, too, was dead, and he carried a double load of grief—and guilt. He didn't think about his parents much, not anymore, but the memories never quite left him.

"Would you like to come inside?"

Her eyes were hopeful, and Matt didn't have the heart to disappoint her.

"I'd offer you a beer, but Maddy told me—" She closed her mouth abruptly and blushed. "Sadie keeps a pot of coffee on all day."

"Coffee would be fine. I can't stay long." Especially if Sadie was going to be giving him the evil eye. What had Maddy told her? he wondered next. That he drank too much? That he couldn't be trusted? Obviously, his reputation had preceded him.

Margaret led the way into the house, stopping just inside the heated porch to remove her jacket and boots; he did the same. She opened the kitchen door and they were greeted by an array of warm, inviting smells. Matt glanced around, relieved that Sadie was nowhere in sight.

Matt noted the coveralls Margaret wore. They were shapeless and about the most unflattering piece of clothing she could have chosen. Yet when she stood on tiptoe to reach for a cup in the top cupboard, he was stunned to see that she had a halfway decent body.

Scolding himself, Matt forced his gaze elsewhere.

"Sadie bakes the most delicious cookies," she told him as she opened the cookie jar and placed a dozen or so on a china plate. "I'd suggest we sit in the den, but neither of us is dressed for it."

Margaret slowly approached the table, carrying a serving tray with two small china cups, sugar, cream and the plate of chocolate chip cookies.

"I'll pour," she announced grandly, as if this feat required unusual skill. She left and returned with the coffeepot and filled each floral-patterned cup to the brim, then smile hesitantly, apparently awaiting his approval.

"Thank you," he mumbled, uncertain what was expected of him. He felt nervous even touching the dainty porcelain cup, afraid he might snap off the delicate handle.

"This set belonged to my mother," Margaret explained as she sat across the table from him.

"It's very nice."

"It's all I have of her, except for the jewelry my father gave her, but I've never worn any of that."

Rather than risk breaking the cup, Matt gingerly lifted it with both hands. There was a long silence. "I hope you're adjusting," he finally blurted out. "To your father's death, I mean."

Margaret didn't reply right away, then said, "I'm trying."

"Is there anything I can do?" His gaze held hers. He was surprised to realize what pretty eyes she had. Huge. A startling clear blue. Dark glossy lashes. She stared at him, her expression completely rapt. Meeting her eyes for any length of time proved disconcerting and he promptly looked elsewhere. The girl had it bad, he thought with a sinking sensation. He wanted to warn her off, tell her she was making a mistake, but he couldn't find the words. The women he dated knew the score, but Margaret was as innocent as a newborn calf. Naive, too, and completely inexperienced; that was obvious. What he needed to do was leave, and the sooner the better.

"I appreciate the offer, but there's nothing anyone can do," Margaret told him.

It took Matt a moment to realize she was answering his question. He nodded. "Well..."

"The ranch is going to be all right," she went on.

Matt took a discreet sip of his coffee. "If you find you need anything, let me know."

Now it was her turn to nod. "I will. Thank you for offering."

"I'm sincere, Margaret," he surprised himself by saying. "You're a capable rancher and I don't mean to imply otherwise, but there are times when neighbors need to rely on one another. I'm here for you, understand?'' He told himself he would have said the same thing to any local rancher who'd suffered a loss or some sort of crisis.

''And I'm here for you,'' she said in a low voice.

Matt downed the last of his coffee in one gulp, eager to be on his way. He'd stayed longer than he wanted, longer than required.

''You're leaving?'' she blurted.

''It's time I headed out,'' he said. Matt could tell she was disappointed, but she didn't employ any clever means of detaining him. That was one of Sheryl's tricks. He'd make noises about going home and she'd find some excuse to keep him with her. He had to give her credit; she was inventive—and often very sexy. Lately he'd been more conscious of her efforts and had become amused at the things she'd said and done to delay him. Sheryl could be one manipulative little devil.

''I'll walk you to your truck,'' Margaret told him, taking the coffee cups and tray to the kitchen counter.

He started to tell her that wasn't necessary, then changed his mind. Being stared at by a woman's adoring eyes was a flattering sensation, and Matt wasn't beyond enjoying it.

Margaret quickly put her mud-caked boots back on her feet. She buttoned her coat all the way to her chin and stuck a knit cap on her head without any concern about what it did to her hair.

''I appreciate your stopping by,'' she told him as they reached the truck.

''I'm sorry I didn't come sooner.''

"I am, too." She blushed then, as if she regretted having said this.

"If you'd like, I could stop by again."

Her eyes flared with excitement. "I wish you would."

Matt wasn't sure what had prompted the offer. His ranch adjoined the Clemens property but this was only the second time he'd come to the house. Dropping by unannounced wasn't a habit he planned to cultivate.

"Come any time," she added, "any time at all." She sounded so pleased and excited.

What happened then was something Matt would always wonder about. One moment he was preparing to climb into his truck and the next he'd wrapped his arms around Margaret Clemens the way he would Sheryl. He kissed her. He wasn't sure why—curiosity, he supposed. He couldn't keep himself from finding out what it would be like to kiss her. Since she hadn't expected a kiss, it wasn't fair to judge. But he did, mainly because he was kind of shocked. As kisses went, it was pretty good. No, damn good. Uncomplicated and—he hated to use this word—sweet. With other women, those with experience, a kiss was never simple. It involved tongues and teeth and it was often explosive with passion and need. A kiss hadn't been innocent for him in a very long while.

He broke it off and released her. Margaret faltered and would have stumbled backward if he hadn't caught her by the shoulders.

An apology would be appropriate, but he wasn't sorry. If he was anything, it was confused.

"I'll check up on you later in the week," he managed to say.

She nodded and pressed the back of her hand to her lips. Her eyes were wide and jubilant, her lashes fluttering as if she didn't know how to react.

Matt drove out of the yard and was halfway down the driveway when he glanced in his rearview mirror. Margaret stood there unmoving, her hand still against her lips, staring after him.

"That's it," Matt said aloud, shaken and bewildered by his own actions. "I'm not coming back. Not for anything."

Calla Stern had expected her troubles to be over when she moved in with her father in Minneapolis. Her mother and Dennis Urlacher had publicly announced their engagement and hadn't even bothered to let her know beforehand. Although she supposed if they *had* approached her, it would have been a wasted effort. She wanted nothing to do with Dennis, and no way did she want to be part of their perfect little family. Not in this lifetime!

Calla had always disliked Dennis. If it wasn't for Dennis, she told herself, her parents might have reconciled when she was younger. She detested them both—Dennis and her mother—for the things they'd done, sneaking around, pretending no one knew they were having an affair. When Calla learned that her mother wasn't even divorced at the time, she'd felt sickened by their disgusting behavior. Later, she'd been insulted and furious that they'd decided to get married and completely excluded her from their plans. Obviously they didn't want her in their lives. Well, that was fine with her; Buffalo Valley was such a hick town and she'd wanted to get out of there, anyway. So it seemed fitting that she'd run away the night Dennis and her mother announced their engagement.

Living with her father, however, had turned out to be less than ideal. She'd been five when her parents separated, and her memories of Willie Stern had been hazy. Over the last eleven years he'd sent her the occasional postcard and intermittently kept in touch. Without realizing it, Calla had placed him on a pedestal—from which he'd quickly tumbled. Her view of Willie Stern had completely changed by the end of her first week with him.

Despite that, she still felt she'd had no choice. After her mother decided to marry Dennis, Calla had packed her bags, borrowed her grandfather's truck and driven into Grand Forks, where she caught the bus to Minneapolis. It would be an understatement to say that Willie was surprised by her sudden appearance on his doorstep, but he'd let her move in with him.

For the first time in conscious memory, Calla had the opportunity to live in a real city with shopping malls, brand-name clothing stores and a school with more than twenty-five students. She didn't need to order an outfit on the Internet or from a catalogue but could walk into a store and try it on in a real dressing room. She had the opportunity to meet lots of other kids her own age, not just a handful. It didn't matter that her father had been such a bitter disappointment. Soon after her arrival she'd run away from Willie's place, but when her mother and Dennis came to collect her, she'd chosen to go back with her father rather than return to Buffalo Valley. She could put up with Willie more easily than she could accept the idea of Dennis Urlacher as her stepfather.

"You get those floors mopped?" Jason Jefferies asked.

Jason was only a year older than she was, but he was

the manager of the BurgerHaven where Calla worked part-time. "Didn't you notice? I finished half an hour ago," she said, unable to contain her sarcasm.

"Don't give me attitude," Jason snapped. "I got three friends who'd jump at the chance to work here. You give me a reason to fire you, Calla, and you're outta here."

"Yes, sir," she said with a falsely sweet smile. Much as she hated to admit it, she needed this job. Her father's income was erratic, its source questionable. And he sure didn't share it with her. The reverse, in fact. Not waiting for a response, she turned and walked away.

Willie wasn't the only disappointment Calla had to face. The high school back in Buffalo Valley had twenty-five students. Twenty-five. The one she attended in Minneapolis had over three thousand—more people than lived in her hometown *and* the surrounding county. Finding her way from classroom to classroom before the bell rang was a major challenge. She'd already gotten nine tardy slips. One more and she'd be ordered to afternoon detention.

One teacher, Mr. Simon, had been totally unreasonable. She had swimming in fifth period, and her sixth-period algebra class was on the third floor in the east wing. A sprinter couldn't have covered that distance in five minutes! Mr. Simon docked her grade one full point every time she was late, and that was totally unfair. Her jaw tightened whenever she thought about it. The only classes in which she got decent grades were art and drama, because she'd volunteered to sew costumes for the senior production. They were doing *The Importance of Being Earnest,* and that meant lots of intricate Victorian dresses.

Calla could lose herself in working with the patterns and fabric, in getting the details perfect.

Jason dimmed the lights and was ready to close the BurgerHaven.

Swallowing her pride, Calla approached him. "Any chance you could give me a ride home?"

He didn't like doing it, she knew, but waiting for the bus by herself unnerved her. A couple of men had harassed her one night, and she'd had nightmares about it ever since. She hated to ask Jason for a ride, but she didn't have any other means of getting home, besides the bus.

"You'll have to pay."

Calla nodded. What a jerk. He collected an hour's wages for driving her one block out of his way. If he charged her any more, she might as well take a taxi.

Jason wasn't the talkative sort and they rode in silence. Calla had hoped to make friends before now, but it hadn't happened. School had been in session nearly three months, and she didn't have one friend. Not even one. Trying to get to class on time was difficult enough.

Her father was sprawled in front of the television when she let herself into the apartment. She brought the mail and the free neighborhood newspaper in with her.

"You bring me anything?" he asked, not moving his gaze from the television screen.

"Not tonight."

That got his attention. "They throw away all the stuff that doesn't get sold, so why the hell not bring me a taco burger?"

Calla wondered if it ever occurred to him that they might not *have* leftovers. "There weren't any," she said, tired and out of sorts. *It's after ten,* she wanted to scream. *Leave me alone!*

"Damn! I was all set for a taco burger, too. I don't suppose you could get me dinner?" He looked beseechingly toward her.

Like she was a magician and could pull a decent meal out of a top hat. "Get you dinner?" she repeated. "With what?"

He leaned back and dug into his pants pocket and tossed her his car keys. "With these."

Calla left the keys on the floor where they'd fallen. She set down her books and sorted through the mail, although it was mostly dunning letters from bill collectors and a few advertising circulars. She paused when she saw the envelope with her mother's familiar writing. This wasn't the first letter she'd received, and her reaction was always the same—hope and excitement. Even though she didn't *want* to feel anything for her mother.

Sarah Stern had lied to her, and Calla refused to forgive her—for that and a truckload of other faults. The biggest of which was marrying Dennis Urlacher.

"You going or not?" her father demanded.

Calla barely heard him. A wave of homesickness threatened to drown her. She missed Buffalo Valley, missed her friends and her old job at The Pizza Parlor and even her old sxchool. Her mother had ruined everything by marrying Dennis. Calla's entire life had been stolen from her and it was their fault.

"What's that?" Willie asked.

"A letter from Mom."

"She send me any money?"

Calla rolled her eyes. Willie insisted that if Sarah wasn't paying him the child support he thought he was entitled to, then Calla had to pay rent. Therefore, Calla paid rent.

"Well, aren't you going to open it?"

"Yes," she said, and headed toward her bedroom. When she did read the letter, she had no intention of doing it in front of him.

Sitting on the side of her bed, Calla stared at the envelope. It was thick, as if it included something extra. Her curiosity got the better of her and she tore it open. Inside were an airline ticket and a letter. She unfolded the letter.

Dear Calla,

I haven't been able to reach you by phone to ask about your plans for Thanksgiving. I'm hoping you can arrange to make it home for a few days. It would mean a great deal to me. I miss you, Calla. I realize I haven't been the world's best mother, and I've made plenty of mistakes, but I do love you.

On the chance you can get away, I've enclosed an airline ticket. The flight leaves Minneapolis Wednesday afternoon and returns on Sunday morning. Dennis and I would pick you up at the airport in Grand Forks. If you're uncomfortable staying with Dennis and me, then your grandfather wanted you to know you could have your old room at his house.

Everything's going well here in Buffalo Valley. Dennis and I bought the old Habberstad house. The two of us rattle around in it, but we both enjoy decorating it. With five bedrooms you could have your pick if you decided you wanted to move back home.

You haven't answered my letters or taken any of my calls. I know you're angry with me, Calla, and I'm sorry. It's time we settled all this. Don't you think so, too?

Love,
Mom

"What did she have to say?" Willie asked, standing in her bedroom doorway.

"Nothing," Calla muttered, stuffing the letter inside her backpack.

"What's that?" he asked, pointing to the airline ticket she'd set beside her on the bed.

"A ticket."

He laughed. "Home for Thanksgiving, right?"

Calla didn't answer.

"Home sweet home with mommy and her new husband. You're not going, are you?"

"I haven't decided."

He glared at her. "I was hoping you and I could spend the day together."

Calla recognized that for the bribe it was.

"It'll be the first Thanksgiving we've had in eleven years. You aren't walking out on me now, are you, kid?"

"I said I hadn't made up my mind yet."

He leaned against the doorjamb, arms crossed. "Did she tell you she's pregnant?"

Calla's gaze flew to her father. He was baiting her and she refused to bite. It would be just like Willie to make this up, but at the same time Calla knew that Dennis wanted a family. She supposed her mother *could* be pregnant. Still, she wasn't sure she could trust Willie.

"She told me so herself," he muttered.

"I don't believe you."

"Ask her, then. She was saving it as a big secret, but she spilled the beans last time she called."

Calla frowned uncertainly. Her father had a habit of lying, of saying exactly what she wanted to hear. Or *didn't* want to hear, depending on the reaction he was after.

"I'll tell you what," Willie said, sounding bored with the subject. "You do what you want for Thanksgiving. Stay or go, it's up to you. But as for your mother having a baby, ask yourself what you think is true." With that, he left.

Calla stared down at the airline ticket. Then, with a deep sigh, jumped to her feet and threw it onto the rickety dresser beside the bed.

Her mother had made her choice, and she'd picked Dennis Urlacher over her.

Three

Rachel Fischer sat in a corner of her restaurant kitchen, where she kept her computer and desk. Writing out a check for the final payment of her loan from the Buffalo County Bank, she signed her name with a flair—and a deep sense of satisfaction. She ripped the check from the book, then stared at it, absorbing the significance of the moment. From this point forward, she was out of debt and free to pursue a relationship with Heath Quantrill, the bank president.

With the last of her bills paid for the month, she put on her hat and coat and headed for the bank. She walked briskly, facing the wind. Normally, the cold cut straight through her, but not today. She hadn't seen Heath in a few weeks and looked forward to personally handing him the check.

He served as the senior loan officer and manager and worked at the Buffalo Valley branch three days a week, spending the other two at the bank's headquarters in Grand Forks.

Rachel and Heath had an on-again/off-again relationship that she'd wasted copious hours analyzing. But over the summer their romance had grown serious and they saw one another exclusively. Since Rachel was a widow, much of her time went into supporting herself and her son. Heath wanted her to go out with him more often, but that was impossible and often a source of conflict. He'd suggested that if she invested as much time in their relationship as she did in her business, she need never worry about working again. The memory of that conversation infuriated her whenever she thought about it.

This last year had been difficult for them. She'd expanded both the hours and the menu of her weekend pizza delivery service—to reasonably consistent success. After paying off her original loan—for the pizza oven—she'd borrowed from the bank again to purchase tables and chairs and had turned her restaurant into a sit-down place serving dinner five days a week.

Her parents owned the building, so her rent was low. They'd operated the Morningside Café for many years, until the diner simply couldn't survive in such a difficult economic climate. It'd broken her mother's heart to leave Buffalo Valley and she'd pleaded with Rachel to join them in Arizona.

A recent widow at the time, Rachel had debated long and hard about uprooting her young son, and eventually decided against it. Mark had endured enough upheaval in his life after the loss of his father. Besides, every book she'd read on widowhood suggested she delay making a major decision for at least twelve months.

In order to support herself, Rachel drove the school bus and worked as a part-time bookkeeper for Knight's Pharmacy. She was barely scraping by when she came up with the idea of starting her own pizza parlor. Actually, it was her son who'd made the suggestion, claiming her homemade pizza was better than the pizza he'd eaten in a fast food restaurant at a friend's birthday party in Grand Forks.

That was when she'd first met Heath Quantrill. Business plan in hand, she'd gone to the bank to apply for a loan. Heath had read over her application, and then, with barely a pause, refused her. True, she had nothing for collateral, although she'd offered her wedding band. She realized that on paper her business venture didn't look promising, but she was young, healthy, ambitious and determined. In addition, she'd been around the restaurant business her entire life. Heath had taken none of that into account.

The next few days had been bleak ones for Rachel. Then, to her amazement, Heath had phoned and announced he'd changed his mind. He'd never actually told her why, but she had her suspicions. Hassie Knight was good friends with Lily Quantrill, Heath's grandmother, and Rachel strongly suspected that Hassie had mentioned the loan to Lily, who had persuaded Heath to relent. Knowing Lily, she didn't think the persuasion had been of the gentle variety.

The bank was busy when Rachel walked in. Both tellers had lineups. Joanie Wyatt was there with her toddler son, and Steve Baylor, a local farmer, stood behind her. Even before she'd opened her restaurant, Rachel knew everyone in town. That wasn't saying much, though, since almost everyone knew everyone else. It was one of the advantages of living in a small town. And one of the disadvantages—when tongues wagged and other people got involved in her personal business. But for the most part she considered it a blessing.

Heath, who was in his private office, was chatting with Carl Hooper, the manager of the J.C. Penney catalogue store. His door was half-open, and he glanced up when she came into the bank. He smiled, clearly pleased to see her.

Content to wait, Rachel took a chair. The bank was the only brick building in town, and one of the nicest, inside and out. Heath's grandparents had founded Buffalo County Bank shortly after World War II and over the years had expanded to ten branches across the state. Their only son and his wife had died within a short time of each other, leaving two sons, Max and Heath. The elder, Max, was the one who'd revealed an interest in the business and Lily, by now a widow, was grooming him to take over as president. Then Max had been killed in a car crash, and Heath, the playboy adventurer, had returned from Europe to take his brother's place. It hadn't been easy to step into Max's shoes, and Heath had struggled with finding his own path these last few years.

Carl Hooper left five minutes later and Rachel sprang from her seat, then walked into Heath's office, approaching his desk.

"Hello," he said, standing to greet her. "It's good to see you."

"Good to see you, too." Oddly, she felt almost shy now that she actually faced him. They stared at each other a moment before Rachel explained the purpose of her visit. "I have two things for you," she announced, pulling out the chair recently vacated by Carl Hooper.

"Two?" Heath raised his brows and sat down himself.

"First of all," she said, opening her purse, "this, as far as I'm aware, is the final payment on my second loan." She handed him the check, stretching her arm across his desk.

"And as far as I'm aware, you're right," Heath said as he took her check. He looked expectantly back at her.

"Also," she said, feeling flustered and excited, "I have an answer for you."

"Really." His voice became suspiciously unemotional. They'd talked about marriage a number of times, but Rachel had always managed to put him off. It didn't seem right to accept an engagement ring while she owed him money. Now the loan was paid off, she felt free to change that.

"I love you, Heath," she whispered, wishing she'd chosen the time and place more carefully. In her excitement, she'd rushed to the bank without careful thought. This *was* a public place, after all—not to mention that Heath's office door was still half-open.

"And?" he prodded.

"Aren't you going to tell me you love me, too?" she asked, thinking it was within his power to make this easier.

"No. If you don't know my feelings by now, then my telling you isn't going to make a damn bit of difference."

She could tell he was enjoying himself. He'd leaned back against his leather chair, playing the role of bank president to the hilt.

"If that's the case, I just might change my mind."

"Before you do, tell me what's *on* your mind," he cajoled.

Rachel figured he was entitled to that much. "Being your wife."

A smile exploded across his face, and he released a long, deep sigh. "At last."

Rachel agreed; it had been a long time coming, but now

she was sure this was what she wanted, what was right for Heath, and for her and Mark.

"What took you so long?" he asked, coming around to her side of the desk.

He didn't know? Hadn't figured it out himself? "I made the last payment," she said, standing to meet him. "I couldn't agree to become your wife while I owed you money."

"Sure, you could have," he argued and then, right there in front of anyone who cared to look, he kissed her.

Rachel quickly became absorbed in the kiss, twining her arms around his neck, but not so absorbed that she didn't notice how quiet the bank had become. When Heath broke off the kiss, he gently disengaged her and hurried to his door. Flinging it wide open, he called out, "We're engaged!"

His announcement was instantly followed by a chorus of congratulations and applause from staff and customers alike. Just as quickly the questions came.

"When's the wedding?"

"Does Lily know?"

"You aren't closing down The Pizza Parlor, are you?"

"You're going to live in Buffalo Valley, right?"

Rachel and Heath glanced at each other, but they didn't seem to have any ready answers. At least Rachel didn't.

"The wedding's soon. Very soon," Heath insisted, his arm around Rachel's slim waist. "Right?"

Rachel blushed and nodded.

"We'll tell Lily this evening," Heath continued, and once more looked to her for confirmation.

"I won't be closing the restaurant," she added. This had

been the subject of repeated arguments between her and Heath. He didn't want her to work, but the restaurant was *hers* and she wasn't willing to give it up simply because she was marrying a wealthy man, although she did plan on hiring extra help.

"You won't?" Heath sounded surprised.

"No," she returned and elbowed him in the ribs.

"They aren't even married yet," Steve Baylor cried, "and they're already arguing."

"Every couple has issues they need to settle," Joanie Wyatt said calmly. She sent Rachel a soft smile. Joanie should know; she'd recently reconciled with her husband after a year-long separation. She and her husband, Brandon, were a good example of a couple who'd worked through the problems in their marriage.

"Rachel wants to stay right here in Buffalo Valley," Heath told everyone.

"I do," she concurred. She hadn't said anything to Heath yet, but she could see several needs arising in the community, prime business opportunities. With the success of her restaurant and Sarah's quilting company, Buffalo Valley was badly in need of a day-care center. Now that she had five full-time employees sewing for her, Sarah was expecting more women to come into town—some to buy quilts and some, eventually, to work for her. All of this meant the bank's, and therefore Heath's, increasing involvement with the town.

"You gonna kiss her again?" Steve asked.

Heath laughed. "I plan to do a lot more than kiss her. Come on," he said to Rachel, reaching for her hand. "If

there was ever a time for a celebration lunch, this is it.''
   Rachel couldn't agree more.

   Matt Eilers had kissed her. Even a week later, Margaret
could hardly believe it had actually happened. In bed at
night, she closed her eyes and relived the kiss. Nothing in
the world could be more wonderful than Matt's wanting
her.

   Sure, she'd been kissed before. Well...once. By a ranch
hand employed by her father. *Briefly* employed. She'd been
sixteen, physically underdeveloped, and as naive as they
come. She was an adult now and eager to have Matt introduce her to adult experience. To show her what being a
woman really meant.

   For seven days she'd kept the kissing incident to herself,
afraid that if she shared it with anyone else, something
would be lost. But when she didn't hear from Matt again,
Margaret knew she needed help in sorting out the significance of what had happened. Since Matt had kissed her
once, surely that meant he'd be interested in doing it
again—didn't it? But she hadn't seen her neighbor since.
The only person she could ask about such things was
Maddy Washburn McKenna.

   Taking the truck, Margaret drove over to Maddy and
Jeb's, hoping to catch Maddy when she wasn't busy with
the baby. Margaret had been present when Julianne Marjorie McKenna was born, and she still considered it one of
the most exciting days of her life. Over the years she'd
helped a lot of calves into this world, but she'd never wit-
nessed a human birth. Julianne's was exhilarating, a truly
spectacular event in Margaret's existence.

   She knew labor and delivery weren't easy on a woman;

she'd been there to see Maddy's struggles. But after holding that precious baby in her arms, Margaret had understood why a woman would willingly undergo such pain.

As she rolled into the McKennas' yard and parked, Maddy waved to her from the kitchen window.

Margaret waved back. She hurried out of the cold and wind and onto the back porch, automatically slipping off her coat, hat and gloves.

"Margaret!" Maddy said, opening the back door for her. "I'm so glad to see you."

Maddy had a way of making everyone feel welcome and...*special,* and Margaret wasn't immune to her enthusiasm.

"This is a wonderful surprise," Maddy went on.

"I'm not interrupting anything, am I?" Margaret was careful to avoid making a pest of herself. Jeb and Maddy hadn't been married long and there was the baby, too. Maddy was her closest friend, and she didn't want anything to disrupt their bond.

"This is perfect timing. Jeb's out with the herd and the baby's napping. How about a pot of tea? The water's already on."

"Sure." She didn't really want tea, but it was one of the rituals of their friendship.

A few minutes later, Maddy carried a steeping pot of tea into the living room and Margaret dutifully followed.

"How have you been?" Maddy asked. They'd spoken on the phone at least once a week, and Maddy always asked that question.

Margaret knew it wasn't her health Maddy was referring to, but her life now that her father was gone. She shrugged, saying what she usually did. "All right, I guess." After a moment's reflection, she continued, "A dozen times a day I find myself thinking I need to talk to Dad about this or that. When I realize I can't ever ask him anything again, this...this feeling of emptiness comes over me." She pressed her hand to her heart. "Some days don't seem as bad as others, but there *are* days I don't think I can go on."

"It takes time."

Margaret knew that. "I'm doing what you suggested the day of the funeral and that's to remember how fortunate I was to have him as long as I did. His life was a blessing to a lot of people."

"I said that?"

Margaret nodded. "Maybe not in those exact words."

Maddy poured the tea and smiled in amusement. "Sometimes I sound so wise, I astonish myself."

"You *are* wise—you understand about people. Actually that's the reason I came over," Margaret said, sitting back on the sofa and cradling her mug with both hands. She paused, hesitant to proceed.

Maddy said nothing, her expression quizzical.

"Matt Eilers stopped by last week to offer his condolences."

Maddy added a spoonful of sugar to her tea. "He's a little late, don't you think?"

"He apologized for that," Margaret said, quick to defend him. She took a deep breath. "When he was ready to leave, I walked him out to his truck...."

"And?" Maddy seemed to sense something important

had happened because she gazed steadily at Margaret as she waited for her to go on.

"Well, before he left—" she paused a second time "—now, I don't want you to misjudge him...I realize Matt isn't one of your favorite people."

"I don't dislike him," Maddy assured her.

"But you don't trust him."

Maddy stirred her tea with no comment, then said, "I can be fair. You'd better tell me."

Margaret was dying to do so. "Oh, Maddy, he kissed me and it was just as wonderful as I dreamed it would be. At first, I didn't know what to think, since it was such a surprise and all. He started to open his truck door, then turned back, took me by the shoulders and out of the blue, he *kissed* me!"

"He kissed you," Maddy repeated in a low voice.

"Yes, and Maddy, oh Maddy, it was *wonderful!*"

"I'm sure it was...."

"I realize every other woman in the entire universe has more experience with men than I do." If it wasn't for Matt, she probably wouldn't care to this day. Being a woman, all that feminine stuff, was something she'd never had any interest in. She'd considered it trivial and, more than that, irrelevant. Most people blamed her father for not seeing to the proper upbringing of a little girl. But that was unfair. Few understood that she'd loved him so much she was determined to fulfill his every wish. Bernard Clemens had wanted a son, so Margaret had spent her entire life trying to be one.

The first time she'd felt a woman's emotions had been a shock. Matt Eilers was the reason for that revelation. One day she saw him and it felt as if she'd been hit over the head with a frying pan. He was the most gorgeous creature she'd ever laid eyes on and she wanted him in the worst way. Wanted him the way a woman wants a man.

"Now all I think about is Matt's kiss...except when I'm feeling depressed about my dad."

"Oh, Margaret..."

"No, listen, I'm happy he did it. Really happy—but I don't know what it means."

Maddy didn't appear to have an immediate answer herself. She kept stirring her tea until any sugar had long dissolved. "I don't know what to suggest," she said finally.

"The problem is, I haven't seen him since," Margaret murmured, unable to hide how discouraged this made her feel. "Do you think he didn't like the kiss—that I might have done it wrong?"

"No." At least Maddy sounded confident about that.

"What should I do?" she asked next. Her friend usually had answers.

"Do?" Maddy echoed, seemingly lost in thought. She set her cup aside and leaned forward, taking Margaret's hand between both of hers. "Listen carefully. I know how you feel about Matt."

"I love him," she stated simply.

"But I want you to promise me you'll be careful about starting any kind of relationship with him."

So Maddy was afraid Matt would take advantage of her. Margaret understood why her friend might react that way, but deep down, Margaret knew otherwise. She'd seen his surprised look after he'd kissed her. He hadn't come to seduce her; she would have bet the ranch on that. Nor was she as naive as others, including Matt, assumed. Inexperienced, yes. Naive, no.

They sat and visited for another thirty minutes before the baby cried and Margaret decided it was time to go. Maddy collected the still-sleepy infant and walked Margaret to the door, promising to call in a few days.

As she drove back to the Circle C, Margaret remembered something her father had often told her. *If you have a question or a doubt, go straight to the source.* She didn't know why she hadn't thought of that earlier. If she had any questions about Matt's kiss or his motives, all she needed to do was ask him.

With renewed purpose, she drove past her own ranch and headed toward his, pulling into the large yard. The Stockerts had been neighbors and friends of her father's for years, but had moved when beef prices plummeted dramatically. The house had sat vacant until Matt arrived, leasing the property from the retired couple. He'd started out small, which was smart, building his herd each year. The house needed plenty of repairs and a coat of paint. But why should he paint a house that wasn't his? Matt put everything he earned back into his herd.

Margaret parked the truck, then got out and glanced around. It appeared that Matt wasn't there. She was about to leave when she saw him walk out of the barn. Once again she was struck by his stunning good looks—stunning at least to her.

Suddenly Margaret felt insecure and self-conscious, and she experienced those emotions as a physical sensation.

She didn't like the uncomfortable feeling that settled in the pit of her stomach.

"Margaret." He touched the brim of his hat in welcome.

"Matt." She touched her own.

They stood three feet apart with the cold drifting in around them. She supposed other people would gradually lead into the purpose of a visit, but she was beyond pretense.

"Why did you kiss me?" she asked, surprised by how cool and even her voice remained. The question had plagued her for days, had practically consumed her, yet she'd made it sound as if she was asking about the price of feed.

His eyes met and held hers. Then, looking discomfited, he shrugged. "I can't rightly say."

"You plan on doing it again?"

His gaze shifted away from hers. "What makes you ask?"

Wait a minute. *She* was the one asking the questions here. "Don't answer my question with one of your own. That's unfair."

"There are rules to this conversation?"

"You just did it again," she cried, exasperated.

At that, Matt burst out laughing.

Despite the seriousness of her concerns, Margaret laughed, too.

"You're fortunate you caught me. I was out on the range earlier, looking for stray cattle."

"We've had a lot of rain lately." They both knew what that meant. The wet weather could bring about symptoms of bloat in the calves; they required careful watching.

As it happened, Matt had brought a sick calf into the barn and before long, Margaret was down on her knees, checking him over.

"What do you think?" he asked.

If Margaret knew anything, it was cattle. "I'd get the vet out here if you hope to save him."

Matt nodded gravely. "I already put in a call to Doc Lenz in Devils Lake, but he said there's not much he could do that I haven't already done."

Talking softly to the sick calf, Margaret stroked his sleek neck. Hardened rancher or not, she hated to see anything suffer. She comforted the calf as it lay dying, tears springing to her eyes. She continued to stroke the calf's face long after it was gone. When she realized Matt was watching her, she got abruptly to her feet and glanced at her watch. "I'd better go home."

He stood, too. "I'll walk you out."

They strolled silently back to her truck, and she wondered if he was as reluctant to let her go as she was to leave. "You never did answer my question," she reminded him.

He grinned and shook his head. "You're right, I didn't."

"It isn't the proper thing for a woman to ask, is it?"

He buried his hands deep in his coat pockets. "I don't see why not. If you'd kissed me, I'd want to know why."

Really. Then perhaps she should do exactly that. Catching him by surprise, she reached for his collar, gripping it with both hands. Then, raising herself on her toes, she slanted her mouth over his, hungry to discover if a second kiss could possibly compare with the first.

Quick as anything, Matt's arms were around her waist,

pulling her against him. He did it with such force that it drove the breath from her lungs. For one wild second, her eyes flew open. Matt quickly took charge of the kiss, seducing her with his lips, introducing her to his tongue and creating an ache in her that reached low into her belly. This was the kind of kiss that would make a woman want to lock the door.

When he released her, it was all Margaret could do to breathe again.

"I shocked you, didn't I?" he said, brushing the hair from her face.

Still breathless, she couldn't answer him.

"I figure you haven't had much experience at this."

His comment irritated her. He seemed to be saying her lack of sexual finesse was obvious.

"I...I should leave now," she murmured, doing her best to sound mature and unaffected, even though her knees were shaking.

"Feel free to stop by any time," he said, opening the truck door.

"By the same token," she said, climbing inside, "feel free to shock me any time."

He was still laughing when he closed the door and she started the engine and drove off. He was laughing and Margaret was smiling. *This could be the start of something good,* a voice inside her seemed to whisper.

The frantic hum of sewing machines filled the workshop at Sarah Urlacher's quilt company. Three machines were in use nearly eight hours every day. Two girls cut pattern pieces while Sarah was busy with the phones. Orders continued to arrive and she was having trouble keeping up. Many nights she stayed late, dying the muslin, soaking the cloth in tea water and other natural concoctions made with lichen and berries and plants. She put in long hours, but she loved it with an intensity that was hard to explain. Quilting was her passion, and her love for it went into every quilt she sold.

No one was more amazed by the almost overnight success of her business than Sarah herself. It'd started out mainly as a hobby, something to occupy her time and employ her talents. Then she'd won first prize at the state fair and sold the quilt for an astonishing five hundred dollars. Soon other sales trickled in. Enough that she'd eventually realized she needed to expand, to move her business out of her father's house. That was when she created the Buffalo Valley Quilting Company.

Although it was a risk, a leap of faith, she'd rented space in one of the abandoned stores on Buffalo Valley's main street. Having her own location with her business name painted on the window had brought her immense satisfaction—and pride. For the first time, she was doing something for herself. The success or failure of this venture rested squarely on her own shoulders. Everything else in her life had been controlled by circumstances, but this company was of her own making. And so was its success.

To be fair, she credited Lindsay Sinclair with those initial sales. Two years earlier, Lindsay had moved to Buffalo Valley and accepted a teaching job. With her, Lindsay had brought hope and vision to the community.

When Sarah started her company, Lindsay had contacted her uncle in Savannah about displaying the distinctive quilts in his upscale furniture store. The first had sold immediately, and everything since had been eagerly snapped up. Soon other retail outlets had approached her.

Already she had a handful of full-time employees and she could use more. But luring women into town to work for her was complicated. Farm wives were often needed at home, and with no day care available in town... A temporary solution was to hire them to do piecework out of their homes, but Sarah didn't feel that gave her the same quality control.

Her thoughts were interrupted by the jangling of the bell above the door. Hassie Knight walked in. The pharmacist visited often, usually without a specific reason; Sarah guessed she just liked seeing all the activity.

"It does my heart good," Hassie had told her once. "This town is coming back to life and it's starting right here in this shop." And then the older woman said something that brought a rush of pride to Sarah every time she thought about it. "I couldn't be prouder of you if you were my own daughter."

"Afternoon, Hassie," Sarah greeted her.

"I brought you a chocolate soda," the older woman said, handing her a tall metal container filled to the brim with ice cream and soda. "I'm betting you didn't eat lunch again today."

Sarah hadn't; she'd been too busy.

"We can't have you getting weak and fainting on us, now can we?"

There was little likelihood of that happening, but Sarah wasn't about to argue. Hassie made the best sodas she'd tasted anywhere. Until that moment, she hadn't realized how famished she was.

"Thank you," she said.

Hassie nodded, then left as abruptly as she'd come.

Sarah stood by the window and watched her. Since her own mother's death, she'd considered Hassie both advisor and friend. In Sarah's opinion, Hassie Knight had held this town together. If not for her, the community would have shriveled up and died the way so many other prairie towns had in the last twenty years.

Sarah's gaze drifted toward her husband's service station. It was difficult even now, three months after speaking their vows, to believe they were actually married. Unfortunately, the joy she felt was almost immediately squelched by regret at her daughter's estrangement. For reasons no one fully understood, Calla disliked Dennis. When they'd announced their engagement, Calla had run away, choosing instead to live with her father in Minneapolis.

Sarah felt an oppressive sadness, a painful despair, whenever she thought about Calla. It was agonizing to see history repeat itself as she watched Calla make the same mistakes she had. Sarah felt so helpless. Nothing she'd said or done had brought Calla home. She shook off the memory; thinking about her daughter made it impossible to concentrate on work.

At five o'clock, her employees packed up and headed home. Sarah stayed behind, catching up on some long-overdue paperwork. An hour after she closed, Dennis joined her.

He walked into the back room, stood behind her, kissing her neck. "You ready to leave?"

He smelled of gasoline and grease, and spicy aftershave. Sarah closed her eyes and enjoyed the loving feel of his arms around her.

"I won't be long. Did you go to the post office?"

His hesitation told her he had.

"There's a letter from Calla," he told her.

Sarah's heart flew into her throat. She'd been so anxious to get a response about Thanksgiving.

"Open it later," Dennis advised.

Sarah whirled around, unable to believe he'd say such a thing. "Why?" He knew she'd been waiting for days to hear from her daughter.

"What if she tells you she won't come?" Dennis asked.

"Then she won't be here." Sarah's flippant reply suggested it didn't matter one way or the other. In reality, it meant everything. She'd only spoken to Calla a few times in the last five months. Despite her best efforts, every conversation had left her feeling guilty, upset and depressed. If only she could get Calla away from Willie's influence, talk to her, reason all this out.

Thanksgiving would be perfect. Her father and her brother, Jeb, along with Maddy and the baby, would be joining them. Even Dennis's parents were coming. A big family dinner, the kind they'd had when her mother was alive. Perhaps it was greedy of her, but Sarah wanted her daughter with them. Surrounded by family, Calla would surely feel the love everyone had for her, would surely realize how much they missed her. Realize how much Sarah needed her. Perhaps they'd even be able to break down the barriers and communicate as mother and daughter.

"Give me the letter," she told him, and held out her hand.

"Sarah..."

"Dennis, please."

His reluctance was obvious. She clutched the small manila envelope and was about to tear into it when she paused. "Perhaps you're right," she said, her voice shaking. All at once she was afraid of what she'd find inside.

"Open it," Dennis said now. "You might as well. Get it over with."

He was as ambivalent as she was. Sarah sighed deeply. Confronting her fear was more difficult than she'd expected. She opened the envelope, reached inside and pulled out half the airline ticket.

Sarah's chest tightened and for a moment she could hardly breathe. Calla had torn the airline ticket in two and returned both halves.

"No letter?" Dennis asked, sounding as discouraged as she felt.

Sarah looked again and shook her head. "Why would she do something so cruel?" she asked.

"Come on, sweetheart," Dennis said. "Let's go home."

"I don't know why she hates me so much," Sarah whispered. "If only she'd talk to me. If only..."

Four

Pastor John Dawson and his family had lived in fifteen different states in the last forty-three years, but he'd never thought of anywhere but Buffalo Valley as *home*. This was where he'd been born, where he'd gone to school, where he'd buried his mother and three years later, his father. From the day he left for the seminary, he'd planned to return to his childhood home—only, he hadn't expected that to take over forty years. He was near retirement age now, and it made sense that he pastor a church in the very town where he'd spent his youth. His life was about to come full circle.

For a time, his return had looked doubtful. It seemed that despite all of Joshua McKenna's and Hassie Knight's efforts, Buffalo Valley was about to be snuffed out, like so many other small towns that dotted the Dakotas. Then, unexpectedly, the community had sprung back to life. John was thrilled and had managed to convince the church hierarchy to send him to Buffalo Valley.

The only church available belonged to the Catholics. It'd been closed for a number of years, ever since Father McGrath, hampered by age and failing health, had retired. Despite circumstances, the elderly priest had continued to stop by every few weeks to celebrate Mass. Recently, however, Father McGrath had entered a retirement home in

Minnesota and the Bishop was eager to sell the property. The Methodist Church had bought it.

Soon after John had accepted the assignment, he'd found a nearby house to rent. The spare bedroom served as his office. The house was smaller than he would've liked, but it was fine for the time being. Fortunately his three daughters were grown and settled in careers and raising their own families. Unfortunately, they lived in three different states—Connecticut, Nebraska and Oregon.

John's first official duty had been to officiate at the funeral of Bernard Clemens. He remembered the rancher, but it'd been years since they'd last spoken. The funeral, sad as it was, had been an opportunity to become acquainted with the people in town, those he'd once known and the younger people, whose families he often remembered. John had spent a good part of the day meeting and greeting his new neighbors.

In some ways, not much had changed in Buffalo Valley. When he'd left, there'd been a reserve toward strangers, a hesitancy. It remained in place to this day. The town...well, it *looked* better than he'd expected, but there was still much to be done. People were pleased with the most recent improvements and planning more. Then there was—

"Lunch is ready," Joyce called from the kitchen, breaking into his musings.

He'd met Joyce while he was in the seminary. His wife had been raised in Boston, but over the years she'd come to love small-town life.

"What are your plans for the afternoon?" she asked as she sat across the table from him. She'd prepared one of his favorites, a chicken salad made with cold noodles and tossed with a soy vinaigrette, but today he had virtually no appetite.

"I thought I'd go over and visit Joshua." A question about a couple he'd met at Bernard's funeral had been bothering John and he could think of no one better to ask than his old friend. After barely touching his lunch, he wandered over to Joshua McKenna's second-hand store. Joshua sold a little of everything. The sign in his window claimed there wasn't anything he couldn't fix, and John believed it.

"Good to see you," Joshua called out when the bell above the door announced John's arrival.

"I'm not disturbing you, am I?" John saw that Joshua was up to his elbows in grease, working on some kind of engine.

"Trust me, I welcome the interruption." Joshua reached for a wadded-up rag, tucked in his back hip pocket. "This," he said, gently patting the huge metal contraption, "is the engine to Gage Sinclair's tractor. Dennis had it two weeks and couldn't get it running. He threw up his hands and asked me to give it a try."

John knew that low prices were killing many of the small farmers in the heartland. Farmers kept their equipment running as long as possible, and then eked out another twenty thousand miles.

"Did you hear I was over at Buffalo Bob's?" John said as Joshua studied the engine. "Went there a couple of weeks ago, after I met them at Bernard's wake." Bob had talked John into trying his karaoke machine. He had no singing voice whatsoever, but bolstered by Merrily, he'd fallen victim. He was fairly confident they wouldn't invite him to sing again.

"They have a little boy, don't they?" John had noticed the child at the Clemens house but hadn't seen him since.

"His name's Axel."

"Unusual name."

Joshua nodded and continued to inspect the engine.

"Haven't seen him around much," John said.

"Seems to me Merrily said he's got the chicken pox," Joshua muttered.

"Poor little boy."

"I've never seen a couple crazier about a kid," Joshua said absentmindedly. He rubbed the side of his face, smearing a smudge of oil along his jaw.

"Bob seems to be a good father," John commented.

"He is," Joshua said. "Especially for being so new to it."

"Axel isn't his child?" John suspected as much, but then, he suspected a lot more.

"No. The boy belongs to Merrily," he said, and reached inside the engine with a long-handled wrench. "No one realized she had a kid until she showed up with him one day."

John's suspicions mounted. When he'd moved into the house, there'd been a pile of junk mail stacked in the post office box, waiting for him once he'd submitted his change-of-address information. Never one to toss a piece of paper without first looking at it, he'd come across some flyers, notifications of several missing and abducted children. The name Axel, being unusual, had stuck in his mind.

Within a week he'd met Bob and Merrily and their boy...Axel.

"Come to think of it, I never saw Merrily pregnant, either," Joshua said. He twisted the wrench again and glanced up. "It used to be that Merrily would drift in and out of town. She'd stay with Buffalo Bob a few weeks, then disappear. He took her leaving real hard and never seemed to know when she'd be coming back."

"You never saw her pregnant?" John repeated.

Joshua paused. "Funny, I never thought about it before, but no."

"She didn't bring the boy with her on earlier visits?"

Joshua shook his head. "No, not once."

"You're sure the boy is hers?"

His friend looked uncertain. "It's clear he belongs to her," he finally said. He held John's eyes for an uncomfortably long moment. "If you've got something to say, then say it."

John wasn't sure this was the time or place to voice his suspicions. For many, he was a newcomer to the community; he had no intention of wading into an explosive situation without being sure of himself.

"Did Sarah hear from Calla?" he asked instead, purposely changing the subject.

"She did." Regret flashed across Joshua's face. "Apparently Calla's not coming."

John had been afraid of that. "Is Sarah upset?"

"Real upset. Frankly, I don't understand Calla. Makes me wonder what lies that no-good father of hers is feeding her."

"You might never know."

Joshua scratched his head, leaving more grease in his hair. "I told you how she ran away from his place, too, didn't I?"

John nodded.

"Sarah and Dennis tried to talk sense into her, but she wouldn't listen. Calla had a choice—either move back here to Buffalo Valley or return to her father. No one understood why she'd choose to live with Willie. I tell you, John, it's got us all worried sick. No one would object if you mentioned it the next time you're talking to God."

"I'll be glad to," John offered. And while he was praying for Calla and her mother, John intended to ask God about the situation with Axel and his parents, too.

In the past few days, Sheryl had phoned no fewer than seven times. She was hounding Matt about Margaret, quizzing him about the relationship and what he was doing to promote it. Heaven help him if she ever found out about those kisses! At first, he'd assumed Sheryl's talk about how he should marry Margaret for her ranch was nothing but that—talk. He'd been wrong. She was dead serious.

That anyone could so blatantly use another for such a mercenary purpose angered him. He should have realized from the beginning that Sheryl was trouble. The evidence was there. Sheryl had bragged about collecting on three frivolous lawsuits, as well as two minor car accidents and a workman's compensation claim. Every single time, she'd walked away with money in her pocket. It was a way of life with her. He'd been unimpressed and somewhat contemptuous, but until now, her proclivity for making easy money hadn't affected him. He refused to get involved.

Friday afternoon he drove to the truck stop, intending to tell her not to call him again. Her attitude toward Margaret Clemens irritated Matt. True, Sheryl was as pretty as a centerfold—and about as two-dimensional. Despite her lovely eyes, Margaret was plain, but unlike Sheryl she was both honest and kind. It surprised him that he felt so protective toward Margaret. One thing he knew for sure: he wasn't going to let Sheryl talk him into using her.

"Sheryl around?" he asked Lee Ann, one of the other waitresses.

"She worked the early shift today," Lee Ann told him. "But I know she'd like to see you."

Matt nodded, and ordered a beer. He wasn't in any hurry.

"Drop in at her house, why don't you?" Lee Ann said as she delivered his Bud Light.

Matt didn't reply. He would've preferred to see Sheryl here, where there were other people, rather than her place—where they'd be alone. She had her own special way of detaining him and he didn't want to fall into that trap. Instead, he went to a local watering hole and drank two more beers. Fortified by alcohol and a strong sense of what was right, he changed his mind and went over to Sheryl's rented house. He drove slowly and carefully, grateful for the lack of traffic—and always keeping an eye out for the sheriff. A drunk driving conviction was something he'd prefer to avoid.

"Where have you been?" Sheryl cried, her face lighting up when she opened her door. Without warning, she hurled herself into his arms, nearly knocking him off balance. "I've been missing you *so* much."

Although she'd been squawking about marriage, Matt was well aware that there were other men in her life. He let her think he was deaf and blind because it suited his own purposes. He was with Sheryl on *his* terms, no matter how much she liked to think she was the one controlling him.

"I haven't seen you in two weeks," she said.

"I've been busy."

"I'm sure you have," Sheryl said and led him into her cozy living room.

He sat down on the sofa and she poured them each a stiff drink, Scotch over ice, bringing the tumblers to the coffee table. He didn't have time to reach for his glass before Sheryl crawled into his lap, straddling his legs.

"So you missed me, too," she murmured, wrapping her arms around his neck and settling her sweet little bottom directly over his crotch.

There was no denying that he had.

"Tell me how it's going with Margaret," she said.

Matt had come to Sheryl's to discuss Margaret, but not for the reason she assumed.

"You'd be a fool to let this opportunity slip through your fingers." She picked up her drink, sipping from it. Her eyes met and held his. "She needs you. Can't you see you'd be helping her?"

It was difficult to ignore his body's natural response to the things Sheryl was doing. His head was clouded with booze and desire, but he couldn't allow her to manipulate him. Bracing his hands against her shoulders, he spoke forcefully. "I'm here to tell you I have no intention of marrying Margaret or anyone else."

"Really?" Her eyebrows arched with the question. "What about me?" She squirmed in his lap, effectively reminding him of all she had to offer...and her willingness to do so. Setting aside her drink, she cupped his face between her hands and directed his mouth to hers.

This was a woman who knew how to bring a man to a full state of arousal—fast. Without the beer and the whiskey, he might have been able to break off the kiss and hold his ground, but his resolve was already weakening.

"I didn't say this was a hard-and-fast decision," he whispered huskily, his eyes closed.

"Good answer." She kissed him again, employing the full range of her talents.

By the time she'd finished kissing him, Matt was putty in her hands.

"I've missed you, cowboy," she said, leading him to the bedroom. "More than you know."

Matt doubted it, but he didn't care, not at that moment. There seemed little excuse to deny himself what he wanted most, and just then it was Sheryl.

The following morning, Matt woke with a hell of a headache. His entire head throbbed. The whiskey bottle, now empty, stood on the bedside table; one of the glasses lay on the floor. The other glass held several cigarette butts, floating in half an inch of melted ice. The sight disgusted him. So did Sheryl, naked beside him. Most of all, he disgusted himself.

Rolling onto his back, he stared up at the ceiling, and silently cursed himself for being so damn weak. He'd never meant for this to happen. He'd never meant to become this involved with Sheryl. But a man had needs—needs Sheryl was always happy to satisfy. What they shared was a mutually pleasurable sexual relationship; that was the extent of it. The more he got to know her, the less he liked her. He worked long, hard hours on his ranch, but every now and then he needed to let loose, indulge himself. Sheryl was always obliging.

"You awake?" Sheryl asked, rolling over and clinging to his side. Her fingers plucked annoyingly at his nipples.

Matt brushed her hand away.

"What are you thinking about?"

He didn't want to talk, and wished now that he'd showered and left before she woke.

"Nothing," he muttered and tried to get up, but she'd wrapped her leg around his and held him tightly in place.

"We need to talk about Margaret."

"She's off-limits," he said in no uncertain terms. His voice was cold, and loud enough to make his head pound even more. He tossed aside the sheet and despite her effort to hold him, Matt scurried out of bed and reached for his jeans.

"You like her, don't you?" Sheryl asked, sitting up and clutching the sheet to her breasts.

"It doesn't matter what I feel for Margaret."

Sheryl was suspiciously silent. "You don't have to marry her, if you don't want to," she said now. "It was just an idea."

"A stupid one."

Sheryl looked repentant. "All right, it was a stupid idea, but I was honestly thinking of her."

"Yeah, I'll bet you were."

"I was," she cried, sounding hurt that he didn't believe

her. "This is a difficult time in Margaret's life. She's alone, and that's scary. She needs someone like you."

"I'm the last person she needs." He fastened his denim shirt, closing the snaps with more force than necessary. When he got to the bottom, he realized he had one snap too many.

"Oh, Matt, don't be in such a hurry to leave me," Sheryl said, smiling softly. Scrambling off the bed, she stood nude before him and unfastened his shirt, then refastened it correctly.

"I have to go."

"When will I see you again?" she pleaded. Pulling on her flimsy housecoat, she followed him to the front door.

"I don't know." That was what he told her, but he'd made his decision. He and Sheryl were finished. He didn't like the way she schemed to bring down another woman. It bothered him that she was so willing to hurt and humiliate Margaret on the patently false pretext of helping her. Sheryl was a user, and he'd been a fool to get involved with her.

The first thing Matt did when he arrived back at his ranch was take a long hot shower. He scrubbed hard to eradicate the scent of Sheryl's heavy perfume. By the time he stepped out of the shower, his skin was red and stung from the scouring.

The phone rang just as he was about to walk out the door. If it was Sheryl he'd tell her not to phone again. Their relationship was over. Finished. No more.

It wasn't Sheryl, though.

"Margaret." He couldn't hide his surprise. Ready to

vent his anger at Sheryl, he was caught off guard by his neighbor's voice.

"I can call back if need be," she said.

"This is as good a time as any," he responded, wondering at the call. They'd been neighbors four years and she'd never phoned him before.

She waited a moment. "You doing anything Thanksgiving?"

The holiday was the following week. Matt wasn't someone who received a lot of invitations. "No."

"Do you want to come to my place for dinner?"

The truth of what Sheryl had said hit home. Without her father, Margaret was alone for the first time in her life. Sure, there were the housekeeper and the ranch hands, but they had their own families. Matt knew what it was to spend holidays alone. It wasn't a good feeling. "You cooking the turkey?" he asked.

"I'd be willing to give it a try, if you're willing to come."

Matt thought about the other ranchers he knew. They all had families to share the holiday with or someplace to go and someone special to see. Matt didn't, and apparently Margaret didn't either.

"I can bring the cranberries," he offered.

"Does this mean you'd come?" Her voice rose with unmistakable pleasure.

People generally didn't get excited about cooking him a meal. "I guess it does."

"I was serious about cooking the turkey, you know."

"I'm serious, too," he told her, grinning. He seemed to be doing a lot of that around Margaret. He'd come to know her a little, and every exposure left him feeling good, a sharp contrast to the way he'd been with Sheryl. "I'll bring a bottle of wine and we can talk."

"Talk?" This seemed to fluster her. "What do you want to talk about?"

"I don't know. Do we have to decide that now?"

She hesitated, as though measuring her words. "We could discuss those kisses...that is, if you want?"

"All right," he returned. It was easy to forget how direct Margaret could be.

"You know what I think?"

"What?"

"That you were just as surprised as me."

"At kissing you?" he asked.

"You liked it, didn't you? That's what threw you for a loop."

He didn't answer her, because he *had* enjoyed their kisses. And because she was absolutely correct: he'd been surprised.

"Am I right, Matt?"

He sighed and wondered if he dared admit it. Past experience had taught him it was better to hide a potentially dangerous fact.

"Why don't we save this discussion for later?" he hedged.

"Okay," she agreed, sounding eager.

The truth was, Matt was sure he'd disappoint Margaret Clemens. He understood why her father had talked to him. Hell, had their positions been reversed—had she been *his* daughter—he would have done the same thing.

* * *

Heath was finally going to tell his grandmother the news she'd been waiting to hear. Thanksgiving seemed the perfect time. During his youth, the two of them were often at odds. It had taken time and distance and more than one clash of wills for him to understand why. They were too much alike. She was a cantankerous old woman, but Heath loved her. He also respected her business acumen and valued her advice—even when it got a little too personal.

He left Rachel and Mark at his house in Grand Forks and drove to the retirement center where Lily Quantrill resided. As far as family went, Lily was all he had.

"I can't understand why you insist on taking me out to eat," she snapped the instant he arrived.

She was confined to a wheelchair now and he knew she hated it, but that was no reason to stay inside when the fresh air might do her some good.

"I thought you'd enjoy getting out for a few hours," Heath told her.

She wheeled toward him and reached for her hat. Posed in front of a mirror, which had been hung deliberately low, she set it on her head and pinned it in place. "Where did you say we were going?"

"I didn't," he reminded her.

Lily paused in her task and glared up at him. "You know I don't like surprises."

"Yes, Grandma."

"Then tell me where we're headed."

Heath sighed. "To eat Thanksgiving dinner."

Her pinched lips told him she wasn't pleased. He ignored her bad mood and laid the heavy winter coat across her lap. No need to put it on until he had her down on the first floor.

"It's a wonder Grandpa ever got to first base with you," he said as he wheeled her toward the elevator.

"Leave your grandfather out of this."

"Yes, Grandma."

"And don't patronize me, young man. I won't put up with it."

Hiding the smile in his voice was impossible. "I wouldn't dream of it."

The elevator arrived and the doors glided smoothly open. Heath maneuvered her chair inside and pushed the button for the lobby.

She twisted around and stared up at him. "Do you seriously think some restaurant is going to fix a turkey the way I remember it?" she barked.

"Thanksgiving is about more than turkey and pumpkin pie."

"Are you lecturing me, Heath Quantrill?"

"I wouldn't dream of it," he said again, his voice light with amusement.

"There was a day you wouldn't dare laugh at me."

"I'm not laughing," he assured her. The doors opened and he stationed her by the entrance while he went to the parking lot to bring the car around. When he returned, an attendant had helped her don her coat and wheeled her outside to meet him.

He didn't realize how thin and frail she was until he lifted her into the passenger seat. Then the attendant folded her wheelchair and loaded it in the trunk.

"I can't imagine why you wanted to take me out to dinner," she muttered for at least the third time.

"Grandma," he told her, "there are women all over town who'd jump at the chance to have dinner with me."

"Well, I'm not one of them."

He glanced over and saw her lips quiver in a half smile.

"Have you been seeing Kate lately?" she demanded.

"No." Earlier in the year, Heath had gone out with a female bank executive a couple of times. The problem was, he'd already fallen in love with Rachel Fischer, but at that point her attitude had been completely and totally unreasonable.

"I've decided I don't like her," Lily informed him.

Heath chuckled. "Few women pass muster with you, do they?"

"Rachel did," she snapped, "but you tried to rush her into bed. It's no wonder the woman won't have anything to do with you." She glowered with disapproval. "What is it with you young people these days? You'd think God gave us Ten Suggestions instead of Ten Commandments."

"Yes, Grandma."

She grumbled something else he couldn't hear. Then, for the first time, she noticed that he wasn't driving in the direction of any restaurants. Instead, they were in a residential neighborhood.

"Where are you taking me?" she demanded again. "And don't give me that story about going to dinner. I want to know exactly where we're headed."

"You'll know soon enough," he promised.

Lily studied the landscape. "This is close to your parents' house, isn't it?"

"It is."

"You're living there, if I remember correctly."

"I am, and you do."

She appeared to relax with that. "How nice. We're having dinner at your home. I always did love that house." She paused. "Haven't been there since I got stuck in this blasted chair."

"I love the house, too." It was the reason he'd moved into it when he returned from Europe. His brother's death had hit him hard and he felt the need to surround himself with what was familiar. The house had been in their family for thirty years. Even now, when it involved a long commute into Buffalo Valley three days a week, he'd chosen to live in the family home.

He pulled into the driveway and paused, watching Lily. She stared at the house and her sharp features softened.

Transferring her from car to wheelchair went smoothly. Earlier he'd rigged a platform to get her up the stairs.

When they reached the porch, the front door opened, and Rachel's son, Mark, stood waiting. The scents of turkey and sage dressing and pumpkin pie were instantly recognizable. Rachel was one fine cook, and dinner promised to be everything he remembered from his childhood.

"Who are you?" Lily demanded of the boy.

Heath admired Mark for not flinching in the face of his grandmother's brusque manner.

"Mark Fischer," Mark returned politely.

"My son," Rachel said, coming to stand behind him, her hands on his shoulders.

Lily turned to look at Heath. "What's going on here?"

she asked, but the question was hopeful, quite unlike her previous demands.

"Please, let me help you get comfortable first," Rachel said, "then Heath and I'll explain."

"All right." All the fire and irritation seemed to be gone.

Ten minutes later, they'd all gathered in the living room. Heath brought out a bottle of champagne and one of sparkling cider, along with four tall flutes. He sat next to Rachel and placed his arm around her shoulders.

Mark sat on Rachel's other side. "Can I tell her?" he asked Heath.

Heath nodded.

"My mom and Heath are going to be married!"

Lily didn't say anything for a moment. "This isn't a joke, is it?"

"No, Grandma," Heath explained, "last week Rachel agreed to become my wife."

Lily nodded, and tears shone in her eyes. "I suspect I don't have time left to hold a great-grandchild, but it'd do my heart good if God allowed me that." She looked away and sniffled, then dug inside her pocket for a fresh tissue.

"Why's she crying?" Mark asked his mother in a loud whisper.

"These aren't tears," Lily said imperiously. "I'm feeling sorry for your mother, that's all. She's going to have her hands full with this grandson of mine."

"I like Heath," Mark told her, leaning forward.

"Now that your mother's agreed to take him on, there's hope for him," Lily said and smiled at the boy through her tears. "This calls for champagne."

"I've already seen to that." Heath held up the bottle.

Lily held Rachel's look, then stretched her hand toward the woman Heath loved.

Rachel grasped Lily's fragile hand with her own.

"I'm so very pleased," she whispered.

"I'm happy, too."

"He loves you, you know."

"I do, and I love him."

"Hey, Grandma, I thought you said you didn't like surprises," Heath said.

"I'm flexible." Her smile was warm and full of love.

Five

Sarah and Dennis's house was brimming with activity
Thanksgiving Day. This was exactly how Sarah had always
dreamed the holidays would be. The turkey, browned to a
golden hue, stuffed and fragrant, sat on the counter, ready
to be placed in the center of the table. While she finished
mashing the potatoes, her mother-in-law, Irene, arranged
serving bowls on the large dining-room table, set with fine
china, a pink linen tablecloth and matching napkins. Small
ceramic pots filled with mauve and gold chrysthanthemums
were situated at intervals, to pleasing effect.

Maddy sat in a corner of the kitchen, nursing Julianne,
an attentive Jeb at his wife's side. Sarah had never seen
her brother happier or more content. Everything she'd ever
hoped for him had come to pass.

The swinging door, which led from one room to the
other, was tossed open every few seconds as Dennis's
mother carried Thanksgiving dishes to the table, an embarrassing array of them. Sarah had been cooking for days,
burying her disappointment at Calla's rejection in the meal
preparation and in setting a table to rival Martha Stewart's.
She'd hoped that if she didn't have time to think, it might
be possible to forget. Unfortunately that tactic didn't work.
Calla's absence left a giant hole in her heart, as impossible
to ignore as it was to fill.

"Everything's on the table," Irene announced as Sarah brought the large bowl of creamy mashed potatoes into the dining room.

Dennis called the family to the table; no one needed further encouragement. Sarah watched as her brother tenderly placed his infant daughter in her carrier, then escorted Maddy into the room. So much had changed in all of their lives this past year.

Once everyone was seated, they joined hands and bowed their heads. Joshua waited a moment, then offered grace. His few simple words were followed by a soft chorus of "Amens."

No one mentioned Calla, although there was a place set for her, in case she changed her mind at the last minute. Sarah wanted everyone to know that her daughter continued to be a part of her life, even though she'd chosen to live with her father.

Soon dishes were being passed around and happy chatter took over. It astonished Sarah that a meal she'd spent days perparing could be consumed in less than an hour. Including dessert.

Once everyone had finished, Joshua looked around the table. His gaze settled on Jeb with Maddy and Julianne, then drifted to Dennis and her. He nodded once, then said, "It seems we have more and more to be grateful for each year."

"That's true," Dennis agreed and reached for Sarah's hand, gently squeezing it.

Jeb held Maddy's hand, as well.

"The only person missing is Calla," Joshua added, glancing toward the empty chair.

As soon as he mentioned her daughter's name, tears sprang to Sarah's eyes, mortifying her. She clutched her napkin and tried to hide the emotion that surged within her. Not only had Calla returned the airline ticket, she'd torn it in half, as if to say that being with her mother was the last thing on earth she wanted to do. She hadn't even bothered to include a letter. Not a single word. The brutal rejection ate at her, tarnishing this lovely time. She'd made mistakes, but she didn't deserve this.

Dennis's fingers tightened around hers. "It's all right, sweetheart," he whispered.

"No, it isn't!" Joshua declared, leaping to his feet. "I don't know what the hell's gotten into that girl, but I intend to find out."

"Dad?" Sarah had rarely heard her father so angry. She watched as he marched across the room toward the telephone. "Get me Willie's phone number," he demanded.

Without questioning him, Sarah did as he asked. Joshua grabbed for the phone and quickly punched in the number.

"What are you going to say?" Sarah asked, standing next to him.

"What someone should have said a long time ago. I'm going to tell her it's high time she came home where she belongs."

"But Dad—"

He held up his hand and blinked, looking uncertain. "Is this the Willie Stern residence?" he asked. He cupped the receiver. "A woman answered. She sounds drunk."

"It isn't Calla, is it?" Horrified, Sarah placed her hand on his elbow.

Her father shook his head. "Willie Stern," he repeated,

then glanced at Sarah. "She went to get him," he explained.

Even this far from the receiver, Sarah could hear the loud, discordant music. Apparently Willie was throwing a party. Sarah hated to think of Calla in that environment. A helpless, sick sensation came over her. Dennis seemed to sense it, because he moved to stand behind her. His hands rested on her shoulders.

Sarah closed her eyes, grateful for her husband's support, for his understanding and love.

"Willie?" Joshua asked, sounding unsure. He turned to Sarah and rolled his eyes. "It's Joshua, Joshua McKenna," he said loudly. "Listen, perhaps it'd be better if you talked to Sarah." With an apologetic expression, he handed her the phone.

Sarah took the receiver but she wasn't happy about it. "Hello, Willie," she said, trying to hide her disgust for her ex-husband.

"Sarah, how are you?" It was difficult to hear him above the music blaring in the background.

"Just great. Where's Calla?"

"Calla? Hold on, and I'll find out." He left and was gone several minutes. Sarah was about to hang up when he came back on the line. "No one knows for sure," he said in a thick, slurred voice.

He was stoned on something, probably a combination of drugs and alcohol. It was enough to make Sarah sick to her stomach.

"Don't you think it's important?" Sarah shouted, despite her best effort to hold onto her temper. With Willie stoned out of his mind, Calla could be missing for days before anyone realized it.

"She has to be around here somewhere."

"Find her," Sarah snapped. "I'm not getting off this line until I talk with my daughter."

"She's *my* daughter, too. You know what your problem is?" Willie asked. "You're uppity. I can't understand how I got involved with an uppity woman."

"I want to talk to Calla," Sarah demanded, barely able to remain civil.

"Fine, you can talk to her. Only I've got to find her first."

"Find her."

"Yes, your majesty," Willie taunted.

The phone made a clanking sound as if it'd been dropped. He was gone for several minutes and then returned. "She's at work," he said. "I forgot."

"Where does she work?"

"BurgerHaven. Not a bad job, either. I asked her if she could get her old man on, but they said I had to have a drug test first." This was followed by uproarious laughter, as if he found the suggestion amusing beyond words.

Sarah closed her eyes until the feeling of revulsion left. "Tell her I phoned."

His laughter died as suddenly as it had begun. "I might," he said.

"Never mind, I'll tell her myself," Sarah said, not wanting to feel beholden to Willie for anything, even the most basic of courtesies.

Everyone was watching her expectantly, especially Dennis's parents. Sarah replaced the receiver. She looked at

Dennis, then her brother and her in-laws. "Apparently...Calla's working today." The words barely made it past her lips before she broke into sobs. Mortified, she retreated into the bedroom, hoping a few minutes alone would help her regain her composure. Normally she was better able to control her emotions.

"Sarah?" Dennis came into the room and closed the door.

"I'm so sorry," she whispered. "It's such a wonderful day and here I am crying...I'm so sorry."

Her husband sat down on the edge of the bed beside her. "You don't have anything to apologize for. Not one damn thing."

"But I embarrassed you in front of your parents—"

"Don't even think that." He placed his arms around her, and Sarah turned into his embrace, breathing in the warm scent of him, loving him until she felt as if her heart would burst. "I don't deserve you," she whispered.

He wove his fingers into her hair and tilted her face toward him. "No, it's the other way around..."

She shook her head. "I don't know what I did for Calla to hate me so."

"You married me. I'm the one she hates."

Sarah wrapped her arms around him, and they clung to one another. Then, sobbing, she pulled away and wiped the tears from her cheeks. "I didn't mean to tell you like this...but, Dennis, I think...I'm fairly sure I'm pregnant."

He stared at her, his face uncomprehending. "You're pregnant?"

She nodded, smiling through her tears.

"When did you find out?"

"Just yesterday... I talked to Hassie and she recommended one of those home pregnancy tests and...and the stick turned blue."

Dennis let out a shout of joy so loud it echoed in the room. Racing to the bedroom door, he hurled it open and stuck out his head. "Mom, Dad, we're pregnant!"

Racing back to her side, he took hold of both her hands. "Oh, Sarah, you don't know how happy this makes me."

She knew Dennis wanted children when she married him. Her doubts were multiple, especially since she didn't seem to be a very successful mother; Calla's attitude proved as much.

"You're pregnant?" Irene asked when Dennis and Sarah reappeared. She held her hands to her mouth, tears trickling down her face.

Sarah nodded.

Irene hugged them both. "This is just *wonderful* news! Just wonderful."

"It is," Maddy agreed, embracing Sarah. "I'm so pleased Julianne will have a cousin close to her own age."

"Congratulations, sis," Jeb said, hugging her, then slapping Dennis on the back. The two men clasped hands.

"Another grandchild," Joshua said, tucking his thumbs inside his suspenders. "Now, this is welcome news. Very welcome." He took a turn and hugged Sarah, too. "I don't suppose anyone would object if I helped myself to a second piece of pumpkin pie."

"I'll join you," Jeb announced.

"Don't mind if I do myself," Norm Urlacher said, trailing Jeb and Joshua into the kitchen.

"I should probably supervise," Dennis said, following

the others. "I want whipped cream on mine," he called, halfway through the door.

"We just ate," Sarah complained to Maddy and her mother-in-law. How anyone could get up from a table laden with a meal fit for royalty and be hungry less than half an hour later was beyond her.

"While they're in there," Irene said, "let's suggest they do the dishes."

"Good idea!"

Soon the three of them were laughing, their excitement about the pregnancy dulling the pain of Calla's rejection.

Margaret Clemens's housekeeper wasn't at all pleased that Margaret had taken it upon herself to invite Matt Eilers to Thanksgiving dinner.

Sadie muttered disparaging comments under her breath all morning as she worked in the kitchen, cooking the turkey, peeling potatoes, slicing green beans and making pumpkin pies.

"You can go now, Sadie," Margaret told her when she'd finished preparing the last of the vegetable dishes and had set a pie on the counter to cool.

"And leave you alone with that scoundrel?" she bellowed, fists digging into her wide hips. "I think *not.*"

"Sadie." Margaret could be just as stubborn. "Matt is a gentleman. Now, go home. Your family's waiting."

Still the housekeeper hesitated.

"Go," Margaret insisted, shooing the older woman out of the kitchen. Sadie had been with the family for as long as Margaret could remember and was as close to a mother as Margaret had. She'd been a blessing, for sure, but distrusted strangers and single men. It didn't help that Matt fell into both categories. He might have lived and ranched in the area for nearly five years, but as far as Sadie was concerned, he wasn't one of them and shouldn't be trusted.

With obvious reluctance the housekeeper removed her apron. "If you need help, you phone."

"I will," Margaret assured her, and edged her toward the door. As soon as Sadie was gone, Margaret sighed with relief, thankful she'd finally managed to get Sadie out of the house. This dinner was important, and the last thing Margaret wanted was a chaperone, especially since she was hoping Matt would see fit to kiss her again.

Her guest arrived promptly at four, the time they'd agreed upon. He brought a bouquet of flowers, along with a can of cranberries and a bottle of wine.

"Thank you, Matt," she murmured, smelling the yellow and bronze mums. Feeling self-conscious, she led him into the kitchen, where she placed the bouquet in a vase. Might as well tell him now and be done with it. "I have a confession to make."

"Already?" he asked, frowning. "I just got here."

"I fell short on my part of the bargain." It probably would have been better if she'd waited until later to own up. "I'm not a very good cook. I'd hoped—actually, I'd planned—to whip up the entire meal on my own, but Sadie convinced me to start with something less demanding before tackling a five-course holiday dinner. So..."

"So in other words Sadie made the turkey?"

Margaret nodded. Well, the turkey and everything else. It hardly seemed surprising that she was pretty much of a lost cause when it came to finding her way around a kitchen. After all, she'd never spent any time learning those skills—she was a rancher, not a cook. The important thing was that, dinner aside, he'd chosen to spend the day with *her*.

Matt glanced at the table already set. "I'm glad not to be alone today. That's what really matters—not the turkey."

His words seemed to echo her thoughts, which flustered her so much, she said the next thing that popped into her mind. "Would you like a beer before we eat?"

"Sure."

Hands and heart trembling, she removed two cans from the refrigerator, emptied them into tall tumblers, then took him to the library. It was her father's favorite room, and hers, too. They sat in the high-back leather chairs, on opposite sides of the brick fireplace. She'd laid a small fire earlier and lit it just before he arrived. It provided a comforting warmth...and a sensation of intimacy.

At first the silence between them was awkward. Then Matt asked her a question about a new worming product for cattle, and before she knew it, they'd talked nearly an hour. Matt seemed as delighted as she by how easily their conversation had gone.

"I don't generally talk cattle with women," he told her, drinking the last of his beer.

Margaret wasn't sure what he was telling her. He seemed to be implying that he didn't think of her as a woman, which she found downright depressing. Especially since she'd taken pains to put on a dress. A dress, panty hose, the whole nine yards. It was the same outfit she'd worn for her father's funeral, although he wouldn't know that, seeing he hadn't attended the services.

"I'd better check on dinner," she said, bolting out of her chair.

"Margaret." He stopped her as soon as she stood. "Did I say something wrong?"

She shook her head, then decided he probably wanted the truth. "If you don't talk cattle with other women, then what *do* you talk about?" She sat on the ottoman facing him, staring at him intently.

Her question appeared to pull him up short, and he avoided eye contact before responding. "We talk about this and that. Nothing important."

"Oh."

"I enjoyed our conversation if that's what concerns you."

The tension eased out of her shoulders. This was as good as a compliment. She blushed and looked away. "I enjoyed it, too." At ease once more, she said, "I'll check on dinner and get us another beer." She reached for the empty tumblers.

"Good idea," Matt called after her.

She wasn't gone long and when she returned they chatted again, this time on a variety of subjects—Buffalo Valley's past and present, the feasibility of raising bison, like Jeb McKenna did, politics, religion and western movies. The beer loosened her inhibitions, and soon they were sharing a few jokes. It felt good to laugh, and to know he considered her a friend. The only other person she felt as comfortable around was Maddy McKenna. But this was different. Better.

"Are you planning to kiss me again?" The beer had given her courage to ask what had been on her mind for weeks.

"Do you want me to?"

"Oh, yes." She nodded eagerly. "In the worst way."

He cast his gaze down at his beer. "I don't know if that's such a good idea."

As far as she was concerned, it was a helluva great idea. "Okay, okay, maybe we should eat first, then check out how we feel afterward."

It didn't help her ego any to see the blatant relief on his face. His attitude was playing havoc with her theory that he'd enjoyed their kisses.

Dinner was superb. Sadie might not have approved of Margaret's inviting Matt for Thanksgiving dinner, but that hadn't stopped her from preparing one of the finest meals in recent memory.

"More wine?" Margaret asked.

"I'll pour," Matt said, reaching for the bottle of chilled chardonnay before she could.

After two beers and two glasses of wine, Margaret's reserve slipped even further. Propping her elbows on the table, she leaned toward Matt. "I want to talk about us kissing again, all right?"

"Margaret…"

"Please. You have to understand that something like this doesn't happen to me every day. I have questions."

He shifted, clearly uncomfortable.

"What did you think?" she blurted.

"Think?"

"You know. How was it?"

He held his wineglass by the stem and seemed to carefully consider his response. "It was…nice."

She couldn't hold back a smile. "It was fabulous for
me, too," she said, trying to sound mature, striving for
sophistication. At the moment she was too pleased to care
whether she succeeded or not. Hot damn, but he was a
looker.

A silence followed, and she guessed he didn't know
what to say next. From her father, Margaret had learned to
respect silence. It didn't always need to be filled, particularly not with chitchat or superficial comments. She let
several minutes pass, watching him, enjoying his nearness.

"Do you know the first time I saw you?" she finally
asked.

Matt shook his head.

"It wasn't too long after you moved here. I was round-
ing up strays and I came upon you and one of our men.
You were knee-deep in mud, freeing one of our calves and
you were arguing with this hand Dad had recently hired."

His face went tight. "I remember."

"Neither of you realized I was watching. As I recall, he
accused you of attempting to steal that calf."

"We threw a couple of punches," Matt said, frowning.
"You were watching?"

"I was." She picked up her wineglass. "You two really
got into it."

"We had a history."

She'd suspected as much, and would have wagered
money that the history they shared was a woman.

"You beat him in a fair fight."

He nodded, but didn't look especially pleased with himself. He should've been, she thought, seeing that he'd come out on the winning side. The other man had hit the dirt after two solid punches. As if the confrontation was irrelevant, Matt had returned to the calf and finished freeing him. His actions told her more about Matt Eilers than all the gossip she'd heard before and since.

"That hand wasn't much of a cattleman," Margaret muttered. "Dad fired him soon after."

"Last I heard, he was working for a fuel distributor in Texas. I think he always liked trucks better than cattle. Not everyone's cut out for ranch life."

That was true enough, and perhaps Margaret should have left it there. She probably would have if not for the drinks she'd had. "I fell in love with you that day," she confessed, "and more so every time I saw you. You might think it's 'cause you're handsome as sin, and that's got something to do with it, but there's more. You're a good person, Matt Eilers. You don't like people to know that— I haven't figured out why. Deep down you're honorable. You don't cheat and I've never heard you say a bad word about anyone—not even when they deserve it."

If Matt had seemed uncomfortable earlier, it didn't compare to the way he responded now. He half rose from his chair, his eyes filled with dread.

"Women aren't supposed to tell a man that, are they?" Margaret said quickly.

"Ah..."

"It's all right," she assured him, regretting that she'd embarrassed him, but not that he knew the truth about how she felt.

"You don't know me," he said. "You don't know what I'm really like, what I've done...."

"I know enough." Matt was no saint, especially when it came to women; she'd seen clear evidence of that. But, as she'd said, he had a good heart. She'd never told anyone what she'd seen that day. Not only had he freed the calf and returned it to its mother, but he'd given the man he'd beaten a hand up, too.

Matt stood and took his wineglass with him.

"I was thinking," she began, then fortified her courage with another sip of wine, "that I'd like to marry you, Matt Eilers."

Matt downed the rest of his wine in one giant gulp. He looked stricken, confused and utterly baffled. Margaret had never intended to propose marriage, but it'd happened and now that it had, she wasn't sorry. If anything, she felt released from a burden.

"I think it's time I left," Matt announced.

"All right," she whispered, and followed him to the kitchen door. Already he had his hat in his hand.

"Dinner was very nice."

Certain she'd embarrassed them both enough, she didn't say or do anything to delay his departure. It'd been a risk; she'd taken her best shot. In all likelihood, she wouldn't see or talk to him again for a long time. That part saddened her.

"Goodbye, Matt."

Without saying anything, he opened the door. The wind moaned and whistled and in its high-pitched rush, she heard it call her a fool. Matt bowed his head against the force of it and hurried toward his truck, parked on the far side of the yard.

Margaret stood at the window and watched as his headlights dimly illuminated the driveway.

Discouraged, she walked back into the dining room and cleared the table. Like her daddy, she was a risk taker, but usually a cautious one. Bernard had always been philosophical about the chances he took. She'd come by his believe-in-miracles-but-don't-bet-on-them attitude naturally. Only this was one miracle she'd really wanted.

An hour later, after she'd cleaned the kitchen and soaked out her disappointment in a hot bath, she heard someone pounding on the kitchen door.

When she went to investigate, she saw it was Matt Eilers. Dressed in her thick flannel robe, she unbolted the lock and hurriedly let him in. His face was red with cold, his jaw tight.

''All right,'' he said abruptly.

Not understanding, she stared at him.

He grasped her by the shoulders and brought her close. His kiss was as wild as his eyes and revealed none of the finesse she'd experienced in their earlier kisses.

''You want me for your husband?'' he demanded roughly. ''Fine, I'll marry you, but you don't have a clue what you're getting yourself into. Not a clue.''

''Don't be so sure,'' she told him, her pulse going crazy. His dark eyes burned into hers. Reaching for his collar with both hands, she jerked his mouth back to hers and kissed him with the same urgency.

She'd waited her entire life for this man and wasn't

about to be shortchanged now. If anyone was in for a surprise, Margaret reasoned, it was going to be Matt Eilers.

Merrily had never thought of herself as an especially perceptive woman, but when it involved Axel she was almost psychic. The Monday following Thanksgiving, she found Pastor Dawson and Bob deep in conversation. They sat at a table on the far side of the restaurant, hunched together, talking quietly.

He knew.

This churchman had figured out that she'd stolen Axel. He knew she and Bob were hiding the boy from his birth parents and from the authorities. What he didn't know was all the whys and wherefores. She doubted the circumstances made any difference to nosy do-gooders like Pastor Dawson. If he'd guessed the truth, he was sure to consider it his God-given duty to call the state police and have her arrested.

That meant she and Bob had no choice. None. They had to protect their son and Merrily was prepared to do so at any price.

Thankfully, Axel was down for his nap when Pastor Dawson finally left. Merrily could barely wait for the other man to walk out the door before she confronted Bob. Her husband still sat at the table, his hands in his hair, staring blankly at the wall.

''He knows?'' She whispered the question.

Bob nodded.

''How?''

''Does it matter?''

Weak and shaky, Merrily pulled out a chair and literally

fell into it. Having Axel taken away was her greatest fear. He was her son. He might not have been born from her body, but he was as much a part of her as if he had.

Bob rubbed his hands down his face, glanced at her and then looked away. Something was wrong, she could see it in his eyes.

"What?" she pleaded.

Her husband shook his head.

"Tell me!" she demanded.

Bob continued to stare at the wall. "Pastor Dawson didn't know for sure.... He asked a few questions...."

"Yes?" she prodded.

"I told him about Axel."

It took a moment for the implication of what he'd said to sink in. "You told him!" The anger inside her was explosive. "Why would you do such a thing?" Bob knew how dangerous that was. He'd purposely put their son at risk. She wanted to lash out at him, slug him, cause him the same kind of pain he'd caused her.

"He'd already guessed."

"You couldn't keep your mouth shut?"

Bob's eyes were empty, his complexion ashen, as if he were about to be violently ill. "He knew, Merrily, he already knew. He just didn't have proof. He asked if there was anything he could do to help. He saw the flyer, recognized Axel's name. He didn't threaten to turn us in...."

She started to tremble, and struggled to control the panic that threatened to overwhelm her. "What kind of questions did he ask?"

"Questions that told me he's figured out what we've

done. He knew you weren't Axel's biological mother…that I wasn't his father.''

''But how?''

''Because of the flyer. And probably because we've made such an effort to keep Axel out of sight lately.''

''That's crazy!'' None of this added up to Merrily. Besides Axel had suffered with chicken pox. It was only natural that they not expose anyone else to the illness.

''He asked about Axel's family and when I didn't answer—''

''You could have explained that we didn't know each other—that you weren't in my life at the time.''

''But you were, and he knew that, too.''

This minister had become a threat to everything Merrily held dear. ''You should have lied!'' she shouted.

''Aren't we living a big enough lie already?'' Bob shouted back. ''I told him the truth because it's the only way we're ever going to be able to live a normal life. Look at us! Axel isn't even three and we're already afraid of what'll happen if anyone recognizes him. Afraid he might be taken away from us. Afraid someone might turn us in. Constantly looking over our shoulders. That's no kind of life, Merrily. Not for Axel and not for you and me.''

''You don't mean that.''

''I do mean it.'' All at once he was on his feet and pacing. His boots made hard, heavy sounds against the floor.

''We're his parents!'' she cried.

''Yes, but burying our heads in the sand is wrong. Wrong for us and wrong for Axel. I love him as much as you do,'' Bob said. ''I'd never purposely do anything to hurt him, but our fear is going to smother him. I can see it happening.''

Merrily wasn't sure what to believe anymore. "How can you say you love Axel after what you did?'' came her high-pitched cry. She looked at Bob, seeing him with fresh eyes. She'd trusted him with everything, her heart, her son, her very life. He'd betrayed that trust. The immensity of it burned like hot coals inside her.

"I did it because I love Axel and I love you.''

Using both hands, she brushed the hair out of her face. Then, taking in a deep breath, she forced the panic from her heart. "Okay, Pastor Dawson knows. Exactly what's he going to do about it?''

Bob continued pacing, but his steps grew slower.

"Bob?'' she asked, when it was clear he hadn't heard her. "He's not going to keep our secret, is he?'' That would be too much to hope for.

"He didn't say he was going to do anything. He offered to help.''

"By turning us in to the authorities, no doubt.'' It was what she expected, what she knew to expect.

"He said if we wanted, he'd be willing to contact the authorities on our behalf.''

"Dear God.'' It felt as though the world had been jerked upside down.

"He wants us to take a week and think it over.''

"A week?'' That meant they had a full seven days to run. In that length of time, they could disappear somewhere in Canada. Bob was good at saving money, better than she was. They could take the cash from their bank account and run.

"Pastor Dawson assured me he wouldn't say anything to anyone," Bob explained.

"Thank God," Merrily whispered. "That gives us time." Already her mind was racing with where they could go and the story they could make up. They'd need a lie that was convincing; they'd have to create a believable background. It would mean a name change, too, for all three of them.

Bob's eyes met hers. She saw his pain, right along with the unasked questions. "What do you mean?"

"We have seven days, don't you see? That's long enough to find a place to hide out, to—"

"Merrily, we can't do that. What kind of life would that be? For any of us? Our lives are here in Buffalo Valley."

"The hell we can't run. Are you nuts? That's exactly what we're going to do! It's our only option." Thanks to him. Thanks to what he'd done.

"Merrily—"

"Do you seriously believe I'm going to wait around for the cops? The social workers? You know me better than that. There's no way in hell I'm going to hand over our son to some stranger. Axel *needs* me. He needs us both."

Bob paled even more. "We're going to fight for him, Merrily, with everything we have. He's our son, and we're going to make a stand right here, surrounded by our friends."

For the first time, the pain gripping her heart lessened, but she still resisted. "It's our only chance. We can make a new life in Canada—or anywhere you want. Running's our only chance."

"Don't you understand that it's only a matter of time before we're found? It's inevitable."

"We can hide—"

"Until the next time. Until someone else figures out that Axel isn't ours."

She slapped at his hand as he reached out to console her. "You broke a trust! You betrayed Axel and me."

"Are you saying I don't love you?" Pain flashed from his eyes. "After everything I've done, after the months we've lived together as husband and wife? Nothing means more to me than you and Axel."

Merrily was sobbing openly now. "My baby, my baby," she whimpered.

Bob embraced her and she buried her face in his shirt.

"I don't want to lose my baby," she wailed.

"I don't, either."

"They'll take him."

"Over my dead body. I'm not going to let it happen," Bob returned adamantly.

Heaving in a shaky breath, she raised her eyes to meet her husband's. In him she saw resolve and determination. He wasn't just going to fight to keep Axel; he was determined to win.

Six

When Margaret went after something, she did so in what could only be called a headlong manner, Matt reflected as he arrived at the Circle C the day of their wedding. She sure didn't let any moss grow under her feet. No sooner had he accepted her proposal than she had them driving into Grand Forks to apply for the marriage license. Shifting schedules, the earliest possible day for the wedding was December seventh. He tried to forget that this was the same day the worst military defeat in U.S. history had occurred.

It didn't help that on the morning of their wedding day, the weather dipped to record cold temperatures. The Grand Forks newscaster stated that it could be the coldest day of the year. One of her uncles, who lived in South Dakota, had planned to attend the ceremony, but he'd phoned that morning to cancel because of the weather. Her other two uncles sent their love and best wishes; since they'd recently made the long trip for Bernard's funeral, they weren't able to come for another visit so soon.

Margaret, never shy, met him at the door, and quickly ushered him out of the piercing wind and into the warm house.

"You haven't changed your mind, have you?" she asked, looking worried. The wind wasn't nearly as penetrating as her eyes. She seemed to gaze straight through him.

"I'm here, aren't I?" The truth was, he *had* changed his mind. Four or five times in the past few hours, in fact, but each time he'd managed to set aside his guilt and his doubts. He was marrying her for all the wrong reasons— and all the right ones. No woman had believed in him the way Margaret did. None had looked past the polished exterior and seen his heart. And dammit, there were all those beautiful cattle. And the land. It wasn't like he could ignore what she had to offer.

Now that he was at the Circle C, he had every intention of going through with the ceremony. If he was making a mistake, then he was doing it with open eyes.

Sadie's disapproval was all too evident and implied that Margaret was the one making the mistake. She didn't even try to hide her distaste for him. He felt her censure the instant he walked into the room. But no matter what the housekeeper thought, it wasn't anything Matt hadn't been saying to himself since the moment he'd agreed to this.

Margaret ignored Sadie, but Matt suspected the two women had done verbal battle over the impending marriage. Clearly Margaret had won the war, but he figured there'd been more than one battle from which she'd walked away wounded. She wanted him and she'd been willing to fight for him; that said a great deal.

"Pastor Dawson is already here," Margaret announced, leading Matt by the hand into the library. "Jeb and Maddy are on their way. Gage and Lindsay are coming, too."

"Hassie?" he asked, and swallowed tightly.

Margaret nodded. "And Leta Betts. Joyce Dawson's here with her husband, as well."

Matt wore his best clothes, a ten-year-old suit, and made

small talk with Pastor Dawson while he waited for their guests. He was tense and tried to hide his nervousness, talking far more than usual. Everyone arrived within the next fifteen minutes. Soon they all gathered in the very room where Bernard Clemens had warned Matt against hurting his daughter. Now he was marrying Margaret and God help him, he sincerely liked her, but he didn't love her. Not the way she deserved to be loved.

Glancing around uneasily, Matt was certain everyone knew why he was doing this. He felt sure that Margaret's friends believed the worst of him, that the words *money, cattle, land* echoed in their brains. It was almost as if they all knew about Sheryl and her scheming ideas, although he swore he wanted no part of that.

Margaret loved him. Bernard Clemens had said as much and Margaret had told him so herself. In time, he hoped to love her with the same intensity. In fact, he was counting on that. He didn't yet, but he would. Dear God, he prayed that would happen.

"Is everyone ready?" John Dawson asked. He stood before them, his open Bible in his hands.

Margaret looked at Matt with such adoration, it was all he could do not to turn and bolt from the room. It amazed him that she couldn't see the truth. He half expected someone to step forward and stop the wedding, claiming he wasn't a fit husband. But he *hoped* to be, wanted to be.

Margaret's friends and neighbors were as somber as if they were attending a funeral. No one seemed happy except Margaret, who, oblivious to the tension in the room, beamed with joy.

His bride wore a long white dress and held a small bouquet of pale rosebuds. White...she wore white. He closed his eyes, barely able to concentrate on Pastor Dawson's words.

Margaret was a virgin. In all his life, Matt had never slept with a virgin. His women were as experienced as he was. He understood there was pain involved when a woman made love for the first time, and the one thing he didn't want to do was hurt Margaret. Marrying her might appear heartless, but he did care for her. She was giving him so much—her life, her trust—and little as he had, he would willingly offer that up to her.

"We are gathered here this afternoon to share in the..."

Matt blocked out the minister's words, his thoughts whirling. This was wrong. He knew it even as he repeated his vows, his voice flat and barely audible. Not wrong for him, but for her. Margaret's loving him was the best luck of his life, but marrying her, pledging himself to her, proved that everything she'd said about him was a lie. A man who was honorable and decent wouldn't do this.

Matt tried to concentrate on the words, but his mind soon drifted. He remembered how love had changed Jeb McKenna and Gage Sinclair. Jeb had been a surly, bitter man until Maddy came into his life. He recalled how Gage and Lindsay Snyder had been continually at odds. Every time Matt talked to him, Gage had predicted that Lindsay would abandon the town after the first snowfall. Yet, months later, when she really was about to go, he'd driven his tractor across a freshly planted field in an effort to stop her. Yes, love had changed both men. The only thing Matt expected Margaret to change in *his* life was the state of his bank account.

Margaret's eyes shone as she held Matt's hand and re-peated her vows, her voice loud, clear, distinct.

After they'd exchanged plain gold bands, Pastor Dawson proclaimed them married. His emotions in turmoil, Matt brought his bride into his arms and kissed her lightly, al-most as if they were brother and sister. He saw the dis-appointment in her eyes and feared this was only the first of many.

It didn't surprise him that none of their guests seemed eager to stay. The ceremony was followed by cake and champagne, and a couple of halfhearted toasts. The weather was a perfect excuse to rush home. They were all polite, cordial, but Matt realized he hadn't fooled anyone, with the exception of Margaret.

A half hour following the ceremony, they were alone.

"Hello, husband," Margaret said, happiness radiating from her. She threw her arms around his neck and gazed lovingly up at him.

"Wife," Matt said. Deception was never his strong suit. He kissed her and felt the muscles of his stomach tighten with dread.

"I don't know about you, but I'm starving. All I've had today is wedding cake."

It was all he'd eaten, too. He couldn't force anything into his stomach earlier, and had skipped both breakfast and lunch.

As they headed into the kitchen, Matt saw that his wife had thought of everything. She had dinner ready to serve, along with wine and music. Nor did Matt need to worry about carrying a conversation. Margaret talked animatedly throughout the meal, bouncing from one subject to the next, asking one question after another; he had merely to reply. They chatted about the ranch, about how he'd give the Stockerts notice and move his things into the house, about combining their herds.

The wine helped relax him, but the tension returned as soon as Margaret mentioned bed. Matt had never experienced problems performing sexually, but with Margaret, his doubts were rampant. His biggest fear was that she'd guess his true feelings and hate him. He had other fears, too. The fact that she was a virgin intimidated him. Any pain he caused her would undoubtedly be followed by plenty of angst—and regret. The mere thought of what might happen was enough to drive away any hint of desire.

"Matt," Margaret whispered, studying him.

He finished the last of his wine and looked up at her.

"I might not be beautiful—"

"It's not that," he said, wanting her to know she wasn't the problem. "You're an attractive woman. Your eyes are lovely. Your hair..." He let his words drift into silence. His hesitation was due to his own failings, which, at the moment, seemed too many to count.

He toyed with the idea of suggesting they put off the wedding night, but couldn't come up with a plausible reason. If she didn't love him so much, Matt thought he could have found a viable excuse, could have invented one. It was out of the question, though, and he firmed his resolve. He would make love to his wife. He was destined to be a disappointment to her in the future, but he was going to give her a wedding night she wouldn't soon forget.

She steered him into the bedroom, then reached over and turned out the light. Matt drew her into his arms and kissed her fully, expecting—he wasn't sure what, but certainly not this strong surge of passion. Her mouth was soft and moist and pliant, her eager response innocent and sweet. What had intimidated him earlier excited him now.

"Margaret," he groaned, shocked at the quick passion she'd created within him. His fingers worked at unfastening the many buttons of her dress. That was a difficult enough task with only the light from a bedside lamp, but nervous as he was, Matt faltered, all thumbs.

"Here," she breathed and whirled around, flipping her hair out of the way. "I told Maddy this dress would be impossible."

Matt chuckled and patiently unbuttoned the dress. Driven by desire, he slipped his hands inside the bodice and cupped her breasts. He was pleasantly surprised to find her lush and full. A sigh escaped him, echoed by a soft groan from her.

"Margaret...Margaret."

"Oh, Matt, this feels so good," she whispered. "I didn't know it would be like this."

He closed his eyes, astonished by the intensity of what he was experiencing.

"You make me feel so beautiful." She turned to face him, the dim light revealing the shape of her features, the perfection of her skin, the brilliance of her eyes.

"You are," he whispered, and she was. It stunned him that he'd ever viewed her as plain, because it simply wasn't so. Her eyes glowing with love, she brought her palms to his cheeks. Rather than trying to understand the curious mix of emotions that swirled inside him, Matt kissed her.

Soon they were devoid of clothes. He pressed her down onto the bed, his engorged penis throbbing.

"I don't want to hurt you," he whispered, his voice husky with need.

"That would be impossible."

"But Margaret..."

"Love me, Matt, just love me."

He brought her satisfaction with his hands and his mouth, reveling in her shudders and cries. Then he poised himself above her, his arms and legs trembling at the knowledge of what he was about to do. Apparently unwilling to wait any longer, Margaret slid her arms around his neck. He murmured, "Not yet," and reached for a condom in his wallet, which he'd tossed onto the bedside table.

As he slipped on the condom, she lifted her head just high enough for their mouths to meet. Urging him with soft sighs, she opened her body to him, giving herself completely. Afraid of causing her pain, Matt kept his movements slow and shallow. Feeling her body suddenly tense, he froze, uncertain how to proceed. It was Margaret who urged him forward, and afterward, it was his sweet, generous wife who comforted him.

Her innocence had been something Matt dreaded, but now he felt honored and more than that, deeply moved.

Usually when he slept with a woman, she clung to him, reluctant to let him go, but with Margaret, he was the one who needed to hold her close. He was determined to be a good husband. He might not have married her for love, but he planned to do his utmost to make their marriage beneficial to them both.

From years of habit, Matt woke at dawn, with Margaret's warm body tucked against his. His arm was around her waist and he grinned, delighted that beneath the ill-fitting jeans and bulky shirts lay the delectable body of a woman. He'd had a hint of it once, during that first visit to her house, but the reality was so much more impressive.

"Morning," she said with a yawn and rolled onto her back. "Morning, husband."

"Good morning, wife," he said and kissed her cheek. "How about I rustle us up some coffee?"

"That sounds wonderful," she said, raising herself to a sitting position. "But before you do, I thought we should talk."

"Talk? Before coffee?" He frowned. Experience had taught him that when a woman sought conversation, she was generally unhappy about *something*. They hadn't been married twenty-four hours. Had he failed her already? "This can't wait?"

She took a minute to mull over his question, then shook her head.

He sat upright and tensed. "Okay, shoot."

"I love you, Matt. I've loved you for nearly five years, and I'm fully aware that you don't love me."

He'd reached for his pants, but let them drop as he sat on the edge of the bed. She knew, and had married him anyway. "Then why'd you go through with it?" he demanded, not sure if he should be relieved or depressed.

"Isn't that the question I should be asking *you?*"

He shook his head. The answer was obvious.

"I already know you married me for the ranch," she told him. "I'm not so beautiful, but those cattle of mine certainly are. I'm not naive enough to think you've fallen head over heels for me in such a short time.''

He said nothing, silenced by her honesty.

''It's always been important to me to make everything as clear and above-board as possible,'' she stated simply, as though reading his mind.

He nodded.

''I had to say these things because I don't want you feeling guilty. I knew how you felt when I asked you to be my husband. It was a risk I was willing to take. Naturally, I hope you'll have a change of heart and that eventually you'll love me as much as I love you.''

Matt stared at his wife, hardly able to believe that he'd been fortunate enough to marry a woman as forthright and plainspoken as Margaret.

''Do you think you *can* learn to love me?'' she asked quietly.

Margaret was almost completely unfamiliar with feminine wiles and manipulative behavior. She was innocent and trusting. Over the years he'd had more than his share of beautiful women and he'd learned that beauty usually faded. Prolonged exposure to a woman he'd once found gorgeous inevitably resulted in disappointment. Look at Sheryl, for instance—as vain and selfish as she was beautiful. Margaret was the first woman he'd ever known who possessed such genuineness.

''I believe I'm halfway in love with you already,'' he said. Then, because it seemed the most natural and perfect thing to do, he made love to his wife.

Sarah sensed almost immediately that there would be problems with the pregnancy. At three weeks she started spotting and, terrified she was about to miscarry, she called Dennis at work.

Her husband, ashen with fear, raced her into the doctor's office in Grand Forks, cursing the lack of a medical facility in Buffalo Valley. After a careful examination, Dr. Leggatt, who'd been the attending physician for both Lindsay Sinclair and Maddy, had ordered complete and total bed rest until at least February, and maybe longer. If Sarah hoped to deliver a healthy infant, there was no alternative.

Never in all her life had Sarah spent this much time in bed.

"Do you need anything before I head out to work?" Dennis asked this particular morning. It was Wednesday in the third week of December.

She managed a smile and casually waved him on his way. So far, she'd been able to occupy herself with designing new quilt patterns. Buffalo Valley Quilting Company had developed to the point that she felt safe venturing beyond the natural-dyed muslin designs she'd started with. These days, she experimented with bright, bold colors and complex patterns.

With Christmas approaching, the company was busier than ever. Jennifer Logan, who'd worked the longest for Sarah, made trips to and from the house twice a day. It helped Sarah stay involved with what was happening. Jennifer, whom Sarah had recently promoted to manager, had a good head for business. Together they talked over every aspect of the daily schedule. If Jennifer was going to be late or needed an immediate answer, she phoned.

The telephone was set up next to the bed for just that

reason. When it rang, Sarah knew it was either Jennifer or Dennis.

"Hello," she said, hoping to sound cheerful and in good spirits, although she'd grown weary of forced bed rest. She followed her physician's orders because she very badly wanted this child. Nothing in her life had ever come easy and she'd learned that what she treasured most often brought her the greatest pain.

"Mom."

Sarah's heart froze at the sound of her daughter's voice. "Calla?"

"What are you doing home? I called the store and Jennifer told me you weren't at work. Are you sick?"

Now, their first conversation in months, wasn't the time to tell her about the pregnancy. Instead, she avoided the question. "Oh, Calla, it's so good to hear from you! How are you?"

"All right." Her voice was flat, dull, and Sarah could only imagine what had been left unsaid.

"Me, too." She'd say anything just to keep the conversation going. "Where are you?"

"Home."

Sarah had to bite her tongue to keep from insisting that Calla's home was and always would be with her. She didn't bother to ask why her daughter wasn't at school this time of day.

"I bought a phone card. Dad doesn't have long distance service."

Probably because he couldn't be trusted to pay the bill, but Sarah didn't say what was already obvious.

"Juliet said you called on Thanksgiving."

Juliet must have been the woman who'd answered the phone at Willie's place. "Your grandfather did—we were hoping to talk to you."

"I was working." Calla sounded none too pleased about that. "Juliet's moved in with Dad, but I doubt it'll last," she added, almost in afterthought. "It never does."

"What about Christmas?" Sarah asked, plunging ahead, hoping Calla would consider joining them, if only for a few days. "Will you be working then, too?"

"I...I was sort of thinking about coming back to Buffalo Valley around then."

Sarah's relief was so great, it was all she could do not to break into sobs. She didn't dare reveal too much emotion. Not to Calla. She cleared her throat. "That would be fabulous. We'd love it if you could."

"Just for a visit, Mom, so don't go hyper on me."

"I won't," Sarah promised, although she wasn't entirely sure what she was agreeing to.

"How's Jessica?" Calla asked about her best friend next.

"Jessica? Good, great," Sarah reported. She closed her eyes, trying to remember the last time she'd talked with the girl. It must be months now. She'd been so busy with the business; she rarely had any opportunity to see the people who'd once been close to her daughter. Jessica and the others hadn't asked about Calla, either. After so many months of not hearing from her, they'd given up.

"What about Joe?"

"Joe Lammerman?" It was a mistake to ask, but Sarah didn't realize that until it was too late.

"Of course Joe Lammerman. I went to the Sweetheart

Dance with him last February, remember? You're supposed to be my mother. I thought real mothers remembered details like that.''

Sarah stiffened. ''Mothers, even real mothers, aren't perfect.''

''So I've noticed.''

''Neither are their children.''

To Sarah's surprise, Calla laughed. ''Touché.''

While Calla was still in high spirits, Sarah decided to finalize the details of her visit. ''It wouldn't be difficult to exchange the airline ticket I sent you for Thanksgiving.'' She wasn't actually sure that was true, but she'd gladly purchase another ticket, if necessary.

''I wouldn't have to stay with you and...and your husband, would I?'' she asked. ''You told me before that Grandpa said I could have my old room back.''

''I'm sure he'd be willing to make the same arrangement,'' Sarah assured her, hoping her excitement didn't show.

''In that case, I'll come home, but only for Christmas.''

''Just one day?'' Sarah shouldn't be greedy, but she wanted Calla to stay much longer. A week, possibly two. Her heart's desire was that her daughter would recognize that she'd been wrong to leave.

''I might be able to stay a bit longer than one day,'' Calla offered, her tone suggesting she'd bestowed a tremendous favor.

''How long?'' she asked warily, fearing Calla would use the opportunity to hurt her.

''A week,'' Calla announced tautly, as though she expected an argument.

"That would be perfect." Sarah couldn't quite disguise her delight. "I'll call the travel agent in Grand Forks today and have the tickets sent to your father's."

"Ah...Mom, listen, would it be possible for you to get the ticket mailed to my job? You know what a slob Dad can be. Things have a way of turning up lost or missing at his place...so it'd probably be best if I could pick up the ticket at the BurgerHaven."

"All right." She reached for a pen and paper and wrote down the address. Then, because she was curious as to why Calla had rebuffed her previous gift of an airline ticket, she asked, "Why didn't you want to come for Thanksgiving?"

Calla hesitated. "Dad told me you were pregnant. I thought it was a ploy to keep me with him, but I wasn't sure."

Sarah closed her eyes and swallowed tightly. It *had* been a lie, but it wasn't now. Clearly this wasn't the time to mention her pregnancy.

"He was lying, wasn't he?"

Willie had lied. He couldn't possibly have known; she hadn't known herself. Sarah suspected it wasn't the first time he'd misled their daughter. "That's why you didn't come here?" she asked, not answering Calla's question.

"No...the ticket went missing, and well, that's the reason I wanted you to have it mailed to the BurgerHaven."

"The ticket went missing?" Sarah repeated.

"Dad said it must have gotten lost..."

That rat! He'd returned the ticket himself and let Sarah believe Calla had heartlessly rejected her offer.

"I'll make sure the new ticket's mailed to the

BurgerHaven,'' Sarah promised. ''Or you could pick it up at the airport,'' she suggested, but Calla seemed to find that an intimidating prospect.

''I want it right here, in my hot little hands,'' she joked. They spoke a few minutes longer and although Sarah didn't want to end the conversation, Calla's telephone card had nearly expired and Willie was due home any minute.

''I'll see you next week then,'' Calla said quickly.

''Next week.'' Sarah replaced the telephone in its cradle and if she hadn't been ordered to rest, she would have danced around the room. She had to let her daughter know about the baby, but she'd bide her time and choose exactly the right moment.

Buffalo Bob pressed the telephone hard against his ear, listening intently. He'd never met Doug Alder, the Savannah attorney Maddy McKenna had recommended, but had talked to him several times over the phone. The case involving Axel was complicated, to say the least, and Doug had decided to work with a California law firm, which meant additional fees and a larger retainer.

During a conference call earlier in the month, both Bob and Merrily had talked to the attorneys regarding their situation.

Merrily had done most of the talking. Her reluctance to work with the authorities was obvious. She didn't trust the lawyers any more than she did Axel's birth parents.

''Well?'' she muttered now, looking to Bob for an answer.

Still listening, Bob held up his hand and shook his head. It was difficult enough to understand the complexity of what Doug was saying without Merrily's constant interruptions.

"As we decided, I contacted Child Protective Services for the state of California on your behalf," Doug Alder continued.

"You didn't mention where Axel was, did you?" Bob demanded.

Merrily's eyes flared wide.

"No...no. I did exactly as we agreed. You tell Merrily I kept my promise to her."

"I will," Bob said, relieved. He'd wanted this to be another conference call, had wanted to include his wife in the meeting, but she'd refused. The first call had ended abruptly, with her nearly in hysterics. Bob had felt trapped—between Doug's recommendation and Merrily's need for comfort and reassurance. He didn't know how she'd cope if they lost Axel.

"I explained the situation," Doug went on, "but it's messy. Merrily not only took Axel, she drove him across state lines. That's a federal kidnapping charge, a serious offense."

Bob realized that if they weren't careful, his wife could end up serving jail time. He wouldn't be exempt from charges himself. His hand tightened around the receiver. "I know there are...problems."

"It doesn't help matters that she didn't get in touch with the authorities when she learned Axel's father intended to sell him."

"She doesn't trust the so-called authorities!" Bob shouted, losing his patience. "Besides, Merrily *did* report what was happening. She called Child Protective Services, but by the time they arrived the bruises were gone. Merrily tried to tell them, and the woman took a report, but nothing ever came of it.'' If anything, her reporting the abuse had made matters worse. Shortly afterward, Axel's parents had decided to sell him to the highest bidder.

''It's understandable, considering her history.'' Doug sighed. ''Merrily's drug conviction could hurt our case.''

Bob's eyes flew to his wife. ''I know.'' He could barely choke out the words. She had a drug conviction—and she'd kept it hidden from him! Throughout the entire ordeal, Bob had been nothing but forthright and honest with Merrily. He'd risked everything for her and the boy, and she hadn't trusted him enough to reveal the truth about her background.

''That's not all.''

A hard knot formed in Bob's chest. ''There's more?''

His question was followed by another heavy sigh. ''In the time you've had Axel, his father's landed in prison on a drug charge.''

This was good news as far as Bob could see. After the way the bastard had abused his own child, prison was exactly where he belonged.

''He has a twenty-year sentence, but he's already been in trouble—fighting with other inmates. It doesn't look like he's going to be paroled any year soon.''

''Good.''

Merrily watched him the way an animal does its prey, pacing back and forth, from the far edge of hope to the brink of despair, frantic to know what was being said, yet afraid to listen herself.

''About Axel's mother—''

"Don't know her, but Merrily does."

"Did," the attorney corrected. "She died of an over-dose."

Bob suffered no regret on her account, either. The woman wasn't fit to be called a mother. From what Merrily had told him, she'd willingly agreed to sell Axel and she'd made no effort to end the abuse.

"This has to be good news, right?" Bob asked. "For us, I mean. Axel has bonded with Merrily and me. We're the only family he knows."

"It *would* be good news if Merrily hadn't stolen the boy."

"She was protecting him," Bob cried. Anyone with half a brain would see that she'd taken the only possible course of action. The child was being physically and psycholog-ically abused. Merrily had contacted the authorities and—because of circumstances, perhaps because of her own lack of credibility—that hadn't resulted in a damn thing. But if she hadn't taken Axel when she did, there was no telling what would've happened to the boy.

"Now listen," Doug said, "I know this is going to be difficult, but I want you to trust me."

Bob could feel it coming. He sensed it the same way he did an approaching storm.

Doug Alder waited as if giving Bob time to adjust to what he was about to say. "The state has asked me to hand Axel over to them."

"No!" Bob's response was loud and instantaneous. "No."

"Bob, listen, if you and Merrily are going to have a chance at adopting Axel yourselves, you have to do this."

"No."

Merrily's eyes had gone wild. She couldn't hear what was being said, but his reaction told her they were in danger of losing their son.

"The state will send a social worker to collect Axel. The courts have appointed what's called a guardian ad litem. That's generally another attorney whose job is to look after the child's best interests. Basically, you have a strong case. Axel loves you and Merrily, and if he's bonded to you, the courts should be willing to consider you as adoptive parents."

Buffalo Bob sat down, his knees too weak to hold him upright. "How...long?"

"How long would Axel be away from you?"

"Yes." His voice shook with the depth of his emotion. This shouldn't be happening. He'd hoped it could all be resolved without Axel's being taken from them. More than hoped, he'd counted on it.

"I can't answer that," Doug told him quietly. "It could be a matter of weeks, but it might take several months."

"Tell me!" Merrily demanded, grabbing Bob's arm. "They want to take him away, don't they?"

He nodded, then gestured for silence.

"It's up to you," Doug told him. "I haven't given the authorities any information that would lead them to you, but I don't think continued secrecy is what you want. You wouldn't have called me if you didn't want to clean up this mess with Axel, and make everything legal and aboveboard. You said it yourself. You're tired of constantly worrying about being found out."

"Either we face it now or we face it later." Bob repeated his own words, although the conviction had gone flat.

"Exactly."

Doug made it sound easy. Made disclosure sound like the only choice they had. If that was the case, then why did his heart feel as though it was being ripped from his chest? If that was the case, why was his wife sobbing at his side?

"The decision is yours."

Bob put down the phone. He looked to Merrily and held open his arms and she came to him. As he held her tight, she stared up at him expectantly, silently begging him not to let them take her baby.

"We have to hand him over until the adoption can be completed," he told her.

Merrily bit down on her lip so hard, blood oozed from between her teeth. "He doesn't know any mother but me."

"He isn't going to forget us."

"But..."

"We have to do this."

Merrily closed her eyes and slowly nodded, sobs shaking her shoulders almost uncontrollably.

"Tell them where we are," Bob whispered into the phone. His resolve was stronger now than ever. It wouldn't be long before they had their son back, before he and Merrily were Axel's legal parents. The interim, the weeks or months without him, would be hard on them both, but that couldn't be avoided.

The state of California scheduled a social worker to pick up Axel two days before Christmas. Doug had tried to talk the authorities into waiting until after the holidays, but his request was denied. Buffalo Bob and Merrily had no choice but to relinquish their son.

Merrily had barely spoken to Bob in days. On the morning of December twenty-third, she silently, dutifully, packed Axel's clothes and toys.

Bob got up early that day, unable to sleep. He found it impossible to stay in one place for long. The flight was supposed to land in Grand Forks at noon, which meant that Beth Graham would arrive between one and two. Maddy McKenna, Hassie and Pastor Dawson arrived at 12:30, hoping to provide comfort and support, but no one seemed to have much to say.

Bob saw the rental car the minute it pulled into town. "She's here," he told Merrily. A few moments later, an older woman walked into the restaurant. She stood at the entrance in her inadequate trench coat, her shoes wet with snow. Despite her obvious discomfort, she had a kind face and her expression was sympathetic.

At the sight of her, Merrily's eyes welled with fresh tears. Bob reached for Axel. "How's my man?" he asked in a choked voice. He held out his palm and Axel slapped his small hand against Bob's. He laughed and hugged Bob tight around the neck.

Bob kissed him, then handed him back to Merrily.

She clung to the boy, sobbing uncontrollably. Axel squirmed in her embrace, not understanding.

The social worker advanced into the room. "I'm Beth Graham from California C.P.S.," she said softly. "I'm here for Axel."

Bob merely nodded.

"No...no! God, please don't take my baby from me! Please!" Merrily screamed as the woman approached.

"I'm sorry, Mrs. Carr."

"Somebody, please... Bob, don't let them do this." Merrily was crying so hard it was difficult to make out her words.

"We have to give him up for now," Bob said as gently as he could. "It'll only be for a little while."

"You promised me it'd never come to this. You promised...."

"I'm sorry." Surely she could see this was just as hard for him.

In the end, Bob was forced to pry Axel away from Merrily's grasp. Thankfully, the social worker left almost immediately. Merrily ran out of the room, and Bob collapsed in a chair, burying his face in his hands. He felt Pastor Dawson at his side, Maddy and Hassie, too. Through blurry eyes, he squinted at the Christmas decorations in the bar, so at odds with the way he felt.

Somehow they made it through the evening, and that first night. Bob didn't sleep and he knew Merrily was awake, too, but they didn't speak. Their emotions remained raw, confused.

Come morning, Christmas Eve, the sun woke Bob. He was surprised to discover he'd drifted off, but he didn't feel he'd gotten any real rest. His heart ached for Axel and for Merrily, who'd placed her trust in him. Difficult as it was, he'd done what he believed to be right.

Rolling onto his side, he reached for his wife and discovered her side of the bed empty. Thinking she'd decided to sleep in Axel's bedroom, he went to look for her. Merrily wasn't there, either.

Nor was she downstairs.

A sick sensation came over him. Hurrying up the stairs,

he ran back to their bedroom. The closet door was half open and he could see at a glance that Merrily's clothes were gone.

His wife had done what she always did. She'd run away.

Rage filled him, and with a wild shout Bob plowed his hand into the wall. His fist slammed into the plaster and as luck would have it, he hit a stud. The last thing he heard before he crumpled to the floor in pain was the sound of cracking bones.

Seven

When Calla arrived in Buffalo Valley on Christmas Eve, she was shocked by how different the town looked after six months away. Christmas lights were strung across Main Street and although it was still daylight, they glowed a festive red and green. The pharmacy windows were painted with a cheery winter scene, and at Maddy's Grocery the entire parking lot was decorated with strings of glittering rope and blinking lights. Even the new beauty shop and the catalogue store had an inviting display of Christmas joy.

Never in her life had Calla seen the town look prettier. She was excited to be back but wasn't admitting it, at least not out loud. In fact, she'd decided to stay cool and impassive and not let anyone know how she felt about being home.

"What do you think?" Jessica asked as they pulled onto Main Street. She'd ridden along with Calla's grandfather to collect her from the Grand Forks airport. Although Calla was curious as to why her mother or Dennis hadn't come, she wasn't about to complain. Actually she was so glad to see her friend that nothing could ruin her good mood.

"The town looks all right," Calla said noncommittally. In reality she thought it was delightful—like driving through a Christmas card. A fresh snowfall had dusted the road and frosted the buildings, and the nostalgic beauty of the scene brought her close to tears.

"You aren't going to get this kind of cozy feel in Minneapolis," Jessica murmured, wrapping her arm around Calla's.

Calla nodded, blinking rapidly.

Jessica couldn't possibly have any idea how glad Calla was to be away from the big city. Phoning her mother had been the hardest thing she'd ever done, but she couldn't tolerate living with her father any longer. She hadn't asked about moving back home yet, but that was what she hoped would happen. If anything, these months away from Buffalo Valley had taught her the importance of checking out a situation before plunging into it. Had she known what her father was really like, she would never have gone to him, would never have made the mistakes she had.

The week before she called her mother, Calla had narrowly escaped being arrested. Her father had held another of his infamous parties. Luckily, she'd been on her way to work when the place was raided. Ten minutes earlier and Calla would have been there when the narcotics officers arrived. The worst of it was that her father had taken the money she'd saved from her job to help bail himself out. Every cent was gone. That money had been her freedom fund, her chance to escape.

Following his arrest, her father had turned ugly. It'd gotten so bad, Calla was ready to swallow her pride and move back to Buffalo Valley. Naturally, she wasn't telling her mother or Dennis the real truth about Willie; if she did decide to stay, she wanted her mother to be grateful.

"Everyone's dying to talk to you."

That bolstered Calla's ego. In six months she hadn't managed to make one good friend in Minneapolis. Between school and her job at BurgerHaven, there hadn't been much opportunity to cultivate friendships. All this time, she'd assumed that attending a big city high school would mean lots of advantages—interesting programs and people she'd never see in a hick town like Buffalo Valley.

True, she had access to programs far beyond the reach of anything offered at school here. Unfortunately, participation in many of those programs required money and time, neither of which was available to her. She could go to Europe with the German class, for instance, but she had to pay her own way. Like her father was ever going to fork over any money! That was a joke. Half the time *she* was the one who supported him.

Calla didn't know why it'd taken her so long to figure it out. Her father was an irresponsible freeloader—and worse.

"Do you want to see your mom a little later?" her grandfather asked when he stopped at his house—the only home Calla had ever known.

"You mean she's not here?" Calla had assumed her mother and probably Dennis would be at her grandfather's waiting, with dinner all ready and a decorated Christmas tree with wrapped gifts beneath it. She felt more than a little hurt that they weren't. She'd been hoping for a resumption of the family's traditional Christmas festivities as part of her "welcome home." She hadn't realized until now how badly she'd wanted that.

"Your...mother hasn't been feeling well lately."

Both her grandfather and Jessica looked at Calla, waiting for a response.

"Is she all right?" Apparently, whatever was wrong seemed to be lingering, because her mother had been at home the day she'd phoned.

"She's fine."

"Actually, everyone's heading over for Christmas Eve service at the church later. You'll come, won't you?" Jessica pleaded.

"Father McGrath is here for Christmas Eve?" Calla asked. The old priest only came into town occasionally, and never for Christmas Eve, not since the church had closed.

"We have a new minister," Jessica told her eagerly. "He used to live here."

"John Dawson," her grandfather cut in. "He was a good friend of mine."

Calla had never heard of him.

"He's great, too," Jessica continued. "There's plans to start a teen group after the first of the year. Everyone's excited about that."

"The whole family's going tonight," Calla's grandfather said. "You comin'?"

"I'll go, I guess."

"Sit by me, okay?" Jessica urged.

Another time, an earlier time, Calla would have found the request childish, but after the trouble she'd had making friends, it felt good to be wanted. "Sure."

"Joe Lammerman will be there."

Calla shrugged as though that was of little concern. Actually she was dying to see him. A year ago they'd gone to the Sweetheart Dance together, but soon afterward Joe had dumped her for some cheerleader over in Devils Lake.

"He's asked about you a few times," Jessica told her, as they walked into her grandfather's house.

"He has?" Joe's interest was the best news yet. She had to hear this, and she didn't want her grandfather listening in. "I'll put everything in my room," she told him, then grabbed Jessica's hand and led her back to her old bedroom.

Everything in her room was just as she'd left it. She wasn't sure how she felt about that—other than grateful.

"What did Joe say?" she asked, hopping onto the bed and sitting there cross-legged.

"He said..." Jessica bit into her lower lip. "You don't want to know."

"Yes, I do."

"All right. He said you were a fool to leave."

Her old boyfriend's remark wasn't far from the truth, and Calla had no problem accepting it.

"But the only reason he said that was because he misses you," Jessica added quickly.

"He's not dating anyone...special, is he?"

"No." Jessica glanced at her watch. "Listen, I've got to run or my mom will kill me. Meet me at the church at seven, okay?"

"Sure." Calla walked her friend to the door and watched as Jessica raced toward the pharmacy where she'd parked. Calla realized she hadn't asked her about Kevin, the one true love of her friend's life. Jess hadn't mentioned him, which suggested that things weren't what they had been. Kevin Betts attended art school in Chicago, and it was difficult to maintain a long-distance relationship. Not long ago, Calla had envied him the opportunity to escape Buffalo Valley.

"Gramps," Calla called, seeking him out. "Do you know if Kevin is still dating Jessica?"

"Don't have a clue," Joshua McKenna muttered.

For the first time Calla looked carefully around the house. Now that her mother was married and living with Dennis, the house wasn't as homey as it used to be. Her grandfather had put up a Christmas tree, but it was a small aluminum one that sat on an end table. That was the extent of any holiday decorations. Her mother had always gone overboard with Christmas and Calla was surprised to realize how much she missed it. She missed silly things, like the two cotton-ball snowmen she'd made in sixth grade. She missed the crocheted and starched snowflakes that added a festive air to the house. Sarah had been ridiculous about the holidays—even placing lights in the windows, including an old gas lamp that had once belonged to Calla's grandmother—and Calla knew now that she loved all the Christmas traditions as much as her mother did.

"I'll bet Mrs. Sinclair could tell you about Jessica and Kevin," her grandfather said. "You'll probably see her at church tonight."

But it would be awkward to ask her old teacher, especially there. Rather than wait, Calla reached for the portable phone and retreated to her bedroom.

Mrs. Sinclair sounded pleased to hear from her. "I didn't mean to bother you," Calla said, getting to her point immediately, "but I need to find out about Jessica and Kevin before I say something I shouldn't."

"Oh, Calla," Lindsay Sinclair breathed, "we've all missed you so much."

"I've missed you, too."

"Are you going to stay?"

"I—I..." Calla could see no reason to delay talking about her problems with school. "I've...my grades haven't been the best. I don't know if I can graduate this year and it'd be too embarrassing to come back and not graduate."

"Yes, you can," Mrs. Sinclair insisted. "I've been on maternity leave and Mrs. Folsom from Devils Lake filled in for me. But I'll be returning after the first of the year. We'll work together and you can get caught up, but it'll take effort on both our parts."

"You'd do that for me?" Calla felt like weeping. She hadn't wanted to say anything, but not being able to graduate with her class was her biggest concern. Because she'd been tardy so often, she'd flunked two classes and her grades other than drama weren't that good. Not the way they'd been here in Buffalo Valley.

"We'll do whatever is necessary to get you back on course. Don't you worry."

"That'd be great."

"Now, listen, about Jessica and Kevin, they broke up in September. Jessica's been dating Bert Loomis."

"Bert?" One of the Loomis twins. That didn't seem possible.

"They're quite an item."

Calla was astonished, and tried to hide it.

"You're coming to the Christmas Eve service, aren't you?"

"I thought I would," she murmured, still adjusting to

the thought of her friend dating Bert Loomis. Funny Jessica hadn't said anything herself.

"I'll see you later, then, and if you want, we can talk some more about school right after the holidays."

"Sure," Calla returned eagerly. They exchanged Christmas greetings, and Calla hung up, feeling a great sense of relief. Her homecoming was going so well, she could see no reason to delay visiting her mother. She wouldn't have admitted it to anyone, but she *had* missed her. A thousand times she'd wanted to call and beg to come home, but had resisted because of Dennis.

"You ready to head on over to visit your mother?" her grandfather asked when she came out of her bedroom.

"I guess." She shrugged, as if to say she'd eventually need to confront her mother and might as well get it over with now.

Calla donned her coat and stuffed a hat over her hair, pulling it down past her ears. They walked the few blocks over to the old Habberstad house. The place had been vacant for a couple of years and was one of the nicest in town. Calla had always liked the two-story Victorian structure, especially the wide veranda. It was the kind of house she'd always thought about living in one day, perhaps when she was married.

Dennis opened the door and shared an enigmatic look with Joshua before greeting Calla. "Merry Christmas."

"You, too," she said, stepping past him. She wasn't actually rude, but she was well aware that her behavior bordered on it.

"Calla!" Her mother was sitting up with her feet on the

sofa, her legs covered with an afghan. She held her arms open for her daughter.

Frowning, Calla hugged her, and briefly closed her eyes, wrapped in the warm embrace. Sarah seemed so pale and thin. "What's wrong?" she asked as she straightened. "Did you break your leg?" Surely that was something her grandfather should have mentioned.

"You'd better tell her," Joshua said, nodding at Sarah and Dennis.

"Tell me what?" She stared at her mother, who looked like she wanted to weep. Dennis came to stand by her and, placing his hand on Sarah's shoulder, he gazed directly at Calla. "Your mother's pregnant. There's been some trouble with the pregnancy and the doctor's ordered bed rest."

Her mother had lied.

"I know what you're thinking," Sarah said hastily, "but I didn't know I was pregnant until the day before Thanksgiving—your father *couldn't* have known. He lied to you."

"Yeah, but you knew when I phoned," she challenged.

"Yes, I did, but it didn't seem the right time to tell you."

Calla glared at her mother. She should have realized. Sarah wasn't any better than Willie. "In other words, you *both* lied to me!"

"Do you have anything you want to say?" Gramps interrupted, coming to stand between Calla and her mother.

"Say?" Calla repeated with a short laugh.

"Like *congratulations, I'm pleased for you,*" Gramps suggested.

"You want me to be happy about this? In your dreams." With that, she raced out of the house. Calla could hear her mother's frantic shouts, begging her to come back, but she ignored her, desperate to get away.

Whatever hope there'd been of rebuilding their relationship was gone now. Completely destroyed. As soon as the new baby arrived, Calla would be old news. They wouldn't want her around. She'd stay in Buffalo Valley, not because she wanted to but because she didn't really have a choice anymore. Her grandfather had said she could live with him and she would until she graduated, but not a minute longer. Once she had enough money for a car and a life of her own, she was leaving Buffalo Valley.

Next time, she wouldn't be back.

Margaret smiled to herself as she sat at her desk doing paperwork, thinking about her life since her marriage. It was the first full week of the new year. Matt was busy working on his truck engine. He enjoyed tinkering with cars. Margaret was fully capable of changing oil and doing other basic maintenance, but it wasn't her favorite task. Matt, on the other hand, seemed to like it.

In the very beginning, she hadn't been sure what to expect from married life. Still wasn't. However, Christmas had turned out to be a wonderful day. Since this was the first Christmas without her father, Margaret had thought the holidays would depress her. But Matt had been sensitive in unexpected ways. Instead of ignoring her father's absence, he'd asked her questions. Before long, she was telling him about holidays from years past. Early on, some or all of her uncles had come, but eventually they'd all married and scattered throughout the country. Then it'd just been Margaret and her father. Matt had talked about his early years with his family, and she'd formed a picture of a small boy torn apart by his parents' divorce. A couple of times she'd been tempted to shed a few tears—for both of them. Even then, her husband seemed to understand and encouraged her to vent her grief.

They'd spent Christmas Day together, just the two of them. They'd eaten a turkey dinner Sadie had left for them—reminiscent of their Thanksgiving repast. And they'd exchanged small, simple gifts. In retrospect, she was pleased they'd been alone.

Marriage to Matt was even better than Margaret could have anticipated. Clearing away any misconceptions regarding his feelings for her, or lack of them, had been a calculated risk. Confronting him the morning after their wedding could easily have backfired. Matt could have lied, could have tried to convince her of his undying devotion. But they both knew he didn't love her. The lie would have oppressed them both.

Margaret realized she should never have proposed when she did. It'd been much too soon, but she loved Matt and needed him. Mostly, she was unwilling to wait. Without her father, she was terribly lonely. Perhaps if Matt hadn't kissed her, she would have been more patient, but he had— and the kiss had been...incredible. So she'd taken a risk and it had paid off.

In the weeks since their wedding, their lives had fallen into a pattern of working side by side. They'd each sold off the better part of their herds rather than feed them through the winter. But that didn't mean they could idle away their time. Most mornings they were either in the saddle or the truck, riding out to check on their breeding stock.

Matt was an experienced cattleman, and they often became involved in lengthy conversations about ranching and cattle. Margaret could hold her own in any such discussion. Matt loved listening to stories about her father and laughed with her, bringing Bernard's memory to life in a way that made her happy rather than sad.

In the evenings, they talked over the events of the day during dinner, then played cribbage. It was a game she enjoyed, one her father had taught her. Almost every night she and Bernard had sat across from each other and counted out the cards, moving the pegs on a huge board he'd made one winter more than thirty years ago. Margaret had been gifted with good card sense; Matt, too, was an accomplished player and they were evenly matched.

Cribbage didn't occupy the entire evening. They sometimes watched television, but not often. Matt had a program or two that he liked and so did she, but for the most part the television was off.

It seemed to her that most of their time together was spent in bed. Margaret had taken to wearing silky concoctions to entice her husband. During the day it was coveralls and flannel, but the nights were made for lace and perfume.

The physical delights of the marriage bed had turned out to be an extraordinary bonus. Margaret supposed it was natural they'd make love often, since they were newlyweds. They were both young and healthy. Although she could have asked Maddy or even Lindsay, sex was a subject she found herself oddly shy about discussing. If what they were doing was too much or not enough—if the intensity and frequency of their love life wasn't "normal" or "average"—she didn't want to know, because it suited her and Matt, and they were the only ones who mattered.

All the books and manuals she'd read about sex had page upon page of description. Although none of the so-called experts had come right out and said it, the implication was there, plain as day. The authors seemed to imply that sex was overrated. Not in Margaret's opinion.

Perhaps because she hadn't had many expectations, she'd been pleasantly surprised by how much she liked it. Apparently Matt did, too, because he was as eager for her as she was for him. He often told her she was a fast learner. Margaret was convinced she'd taught him a thing or two herself, although he probably wouldn't admit that.

Her husband might not have married her for love, but she was determined to win his heart. Every day she grew more and more encouraged. Eventually he *would* love her; she was sure of it.

The phone pealed and Margaret automatically reached for the receiver on her desk.

"Hello," she said in her usual no-nonsense tone.

Sadie picked up at the same time. "Hello."

"I'm calling for Matt Eilers." The voice on the other end of the line was decidedly female. Decidedly sexy.

"I've got it," Sadie said gruffly.

Margaret was about to replace the receiver, but hesitated, listening for a moment longer while Sadie informed the woman that Matt was out for the day. Lately, she noted, the housekeeper made a mad dash for the phone any time it rang. Now Margaret wondered if there was a reason she knew nothing about.

"Have you given Matt my messages?" the other woman asked, her voice defiant and angry.

"I have." This came from Sadie.

"But I have to talk to him!"

"I told Mr. Eilers about your calls and he said he didn't want to speak to you. He asked that you not phone here again."

"Then you tell him that either he gets in touch with me soon or he'll live to regret it."

Margaret had already listened to more than she should have. Quietly putting down the receiver, she kept her hand poised over the phone. She should be pleased Matt didn't want to talk to another woman but she wasn't. She wanted to know more.

Before doing anything rash, she tried to reason out her feelings, sorting through the days for any evidence that her husband had been unfaithful. She knew for a fact that he hadn't been with anyone else since their wedding. There hadn't been a day in which they weren't together almost every hour.

Jealousy burned in her. Margaret had never thought of herself as the suspicious type, but she couldn't just ignore this. Her father had taught her to go to the source and that was exactly what she intended to do.

Margaret got up and retrieved her hat and coat from the hallway, then marched outside.

Matt had pulled his truck into one of the outbuildings and was bent over the side, working on the engine. He didn't hear her approach or if he did, he was too involved in what he was doing to acknowledge her.

"Who's the woman who keeps phoning the house asking for you?" Margaret demanded.

Matt straightened and reached for a rag to wipe the grease from his hands. "I thought you were clearing your desk."

"I did, but the phone rang."

"Oh." The red in his ears wasn't from the cold; Margaret would have wagered money on that.

"You'd better tell me." Her eyes hardened and she refused to release his. Anger settled in the pit of her stomach. She knew what people said about her marriage. She didn't want to look any more of a fool than she already did.

"Maybe we should wait and discuss this later," Matt suggested.

Margaret shook her head. "We'll talk about it now."

He stared at her a moment, then a slow, sexy grin widened his mouth. He was obviously about to say something.

She didn't give him a chance. "Nor am I willing to be sidetracked."

Matt sighed. "Dammit, Margaret, there's nothing for you to get upset about."

"I'm not upset." She crossed her arms, disliking this unpleasant feeling that came over her.

"She isn't important—"

"Does *she* have a name?"

Matt met her gaze straight on. "It's Sheryl, but I swear to you I haven't seen her in weeks."

The uncomfortable tightness in her chest lessened slightly. "Have you seen her since we've been married?"

"No." He was adamant about that. His face softened

and he offered her a second, tentative smile. "You're all the woman I can handle."

Slowly Margaret grinned. It could be a ploy to bolster her ego, and if so, it had worked. She felt better already. "I—I never knew I'd be a jealous wife."

"You don't need to be, I promise you that."

She relaxed.

"Any more questions?" he asked.

"No." She started toward the house, but a few feet away she turned back. "You don't plan on seeing Sheryl again, do you?"

"No," he said. "Not on purpose anyway."

"One more question." She looked down, embarrassed to be asking it, but needing to be sure. "Am I really all the woman you can handle?"

He took his time answering. Meeting her eyes, he didn't say anything for a long moment. "In all my life I've never had anyone believe in me the way you do. Without conditions. Without expectations. I figured I was lucky to marry you, but I had no idea how damn lucky."

He didn't kiss her, didn't so much as touch her. Without another word, he returned to the truck and resumed his task.

Reassured, Margaret headed back to the house. Sadie was waiting in the kitchen. "Did he tell you about her?" the housekeeper demanded as soon as she hung up her coat and hat.

"This is between me and Matt," Margaret told her, tired of the same old argument, resenting the housekeeper's disapproval of her marriage.

"He's playing you for a fool." Sadie made a soft belligerent sound. "Mark my words, you're going to rue the day you ever laid eyes on that man."

Rachel and Heath were married in a private ceremony the third week of January. The reception that followed was in a posh Grand Forks hotel. Against the advice of her physician, Lily Quantrill attended both the wedding and the reception, looking frailer than Heath could remember.

The reception was well attended, with friends from Buffalo Valley as well as Grand Forks. The Sinclairs were there and Hassie Knight and the McKennas and more. Best of all, Rachel's parents had flown in from Arizona. Heath divided his attention among his bride, his guests and his grandmother.

"I think it's time you went back to the retirement center," he told Lily, ready to call for the attendant. Heath didn't want to make a fuss, but he was worried. Her health had declined rapidly in the past few weeks.

"Would you kindly allow me to make my own decisions?"

"Grandma..."

"What are you doing spending time with me, anyway? You have a bride."

Heath glanced toward Rachel who stood in the center of a group of men, his business associates, completely winning them over. "She'll have me the rest of my life," he countered. But he didn't know how much longer he'd have Lily.

"Before I go, there's something I want to tell you," Lily said.

Heath had to strain in order to hear her and crouched by her wheelchair so they could look eye to eye. "Then you'll go back to the center and to bed?"

"You make me sound like a disobedient child," she muttered, scowling at him.

It was a scowl he knew well. She'd been critical of him nearly his entire life. In his youth, Heath had watched his parents and brother kowtow to Lily Quantrill. He never had. He viewed her as cantankerous, opinionated and wonderful, but he'd always been his own person, even as a boy.

"What's so important that you have to say it right now?" he asked.

Lily reached out and touched his cheek with an arthritic finger. "You always were my favorite."

"Me!" The shock of it nearly bowled him over.

"You were the only one with enough grit to stand up to me."

"That being the case, you might've occasionally let me win an argument."

Lily's face beamed. "You won your fair share."

Heath had never thought of it that way.

"Rachel will make you a good wife."

Heath smiled at his bride, loving her with an intensity he'd never known. "I think so, too."

"I'm proud of you for not settling for second best."

He'd been tempted a number of times to search out another woman, especially when it seemed Rachel wasn't interested in him.

"You've made me proud in more ways than one, Heath," she continued. "I'm confident that Buffalo County Bank will prosper with you as president." Her eyes were steadfast on his.

"President?"

"You're ready. You have been for a long time."

Heath looked at Rachel. They'd decided, because of her restaurant and Mark's school, to make their home in Buffalo Valley. His grandmother was moving him into the leadership of the bank, and the head office wasn't in Buffalo Valley. Such a promotion would mean many long hours on the road, commuting to and from Grand Forks, not to mention the other eight branches across the state.

His frown must have said it all.

"Your grandfather and I started the business in Buffalo Valley," she reminded him.

He nodded. "Yes, Grandma," he murmured, "I know that. But things are different now...."

Her smile was fleeting. "You'll figure it out. Michael and I did, all those years ago." Her eyes were tired and slowly drifted closed. "Now I think it's time I went home."

Long past time, but Heath had already said so earlier. As it was, she seemed to have fallen asleep in her wheelchair.

"Heath?" Rachel joined him. He stood and slid his arm around his bride's waist, taken aback once again by her beauty. "Lily's tired," he whispered. "She needs to go home."

Rachel pressed her head to his shoulder. "Perhaps you'd better see her out."

"You don't mind?" He hated to leave his wife of only a few hours. She'd been more than patient already.

"Lily needs you."

Grateful for Rachel's understanding, Heath kissed her cheek and accompanied his grandmother to the car the home had sent for her. Not allowing the attendant to place her in the vehicle, Heath gently lifted her from the chair himself and set her inside.

As the car pulled away from the curb, it occurred to him that he was now officially the president of Buffalo County Bank. For nearly three years, he'd served on the board of directors, sat in on meetings, offered his recommendations. Apparently his grandmother was confident that he was ready to take over.

This was no small matter. In his hands she'd placed fifty years of banking history and the future of one of the largest financial institutions in the state. Along with faith, love and trust, she'd presented him with a huge personal dilemma.

"You're a crafty little devil," he whispered aloud. "Your favorite relative, am I?" Then the laughter came, bubbling up inside him. He was her *only* relative. And he doubted very much that he'd *always* been her favorite, as she'd claimed. Still, that made no difference. He adored Lily Quantrill as much as he ever had—more—and was thankful for the influence she'd had on his life.

Rachel was waiting for him when Heath returned to the reception. "Is everything all right?" she asked.

Heath nodded. "Just fine," he said, and unable to resist, he kissed her.

"How much longer do you think we're going to have Lily?" Rachel asked.

Heath shrugged; he'd been wondering the same thing all evening.

The question was answered a week later when Lily Quantrill died quietly in her sleep.

Eight

It soon became apparent to Matt that Sheryl had no intention of staying out of his life. Sadie took considerable delight in letting him know his "girlfriend" continued to phone the house. Her pinched lips suggested it was all she could do to keep her opinions to herself.

"If she calls again, hang up on her," Matt instructed.

"Very well," Sadie returned flippantly. Everything the housekeeper said and did spoke of her disapproval. If it was up to him, he'd fire the woman, but she'd been with the family for years, and Margaret felt a strong loyalty toward her.

"I think you should know she isn't going to give up easily," Sadie told him. This was the day after his confrontation with Margaret, and Matt was particularly sensitive to the subject of Sheryl—and sick of it. "She wanted me to tell you that if you didn't see her soon, you'd regret it," the housekeeper intoned with far too much pleasure.

Great. It'd come down to threats, had it? Matt didn't know what the hell he was supposed to do. Margaret wasn't a woman who'd casually accept a dalliance on his part. Not that he had any desire to cheat on his wife.

In fact, this entire marriage had turned out to be a shock. He'd respected and liked Margaret when he'd married her, but he hadn't really *known* her. He'd discovered since that every day with her was an adventure. The best kind of adventure. Not only did she know cattle and ranching, but she was one hell of a worker. She put in twelve-hour days without complaint, working as hard and long as he did. There was something about having a partner, an equal partner, that lightened the load and allowed him to find enjoyment in ordinary things. At night Margaret proved she was one hell of a woman, too. She'd been a virgin when they got married, but her appetite for the physical side of marriage was strong and inventive.

When he married Margaret Clemens, Matt hadn't known what he was getting. He hadn't expected to acquire a knowledgeable and intelligent partner any more than he'd anticipated finding a best friend. That was what Margaret had become. His wife, his partner and his best friend.

The first week of February, Sadie fended off two more calls from Sheryl. Matt knew the housekeeper had reached the end of her limited tolerance when she pulled him aside to suggest he "take care" of the situation. For once Matt found himself agreeing with the woman. Enough was enough. He decided to talk to Sheryl himself and put a stop to her harassment.

Late the following afternoon, when Margaret went over to visit Maddy McKenna, Matt hopped in the pickup and headed into Devils Lake. This was better done in person; he'd settle matters with Sheryl and when he was finished, there'd be no room for doubt. Whatever had once been between them was long over. He was married now and he wasn't interested in a relationship with anyone else.

He would never have believed Sheryl was capable of

this. The closer he got to Devils Lake, the angrier he became.

Pulling into the parking lot at the truck stop, he saw that the place was crowded. Five o'clock on a Friday—he should have known it would be. Although the bar and grill catered to truckers, it was a favorite watering hole. The locals often came by for a reasonably priced dinner and a couple of beers to wash it down.

The bar was filled with cigarette smoke so thick it stung his eyes. He thought he saw Sheryl by the bar and he edged past a burly cowhand to get there.

"Matt!"

He whirled around to see Sheryl's friend, although for the life of him, he couldn't remember her name.

He shouldered his way over to the waitress, who wore a cowgirl outfit with a too-short skirt and a fringed vest. "Sheryl's going to be so happy to see you," she said as Matt reached her. "Stay here and I'll find her for you."

He was close to the bar, and would have stepped up to it and ordered a beer if there'd been room. On second thought, maybe that wasn't such a good idea, since he didn't intend to stay any longer than necessary.

"Matt." Before he had time to respond, Sheryl hurled herself into his arms. "I knew you'd come. I told Lee Ann you'd come by and I was right." Her heavily made-up face was bright with happiness.

"We need to talk," Matt said, tugging her arms free from his neck. He surveyed the room and realized it would be impossible to hold a private conversation.

Sheryl seemed to realize the same thing. "Follow me," she said, and when he hesitated, she reached for his hand, linking their fingers. She led him behind the bar, pausing long enough to lean forward and whisper something to the bartender. The other man glanced at Matt, frowned, then reluctantly nodded.

"Sam said we could talk in his office," Sheryl said, dragging Matt through the kitchen.

He walked past two chefs and the stove, obediently following Sheryl. Still, he argued with himself every step of the way. What he had to tell her would only take a minute. He'd rehearsed his statement on the drive in: They'd shared a short-term relationship that was mutually enjoyable while it lasted, but it was over. It'd been over well before he married Margaret, he'd tell Sheryl, and he'd explain that he planned to honor his marriage vows.

Sheryl turned to smile at him. She opened the office door and laughing, yanked him inside, closing the door after him. The room was pitch-dark. His back was against the wall, and before Matt had a chance to find his bearings, Sheryl's arms were around him.

"Oh, Matt," she cried. "I've missed you so damn much." She moved against him, seducing him with her body, kissing him while her breasts massaged his chest.

"Sheryl..."

He wasn't allowed to finish. Her mouth was all over his, open, moist, insistent. He jerked his head back and forth, but all that did was encourage her. Backed against the wall, he couldn't easily pull away.

"Tell me you've missed me. I need to hear it," she begged.

"Sheryl, stop!"

"No," she whimpered, "I need you so much." Sheryl's

hands were busy in the dark, tugging his shirt free of his waist. Then she was rubbing her palms up his bare chest.

"Stop!" he shouted, gripping her hard by the shoulders, finally disengaging her with a shove.

Breathing hard, Sheryl went still.

"I don't want to do this," he told her, struggling to hold back his irritation.

"I know this isn't the ideal place to make love, but I'm so hungry for you, I—"

"I'm not making love to you, Sheryl. I'm married now."

He heard her sigh. "Don't I know it. But that doesn't have to change anything. Not with you and me. We have an understanding."

"No, we don't."

"You don't mean that," she insisted, sounding close to tears.

By this time, Matt's eyes had adjusted to the dark, but he still had trouble making out details. He felt behind him for a light switch. Nothing.

"You want me," Sheryl whispered. "Your body tells me you do." As if to prove her point, she started to unbuckle his belt. He stopped her.

"Like I said, it's over. Don't call me again."

"Oh, am I causing problems between you and Margaret?" she asked in a falsely sweet voice.

"The only person you're causing problems with is the housekeeper."

Sheryl obviously thought that was a joke and laughed softly. "Okay, okay, but I had to see you."

''No, you didn't. And like I said, I don't want you phoning the Circle C again.''

''It got you here, didn't it?''

Matt groaned, understanding her game. She intended to use those phone calls to blackmail him. Either he went along with her little scheme or she'd continue making trouble for him.

''Come on, Matt, give me what I want.'' Her arms began to slither around his neck.

He closed his hands on her wrists and wrenched himself free before she could kiss him again. As it was, he feared the heavy scent of her perfume would cling to him. He didn't want to think how Margaret would react if she happened to catch a whiff of that. His sole purpose in being here was to get Sheryl out of their lives, not to create more problems.

''I mean it,'' he growled. ''Don't call me again.''

''You can't be serious.'' Her voice held a sharp edge.

Good! Maybe she'd finally believe him. ''I'm not the right man for you.''

''The hell you aren't,'' she snapped. ''Don't tell me you've forgotten our plan.''

''Plan? We didn't have any plan.''

''You were going to marry Margaret, and then divorce her in a year and marry me.''

Matt shook his head firmly. That he'd even listened to anything so outrageous nauseated him.

''You married her, and there's no way in hell you'll ever convince me you did it for love.''

''I'm not divorcing Margaret,'' he insisted. ''Certainly not for you.''

Matt winced as Sheryl swore, using language he'd rarely heard, even from the toughened cowhands. ''You can't cut me out of this now,'' she yelled.

He was astounded—she honestly believed he'd followed through with her callous scheme. ''It's over, Sheryl,'' he said quietly. ''Way over.''

''That's what *you* think,'' she said in vicious tones. ''We haven't even started yet. No one double-crosses me. No one. You're going to be sorry you did this, Matthew Eilers.''

''Yeah, whatever, but I'm telling you for the last time that I'm not going to let you blackmail me. If you're thinking of telling Margaret about our so-called plan, then feel free. She knew I didn't love her when we got married. And you know what? It doesn't matter to her. Nothing you say now will make one bit of difference.'' Not caring if he stumbled over furniture, he blindly moved forward, arms outstretched. With a minimum of fuss he located the door, and jerked it open.

Squinting against the bright hallway light, he hurried through the kitchen and bar, eager to make his escape. He regretted ever coming to Devils Lake. The first thing he wanted to do when he got home was have a long, hot shower—to wash every trace of Sheryl from his skin.

If only he could as easily remove her from his life.

The biggest news in Buffalo Valley after the first of the year, Calla learned, was that Joanie and Brandon Wyatt were opening a video rental store. Brandon would continue to farm, and Joanie would manage the store. Apparently they'd been able to buy the inventory of another store in a nearby town, one that was going out of business. In addition to renting videos, Joanie would be carrying a number of craft items, such as knitting yarn and cross-stitch supplies.

The new store created quite a buzz. Calla enjoyed crafts and actually showed a talent for that kind of activity, which she supposed wasn't surprising, since her mother was artistic. The one bright spot about attending school in Minneapolis had been the drama class and her work designing and sewing costumes. Her projects had received high grades and lots of praise.

The very best thing about the video store was that Joanie hired Calla part-time. Calla loved it. She could have spent her entire paycheck on craft supplies. In fact, the first week she collected her pay, she discovered she actually owed the store money.

Between her job and school, with the extra assignments Mrs. Sinclair had given her in order to make up the credits she'd lost while living in Minneapolis, Calla didn't have time to worry about her mother. They'd talked maybe twice since she'd moved back, but their conversations had been stilted and uncomfortable. Calla had the impression her mother was glad to be rid of her.

Not that it mattered. She lived with her grandfather, and that was working out all right. Without her mother to see to his meals and the other household duties, Joshua McKenna was in pretty sad shape. He needed her, and frankly Calla needed him. Not only that, life with Gramps was a thousand times better than it'd been at her father's. Calla wouldn't even consider living with her mother and Dennis.

No, the situation at her grandfather's house was fine; it suited them both.

Friday afternoon, Calla was leaving the video store when she ran into Joe Lammerman. She played it cool with Joe these days. He kept his distance from her, too, although he was friendly whenever they happened to meet.

"How's it going?" he asked, stopping in front of her. He wore a too-big jacket and a knit cap that fit over his ears. He'd grown taller since she'd left and now stood a full head higher than Calla.

"All right," she responded without a lot of enthusiasm.

"You thinking about going to the Sweetheart Dance this year?"

"I guess so," she said with a casual shrug. If he was inviting her to attend the dance with him, he'd left it till the last minute. Either it'd taken him that long to find the courage, or she wasn't his first choice. She found neither option acceptable.

"I thought I'd go," Joe muttered.

"Great. I'll probably see you there." She stepped around him and moved on without giving him the opportunity to invite her, if that had indeed been his intention.

With her spirits high—Joe was still interested in her!— Calla walked over to Knight's Pharmacy. She was out of mascara.

"Hi, Hassie," she called as she came through the door. The pharmacist stood at the back, behind the counter where she filled prescriptions.

"Hey, Calla," Hassie greeted her. "Good to see you. Listen, could I impose on you to do me a favor?"

"What?" Calla had learned the hard way to ask what

kind of favor first. Her stay in Minneapolis had made her wary of even the most innocent-sounding requests. She strolled purposely toward the far side of the store, where Hassie displayed several lines of cosmetics.

"I've got a new prescription for your mother," Hassie told her. "Would you drop it off for me?"

Calla placed the mascara on the counter and pulled a wad of dollars from the hip pocket of her jeans. "Can't Dennis get it for her later? Let him do it." Calla wasn't stupid. Hassie was trying to manipulate her into visiting her mother—something Calla would prefer not to do.

Her response seemed to stun Hassie. Not saying a word, she stared at Calla with a directness that made her squirm.

"Oh, all right," Calla said irritably. "I'll take over the prescription." But she was annoyed Hassie had asked her to do this, and made her feelings very clear.

Muttering under her breath, she grabbed the small white sack and her change and slammed out of the store. Still annoyed, she walked the few blocks to the old Habberstad house.

She stomped onto the porch, where she paused to ring the doorbell. Then, without waiting for an answer, she let herself inside. "It's me," she shouted, stepping into the house.

Her mother lay on the sofa where she'd been the other two times Calla had talked to her.

"Calla!" Her mother's eyes lit up when she saw her.

Calla hated that and she loved it. She wanted her mother to be happy to see her, but at the same time, she didn't want to feel anything for Sarah. Nevertheless, Calla had to admit that she did, and she resented it. "Hassie asked me to drop off this prescription,'' she said, wanting to be sure her mother realized this wasn't a social call.

''Thank you.'' Sarah was pale and drawn, much paler than she'd been on Calla's last visit.

''How are you?'' Calla hesitated, then set the small package on the coffee table.

Her mother glanced up toward the ceiling. ''I'm going stir crazy. Another month and everything should be better, but this inactivity is so boring. I've read every book and magazine in the house, until my eyes feel like they're about to fall out of my head.''

''Can't you work on the quilts?''

''Some,'' her mother said, ''but my concentration is so poor these days.''

''You could always watch TV or videos.''

''I could,'' she agreed. ''But there's very little I want to see on television.''

''Daytime television is the pits,'' Calla murmured, remembering her own attempts to watch it in Minneapolis. She also remembered that her father had found it enthralling, especially the sports channels. He could sit in front of the TV for eight hours straight.

''I'll manage,'' Sarah insisted.

Calla frowned. ''One would think Dennis would be happy to get you some videos, then,'' she said waspishly, eager to put her stepfather in a bad light.

''He would if I asked,'' Sarah returned.

''Why don't you?''

Sarah looked down, shaking her head. ''He has enough to do with keeping up the house, cooking, cleaning, plus working all day. I don't want to ask anything more of him.''

Calla walked about the room and picked up discarded sections of the newspaper. It didn't look like Dennis was all that great a housekeeper, but she didn't say so.

''Dennis should spend more time with you,'' Calla muttered instead, her tone challenging. He was the one responsible for this—her mother being pregnant and all. The least he could do was be there for her.

''He tries.''

Calla snorted softly, hating the way her mother was so quick to defend him. ''In my opinion, he doesn't try hard enough.'' She picked up the empty juice glass on the table and carried it, along with the newspaper, into the kitchen. The sink was filled with dirty dishes. There was no excuse for that. It wouldn't take three minutes to load the dishwasher. If her mother saw the state of the kitchen, she'd have a conniption.

Calla ran the sink full of hot, soapy water, rinsed the dishes and loaded them, then wiped down the counter. She should probably leave this mess for Dennis but knew how upset her mother would be if she were to see all these dirty dishes.

''What are you doing in there?'' Sarah called.

Not wanting to admit she was washing dishes, Calla made up an excuse. ''I thought you'd enjoy a cup of herbal tea.''

''Oh, Calla, how thoughtful. I'd love one.''

She hadn't wanted her mother to think of her as thoughtful, but there was no help for that now. Feeling as though their roles had been reversed and *she* was the adult in the situation, Calla brewed a pot of mint tea and carried it out on a tray—with a cup and saucer and a plate of cheese and crackers. Her mother should be gaining weight, not losing it. She looked wretched, almost gaunt.

"Calla," her mother whispered, "this is lovely. Thank you."

She shrugged, dismissing the gratitude.

"Could you stay a few minutes and talk?" Sarah implored.

"What's wrong with the baby?" No one had bothered to explain it to Calla—but then she'd made a point of not asking until now.

Her mother seemed happy to supply the answer and outlined what the physician had told her. Apparently, what she had was called an irritated uterus, which was a broad term describing the symptoms. It'd started with spotting early in the pregnancy. During even the slightest activity, the uterus underwent contractions. When Sarah lay down and kept still, the baby was safe, but the minute she was up and about, her uterus reacted. Sarah spoke about this at greater length than Calla considered necessary; it made her realize how lonely her mother was, how hungry for company.

Calla had intended to leave almost immediately, but now she was glad she'd stayed. Her mother was going crazy with all this unproductive time on her hands, and Calla discovered that she enjoyed being useful—and appreciated. Before long, she had a cup of tea herself.

She reached for a cracker with cheese. "Joe asked me about the Sweetheart Dance," she commented, unsure why she mentioned the fact. It was something to talk about, she decided, something noteworthy.

"Was he inviting you?" Sarah's look held hers.

Calla set the teacup aside and tucked her hands beneath her thighs. "If he was, I didn't give him the opportunity to ask."

"He's a little late, isn't he, seeing that the dance is next week?"

Calla nodded. "That's what I thought. I didn't want to give him the impression that he could ask me at the last minute and I'd leap at the chance to go out with him again." Calla lowered her gaze. "But I would."

"You're still interested in him?"

Calla shrugged. Joe had hurt her, dumping her the way he had. He'd made her feel foolish...and undesirable. It wasn't because of the things they'd done physically that she felt bad, although she had regrets in that area, too, but because she'd shared her thoughts. He'd gotten her to talk about her feelings and her problems. He'd seemed to understand and sympathize. She'd felt close to him, closer than she had to anyone, when out of the blue he'd announced that it might be best if they started seeing other people. Translated, that meant he'd met a cheerleader type with a lot more sexual experience. A girl who was willing to put out.

"I'm over Joe," she said, although that wasn't entirely true. "What I want is for him to be sorry that he broke up with me."

To her surprise, when she glanced up she found her mother smiling. Calla bristled. "Is that funny?"

"No, no," Sarah said, obviously hurrying to correct the

impression. "It's just very human. Everyone feels like that when someone's done them wrong."

They talked more about Joe, and drank another cup of tea. This was the longest conversation Calla had had with her mother in years. When she checked her watch, she was shocked to see how late it was.

"Would you like me to get dinner started?" She'd found a roast defrosting on the kitchen counter. If she stuck it in the oven now, it'd be done by about 7:30.

Sarah looked amazed at the offer. "That would be very nice. Meals have been pretty haphazard recently."

Calla could well imagine. She knew what her grandfather was like when he came home from work; the last thing he wanted to do was cook dinner. Apparently Dennis felt the same way. Calla was absolutly certain that until she'd returned, her grandfather had eaten every meal out of a can or the freezer, unless he went over to Buffalo Bob's or The Pizza Parlor.

Thirty minutes later, just as Calla was about to leave, the back door suddenly opened and Dennis walked in. He paused when he saw her, almost as though bracing himself for a confrontation.

"My mother's too pale," Calla said, accusing him.

"I know," he muttered, frowning. "The blood test showed she's anemic. That's what her new prescription was for." He looked around the kitchen. "You clean up here?"

She nodded. "Someone had to do it. My mother doesn't like a mess. You're her husband, you should know that."

"I do—I just wish there were more hours in a day."

Calla wasn't interested in listening to his excuses. ''You take care of her, understand?''

''You'd better believe it,'' Dennis said grimly. Then he paused. ''Listen, Calla. You and I might have our problems, but we do have one thing in common.''

Calla doubted it.

''We both love your mother.''

Five weeks after Axel had been pulled from her arms, Merrily woke up in Oklahoma City, sleeping in a cheap hotel and working at a job she hated. More and more, her thoughts were of Bob and Buffalo Valley, and the life she'd abandoned. She'd left with no intention of returning, but now, going back was all she thought about.

It was a revelation to her: she'd lost the taste for running. Despite what she'd been telling herself every day of these five miserable weeks, the only place she wanted to be was with Bob, her Buffalo man in North Dakota. Somehow, without her noticing it, Buffalo Valley had become home.

Merrily believed Bob had betrayed her. So she'd done what she'd always done—and that was to escape. To run as far and as fast as she could. If Bob had kept his mouth shut, they'd still have Axel. If he hadn't insisted they work this out through the legal system, no one in California would ever know what had become of the boy. Not a single person there cared that Axel was being abused by his father. Not until it was too late and the evidence was gone. The state had refused to listen when she'd reported that his mother was a drug addict. Because of her own previous conviction? Why should that matter? No one gave a damn about Axel—not the police and not Child Protective Services—until she'd risked everything and taken him. Overnight she was a criminal.

The people of California should be thanking her for saving his life; instead they called her a kidnapper and threatened her with a jail term that would make her an old woman by the time she was released.

What hurt most was that her husband, the man she loved, was responsible for this, the biggest loss of her life. He'd insisted they couldn't be constantly looking over their shoulders, worrying, wondering.

Bob didn't want anything hanging over his head; he hated living like a fugitive. He was also braver than she was, more trusting. Apparently he hadn't gotten kicked in the teeth as many times as she had. He actually seemed to believe that once the courts heard the evidence, the two of them would get Axel back.

Merrily tried not to think about Axel, because every time she did her eyes filled with tears. In the last five weeks, she'd shed more tears than she would've guessed possible. They'd taken away her baby and despite all the promises, despite all the reassurances, she knew deep in her heart that she'd never see Axel again.

That was why she'd run. When the pain got too bad, that was what she always did. Her entire life had been spent racing from one "geographical cure" to another, seeking a new beginning, a fresh start, a way out. Not until she'd met Bob had she ever returned to one place. One man.

Sitting on the edge of the thin mattress, Merrily rubbed her face. She missed Bob and their home. She missed Axel, too, but there was nothing she could do about that, and the ache in her heart was even worse without Bob.

It didn't take long to stuff her belongings in a bag. She paid the bill with cash, then worked an eight-hour shift at the all-night diner. Before she left, she filled her car with gas and headed north to Buffalo Valley. Headed home.

Not until she reached Sioux Falls, South Dakota, did she allow herself to wonder what Bob would say or do when he saw her. After five weeks of no contact, she couldn't be one-hundred-percent sure of her reception.

Bob had made it plain when he married her that from this point forward they were partners in life. Her disappearing acts were over. She'd agreed to those terms, welcomed the opportunity to be a wife and...a mother to Axel. She would have done anything, signed any contract, to ensure a stable life for her son.

In the weeks she'd been away, a whole lot could have changed. Merrily didn't know what Bob had told their attorney about her being gone, or if he had. All that money spent and for what? It wouldn't get Axel back. Nor did she know what awaited her in regard to possible jail time. There was every likelihood that there'd been an arrest warrant issued in her name. That was all part of the risk she was taking. Nevertheless she headed back because the life she had now was no life. With Bob there was a chance— there was love.

It was late when she hit Buffalo Valley. Almost midnight. The only light came from the street lamps, which she saw even before she turned off the highway. Bob would have closed the restaurant for the night, but the bar might still be open.

Sure enough, the neon sign for 3 OF A KIND glowed in the window. Merrily studied each store, each business, on Main Street. So Joanie Wyatt had gone ahead and opened a video rental place. Although the sign was turned off, Merrily saw the storefront. In the years she'd known Bob, she'd watched this town grow. She'd taken comfort in that, seeing the changes in Buffalo Valley, believing they paralleled the changes in her own life. Changes for which she thanked Buffalo Bob Carr.

Winter in North Dakota was dark and cold. Barren. Snowbanks lined the sides of the streets. Merrily parked with difficulty and climbed out of her car, then walked the short distance toward 3 OF A KIND. A look through the window revealed a couple of men sitting at the bar, drinking beer.

Bob was nowhere in sight.

Taking a calming breath, Merrily stepped inside. She saw him immediately and just as importantly, he saw her.

His eyes narrowed as he paused, a beer mug in one hand. That was when she noticed the cast on his right arm. Apparently he'd broken it. A chill went through her that couldn't be attributed to the cold or the wind; she knew it was brought on by the realization that the man she loved had endured terrible pain.

"What happened?" she asked, walking toward him, her gaze on his arm.

His eyes held hers. "You left."

The two men sitting at the bar stared at her and then each other. Merrily had seen them before, but she didn't remember their names. She ignored them and they turned away and pretended to ignore her.

"I'm back now," she told Bob, hoping he understood that this time it was forever.

"Should I throw a party?" he asked.

She deserved his sarcasm. "I realized something important," she said in a low voice. "I don't belong anywhere but with you."

He looked as though he didn't believe her and she couldn't blame him. "I love you, Buffalo Bob Carr."

He set the frosty mug down and turned away. "I'm sorry, fellows, but I'm closing up early tonight. I got a problem here that's going to demand my full attention."

"Sure thing, Bob."

"Yeah. I should be leaving, anyway. See ya, Bob."

Both men left cash on the counter, although he hadn't presented either one with a bill. Casting a wary eye in her direction, they ambled out the door.

After the men had gone, Merrily stood in the center of the room, waiting. Unable to read Bob's response, she wasn't sure what to do.

He frowned, standing behind the bar as if it offered him some defense. "I risked everything for you, and then you walked out."

"I know—I thought you'd betrayed me."

"I was protecting you, protecting Axel. Protecting us."

She didn't want to hear it, hadn't traveled all this way to argue. "I'm not leaving again."

"I've heard that before," Bob muttered.

"This time I know there's nothing out there that isn't a thousand times better right here." She stepped toward the end of the bar, hoping for a sign that would tell her he wanted her back. That he'd been as miserable as she had.

Merrily's arms had felt empty from the moment Bob pried Axel from her embrace. They'd ached for five very long weeks. "I'm so sorry," she whispered and broke into sobs.

It was the sound of her tears that seemed to break the spell. Bob stepped around the bar and strode toward her, and she fell into his arms, the tears burning her eyes, streaming down her face.

The instant Bob's arms closed around her, Merrily felt the throbbing pain in her heart diminish. For the first time since Axel had been taken from her, she felt as though she didn't stand alone. Her husband was with her, and to her amazement he loved her. Still loved her. He was willing to forgive her, and take her back.

They clung without words, like the lone survivors of an accident, trembling and in shock. The cast on his right arm dug into her back, reminding her that she should find out what had happened. Had he fallen? Been in a fight?

"I lost Axel," Bob whispered, "and then you."

"Oh, Bob." He didn't understand that he hadn't lost her. Couldn't. Not anymore. She was a part of him and he a part of her.

"Don't leave me again...I can't bear it."

"Never," she promised, and this time she knew it was true.

Nine

"You ready?" Jeb asked, coming inside, out of the cold, to collect his wife and daughter. In addition to a number of business-related errands she needed to do, Maddy planned to visit Sarah—and she was anxious to talk to Buffalo Bob and Merrily. They'd phoned the night before and asked if she could stop by for a few minutes to answer their questions. They were looking for advice to help them win back Axel.

"Ready," Maddy told her husband, carrying a bundled-up Julianne in her combination car seat/baby carrier. Jeb had thoughtfully gone out to start the car for her.

He took Julianne's carrier from Maddy and tucked their daughter safely into the Bronco's back seat. Maddy waited by the driver's side and glanced at her watch. It was now 12:30. "I'll be back by four," she told him.

He nodded, his eyes serious. "Drive carefully."

"I will," she promised, and they briefly kissed before she climbed into the driver's seat. The vehicle was warm inside; she was grateful to Jeb for that. She didn't know if she'd ever become accustomed to the frigid winters in North Dakota. The blizzard a year earlier, in which she'd almost died, had been an accurate indication of what the weather could be like.

Jeb remained standing in the driveway, watching her

leave. Although he'd encouraged her to talk to Bob and Merrily, she knew he'd rather she stayed off the icy roads. But he, too, was concerned about the couple.

Maddy had been the one who'd recommended Doug Alder. From her work with Child Protective Services in Savannah, Maddy knew and trusted the attorney. He was the best—compassionate, yet tough and realistic. The situation with Axel was complicated, but she'd seen Doug succeed in similar cases. Still, the main thing Bob and Merrily— *all* of them—needed to remember was that Axel's welfare came first.

Bob had sounded worried when he'd phoned. Maddy wasn't sure if she should stop by to see him right away or wait until she'd talked to her sister-in-law, Sarah Urlacher. Sarah's pregnancy continued to have problems, and between boredom and physical weakness, she found the required bed rest increasingly difficult.

Rather than delay talking to Bob and Merrily, Maddy decided to drive over to 3 OF A KIND immediately. Merrily hugged her, and it seemed she clung an extra moment before she left to get Bob.

The three sat at a table in the restaurant, nursing cups of coffee. Nine-month-old Julianne sat in the high chair, gnawing contentedly on an arrowroot cracker. Several times Maddy caught Merrily glancing toward the toddler with a look of longing.

"We heard from Doug Alder," Bob explained. He met his wife's eyes and she reached for his hand. He clasped her fingers tightly.

"I think I told you Axel's father is in prison," Bob went on.

Maddy nodded. "And his mother is dead."

"From what we understand, Axel has been made a ward of the state and is now available for adoption."

Maddy's heart leapt with gratitude. The possibility of adoption was what she'd hoped for. She'd also learned from Bob that the lawyer in California had talked to the prosecutor before they'd surrendered Axel. He'd worked a minor miracle in having the federal kidnapping charges against Merrily reduced to a suspended sentence; she wouldn't have to serve any jail time.

"Axel's in a foster home now," Merrily blurted out. Her knuckles were white from the pressure with which she held onto her husband's hand.

"Apparently he isn't doing well," Bob added.

"We asked Doug to get us a report..." Merrily paused, and tears filled her eyes, threatening to spill over. "He was able to talk to Axel's caseworker and she said he isn't eating or sleeping well."

"You've applied for adoption?" she asked, certain they had.

"We've spent two days filling out all the forms," Bob told her.

"Doug thinks that given our history with Axel, we'd be seriously considered," Merrily said.

"But he also explained that it was no guarantee we'd be chosen," Bob pointed out. "Apparently there are very few children available for adoption these days, but no lack of applicants."

"Axel loves us as much as we love him," Merrily rushed to add. "I'm sure the judge will take that into consideration, don't you think?"

''Naturally the caseworker will be interviewing us,'' Bob said, not giving Maddy an opportunity to respond to Merrily's question. ''We were hoping you could tell us what they'd want to hear.''

''I'll be happy to help in any way I can.''

''Pastor Dawson has been...helpful,'' Merrily said with a guarded smile. ''He said we'd done a brave thing and that he respects and admires us for the way we've handled the situation. He...thought it might help if he got a letter-writing campaign going. You know, having people from the community write letters of recommendation on our behalf.''

''That's an excellent idea.'' Maddy would gladly send one herself.

''We have to travel to California for the interview, of course.''

Maddy knew this entire process was expensive. Attorney's fees were high, and it had to be costing them plenty, along with all the fees involved in the adoption process.

''The church took up a donation to help with the traveling expenses,'' Merrily told her. ''We weren't expecting anything like that. We were really touched by what they did.''

Julianne had been running a fever the previous weekend, so Maddy had missed Sunday services and hadn't heard about the collection.

''Everyone's been great,'' Bob said, his voice gruff with emotion. ''I don't know what we would've done without all our friends.''

''The town wants you to bring Axel home, too.''

Merrily nodded tearfully. "I can't tell you how much everyone's support has meant to us."

Bob stood and disappeared for a moment, then returned with a file. "This is the paperwork we've completed for the state of California." He handed it to Maddy. She read through the questionnaire and was impressed with the straightforward, honest way in which he'd revealed his past, including his run-ins with the law. At the end of the application, he'd listed improvements he'd made in his life during the past few years, since taking ownership of 3 OF A KIND. He described how he was now a successful businessman, a member of the town council, a member of the school board, a married man. The letters of recommendation Pastor Dawson was collecting would underline those constructive changes.

Merrily's portion of the form supplied all the necessary details, plus a heartfelt plea that the judge make her and Bob legally what they already were in every other way, and that was Axel's family.

"You've done an excellent job with this," Maddy said when she finished.

"Would you let us adopt Axel if you were the one making the decision?" Merrily asked.

It was a difficult question, especially since she knew how badly they needed to hear a positive response. The fact that they both had police records didn't help their case. But anyone who bothered to read their application would be able to tell how much they loved Axel. The child had clearly bonded with them, which was also in their favor.

Bob and Merrily studied her, anticipating her response.

She nodded and smiled. "I think I would. I believe you have an excellent chance."

For the first time since her arrival, they both smiled.

"That's what Doug told me," Bob said, sounding vastly relieved.

"Now, let's go over the kinds of questions that are likely to be asked in the personal interview," she suggested.

When she'd spent an hour or so rehearsing questions and answers with Bob and Merrily, Maddy left, their effusive thanks echoing in her ears. She'd take care of her errands next, then drop in on Sarah. She walked across the street to her grocery, planning to discuss some business issues with Pete Mitchell, her manager. She wanted to switch one of her suppliers, plus try out some new inventory-control software. As well, she and the Loomis boys were going to talk over their ideas for a Valentine's display. She missed the everyday interaction with people in town, but loved her role as wife and mother. In time, she'd return to the store, but for now she was content. She had an excellent manager and the Loomis twins were an unexpected asset.

"Afternoon, Maddy," Pastor Dawson called out when she entered the grocery.

"Hello," she called back. Julianne rested against her side and cheerfully waved her arms in greeting.

"My goodness, Julianne is growing," he said as he approached them.

"She's going to be walking any day now." Maddy wasn't sure if she should be thrilled or not that her daughter was an early walker.

"You talked to Bob and Merrily?" Pastor Dawson asked.

"I did. What you're doing with the letters is extremely generous."

The minister brushed off her praise. "You'll write one on their behalf, won't you?"

"Of course. I'll have it to you before the end of the week."

"Terrific." He hesitated, his expression sober. "What do you think of their chances?"

That seemed to be the question of the hour. "I don't know... I'd like to believe the judge would take into account more than meets the eye. More than their police records, in other words."

"Merrily stole Axel," the pastor said bluntly.

"There were extenuating circumstances." She sighed. "But..."

"Do you have doubts?" he asked.

Maddy shifted Julianne from one side to the other while she considered his question. What *were* the chances of Bob and Merrily being selected as Axel's parents? Worrying her lower lip, she slowly shook her head. "I just don't know."

"We'll leave it in God's hands," the pastor told her.

That sounded like the best solution to Maddy.

As February drew to a close, Sarah grew more and more restless. She'd hoped to get back to her normal life after the first of the year, but the doctor advised against it. He felt that continued bed rest would give her baby the optimum chance of a safe delivery. On this particular Monday, she picked up the remote control and turned off the television. Another four months of this forced inactivity and she'd go stark raving mad. If not for her designing board, she'd have reached that point long before now. Thankfully, she'd had plenty of company in the last two months. Maddy visited her once a week, and even her brother had deigned to stop by and chat. Now, that was a rare treat.

Jeb was happy—happier than he'd been in years. Maddy was perfect for him, and Sarah felt vindicated; she'd recognized it long before her hardheaded brother did. Marriage and fatherhood required a serious adjustment, but he genuinely loved Maddy and was crazy about their baby.

Within a few months she'd be a new mother herself, but it didn't seem quite real to her. Although Dennis was thrilled with the pregnancy, he worried constantly. He'd waited for this child a long time and, God willing, she'd give him the family he wanted.

Unfortunately, he was short-staffed and worked long hours. Her being trapped in the house made his life more difficult. Not only was he responsible for supplying fuel to the outlying areas, but he owned and operated the only gas station in town. After a full day he came home and had to see to her needs, both physically and emotionally. Sarah knew he worried about her when he was on the road, and tried to check in at least twice a day. Some days it just wasn't possible.

Leta Betts and Hassie Knight made frequent visits, and for that Sarah was grateful. Leta had decided it was time Sarah learned how to knit, and had undertaken to teach her, the way she had so many others. Joanie sold more yarn than anything else, and she had Leta to thank for that. Despite Sarah's aptitude with a needle, though, knitting didn't come naturally. Leta had encouraged her, and soon

had her working on a blanket for the baby. However, looking at her humble effort now, Sarah realized she must have
done something wrong because it resembled a triangle
more than it did a square. Until she saw Leta again, she'd
have to set the project aside.

Releasing a deep sigh, Sarah closed her eyes, attempting
to nap. She was on the verge of falling asleep when the
doorbell chimed. She raised her head as Calla walked into
the house.

"Hi," Calla said, sounding only slightly belligerent.

"Hi," Sarah returned, hardly knowing how to respond
to her anymore. She was afraid her daughter would know
how pleased she was to see her and decide not to visit
again. Either that, or she'd be outraged that Sarah hadn't
revealed the proper delight. Sarah just couldn't predict her
reactions.

"I brought you some videos," Calla announced in an
offhand manner, as if it embarrassed her to admit she'd
actually thought of Sarah. She stepped forward and set the
plastic sack on the coffee table, then quickly stepped back,
hands in her pockets.

Stunned into speechlessness, Sarah stared at her daughter.

"I thought...you know, watching movies might help kill
time."

"That's so nice of you."

Calla shrugged off her gratitude. "I work at the video
store, Mother. It's no big deal."

Sarah reached for the bag and sorted through the titles.
These were the very ones she would've chosen if she'd
picked out the movies herself. The original *Sabrina* star-

ring William Holden, Audrey Hepburn and Humphrey Bogart. *The Rainmaker* with Katharine Hepburn and Burt Lancaster. Plus *Father Goose* with Leslie Caron and Cary Grant.

"Oh, Calla, these are perfect!"

"They're old movies—no one ever rents them."

"Get my purse and I'll pay you. I wouldn't want you to take this out of your own wages."

"No need to do that." Calla sat on the edge of the chair, as if she anticipated needing to make a quick escape. "Joanie told me to tell you there's no charge. She's been meaning to come by and visit but hasn't had a chance."

"That's so sweet of her."

Calla looked about the room and frowned. Sarah could only imagine what displeased her now.

"Is Dennis treating you any better?"

She opened her mouth to argue but decided that wouldn't help. "He's been his usual self." Which was wonderful, gentle and patient, but her daughter didn't want to hear that.

Calla snorted. "That's what I thought." She jumped up from the chair and went into the kitchen. "Look at this!" she cried, sounding disgusted.

"What?" Sarah called out to her.

"Did you know he stacks dirty dishes in the sink?"

Sarah was a meticulous housekeeper and no one knew that better than Calla. Before she could respond, she heard running water. Apparently her daughter had taken it upon herself to wash those unsightly dishes. Calla was more like her than she cared to admit.

The child moved within her and Sarah pressed her hands

against her abdomen. "That's your sister making all the racket out there," she whispered. Almost five months into the pregnancy, and the baby moved quite a bit now. Sarah found it reassuring. Feeling her baby eased her worries somewhat.

"Do you want me to put in one of those movies for you?" Calla asked a few minutes later.

"Please." Sarah was definitely in the mood to be entertained.

Calla reappeared and grabbed the top video. Using the remote control like an expert, she slipped the video into the VCR and set it on Play.

"Have you ever seen *Father Goose?*" Sarah asked as the credits rolled and the music began.

Calla shook her head, implying that any one of these movies would be completely boring to a girl her age.

"It's quite humorous."

The opening scenes came on, and Calla watched the first couple of minutes. "This takes place during World War II?"

Sarah nodded.

"We're reading about that in our history class. Did you know Hassie's husband fought in the war?"

"Yes. So did other men from this area."

"Hassie had a son who died in Vietnam, too. His name was Vaughn. She came to talk to us last Friday and brought pictures of him. I knew she was the one who put up flags at the cemetery every Veterans' Day, but I never really understood why."

Sarah was sure she'd mentioned Hassie's son at one time or another. Perhaps not.

"She had photographs of him when he was in high school. He was a really good football player. He wasn't bad-looking either."

"She doesn't talk much about Vaughn anymore," Sarah said. "I think she still finds it too painful."

"Hassie told us how his girlfriend stayed in touch with her for years after Vaughn died, even after she married someone else and had children. She named one of her children after him—Thomas Vaughn. That has a nice sound, doesn't it?"

Sarah nodded.

"When she left, Mrs. Sinclair talked about the effect war has on people," Calla said quietly.

The Friday afternoon sessions at the high school had been a real hit with the community, for a number of reasons. Lindsay regularly invited people to come in and talk to her students—about their jobs or their family histories or their interests. Sarah had spoken herself and her father had, too, more than once. Almost everyone in the community had. Farmers, cattlemen, business owners. Everyday people. Lindsay was a master at convincing folks they had something beneficial to contribute. And in doing so, she'd helped foster the town's new and growing sense of pride.

"Would you like some popcorn?" Calla asked.

Taken aback by the question, Sarah blinked. "Sure."

"Me, too." She put the VCR on Pause and walked out to the kitchen.

Calla was staying? Sarah could hardly believe it. Soon the popping of kernels could be heard from the microwave in the background, and the scent drifted through the house.

Calla returned a few minutes later with a small bowl for each. "Do you have a name picked out for the baby?"

"Not yet." Both she and Dennis had gone around and around about names. "Do you have any suggestions?"

"Me?"

"Sure, you might as well put in your two-cents' worth," Sarah said. "Everyone else has."

Calla munched on her popcorn, seemingly deep in thought. "I'd suggest that if it's a girl you name her after Grandma, but Jeb and Maddy beat you to the punch."

"I thought of that already."

"What about Denise? Isn't that the female form of Dennis?" Calla asked with a sneer. "Doesn't he want to name the baby after himself?"

Sarah ignored the sarcasm. "Denise..." she murmured, trying to come up with a middle name.

"Denise Sarah," Calla threw out. "Might as well get your name in there, too."

"What about a boy's name?"

Calla mulled that over for a moment, then said, "I've always liked the name Joseph."

Sarah wasn't fooled. Calla was thinking about Joe Lammerman, who'd been her first love. She hadn't mentioned him much lately, but Sarah knew her daughter still cared for Joe. Through the grapevine, Sarah had learned that Calla and Joe had both showed up at the Sweetheart Dance without dates and then spent most of the night dancing with each other. She'd also heard from her father that they'd gone out to the movies one evening last week.

"I've been dating Joe again—well, sort of dating him." This information was offered casually.

"You always did have a soft spot in your heart for him."

"A soft spot in my head, you mean," Calla muttered. "I promised myself that if Joe ever asked me out again, I'd take real pleasure in rejecting him. Then he called to invite me to a movie and I couldn't say *yes* fast enough. Sometimes I don't know what's wrong with me," she said in disgust.

"The same thing that's wrong with most of us when it comes to men," Sarah said wryly. Calla nodded without comment and pressed Play, as though to end a conversation that was becoming too personal.

They were silent for a few minutes as the movie began again. Soon they were both laughing.

"This isn't such a bad movie," Calla commented, sounding surprised.

"It's actually pretty wonderful," Sarah added, glancing from the television screen to her daughter.

Calla's visit felt like a gift to Sarah, an unexpected and welcome surprise. The baby moved, this time for several moments as if exploring his or her cramped space. As Sarah cradled her stomach, she noticed Calla staring at her, but she said nothing.

The movie was almost over when Dennis returned from work. He saw Calla in the living room with Sarah and stopped short. "Hello," he said cautiously.

"Hi." Calla's greeting was equally stiff. "I brought my mother a few videos."

He looked at Sarah and she saw the merest hint of a smile. "I heard you were working for Joanie," he said.

"Yeah," she said and stood. "I'd better be going."

"Don't let me rush you off," Dennis told her. "I've got to shower and then make something for dinner. Stay as long as you like."

Calla wavered, visibly unsure about what she should do. "I'll just watch the end of the movie."

Before Dennis turned away, his eyes caught Sarah's and he winked. Humming, he walked down the hallway to the bathroom, wearing a huge grin.

There were already hints of spring, and it wouldn't be long before the first calves of the season arrived. When Margaret woke Monday morning, she suggested they work on cleaning out and preparing the calving barn. Matt agreed. After breakfast, they started, working side by side, laughing and teasing one another.

"How many calves have you delivered?" Margaret asked.

Matt doubted it was as many as his wife. He was about to answer when Sadie appeared, looking more than a little displeased.

"Phone call," she said in that spiritless monotone of hers. "For you," she added, pointing at Matt.

Matt could easily guess who the call was from.

Sheryl.

"Take a message," he said curtly.

"Who is it?" Margaret wanted to know, staring from her housekeeper back to Matt.

"The call is for Mr. Eilers," Sadie responded diplomatically.

"Matt?" Margaret looked at him. "Problems?"

"No," he muttered, and without another word, followed

Sadie toward the house. His steps were heavy with dread. When he hadn't heard from Sheryl for several weeks, he'd hoped that meant she'd accepted his decision. Apparently not.

The phone was just inside the kitchen, and by the time he reached it, he was furious.

"Hello!" he half yelled as he picked up the receiver.

"Matt..."

It was Sheryl, all right, and hearing her voice was enough to set him off.

"What does it take, Sheryl? I can't be any more blunt than I was before. There's nothing between us and there won't be in the future. Don't call here again, understand?"

"But, Matt—"

He didn't wait to hear her response; instead he slammed down the phone. Sadie stood with her back to him, slicing vegetables, but Matt knew she'd heard every word. Good. He wanted the housekeeper to realize he wasn't cheating on his wife.

"Sadie."

She turned and for the first time since he'd married Margaret, he thought he saw her smile. "I told you before, if Sheryl phones again, hang up on her."

"Hang up?" The housekeeper gave him a sour look. "I didn't know if you meant it or if that was just for show."

"I meant it, all right. Would you please do as I ask?"

Sadie muttered an unintelligible response, and Matt wondered, not for the first time, if the woman was trying to make trouble.

Margaret was waiting for him when he returned to the calving barn. "Who was that on the phone, Matt?" she demanded the moment he walked into the stall he'd been hosing down with antiseptic.

"Just now?" he hedged.

"Of course just now!" She scowled. "It was a woman, wasn't it?"

He was tempted to lie. That would have been an easy out, but then he remembered what Margaret had said—she considered him an honorable and decent man. He felt obliged to live up to that, even if it cost him. He lowered his gaze and nodded.

Margaret didn't say anything else, simply turned her back and continued to work.

"It's not like it sounds..." Matt tried, hating the look of hurt and disappointment in her eyes, hating the way her shoulders slumped forward. "I was hoping you'd hear me out."

"Answer me another question first," she insisted, slamming the pitchfork into the ground.

"All right," he said, determined to be as forthright with her as he'd been with Sheryl.

"Is this the same woman you went to see a little while back?"

The question caught him off guard. So much so, that he literally took a step in retreat. Margaret knew he'd driven to Devils Lake to see Sheryl? It was the first she'd mentioned it.

"You think I didn't smell her on you?"

"Ah..." He'd worried about that.

"Wasn't I supposed to figure out why you suddenly felt the overwhelming urge to take a shower the instant you walked in the house?"

She had him there.

"What's her full name?" Margaret asked. "Sheryl what?"

"Margaret, listen…"

"Don't give me excuses." She was stiff with anger. Rarely had Matt seen her in such a rage. If he didn't watch out, she was liable to stab him with the pitchfork.

"Her name's Sheryl Decker."

"Sheryl Decker," she repeated as if the sound of it was repugnant. "Did you sleep with her, too?"

"No." His response was immediate. From the moment he'd taken his wedding vows, he'd been faithful to Margaret.

"Do you love her?"

"I swear to you that I don't."

"Then why's she calling you?"

"I don't know," he cried, and it was the truth. "I don't *want* to know. I didn't talk to her just now and I won't. I told her not to call here again and I slammed the phone in her ear. You can ask Sadie if you don't believe me." He didn't entirely trust the housekeeper, but surely she wouldn't tell an outright lie.

"I swear to you I didn't sleep with her."

Margaret blinked a couple of times, her face vulnerable, uncertain.

He held out his palms, silently imploring her to believe in him.

Margaret cast down her eyes. "I don't like this feeling," she said, her voice low.

"What feeling?" If he could get her to talk about it, perhaps they could come to an understanding. He desper-

ately wanted her to believe him, needed her to. She was
the only woman who'd ever really loved him. The one
thing she'd asked of him was that he marry her. Even then,
she seemed to think *he* was doing *her* the favor. That was
incredible enough, but then he stopped to consider what
she'd brought into the marriage—the cattle, the land, the
house and everything else. It was more than Matt had expected to accumulate in a lifetime.

"The feeling here," she said, pressing her hand to her
heart. "I hate it when I think of you with another woman.
It makes me want to be sick."

"No, Margaret, no..." He didn't care what she did with
that stupid pitchfork, but he wasn't keeping his distance
any longer. He walked right up to her and backed her
against the wall. Before she could argue, he kissed her. By
this time they were lovingly familiar with each other's bod-
ies. Matt savored the taste of her lips, inhaling the smell
of hay and fresh soap—as seductive as anything he'd ever
encountered.

"You wearing your lace underwear?" he whispered.

She nodded, then said, "Don't try to sidetrack me."

"I'd never do that," he murmured. As he spoke, he
opened her coat and made short work of the buckles holding up her coveralls. Before long, her breasts were in his
hands.

"This is unfair," Margaret protested, but he noticed she
didn't say it with real conviction.

"Is it now?" he asked, kissing away any further objec-
tion.

An hour or so later, Sadie came to the barn to call them

in for lunch. The housekeeper's eyes narrowed when she saw them.

"We'll be there right away," Margaret promised.

"Take your time," Sadie muttered, pulling a piece of hay from the back of Margaret's hair. Then she glanced at Matt and shook her head, as though to suggest he ought to know better.

That afternoon Maddy McKenna came for an unexpected visit. The two women disappeared into the house and Matt busied himself with routine chores. At the sound of a car engine, he peered outside the barn—and froze. It was Sheryl.

His heart went into a tailspin. So, it had come to this, had it?

She'd parked the car and started for the house when he stopped her. The last thing he wanted was a confrontation in front of Margaret and her friend. "What do you want?" he demanded, letting her know he wouldn't tolerate her interference.

"Want?" she asked with a short, humorless laugh. "I don't want anything from you, Matthew Eilers."

"Good." Then she could be on her way and out of his life.

"I'm here to give you something," she told him, opening her purse. She withdrew a thick envelope and slapped it into his palm.

"What's this?"

"I'm serving you with papers."

"Papers?" She was *suing* him? For what?

"It's a paternity suit. I'm pregnant, Matt, and you're the father."

Ten

The minutes of the March meeting of the Buffalo Valley Town Council as recorded by Hassie Knight, Secretary and Treasurer, duly elected.

The meeting was brought to order by council president Joshua McKenna with the Pledge of Allegiance to the American flag. Council members in attendance as listed: Joshua McKenna, Dennis Urlacher, Heath Quantrill, Robert Carr, Gage Sinclair, and Hassie Knight. Reverend John Dawson and Rachel Quantrill sat in as observers.

1. In the matter of old business, Joshua McKenna reported that he'd heard back from the Doctors' Clinic in Grand Forks, and it has now been confirmed that Buffalo Valley has been chosen as a branch site for the health organization. This means that a general practitioner will be scheduling regular office hours in Buffalo Valley three days a week, starting the first week of April.

   This is a major step for Buffalo Valley, and a much-needed service. Council members congratulated Joshua on his persuasive efforts and the many hours of meetings that went into convincing the Doctors' Clinic to choose Buffalo Valley.

2. Also in the matter of old business, Heath Quantrill stated that he will be working four days a week at the Buffalo County Bank and traveling into Grand Forks only one day. He was asked about his announcement from last month's meeting. Heath explained that a consulting firm has been hired by the ten-branch bank to explore the possibility of moving head office from Grand Forks to Buffalo Valley. Heath did explain that this is only in the beginning stages and that it would be two to three years before the move, if it does happen, is completed.

3. In the area of new business, Hassie Knight suggested that the community should plan a celebration. Buffalo Valley has experienced tremendous growth in the last three years. Her idea is to have a Summer Fest.

4. Heath Quantrill has other news. His grandmother's will has recently been read, and she donated two square blocks of land to Buffalo Valley, with the stipulation that the town utilize the property as a park. Robert Carr (Buffalo Bob) added that with the number of marriages and births taking place, a park would benefit families and draw more people into town.

Much discussion followed, and the idea for the Summer Fest and the park were shelved until next month. The meeting adjourned at one o'clock.

Respectfully submitted,
Hassie Knight

* * *

Bundled in her coat, gloves, scarf and boots, Hassie stood on the sidewalk outside the pharmacy that had been in the Knight family for more years than she wanted to think about. Her daughter had been after her to retire, move to Hawaii and spend the rest of her days soaking up the tropical sun. As if Hassie could do such a thing! In all her life, she'd never been one to sit back, relax, take it easy. She'd be bored to death. Valerie loved Hawaii and often mailed postcards of the turquoise-colored water, white beaches and sloping palm trees, hoping to lure her to the islands. Hassie wouldn't be opposed to another visit, but all that sunshine would be more than her system could handle. No, Buffalo Valley was her home, and recent events here were downright exciting.

The Doctors' Clinic was open for business now. Joshua McKenna could be proud of that. The council president had negotiated long and hard to convince the clinic to set up a branch office in town. Hassie knew that Sarah's troubled pregnancy had been his incentive; both he and Dennis were worried about her and the baby. The town needed a doctor, and even one on a part-time basis was better than none. At the rate Buffalo Valley was growing, it made sense to plan for a clinic that would eventually have office hours five days a week.

The Doctors' Clinic wasn't the only new sign on the block. Harvey Hendrickson had sold his farm, and instead of moving his family out of the area, he'd opened a hardware store. The town needed that almost as badly as it did the clinic. The entire Hendrickson family had moved into

Buffalo Valley, and with six children, they had plenty of homegrown employees.

"What's so interesting out here?" Leta asked, coming outside to stand on the sidewalk with Hassie. She wore several layers of clothes and only her nose was visible beneath the thick woolen scarf tied around her head and draped across her neck.

"I was just taking a gander at Main Street," Hassie explained. It was a joy to look up and down the street and see new businesses popping up every few weeks.

"I heard talk that Rachel's thinking about building a drive-in hamburger place."

Hassie grinned. She'd heard the same rumor herself. Rachel had a good head for business; the success of The Pizza Parlor proved as much. "My guess is she'll set it up across the street from the proposed park."

"Ready to go in?" Leta led the way back into the warm store. "This town could use a fast-food restaurant. The teenagers would love it. Families, too. And tourists in the summer."

"What do you think of Rachel as the new council president?" Hassie asked. The annual election was coming up, and Hassie had been giving some thought to potential candidates. Who was the best person to take this town into the future? The person who kept rising to the top of her list was Rachel Quantrill. Hassie walked to the back of the store, where she removed her coat and reached for her white pharmaceutical jacket.

"Wouldn't Joshua take exception to that?" Leta asked, after shedding her own coat.

Hassie shook her head. "I doubt it. He's commented a

number of times that he's ready to retire from the council. Can't say I blame him. He's been president nearly five years now.''

''I think she'd do a good job,'' Leta said.

Hassie agreed; Rachel loved Buffalo Valley with the same passion and loyalty as Hassie. Like so many other towns across the Dakotas, Buffalo Valley had seen its share of troubles. But overall, living here had been a blessing. Even during the very worst times, a sense of community, of neighborly cooperation, had never entirely disappeared. And now...now things were looking up.

''How's Sarah doing?'' Hassie asked, knowing Leta had recently been to visit.

''Better, I think. Her mood was good.''

''Calla's stopping by more often, is she?''

Leta nodded. ''Thankfully, yes. She tries to avoid Dennis, though. Sarah said she always has a convenient excuse for coming over. Usually it's something to do with the video store. Either she's dropping off a movie or picking one up. Although, as I understand it, she usually doesn't stay long.''

''Still, they're communicating.''

Leta flashed her an easy smile. ''So it seems. You know who I haven't seen much of lately? Margaret Clemens.''

''It's Eilers now,'' Hassie reminded her.

''Right.'' Her tone conveyed her lack of enthusiasm for Margaret's choice of husband.

To be fair, Hassie had entertained her own doubts about Margaret's marriage to the rogue rancher. The girl deserved better. Bernard had certainly been unimpressed by him. Hassie recalled a time, nearly a year ago now, when

he'd sat at her soda fountain and asked Hassie her opinion
of Matt Eilers. Hassie hadn't been sure what to say. She
knew who Matt was, knew his reputation, but not much
more.

Most people tended to think of him as an outsider, the
same way they'd looked at Lindsay Snyder and Maddy
Washburn when they'd first arrived. It hadn't taken Lindsay long to win the respect and affection of the townspeo-
ple. Maddy, either. Matt was a different story. He'd been
part of the community far longer but was less well known,
and certainly not as well liked.

Anyone with a lick of sense knew he hadn't married
Margaret for love. Apparently Margaret knew it, too. And
this was the kicker—it didn't seem to matter to her. She'd
been blinded by hormones, Hassie suspected. Poor thing.
However, Hassie had to admit she'd seen a softening in
Margaret since her marriage.

"Lots of changes..." Leta was saying.

Distracted from her thoughts, Hassie paused, wondering
what she'd missed.

"Changes in Margaret and for that matter Matt, too,"
Leta went on.

"Change isn't always bad, you know."

Leta's smile said she agreed. "In their case, I think it's
for the better. Those two actually seem happy. I would
never have believed it, but I'm delighted."

Hassie was pleased for them, too, and hoped that whatever they'd found would last.

If ever there was a time Matt Eilers needed a drink, it
was now. He stepped into the Doctors' Clinic for the

scheduled blood test that would dictate his future and claimed a seat in the waiting room. The collar of his shirt felt like a noose around his neck and his hands sweated with the agony of the unknown. He hadn't come by choice, that was for damn sure. He'd been ordered here by the court.

A number of people sat in the waiting room, most of whom he didn't recognize. Thank God. The last thing he wanted was for Margaret to get wind of this. He'd taken a chair as far removed from the others as possible. He felt so worried that he was sick to his stomach. He removed his hat and, for something to do, rotated the brim while he waited for his name to be called.

Under normal circumstances, Matt wasn't a praying man, but today he was. He'd willingly fall to his knees before the Almighty if this blood test proved he wasn't the father of Sheryl's baby.

Needless to say, he hadn't mentioned the paternity suit to Margaret. Hell and damnation, he couldn't tell his wife of only a few months that he might have gotten another woman pregnant. Seeing how Margaret had reacted to Sheryl's phone calls, Matt didn't want to even *think* what she'd say or do if he told her about the pregnancy. He gripped his hat tightly and prayed like never before.

Okay, so he'd slept with Sheryl, but he wasn't fool enough to believe he was the only one. And yes, there'd been a time or two when they'd been careless about birth control. That made him feel both weak and stupid. Sheryl had a reputation—and not just for being an easy lay. He knew about her opportunistic and frivolous lawsuits, her willingness to lie and manipulate others. More fool he for ever getting involved with her.

"Matt Eilers."

At the sound of his name, Matt nearly stumbled out of his chair in his eagerness to get this over with.

"Hello, Mr. Eilers." The nurse greeted him cordially, leading him to a small cubicle at the end of the hallway. She motioned for him to take a chair. "I understand you're here for a court-ordered blood test."

"Yes." Matt nodded for good measure. "Isn't this a bit unusual? I thought the normal procedure was to wait until after the baby's born to determine paternity?"

"Generally, yes," the nurse informed him. "It *can* be decided early, but for the baby's sake, that's not recommended. It causes a risk to the pregnancy." Frowning, she glanced down and read over the court document. "Apparently, in this case, the mother insisted paternity be determined right away and went against the advice of her physician."

It was already clear that Sheryl was bent on getting revenge—and money—as quickly and efficiently as possible. It was equally clear that the well-being of her baby was not her priority here. Matt swallowed hard and tensed.

"If you'll roll up your sleeve?"

He did as instructed.

The procedure took only a minute. The nurse then taped a piece of gauze to the inside of his elbow, and Matt rolled down his sleeve, refastening it at the wrist.

"How long will it take before I get the results?" he asked. He had no doubt that Sheryl would be on his doorstep the minute the report came in. She was willing to put the baby at risk to prove that he was the father, just so she could drain every possible penny from him. He'd already received the bill for her test, which had been done at the Grand Forks hospital. Thank God he'd intercepted the mail that day!

"It shouldn't be more than a week."

So all he had to do was live with this threat hanging over his life—and his marriage. A few more days of repressed anger and pretended normalcy. Margaret *couldn't* know.

When he was finished, Matt walked over to 3 OF A KIND, needing a stiff drink. To his surprise, the building was locked up tighter than a bank.

"What's going on?" he asked Steve Baylor, who happened to be walking by.

"You didn't hear?" Steve asked.

Obviously he hadn't, or he wouldn't be asking. "Hear what?"

"Buffalo Bob and Merrily are in California. They're looking to adopt that kid."

"They closed down completely?" Matt needed something to calm his nerves. That and some quiet to think about this situation.

"I understand they won't be back for several days."

He muttered a curse under his breath. "Anyplace else a man can get a drink?" He wasn't aware of one, but Steve had lived in Buffalo Valley his entire life and would know better than he did.

Steve lifted the brim of his hat, frowning heavily. It shouldn't be this difficult, Matt thought irritably.

"Hassie's," Steve said, after a moment.

"She serves beer?"

"Root beer," Steve answered and laughed. "But she makes a mean chocolate soda. If you're desperate you might check it out."

Matt didn't have much choice. Really, the drink wasn't that important. What he needed most was a few minutes to compose himself before he returned to the ranch and Margaret.

Matt had lived in the vicinity of Buffalo Valley five years, and not once had he been inside Hassie's place. No reason to before now. His ranch was equidistant from Buffalo Valley and Devils Lake. Most of the time he steered toward the larger of the two towns. Not so with the Clemenses. They seemed to have some link with Buffalo Valley.

"Hello there, Matt," Hassie said in a friendly voice when he walked through the pharmacy's glass door, past a couple on their way out. "What can I do for you?"

He ambled over to the soda fountain and sat down. "I heard you make an exceptional soda. I've been meaning to try it," he said, hoping not to give himself away. He didn't need Hassie reporting to Margaret that he'd come in looking drawn and worried.

"That I do," she agreed, striding around the counter. "Business has been good the last few days with Bob gone."

"Do you have anything stronger than root beer?" Might as well ask.

"Afraid not." She reached for a tall glass. "So, you interested in one of my famous sodas?"

"Sure," he agreed. Why not?

"You're not such a bad guy," she said casually, bending forward to scoop up the ice cream.

Matt could have asked her what she meant, but he wasn't in a talkative mood. Not today. Once he had his soda, he'd make sure Hassie knew he was looking for privacy.

"A lot of us had our doubts when you married Margaret."

Matt could well imagine. "She's one helluva woman," he said, wanting Hassie to know he appreciated his wife. Okay, so Margaret she had her faults. He laid claim to a fair share of his own.

"Where is she?" Hassie asked.

Matt lowered his eyes, wishing he could come up with some plausible reason for being in town while Margaret was busy at the ranch, fighting the cold and wind as she and a couple of the hands rode across the north and east pastures, checking for early calves.

He stared up at Hassie and realized she was waiting for him to answer. "She's home...I had to come into town for a doctor's appointment." That much was true. He'd told Margaret the same thing.

"Like I was saying," Hassie continued as she assembled the soda. "I'm really pleased about the way things have turned out between you two."

"I'm pleased myself," Matt said, just to be conversational.

"I've always been fond of Margaret. Her daddy used to bring her into town, back when she was a little girl."

Matt listened, wondering what his wife had been like as a child.

"She used to try to imitate Bernard's walk. It was the cutest thing I've ever seen. She dressed just like him."

Still did for that matter, Matt mused, grinning to himself. He'd never known a woman more comfortable in coveralls, but it was what she wore underneath that enthralled him.

"I'm not sure how well you knew Bernard Clemens."

Matt wished now that he'd had the opportunity to know Margaret's father. He felt sure he would have enjoyed a friendship with the man.

"His wife, Maggie, was nearly twenty years his junior and as pretty as a picture. I remember when he brought her into town the first time. He was the envy of every man in the county. Maggie was a gentle creature, very elegant and refined. It damn near killed him when she died." She shook her head. "I don't think he ever recovered from her death."

Matt's heart ached for the father-in-law he'd only briefly met. "He had Margaret."

"That he did. And to give him credit, he did the best he could with her, but I've often wondered what her life would have been like had her mother lived."

One thing was certain: she wouldn't be married to Matt.

"It's worked out for her, though."

Caught up in his own thoughts, Matt had lost track of the conversation. "Beg your pardon?"

"For Margaret," Hassie said as she set the bubbling soda in front of him.

"What's worked out for her?" he asked.

"Well...you fell in love with her, didn't you?"

Her words hit him like a fist in the face and he blinked back his surprise. Circumstances being what they were, he didn't feel he'd done Margaret any favors. "I'm not sure what you're getting at," he murmured.

Hassie gently patted his hand. "You love her."

Matt nearly swallowed the straw. *Love Margaret?* He narrowed his eyes, wondering what the old woman knew that he didn't.

"You seem a little shocked," she said, apparently finding his reaction amusing. "But you couldn't hide your feelings if you tried. She's got you, Matt Eilers, hook, line and sinker."

Until Hassie said it aloud, Matt hadn't thought about it, but she was right. "I do love her," he said, and found it only slightly amazing that the first person he told was a busybody old-lady pharmacist.

The person who deserved to hear this was Margaret. The woman he loved. His wife.

"We can't put it off much longer," Rachel said, finishing her breakfast coffee.

Heath nodded, wandering into the living room. He knew his wife was right, but he didn't think he was emotionally capable of sorting through his grandmother's things. She'd been gone two months, and he was only now becoming accustomed to her loss.

For three years, he'd talked with her on a daily basis. Until the very end, she'd been involved in the business. Countless times Heath had gone to his grandmother for advice and guidance. She'd shown him that he possessed every bit as much financial sense as Max, although she'd rarely mentioned his brother's name. There'd been a valid reason for that.

Neither Lily nor Heath would ever forget Max—that would have been impossible—but his older brother's death remained a painful subject for them.

Max had been the one with the brains. The brother who'd been groomed from his school days to take over the bank. Then, in an instant, Max was gone.

Heath had hurried home to North Dakota.

Lily hadn't been easy on him during those early years. The first thing she'd done was appoint him loan manager at Buffalo Valley. In the beginning he'd been insulted. Outraged. He was the only surviving heir, and his grandmother had sent him to work at a minor branch in a town that was all but dead. Every farmer in the area needed money. It was a terrible position to find himself in, and after a few months he'd hardened his heart. Being appointed to this less-than-desirable job had been a punishment, he guessed, for having left, for not allowing her to control his life the way she had Max's. They'd started off on hard ground, the two of them, but Heath soon recognized that Lily was teaching him some of the most important lessons he'd ever learn about the banking business.

"I can help if you want," Rachel said, coming into the living room and sitting across from him. "But you really need to do this soon."

"You're right, I shouldn't put it off any longer," Heath replied without enthusiasm. The retirement center had already packed up everything in Lily's small apartment and Heath had stored it all in the large basement of his parents' home. He'd eventually be selling the place but wasn't ready to let it go quite yet.

"So do you want me there?" Rachel stood behind him

and wrapped her arms around his waist. Heath breathed in her familiar scent and realized that having her with him was important. He not only wanted her company, he needed it.

His stepson had spent the night with a friend and wasn't coming home until late in the afternoon, which gave him and Rachel at least half a day. They drove into Grand Forks, chatting as they went.

Midmorning they arrived at the family home. Until their wedding, he'd been living in this very house and he still maintained it, but most of the time he stayed in Buffalo Valley with Rachel and Mark.

Cartons were stacked all about the recreation room in the house's daylight basement. "Where would you like to start?" Rachel asked, hands on her hips. She'd pinned her hair up and wore faded blue jeans, ready to tackle the work with the same energy she brought to everything else.

Heath glanced at the first stack of boxes. There was no need to keep Lily's clothes, which he intended to pass on to a charitable organization. But he wanted to be sure he wasn't unintentionally giving away something personal.

They worked silently for an hour before Rachel commented, "Look, this box has your name on it."

"Mine?" Heath didn't think he'd left behind anything of importance when he'd gone to Europe.

"Aren't you curious?"

He had to admit he was. He lifted it down and slit open the sealed top with a knife, then peeled back the cardboard. To his amazement, he discovered an assortment of expensive leather-bound scrapbooks. His name was embossed in gold on the cover of each one.

"These are yours?" Rachel asked.

"No." Heath had never seen them before. He opened the top book and his breath caught at the newspaper photograph on the first page. He was in his high-school basketball uniform; he and three other players were grinning wildly, clutching a trophy.

"Heath," Rachel breathed in awe. "Is that you?"

They sat down together and flipped through the pages. Each one showed Heath. If not a picture or an item from the local newspaper, then the school paper. Every program of every game he'd ever played was there. High school and college.

"I had no idea you were a sports star," Rachel said, smiling at him.

Heath didn't remember being especially talented; certainly he wasn't the star. He'd been a member of the team and a hardworking athlete, but he hadn't sought the glory.

"Your mother kept these scrapbooks?"

Heath suspected she hadn't. Most likely it'd been Lily.

When he didn't respond, Rachel tucked her arm through his. "Lily?"

He nodded. The second book revealed every letter and postcard he'd mailed home. Lily had kept them all. Treasured each one. All this time, all these years, she'd loved him. It shouldn't have come as such a shock, but it did. For much of his adult life, Heath had considered himself the black sheep of the family. The one who didn't fit in and probably never would. Max, his intelligent, perfect-in-every-way brother, had been the Quantrills' golden boy.

Then Heath recalled his wedding day and those few minutes when he'd stolen away to be with Lily. She'd been weak, growing more and more feeble. He remembered her taking his hand and whispering, telling him he'd always been her favorite.

Heath had listened with skepticism, considered her words the rambling of an old woman at the end of her life, holding on, clinging to her family. But she *had* loved him, loved him from the first, long before he was ready to accept that love.

If it hadn't been for Max's passing, he might never have known.

Eleven

Margaret knew something was terribly wrong with Matt. She sensed it. Felt it in every pore, every nerve, especially when she lay in his arms. As always, he was loving and attentive, but a part of him was missing—that was the only way she could describe it. Lacking confidence, she assumed the problem, whatever it might be, originated with her. If not, perhaps that other woman was somehow involved; she was afraid to find out, afraid of what it would do to her and Matt. To their marriage. For the first time in her life, she felt like a coward.

The only person Margaret could talk to was Maddy. She couldn't stand this silent tension between her and Matt. It terrified her.

Not bothering to drive over, Margaret saddled Midnight, a favorite gelding, gaining purpose as she rode, her face to the wind, her shoulders hunched. The cold stung her eyes, and her lips were badly chapped, but she hardly noticed. She'd entered this marriage convinced that her love for Matt was the only thing that mattered. As long as he was her husband, she'd believed she could accept whatever happened. Naturally she'd hoped that one day he'd love her, too.

When they were first married, everything had gone so well, but lately—in the last couple of weeks—she felt she'd failed both Matt and herself. The worst of it was not knowing what she'd done or why Matt had closed her out. Outwardly he behaved as if their lives were the same as always, which made it difficult for Margaret to broach the subject.

"Hi, Margaret!" Maddy called out from just inside the kitchen. She'd scooped Julianne into her arms, and the child gurgled happily in greeting.

"I shouldn't have come unannounced." Margaret felt a bit awkward now that she was here. "I...I could come back later."

"Don't be silly. I'm dying for company and Jeb's out with the bison." She steered Margaret toward the kitchen table and buckled Julianne into her high chair.

Margaret should be with her own herd. Matt was probably wondering where she'd vanished, and why. Not wanting him to worry, she'd told Sadie where she was, asking her to pass the message on. Margaret didn't think she could face Matt herself. Not right now.

"How about tea?" Maddy asked, already filling the kettle and setting it on the burner.

"Sure," Margaret answered.

"I baked cookies this morning. We'll indulge in those, too," Maddy said as she brought down two cups and saucers from the high cupboard.

"That'd be nice," Margaret said politely. Some emotion must have echoed in her voice because Maddy abruptly turned around.

"I take it this isn't a social call?"

Margaret shrugged.

"What's wrong?" Being the good friend she was,

Maddy abandoned her task and moved to Margaret's side, taking the chair across from her. She clasped Margaret's hands in her own.

"If I knew what was wrong, I wouldn't be here," she snapped, and instantly regretted her outburst. "Maddy... something's not right between Matt and me, and I don't know what it is."

Maddy stared at her in silence for a moment, eyes narrowing at the pain and confusion Margaret didn't bother to hide.

The kettle started to whistle, and Maddy quickly rose and tended to it. She let the tea steep, then poured it and brought the cups to the table. Margaret said nothing all this time, sunk in her own misery. Maddy slowly stirred in a heaping teaspoon of sugar, still frowning.

"I'm positive Matt's keeping something from me. At first I thought it had to do with a woman, but now I'm not sure," Margaret finally said. "I've asked him what's wrong, and he just tells me I'm imagining things."

"You aren't."

"I know I'm not," she muttered.

"Trust your instincts," Maddy said. "But what could he be holding back? Do you have any idea?"

"The only thing I can think of..." She hesitated, afraid to even say the words aloud. "There might be another woman."

Maddy's eyes widened. "You mentioned something about a woman."

Margaret nodded. "She was phoning the house for a while."

"No longer?"

Margaret shook her head, then quickly lowered her eyes. "Matt came home one afternoon, smelling of perfume."

"Did you ask him about it?"

"Not right away, but he swore all he'd done was tell her to leave him the hell alone."

"You believe him?"

Call her a fool, but she did. Once more Margaret nodded.

"Whatever's wrong will eventually come out," Maddy said. "If you trust him, and you say you do—"

"Yes, but..." Margaret stopped and bit her lower lip.

"But what? Are you afraid this is all tied to some lacking on your part?" Maddy asked gently.

"Yes!" Margaret was astonished that Maddy knew her so well. "I'm afraid I'm not woman enough to keep him happy."

"Nonsense!"

"But—"

"Don't allow your own insecurities to blind you to what's really happening. I'm pretty sure this has nothing to do with you. Men aren't very good at sharing their troubles—unlike women. Most of them prefer to handle things alone, at least in my experience. In his own male way, Matt is asking for space and time. Men seem to need that. Step back and give it to him."

"But—" Stepping back was the last thing Margaret intended to do. She wanted to hog-tie her husband and not release him until he told her what was wrong. She wanted Maddy to advise her to confront him—until she suddenly realized the wisdom of what her friend was telling her.

"You love him, you trust him," Maddy said simply. "Now prove it."

Margaret exhaled a deep sigh. Already she felt better.

"I was talking to Hassie about Matt the other day," Maddy continued. "Hassie mentioned the positive changes she's seen in him since the two of you got married."

"What kind of changes?"

"First, Matt used to spend a lot of time away from his ranch. If he wasn't at Buffalo Bob's, then he was drinking in Devils Lake. That's not to say he wasn't a hardworking rancher, but he didn't let his responsibilities stand in the way of a good time."

Margaret couldn't say anything in his defense because it was true.

"He used to be a real loner, although he certainly had acquaintances—mostly in bars. He's a lot friendlier now, much more part of the community."

Margaret had noted that herself.

"Those are only a few. But it's the changes I've seen in *you* that I mentioned to Hassie," Maddy surprised her by adding.

Margaret pressed her hand over her heart and attempted a smile. "Me?"

"There's a softness in you I've never seen before," Maddy said. "A...sweetness."

"Sweet? Me?" Margaret was ready to laugh out loud and would have, if not for the challenging look from her friend.

"It's true! Oh, Margaret, you mean to say you don't see it? I do. So does Hassie. Marriage is what's made the difference. When you announced that you were marrying

Matt, I have to tell you I had my doubts. I prayed you were making the right decision. Without even thinking, I could come up with a dozen men who would, in my opinion, have made you a better husband.''

''But I love Matt!''

''I realized that. Which is why I knew it wouldn't do any good to try to change your mind.''

Margaret couldn't argue. She wanted Matt and no other husband.

''Actually I'd planned to phone you later in the week,'' Maddy said. ''Jeb and I wanted to invite you and Matt over for dinner next weekend.''

Margaret felt her heart lighten. ''Yes...I mean I'll ask Matt to make sure he doesn't have a conflict, but it should be fine.'' This was exactly what Margaret had hoped would happen. She yearned to be like other couples, to make close friends in the community, to belong.

Not long after she finished her tea, Margaret returned to the house, looking forward to telling Matt about the McKennas' invitation. When he saw her, Matt immediately came out from the barn to meet her.

''Where'd you go?'' he asked, although Margaret suspected he already knew.

''I went to Maddy's for tea,'' she said, as if it was a very womanly thing to do and she regularly took part in such activities.

''You might have mentioned it.''

''I might have,'' she agreed as she led Midnight into the barn and unsaddled him. ''In fact, I asked Sadie to let you know.''

Hands in his hip pockets, Matt followed her as she went

about her tasks of rubbing down the gelding and feeding him oats.

"I didn't talk to Sadie," he muttered.

"Well, it's no big mystery. I just needed to get away," Margaret confessed as she gave Midnight a final pat and let herself out of the stall.

"Any particular reason?"

"Actually, I was worried about us."

Her husband tensed. "Us?"

"It's all right, Matt," she said, and slipped her arm around his waist to hug him. "Really. I don't know what's bothering you, but I can tell that something is. I'm giving you space to deal with it in your own way. When you're ready to discuss it with me, I'll be here."

He stared at her as though he wasn't sure he should believe her.

"If you choose not to tell me, that's fine by me, too."

He frowned. "You're okay with that?"

"I'm fine with it."

He looked down at her, shaking his head. "I don't know what I ever did to deserve you," he said, his voice low and barely controlled. "But whatever it was, I'm grateful."

Sarah and Dennis sat in Dr. Leggatt's Grand Forks office and anxiously awaited his decision. "I'm feeling much better," she told him. The cramping and contractions had lessened over the weeks of continued bed rest.

"The pregnancy seems to be progressing normally," Dr. Leggatt said, sitting across the desk from Sarah. She looked at her husband and flashed him a huge grin.

"Then I can go back to being a regular person again?"

That might be pushing her luck, but she couldn't help asking.

"Back to work?" he repeated with a short laugh. "Not quite."

"I can leave the house?"

He hesitated. "Some."

Her shoulders sagged with disappointment, and Dennis's hand tightened around hers.

"You're the best judge in this situation," the doctor said. "No one knows better than you exactly how much activity you can undertake. As soon as you feel any contractions, you know what to do. The most dangerous time has passed, but we still have to be careful if you're going to carry this child to term."

Sarah wanted that more than anything, even if it meant risking her sanity. This afternoon was the first time in weeks that she'd stepped outside. The first time she'd stood in the afternoon sunshine and breathed in fresh spring air. It made her feel nearly giddy with happiness. Giddy with love. It turned her thoughts to her husband and how long it'd been since they'd last made love.

They rode the elevator to the lobby and as luck would have it, they were alone. "Dennis, I want you to kiss me."

"Here? Now?"

This joy was almost more than she could contain. "Yes, right here. Right now. Hurry." It didn't matter that she was five months pregnant or that the elevator could stop any second.

"Sarah, I..." Dennis paused, glancing over his shoulder as though he half expected someone to suddenly appear, then wrapped his arms around her. The kiss started gently but quickly grew as wild as their passion. Sarah slid her hands around his neck and gave herself fully to this man she loved beyond reason. One kiss, however, wasn't enough. Their dilemma was ironic; before their marriage they'd made love often and with abandon. Now that they were legally husband and wife, their relationship was strictly platonic, for fear lovemaking might disturb the troubled pregnancy.

By the time the kiss ended and the elevator doors opened, Sarah was weak with longing. Somehow they managed to step out and allow others to enter. Smiling to herself, she wondered if anyone had noticed. Dennis didn't look any more in control than she felt.

The ride back to Buffalo Valley was jubilant. The tests showed the baby was healthy and developing at the proper pace. The release of tension and worry was enough to make Sarah feel light-headed. With caution, she could carry the baby to term and they'd have the child they both wanted so much.

"I'd like to go to the shop," Sarah told her husband as they drove into town.

He frowned in her direction and seemed about to object, then changed his mind. "Dr. Leggatt said you'd know your own endurance."

"And I do," she assured him.

Dennis pulled into a parking space in front of the Buffalo Valley Quilting Company. Although Sarah talked to her manager every day, she hadn't actually been inside the shop since December.

No sooner had she walked in than she was surrounded by her staff. Everyone was talking at once. Most of her life, Sarah had maintained a distance from people, but none of that reserve was in evidence this afternoon. She felt free and alive and very much in love with her husband.

Jennifer proudly showed her the quilts in progress. Sarah examined each one, amazed at their beauty and the talent of her staff. She couldn't have done a better job herself and said so.

Dennis stood at her side, his arm about her waist. He, too, appeared impressed with the work that had been done in Sarah's absence.

The doorbell above the shop chimed and Sarah glanced over her shoulder to see Calla. Her daughter looked upset and near panic.

"Jennifer," Calla cried, "does anyone know where my mother—" She stopped talking when she saw Sarah.

"I'm here," Sarah said and stretched out her arm to her daughter.

Calla hesitantly advanced toward her. "I stopped at the house after school and you weren't there. I...I didn't know what to think."

"I'm fine," Sarah told her, struggling to hold back tears. This was the first sign she'd seen of Calla's love in a very long while. "I should've let you know I had a doctor's appointment this afternoon."

"I'd better get back to work," Dennis said, and squeezed her hand, aware of Calla's feelings toward him. Whenever possible, he tried to give her plenty of breathing space.

"You'll get a ride home?" he asked. "Lie down for a couple of hours?"

Sarah assured him she would, although at the moment she felt like celebrating, not resting.

"I...I didn't mean to interrupt anything," Calla said, sounding self-conscious. She backed away from her mother as though she'd suddenly remembered their estrangement.

"You didn't. How about one of Hassie's sodas?" Sarah asked, and then for incentive, she added, "just you and me. I'll tell you what the doctor had to say."

Calla shrugged as if to imply that she didn't have anything better to do.

"Great." Sarah smiled at Jennifer, then walked over to Hassie's with her daughter.

Unfortunately Hassie was gone for the afternoon, but Leta Betts put together a darn good soda herself. She served them, then hurried to help a customer who seemed bewildered by the different kinds of film on display.

More like longtime friends than mother and daughter, Sarah and Calla sat on the padded stools and sipped their sodas and chatted. "The baby's going to be all right?" Calla asked.

"So far, so good."

Calla's lips formed a smile. "What's it like being pregnant?" she asked.

"Actually, it's pretty incredible."

"Do you really feel the baby kick?"

"All the time."

Calla's questions revealed thought and sensitivity. Apparently she'd done quite a bit of thinking about this baby. That pleased Sarah. In the last months, Calla had revealed no indication of jealousy or sibling resentment.

Then, in a carefully casual voice, Calla said, "Dad phoned the other day."

Involuntarily, Sarah tensed. If Willie had gotten hold of Calla it could be for only one reason. He wanted something. It didn't take a brain surgeon to figure out what it was, either. He was after Calla's hard-earned paycheck.

"Do I dare ask why he called?"

"He said he needs money. A loan."

"You didn't give it to him, did you?" It wasn't any of Sarah's business, but she'd blurted out the question before she could think better of it.

"Mother, please," Calla returned, rolling her eyes. She held onto the straw with one hand and the glass with the other. "Do I look like I was born yesterday?"

So Willie didn't get a dime. "Good for you."

Calla didn't say anything for a couple of moments, then glanced in Sarah's direction, her eyes sober. "It wasn't easy, you know?"

Sarah did know. Calla was Willie's daughter and any daughter sought her father's approval, even if that father was as inadequate as Willie. Refusing him money must have been difficult.

"He asked me to get it from you," she added. "He seems to think you'd give it to me if I asked."

Willie was right; if Calla had asked for money, Sarah might well have forked over her own cash without asking a lot of questions. She would have seen it as a way to build a bridge in their relationship, a way she could prove her love.

Calla was staring at her, waiting. Then Sarah understood. Her daughter was asking. Despite everything Willie had done to her, Calla wanted to help him.

"I won't give you money for your father," she said flatly.

Calla looked away.

Feeling she had to explain, Sarah said, "It's as hard for me to turn you down as it was for you to say no to your father. I understand what you must have felt when he pressured you, because that's how I feel right now."

Calla looked back and surprise flickered in her eyes.

"I love you, Calla. You're my daughter and the fact that you've decided to live apart from me hurts. It hurts really badly. I'd do just about anything to regain your affection."

That seemed to require some digesting on Calla's part. "You won't give my father money?"

"No."

Calla's eyes narrowed. "Because you're married to Dennis."

"I did marry Dennis, but my decision has nothing to do with him." She paused, trying to make sense of Calla's reactions. "I wasn't choosing Dennis over you, if that's what you're thinking."

By now Calla's eyes had turned cold. "Think what you like, Mother, but that's exactly what you did." She slipped off the stool and stalked outside, as though she couldn't get away fast enough.

Buffalo Bob felt good. Better than good. He felt terrific. He'd taken the biggest gamble of his life by contacting the California authorities about Axel. Even bigger than buying into that poker game when he won 3 OF A KIND from

Dave Ertz. He'd made an honest go of the business in a town that was practically dead. Now, as March progressed, he had real hopes that the courts would choose him and Merrily as Axel's adoptive parents.

Merrily rushed into the kitchen. "Pastor Dawson is here."

Bob nodded and carried a tray laden with an assortment of baked delicacies into the restaurant. His cast had been removed several weeks before but his arm was still weak, and several people rushed to take it from him. Everyone he'd contacted upon his return had shown up. Bob figured this meeting was the best way to thank the community for all the help and support he and Merrily had received.

The low buzz of chatter died down when he walked out of the kitchen. He set the tray on the counter, alongside the large urn of coffee.

"Help yourselves, and once everyone's served, Merrily and I will tell you about our trip."

"I'm not shy," Hassie announced as she reached for a plate.

"Me, neither," Joshua McKenna said and followed suit.

Soon Lindsay and Gage Sinclair, along with Maddy, had helped themselves to the pastries and cookies. Bob noticed that it was difficult for Merrily to keep her eyes off the two infants. His wife hungered for their son, but Bob didn't think it would take much longer for Axel to come home.

"First of all," Bob said after everyone was seated again, "Merrily and I want to thank you from the bottom of our hearts for the way you've stood by us and supported us."

Merrily's arm was around his waist. "It meant more to us than you'll ever know to have your letters of recommendation there before the judge. We know he was impressed."

"He said he was," Bob told them and noticed the quick exchange of smiles. He grinned at Pastor Dawson, who'd originally come up with the idea. "The money the church collected was a huge help, too."

"California is expensive," Merrily said. "Compared to North Dakota, anyway."

"What else happened?" Pastor Dawson asked.

Merrily cleared her throat and when she spoke, the muscles in her face tightened. "I—I had to stand before the judge because of what I did."

Even with the plea bargain in place, Merrily had been terrified. The federal kidnapping charge was a serious crime. It was only the testimony she'd provided in the plea agreement regarding Axel's natural father that had saved her from jail.

"Did you see Axel?" Leta Betts asked.

"No," Merrily replied, and that one word revealed a world of pain and regret.

Bob put his arm protectively around his wife's shoulders. This had been the hardest part of the entire ordeal. Merrily had assumed she'd have some time with Axel. Bob had, too, but it didn't come to pass.

"We talked to the social worker and it was felt that a visit from us now would do him more harm than good," he explained.

"He's...doing better, we understood." Merrily forced a brave smile.

Bob loved her all the more for trying to conceal her bitter disappointment. He saw several heads nod in agreement and noted the pained looks their friends shared with him and Merrily.

"We were able to get a couple of pictures of him, though," his wife added excitedly. She went from table to table, showing off the latest snapshots of Axel. "I couldn't believe how much he's grown."

"You're being considered for adoption?" The question came from Gage Sinclair.

"Yes, oh, yes." Again it was Merrily who responded.

"We were interviewed individually," Bob said.

"And then together," Merrily told him.

"Are they doing a home study?" Maddy asked.

"Apparently so." Bob explained that the last thing he'd heard from Linda Beck, the social worker assigned to Axel's case, was that she'd be getting in touch with them soon about a home study.

Grinning, Maddy flashed them a thumbs-up.

"If she wants to interview character witnesses, give her my name," Pastor Dawson said.

Bob felt his wife's arm tighten about him. "You'd do that for us?"

"Of course."

Each person in the room made the same offer. Bob was deeply moved by these actions of genuine friendship. Never would he have guessed that he'd meet such good people in this down-on-its-luck town. Everyone here was as much family as he'd ever hoped to find.

"Bob and I are grateful, but the battle hasn't been won yet," Merrily went on to say.

"We'll do everything we can to help," Hassie called out.

Their friends lingered for another hour, asking questions and making suggestions. Before they left, each one in turn hugged him and Merrily.

Before she went home, Maddy said that with the state willing to do a home study, it was advisable to make their living quarters as attractive as possible. An apartment above a bar probably wouldn't be considered the best environment for a toddler. Maddy hadn't come right out and said that, but Bob had gotten the message.

Axel's old bedroom could use a fresh coat of paint. Merrily had thought of a dozen ways to add homey touches about the place, too. Funny, he'd never given the matter much thought, but Maddy was right. Their living quarters could definitely use a bit of sprucing up. Nothing extravagant. They couldn't afford that.

The attorneys' fees, plus the trip out west, had set Bob back plenty. The fact that they'd been forced to close down the business while they were away didn't help, either.

"Notice any changes?" Merrily asked when he walked into their bedroom later that night.

Bob looked around, not sure what was different. "You'd better tell me," he suggested tiredly.

"I removed the painting."

Bob's gaze flew to the wall. He loved the painting that depicted a saloon in the old west, with men crowded around the bar, their shot glasses raised in a silent toast. The bartender reminded Bob of himself, only his belly wasn't as big and his hair was longer. Above the bar was a painting of a naked woman posed to reveal the most seductive parts of the female anatomy.

"You moved my picture?" he cried, unable to disguise his outrage.

"We can't have the social worker walking into the bedroom and seeing a picture of a naked woman."

"It's more than a painting of a naked woman," he argued. Certain things were worth fighting for, and that picture was one. "What's that?" he asked with disgust, pointing to the still life of some fruit bowl she'd replaced it with.

"Fruit."

"I know that. It's insipid. Stupid."

"You like that naked woman?"

"Damn straight I do."

Merrily arched her brows, then slowly released the sash holding her silk robe together. "I was hoping you'd find a *real* naked woman more enticing than a painting."

"Oh, no, you don't," Bob said. He wouldn't be that easily dissuaded. He wanted his picture back. Okay, okay, he'd move it for the home study, but not until absolutely necessary.

"I'll rehang it after the interview if you insist." Merrily shrugged her shoulders and the robe pooled at her bare feet. He'd been with Merrily for years now, and there were damn few secrets when it came to his wife's naked body. Nevertheless, Bob found himself as eager to make love to her as he had the very first time.

"You'd put it back later?" he asked, surprised at how weak his voice sounded.

"I would."

"Then I can't see any harm." As he spoke he threw off his own clothes with an urgency that left him trembling. "Come to your Buffalo man," he coaxed.

His wife didn't need any further encouragement.

Twelve

Sarah didn't take one minute of her newfound freedom for granted, limited though it was. Wanting to protect her pregnancy and at the same time have some semblance of a life, she paced herself carfully. Mornings were spent at the Buffalo Valley Quilting Company.

Orders for her quilts continued to pour in and the thrill never waned. People loved her simple designs and the fact that each quilt was individually constructed, each unique in its own way. At noon she returned to the house for what she called quiet time. Dennis assumed she napped, and sometimes she did, but mostly she worried about her relationship with Calla and wondered what she could do to repair the damage.

In the afternoons she prepared dinner and if she was feeling up to it, she took a short walk or went to visit friends. The last week of March, Sarah stopped by Joanie's video store. It had only been open a few months and was an unqualified success. Sarah had gone there two or three times in the last weeks, but catching Joanie during a quiet moment was rare.

Sure enough, Joanie was busy ringing up a sale when Sarah stepped in. She liked the way the videos were displayed; Brandon had built the cases himself. In the back of the store was an area set up for crafts. Needlepoint kits hung from a peg board on the wall and there was a bulletin board filled with demonstration greeting cards created with rubber stamps. Joanie had bins of yarn and pattern books, with a completed sweater hanging up on display. Even while making the most of her space, she'd managed to create a homey and comfortable atmosphere. A couple of big, overstuffed chairs marked the entrance to the crafts section, issuing a silent invitation to sit down and relax.

"Hi, Sarah," Joanie called out when she'd finished with her customer. "It's great to see you."

"You, too," she called back. "I'm admiring your store."

Joanie walked toward her. "The crafts are where my heart is. Brandon and I both felt the videos were where we'd make the most profit, but I've always loved crafts. Can I help you find anything?"

"No, thanks. Actually I was hoping we could chat for a few minutes."

"Sure." Joanie glanced at the front of the store, where two people were choosing videos.

"Whenever it's most convenient for you," Sarah suggested, knowing that if she were to attempt the conversation now, they'd be constantly interrupted.

"Would you like me to drop by your house on my way home?" Joanie asked. "Calla comes in about four. I could be there shortly after that."

"Perfect."

By the time Joanie arrived, Sarah had made tea and baked currant-filled scones. "Oh, this is lovely," Joanie said, joining her in the living room.

Knowing she was taking Joanie away from her family,

Sarah came directly to the point. "To begin with, I wanted to thank you for sending me videos while I was laid up. I can't tell you what a different they made."

Joanie brushed aside her gratitude. "It was no problem, and truthfully, the idea was Calla's."

Sarah had suspected as much, and her spirits soared at Joanie's confirmation. Despite her overtures, her relationship with Calla remained fragile and tentative. Anytime she saw progress, something would happen to upset Calla. Almost every conversation seemed to end with her angry. Regretfully, Sarah realized that nothing she could say now would undo the past. All she could do was swallow her irritation and hope that Calla would look beyond her failings as a mother. Sarah wanted her daughter to know that no one would ever love her as much as she did. Calla could trust her, talk to her, come to her. Anytime. Anyplace. Unfortunately, with a girl as moody as Calla, that kind of trust didn't come easily.

"Calla's a good kid," Joanie said.

Sarah nodded. "What I really wanted to talk to you about is a day-care center," she said, diverting the conversation from the uncomfortable subject of her daughter.

"Really? Rachel Quantrill mentioned starting one, too."

"Did she?" This was welcome news to Sarah.

"There's definitely a need. I'm driving over to Bellmont every day to drop Jason off with a friend who has a toddler herself. Brandon picks him up in the afternoons, but it's inconvenient all the way around."

Sarah had her own concerns. She had to find more employees, and she couldn't do that unless there was someplace women felt comfortable leaving their children. With orders coming in at such a steady pace, her quilt company was having trouble meeting the demand. But it wasn't only her business she was thinking of. Within a matter of months, she'd need someplace she could leave her own baby and feel confident that he or she would receive the best possible care.

"I've been meaning to talk to Rachel," Joanie said. "Perhaps we both can."

"That'd be great."

Joanie reached for her scone and broke it in half. "I realize you invited me over to discuss day care, but you're worried about Calla, too, aren't you?"

Sarah's distress must be more obvious than she'd realized. A lump thickened her throat and she nodded; it was the only reply she could manage.

"I meant what I said about her," Joanie murmured.

"She *is* a good kid, but we just don't seem to get along," Sarah whispered, then averted her gaze, embarrassed and dismayed that everything had gone so wrong between her and Calla. "I can't tell you how many times I've tried." She weighed the advisability of baring her soul to someone she viewed more as acquaintance than friend. But keeping everything to herself, the way she had in the past, hadn't worked, either.

"Calla feels I chose Dennis over her. You see..." Sarah hesitated. "I wasn't legally divorced when I first got involved with him and..." She stopped rather than allow her emotion to take control. After a moment to compose herself, she continued. "I know you and Brandon were separated for a while and I'm so pleased you worked out your problems, but—"

"But," Joanie finished for her, "a reconciliation isn't always possible. I know that better than anyone. I loved Brandon and he loved me. We had a lot of years and three children invested in this relationship. Neither one of us wanted a divorce, but we simply couldn't continue the way we were."

"You see," Sarah whispered, fearing her voice was about to crack, "I loved Willie, too—or the man I thought he was. I was young and stupid, and in the beginning I put up with a lot more than I should have. I guess I was hoping he'd...change.... It seems ridiculous now, but deep down I prayed he'd realize how much he loved Calla and me. Needless to say, that didn't happen. When it became obvious that I didn't have any choice but to leave, I moved home. I should have gone ahead with the divorce then, but I put it off. There were complications with money that made it easy to delay."

"Dennis didn't know?"

Admitting she'd lied to him was a painful thing. "I didn't tell anyone, not even my father. I let everyone assume I was divorced. A few years later—once I started seeing Dennis—I desperately wanted out of the marriage, but by then I was trapped in the lie." She reached for her tea, humiliated to be confessing her sins.

"Is this why Calla's so upset with you?" Joanie asked softly.

Sarah shrugged. "Partly. Willie never bothered to keep in touch with her, and because she wanted a father who loved her and cared about her, she built him up in her mind. He became the perfect father—a complete fantasy.

Later, when she discovered we *weren't* divorced, she felt I'd purposely withheld her father from her.''

"That was why she moved in with him?''

Sarah nodded, putting down her cup. "There was more to her decision to run away. She was furious with me for...being involved with Dennis while still legally married to her father.''

"You can't beat yourself up over that. We all make mistakes. It's part of life, part of the maturing process. Trust me, I've made plenty of mistakes with my own children.''

"I'm sure you can understand why Calla believes I chose Dennis over her.'' It didn't help that they'd announced their engagement without talking to Calla first. Neither of them had intended to slight her, but they'd suffered the consequences ever since.

"None of us are perfect parents,'' Joanie reassured her. "We try, but we're only human.''

"I wish I could get her to look at things differently....''

"Calla's still young. And she's got some issues to resolve. Teenagers don't have much perspective, anyway, but toss in divorce and what she assumes is betrayal, and you end up with the kind of confusion Calla's feeling.''

Sarah didn't know how to react to Calla's contradictory emotions. Her daughter's coming to her, asking for money to give Willie, had hit her hard. Even knowing the kind of man he was, Calla had wanted to rescue him and planned to use Sarah to do it. She was afraid that Calla had given Willie her own meager paycheck. If she had, Sarah would prefer not to know about it. She just couldn't handle that right now.

"Is...is she dating Joe Lammerman?" Sarah hated to ask, but Calla hadn't been exactly forthcoming about the on-again off-again relationship.

"She hasn't seen much of him since the Sweetheart Dance. In fact, I'm fairly confident she's interested in Kevin Betts."

"Kevin?"

"I can't say for sure, but last month she told me they were writing."

"When did that start?"

"Not long ago. I do know the letters have been coming fast and furious lately."

So Calla was corresponding with Kevin. Sarah experienced a sadness that was difficult to define. Having always liked Kevin, she was pleased, but at the same time, she wished Calla had mentioned this to her. She couldn't help wondering when she would. If she ever did.

The Doctors' Clinic had told Matt he should have the results of the blood test within a week. He'd figured they'd either phone him or mail him, but it was almost two weeks now and he hadn't heard. From anyone.

No news was good news, or so he'd always been told, but as the days progressed, his thinking took a decided turn toward reality. No news was no news.

When he couldn't stand the suspense any longer, he invented an excuse about needing something from the hardware store and drove into town. The receptionist at the clinic glanced up as he approached the desk. His heart pounded with dread.

He gave his name, then said, "I'd like to talk to Dr. Kaplan."

The middle-aged woman ran her finger down the appointment schedule. "I'm sorry, but I don't see your name. What time was your appointment?"

"I don't have an appointment," he said with controlled impatience. "All I need is a few minutes of his time."

"But..."

"I don't mean to cause a ruckus, but I *will* talk to Dr. Kaplan."

The woman heaved a deep sigh, and Matt knew she'd gotten his message. "If you'll wait here, I'll see what I can do."

"Thank you." He remained standing at the desk.

A minute later, the receptionist returned. "Please take a seat. He'll be with you as soon as possible."

Kaplan's ASAP turned out to be ninety minutes. Twice Matt was ready to walk straight through the door and corner the physician, but he managed to curb his irritation. He'd waited this long; a few more minutes wasn't going to matter. What surprised him was the number of people coming in and out of the clinic—including several he recognized. Apparently the place was doing a good business.

"Dr. Kaplan will see you now," the receptionist announced.

Matt stared at her and his legs refused to budge. After waiting more than two weeks and ninety minutes, he'd expected to race inside when the opportunity presented itself.

"Mr. Eilers?"

"Yes...thank you." He stood and followed her inside as she led him past the cubicles to the physician's private office.

He was pacing when the harried doctor walked in. ''I understand you have a problem,'' he snapped.

''I was told,'' Matt said, his own voice raised, ''that I'd get the results of my blood test a week ago. I've heard nothing. As you might well understand, I'm anxious to know the verdict.''

''You haven't received notification?'' He flipped open the chart.

''Not a word.''

''Ah.'' Dr. Kaplan glanced up. ''The results were sent to the court. They'll send you notification soon. It's our policy—''

''Tell me.'' Matt wasn't willing to wait until he was contacted by an attorney. He needed to know if he'd fathered Sheryl's baby. He'd come this far and wouldn't retreat now.

''Mr. Eilers—''

''Either you tell me or—''

''All right, all right.''

The physician must have recognized that Matt was frustrated, stressed out and damn near sick with worry.

Sitting down at his desk, Dr. Kaplan pushed up his glasses and read through the report.

''Well?'' Matt demanded in a growl.

''The test is positive. You're the child's father.''

It was as though Matt had suddenly been tackled from behind. His legs simply went out from under him and he slumped into a chair. If there hadn't been a cushioned seat to catch him, he would have fallen to the floor. ''There isn't any chance of a mistake?''

''None.''

The shock was almost immediately replaced with a numbness that quickly spread to his extremities. He'd always thought that if and when he ever learned he was going to be a father it would be a joyous moment. Instead, he felt a sense of impending doom. His life as he knew it was about to change drastically—and not for the better.

He should have realized the happiness he'd found with Margaret wouldn't last. Nothing this good ever did. Dear God, how was he going to tell his wife?

"Mr. Eilers?"

He looked up and noticed that Dr. Kaplan was standing beside him.

"Thank you for letting me know." He managed a hoarse whisper and staggered out of the chair. When he walked outside, the cold air hit his face but he was only distantly aware of it. Sheryl was having his baby.

After leaving the Doctors' Clinic, Matt sat in his truck, hands clenching the steering wheel while he mulled over what to do next. Obviously he had to tell Margaret. His wife wasn't going to take this news well and he couldn't blame her. Briefly he considered hiding the truth from her until he was better able to deal with it. Until *they* were better able, he amended.

The numbness started to dissolve, replaced with an anger that began to build in the pit of his stomach. Sheryl had purposely gotten pregnant. Nothing would convince him otherwise. She was the one who'd suggested he marry Margaret, then obtain a divorce and marry *her*. He cringed every time he thought about that ridiculous scheme. He remembered that when he'd teasingly asked Sheryl why he should leave a wealthy wife to marry her, she'd claimed she had ways of bringing him back.

She had ways, all right. Getting pregnant was the trick she'd held up her sleeve. She planned to use this child as a weapon against him. He clenched his jaw so hard his teeth ached. *A child.*

It became clear to him that he had no choice but to tell Margaret and the sooner the better. If he didn't, Sheryl would take great delight in doing it for him. The woman wanted to make as much trouble for him as she could. What was the old expression about a woman scorned? He had to protect his marriage from Sheryl's fury, and that meant, first and foremost, telling Margaret the truth.

Decision made, he closed his eyes, wondering how he'd ever find the strength to face her with this news. Two minutes later, he was out of the truck and inside 3 OF A KIND. This task required the kind of courage only hard liquor provided.

"What can I do for you?" Buffalo Bob asked as Matt approached the bar.

"Give me a shot of whiskey."

"Ice?"

"No." He needed fortification—the courage weak men found in the bottom of a bottle.

Bob eyed him suspiciously as he set the shot glass down on the counter. "You don't look so good," he commented. "You sure you want this? I've never known you to drink anything but beer."

Matt's response was to reach for the whiskey and toss it down his throat. It burned, and he shook his head in an effort to cut the effect. "Another."

Bob hesitated.

"What's the matter?" Matt demanded. "Isn't my money good enough?"

"It isn't your money I'm worried about."

"Just give me the damn drink." He downed that glass, then shook his head again, coughing violently. He heard his name shouted from outside the restaurant.

"Matthew Eilers, come out here!"

Margaret? He whirled around and found his wife looking straight at him through the large window. One glimpse of the anger and outrage that flashed from her eyes told him he could stop worrying about breaking the truth to her. She already knew.

No sooner had he stepped out the door than she sprang directly in front of him.

"Is it true?" Her anger was fierce, unrelenting. "Is it true?" she screamed again.

"Margaret, perhaps we should talk about this someplace less public." He glanced around, and it seemed everyone in town was watching. A couple of store owners stood in doorways. People crowded nearby, wanting to know what all the noise was about.

"Answer the question, dammit!"

"Is what true?" he repeated, buying time while he could.

The words had barely left his mouth when she grabbed hold of his shirt collar and jerked him toward her. Her face was scant inches from his own.

"You know what I'm talking about, so don't play dumb with me."

Matt closed his eyes and nodded.

"You son of a bitch." She dragged out each word—and then slammed her fist into his belly with enough force to double him over.

Too stunned to react, Matt staggered backward only to have her immediately plow her fist into him a second time. Clutching his middle, Matt fell to his knees and groaned.

He looked up, silently pleading with her to let him explain, but he could see it would do no good. Nothing he had to say now would make a damn bit of difference. He closed his eyes, expecting her to kick him next.

Instead she whirled around and stalked off.

"You okay?" Buffalo Bob asked as Matt rose painfully to his feet.

Not only had Margaret slugged him as hard as a man, she'd humiliated him in front of the entire town.

"You need a place for the night?" Bob asked.

Matt shook his head. He was going after his wife, and they'd talk this out. Sheryl might try to screw up his life, but by God, he wasn't going to let it happen. He loved Margaret and would do everything in his power to save his marriage.

He couldn't have been more than ten minutes behind her, but by the time he pulled into the yard, she'd managed to drag the contents of his closet outside and dump it all on the ground.

Matt parked and advanced cautiously toward her. "Margaret..."

In return she glared at him with such ferocity he swallowed his plea.

"I want you out of here, understand?"

He raised both hands in a pleading gesture. "Can we talk about this?"

"No!"

"All right. I can see you're upset.... Perhaps this isn't the best time for us to—"

"I want you off my land! Now get the hell out."

Matt rubbed his face. He felt as if he'd walked directly into a full-blown nightmare. "Margaret, I know you're angry. I don't blame you, but the least you can do is hear me out."

"The *least* I can do? That's rich." Her laugh was high and hysterical. Next she proceeded to stomp all over his clothes, grinding them into the mud and dirt. "Get out...of my sight...before...I do something I regret."

The tears in her voice damn near broke his heart. Not caring what she did to him, Matt moved toward her, taking her in his arms. As he knew she would, Margaret started to pound at his chest with her fists. He took each hit, not caring about the pain, more concerned with the agony he'd caused her.

Margaret was sobbing now. Matt felt like weeping himself. He tried to hold her, but she wouldn't allow it. She pushed away from him with such vigor that she stumbled backward. He reached out to balance her, but she slapped at his hands.

"I hate you!" she cried vehemently. "I can't believe I could ever have loved you."

"Margaret, please..."

Shaking her head wildly, she burst into sobs and raced toward the house.

Matt hurried after her, not knowing what he'd say or do

if he happened to catch her. He didn't have a chance to find out. Margaret got to the porch first and slammed the door in his face.

Resting his head against the screen, he bent over, balancing his hands on his knees as he exhaled. His head swam, and he was beginning to feel sick to his stomach. Sick enough to step off the porch and heave into the bushes. It wasn't long before he lost what remained of his lunch, plus the whiskey.

Wiping his mouth, he walked over to where Margaret had dumped his clothes. He crouched down to pick up a shirt. The door opened and he glanced up, hoping it was Margaret.

Sadie stood on the porch, hands on her broad hips. "Quite the mess you've gotten yourself into."

He straightened. "Is Margaret okay?"

"No, but there's nothing you can do now."

Even with all the evidence to the contrary, he had to say it. "Despite what she thinks or what anyone says, I love her."

"You have a fine way of showing it."

"I never touched another woman after we were married." Sheryl had tried to tempt him, had kissed him, but he'd wanted nothing to do with her. He'd always known what a conniving bitch she was. Why had he ever gotten involved? What an idiot! He kicked at his clothes, disgusted with himself.

Sadie snickered.

"Go ahead and say it," he yelled. "You never approved of me. The old man didn't either."

"You don't deserve her."

Matt hauled what clothes he could to the bed of his pickup, throwing them inside.

"You running?" Sadie taunted.

"No. Like I said, I love my wife and by God, I'm going to fight to save this marriage."

"So you're leaving?"

"She kicked me out."

"There's always the bunkhouse."

Matt hadn't thought of that and appreciated the suggestion. He nodded. "Thanks."

"You've accomplished quite a feat, Matt Eilers," the housekeeper commented as he grabbed another bundle of mud-caked clothes.

Frowning, he looked in her direction. "What makes you say that?"

"You've managed to get two women pregnant at the same time."

Because his head was reeling and his heart was aching, it took him a moment to understand. Shock raced through him. "Margaret's pregnant?"

"Two women at once. You must be real proud of yourself." With that, she returned to the house.

Matt heard her turn the bolt, locking him out.

Curled up tightly in the middle of the bed, Margaret wrapped her arms around her middle and stared at the wall. Sleep was out of the question. Every time she thought about the letter that had arrived in the mail—a letter addressed to them both—the pain started all over again. Sheryl hadn't missed a trick. She was after Matt—and Margaret's money.

After spending several minutes sorting through the legal jargon, she'd realized it was a paternity suit against Matt. Not only was Sheryl Decker looking for child support, she sought income to cover her expenses during the pregnancy, plus all medical costs. Seeing that Matt had married a wealthy woman, the amount Sheryl's attorney requested was a substantial sum.

Margaret wasn't stupid. She tallied up the numbers and figured out that she and Matt weren't married yet when he'd slept with Sheryl. But that didn't make the pain any less. He'd fooled around before the wedding, and she couldn't trust that the affair hadn't continued afterward. He'd lied to her! Hadn't he claimed that he'd never slept with Sheryl?

Margaret felt like an idiot. How she'd loved him, wanted him. All the years she'd wasted pining for him. She'd been willing to do *anything* to get Matt to notice her. All the work and effort she'd put into changing her appearance had been for him. Why? So he could devastate her? Betray her trust? He'd humiliated her, publicly humiliated her! Margaret didn't know how she'd show her face in town again.

Dear heaven, she had no idea what to do.

The tears came in earnest then. Margaret hated that she couldn't make herself stop crying. Hated the way her nose ran and her eyes hurt and her shoulders shook. All her emotions were out of kilter. Because of the pregnancy, no doubt. She blamed Matt for that, too, taking risks with birth control. He'd gotten her pregnant—her *and* his lover.

Closing her eyes, she forced herself to try to sleep, but only managed to doze fitfully.

"Margaret." Sadie's voice gently woke her.

Her eyes flew open. Sunlight poured into the room. Her mouth felt dry and her eyes ached. Propping herself on one elbow, Margaret looked around. "What time is it?" she demanded.

"Long past the time you normally rise."

Throwing off the covers, she reached for her jeans, but stopped when the room started to sway. She fell back onto the bed.

"Don't hurry. Everything's under control."

"What about the men?" This was calving season; she had responsibilities.

"Matt's with them."

At the sound of his name, Margaret clenched her fists and vaulted upright. "What's he doing here? I told him to get the hell off my land!"

"He's your husband," Sadie stated calmly.

"Thanks for reminding me."

The housekeeper smiled sardonically. "You're welcome."

With her head swimming and her stomach heaving, Margaret grabbed the bedpost and hung on, certain she was about to be ill. It took a determined effort to breathe normally.

"I'd like you to make an appointment for me with the best divorce attorney you know," she said.

Sadie calmly shook her head. "I'm your housekeeper, not your secretary."

"Fine, I'll do it myself." She'd assumed Sadie would be only too happy to comply.

"You're the one who married him."

"Go ahead, rub it in. I was stupid, but believe me, this isn't a mistake I plan to repeat." She'd already made one colossal error in judgment and she'd pay for it the rest of her life. She'd learned her lesson. Love wasn't what it was cracked up to be. It was like a wild animal that you thought you'd tamed—you could never completely trust it.

"What about the child?" Sadie asked, focusing her gaze on Margaret's abdomen. "That's his child, too."

"Are you sticking up for him?" Margaret cried. Not only had her husband lied to her, now her staff had taken his side.

Sadie grimaced. "Matt Eilers is a bastard and he deserves to be shot."

"Let me be the first one to volunteer," Margaret said, and she'd let Sadie guess exactly where she intended to aim the gun.

"You married him."

If Sadie reminded her of that one more time, Margaret thought she'd scream. "It was a mistake!"

"Yes," the housekeeper agreed, "but not nearly as big a mistake as divorcing him would be."

"How can you say that?" Margaret asked. The one person she'd counted on was Sadie. They weren't close, but the housekeeper had known her longer than anyone. This betrayal cut her to the bone; surely Sadie could see that. She needed comfort and sympathy, not judgmental comments and bad advice.

"Right or wrong, you married him, and you loved him. The child you carry is his. The baby deserves a father."

"Tell Sheryl that."

"That's something I'll leave up to you and Matt," Sadie said gravely. "That's for you to work out."

Thirteen

Matt thought he'd lose his mind if he spent another night sitting in the bunkhouse staring at the wall. It was April now, and Margaret hadn't said a word to him in two weeks. Correction. She'd said several words he didn't care to repeat. Every effort he'd made toward reconciliation had been rebuffed.

He'd realized early on that his wife wouldn't react well to the news of Sheryl's pregnancy, but he'd had no idea that the line between love and hate could be so thin. Margaret passionately hated him. He felt it in her contemptuous stare every time he met her eyes. She wanted him off her ranch, and after two weeks of constant rejection, he was at his wits' end. Perhaps it would be best if he did leave. Margaret had made her intentions clear: His life would be hell as long as he stayed there. She'd personally see to it.

His friends were few, and not knowing where else to turn, Matt headed into Buffalo Valley. He didn't have any place to go, so he went to 3 OF A KIND. The music was blaring and Buffalo Bob had cranked up the karaoke machine.

Some cowhand belted out an off-key version of a Jim Reeves hit. Matt didn't know him, and didn't plan to seek out any company. He took a table in the back of the room, letting it be known that he was there for the booze and not for local chitchat. It wasn't long before Merrily approached.

"How you doing?" she asked, friendly as ever.

His reply was a forced smile. "I could use a beer."

"Coming right up."

Sitting in the shadows, Matt nursed three drinks, one right after the other, but they didn't make him feel any better. If anything, he was more miserable now than he'd been when he arrived. Margaret wasn't his only worry; already Sheryl and her attorney were determined to bleed him dry. She was after child support, money for her medical bills and living expenses. It wouldn't stop there, either. He knew damn well this was only the beginning. She was going to exploit this situation for every dime she could get, just like she had in those lawsuits she'd filed in the past. And if she didn't get any money out of Margaret, she'd try for whatever she could get out of him. It was all about money for Sheryl. She didn't give a damn about the kid.

It must be near closing time. The bar was mostly deserted and Bob was counting out the till. Matt should be clearing his own tab and moving on, but the thought of returning to the ranch held little appeal.

Trapped in his own murky thoughts, Matt didn't notice Bob walking over to his table.

"I'll settle up with you now," Matt said, reaching for his wallet.

"Anytime is fine. I'm in no hurry," Bob said, and surprised him by pulling out a chair and taking a seat. "Seems you got something on your mind."

Matt didn't respond. He hadn't meant to be this obvious—but what did he expect after half the town had seen

Margaret beat the hell out of him in the middle of Main Street?

"Trouble at home?"

Matt stiffened. "That's my business."

"I don't mean to pry," Bob continued, sounding apologetic. "Nor am I about to offer you advice—"

"Good," Matt said, cutting him off.

"But," Bob went on, unfazed, "I don't think it's a good idea for you to be driving."

"I only had three beers."

"It's not the alcohol I'm worried about, it's your state of mind. You look about as low as a man can get. Merrily thinks it'd be best if you spent the night, and I agree. We have a room for you—on the house. In the morning, if you feel like talking—"

"I already said—"

"You don't have to discuss your troubles with me," Bob said, holding up both hands. "But if you *want* to talk, I'm here, and there are others, too."

Matt frowned. "Who?"

"Hassie for one. She won't judge you. And the new pastor. He's been a real help to Merrily and me." Bob looked down at the floor. "You might've heard our boy was taken away from us."

Matt had heard about it, but not the details.

"We were both pretty upset, as you can imagine."

"That was when you broke your hand?"

Bob smiled briefly. "Put it through the wall. I was feeling worse than I've ever felt. I'm embarrassed to admit it now, but for a while there, I wondered if life was worth living."

"I can't see myself talking this out with a pharmacist."
He didn't want to hear what a preacher would have to say,
either. Especially when it wasn't four months ago that John
Dawson had officiated at his wedding. Just married, two
women pregnant—there had to be an entire section of hell
ready and waiting for the likes of him.

"Just think about it," Bob advised. "It might help."

"Thanks for the suggestion."

"I don't know what I would've done without my friends
during that time. They got me through some rough days
when I didn't care what the hell happened to me anymore."

With Bob's words echoing in his mind, Matt took the
room key and wandered up the stairs. Normally he wasn't
one to accept charity, but even in his pain he recognized
that Bob offered friendship and understanding, not pity.

The phone on the nightstand seemed to taunt him. He
would have given anything to call Margaret. Anything simply to talk to her and share bits and pieces of their day,
the way they had for those few months. She represented
everything that had ever been good in his life. He was
weak, but her love made him strong. Without her, he was
nothing and never would be.

Sitting on the edge of the bed, Matt buried his face in
his hands. Margaret was having his baby and this should
be the happiest moment of his life, but whatever glimmers
of joy he experienced were tainted by Sheryl. Dear God,
could he have screwed up any worse?

Things didn't look much better in the morning. Matt
thanked Bob and Merrily, left the room key on the counter
and headed toward his truck. Part of him wanted to escape.

Change his name, move to a different town, start all over again. The thought was tempting, but he knew running was a coward's trick. Besides, it wouldn't solve a damn thing.

On his way out of town, he drove past the old church, same as he always did, went a block farther, then abruptly stepped on the brake. He skidded to a stop.

That he'd even consider talking to the minister was evidence of how deep his troubles went. Just as fast as he'd braked, he put the truck in Reverse and turned around. He parked outside the church, suddenly besieged by second thoughts. He sat in his vehicle while he weighed the idea of spilling his guts to a man he figured would likely condemn him—despite Buffalo Bob's claim to the contrary.

He might have changed his mind and driven on if Pastor Dawson hadn't walked out of the church that very moment. Figuring he had nothing to lose, Matt climbed from his truck.

"Pastor Dawson?" he called.

John Dawson turned around. "Good to see you, Matt," he said warmly. "What can I do for you?"

"Do you have a few minutes?" he asked.

"Of course. Come inside. I'll ask Joyce to bring us some coffee."

Like a schoolboy headed into the principal's office, Matt followed the minister. A few minutes later, he was sitting in a comfortable chair, a mug of hot coffee in his hand.

To his relief, the pastor didn't drill him with questions. Matt needed a few minutes of silence and false starts to dredge up the courage to tell him about Sheryl. He was sick at heart by the time he finished.

"Go on, say it," Matt murmured.

''That you're a fool?'' John Dawson asked, then surprised him by laughing. ''Why would I call you a fool when you've already done that half a dozen times yourself?''

''I don't know what to do,'' Matt confessed, leaning forward and bracing his elbows on his knees. ''Margaret isn't speaking to me...hell, I don't blame her. I try to think how I'd react if I learned she was pregnant with another man's child.'' He closed his eyes, unable to bear the thought. Yet that was the very thing he'd done to her. The relationship with Sheryl had taken place before he married Margaret, but somehow that didn't make it hurt any less—especially since his dishonesty had left her feeling so betrayed.

''First thing you need to do is get yourself an attorney,'' Pastor Dawson said with the authority of a man who'd advised countless others. ''You have legal rights, too. I suspect you're correct in guessing that Sheryl did intentionally plan the pregnancy. From everything you've said, it looks like she'll try to use the child as a means of controlling you. As much as possible, don't let it happen.''

Matt nodded. That had been his own thought, but he'd felt too helpless and confused to think clearly. An attorney was necessary and he wondered why he hadn't considered hiring one sooner.

''Another thing. Don't let Sheryl drive a wedge between you and Margaret. If you're thinking about moving out, don't.''

''I am,'' Matt confessed. ''Every time Margaret deigns to speak to me, she lets it be known that she wants me out of her life.'' For the first time in days he managed a small if genuine smile. "My wife has her own way of expressing her wishes."

John Dawson's look grew intense. "If you love her the way you claim, then it's time you proved it."

"I'd do anything to make this right with Margaret," Matt told him, feeling the first signs of optimism since he'd learned about Sheryl's baby.

"Be patient," the minister continued. "Do what you can to make amends. But remember, it isn't going to be easy. Show her how committed you are. If you love her, though, stick it out."

"I do love her.... I'm not giving up on our marriage," Matt said. He stood and offered the pastor his hand. "Thank you." John Dawson had been refreshingly non-judgmental, kind and helpful. He'd told Matt what he needed to hear, given him a plan of action and promised to pray for him.

Leaving the minister's, Matt drove into Grand Forks, met with an attorney he chose from the Yellow Pages and began to feel some hope. He arrived back at the ranch just as Margaret was leaving the barn. He paused when he saw her, wondering if he should say anything.

Scowling at him, she removed her gloves. "I thought I was finished with you once and for all."

"I spent the night in town. Had some thinking to do."

She snickered as though she didn't believe him.

Matt followed her to the house and stopped on the front step. "I thought you should know I saw an attorney this afternoon."

"Good. When's the divorce final?" She looked straight through him, her face emotionless.

"It wasn't a divorce attorney."

"More's the pity." She started inside.

"Margaret, for the love of God, would you listen to me?"

She hesitated, her back to him. "I have the distinct impression I'm not going to like what you have to say."

"What will it take to make this right with you?" he shouted.

"Take?" she shouted back, finally confronting him. "You think you can buy your way out of this? Do you think I can pretend this never happened? Do you seriously believe I can put it out of my mind? Haven't you figured it out yet? *Nothing* you say or do could possibly make this right with me."

"Look, I realize it isn't an easy situation. I'd give anything to have spared you this, but it happened and I can't deny it. Keep in mind that I wasn't married to you at the time, and once we got married I didn't see Sheryl again. Still, we're both going to have to deal with this pregnancy. I'm sorry. Sorrier than you know."

Slowly, thoughtfully, she shook her head, dismissing everything he'd said. "What about *my* pregnancy, Matt? What about *my* baby? This should be a happy time for us…. But all I can think about is that another woman's having your baby, another woman is giving you a child first." Tears shone in her eyes and she seemed about to say something else. Instead, she stormed into the house and slammed the door.

More than ever, Matt had the feeling he was going to need the prayers Pastor Dawson had promised.

*   *   *

Dennis Urlacher and Jeb McKenna had been friends most of their lives. When he wanted to talk about Sarah's pregnancy, Dennis figured the one person who'd understand his fears would be her brother.

Driving out to the bison ranch for a fuel delivery, Dennis couldn't stop worrying about his wife and child. Sarah's pregnancy had been difficult from the start. They'd feared with the first spotting that she'd miscarry. The trauma of those few weeks had taken an emotional toll on them both. When Sarah became bedridden, it'd been a hardship in more ways than one.

In the last months, the pregnancy had taken a turn for the better and Sarah was allowed to get around to a limited degree. After a huge number of expensive tests, it was determined that the baby was developing normally. For Dennis, relief alternated with panic about what *could* still happen. He desperately wanted this child; he'd waited a long time for a family and he deeply loved Sarah.

Knowing he was due to deliver fuel that afternoon, Jeb was waiting for him when he arrived. Dennis wasn't usually one to chat. Jeb knew and understood that. Perhaps it was one reason they'd remained such good friends—they didn't need a lot of conversation to be content.

Marriage had changed Jeb. After the farming accident that cost him his leg, he'd become something of a recluse. But in the months since he'd married Maddy, Dennis had seen the old Jeb, with his subtle sense of humor and gruff charm, reemerge. There was a brightness in his eyes again, a sense of life that had virtually disappeared. A laugh that came more easily now and a pride that shone every time Jeb mentioned Maddy or their daughter.

Dennis parked his gasoline truck close to the tank he was scheduled to refill. Jeb didn't run much farm equipment anymore; as much as anything, filling the tank was an excuse for them to visit. Dennis noticed that men needed excuses to get together. Not so with women. They seemed to throw a party for every reason imaginable.

"About time you got here," Jeb said by way of greeting.

Dennis grinned as he pulled out the nozzle and went about his business. "You talk to Sarah lately?" he asked casually a couple of minutes later.

"Last week."

"How'd she sound to you?"

Jeb shrugged and his brows came together in a frown. "Same as always. Is everything all right?"

Dennis wished he knew. "I think she's doing too much. She won't slow down. The doctor said she should use her judgment, but...I'm worried. I've tried to convince her to let me do more around the house—she won't hear of it."

"How's the pregnancy going?"

"Supposedly everything's as it should be. But..." Dennis sighed. His fears were rampant. He didn't go to sleep without worrying about Sarah and the baby. He feared the unknown, feared some unexpected complication that would cost him either the life of his child or that of his wife. Perhaps both. There were nights he'd lie awake for hours, consumed by dread.

Dennis wasn't the kind of man who could bear the grief of losing a wife or child. He wasn't the kind of man who could ever get over it, whose personality would remain intact.

"You want me to talk to her?" Jeb asked.

"I want you to tell me everything's going to be all right with her and the baby," Dennis snapped. He ran his hand over his face and glanced apologetically at his friend. "Sorry."

Jeb slapped him on the shoulder and waited until Dennis had finished with the pump. He sat on the fuel truck's bumper, where Dennis joined him.

"I worried about Maddy, too," Jeb said quietly.

"She had complications?"

"No," Jeb admitted, "but that didn't keep me from worrying. When I learned she'd gone into labor and refused to leave for the hospital without me, I nearly lost it. Luckily everything turned out all right. I told her never again, but she's already after me to have another baby."

"So soon?"

"She was an only child and she wants to be sure Julianne has siblings." Jeb stood, paced two or three steps, then turned around. "The problem is, Maddy knows there's damn little I can refuse her, so give or take a few months I figure she'll be pregnant with our second baby."

Dennis chuckled.

"What's so damn funny?"

"You. I never would've believed a woman would get to you like this."

"Maddy isn't just a woman. She's...Maddy."

Dennis nodded, understanding far better than he let on. He felt the same about Sarah. He was crazy in love with her. Nothing could change that.

An advancing car sounded in the background, and Jeb peered around the fuel truck. "That's Calla."

A heaviness settled over Dennis's heart. "Did you know she was coming?"

"She called earlier and mentioned stopping by this afternoon sometime."

Dennis stood. "You might have said something."

Jeb frowned. "Why? She's your stepdaughter."

"True enough, but we don't get along, never have. I don't know what I did that was so horrible—other than love her mother." He shrugged helplessly. "She seems to think we're in competition."

Calla parked her grandfather's truck and climbed down. Dennis noticed her hesitation when she saw him, as though she wasn't pleased to be running into him, either.

"What's he doing here?" she demanded of Jeb.

"I have a name, Calla," Dennis said mildly.

She glared at him. "Whatever."

"No, it's Dennis, and like it or not, I'm your stepfather."

She sighed, signalling that she was bored with the subject. "Whatever," she said again, infuriating him with her rudeness.

"Dennis is here delivering fuel," Jeb said, coming to stand between them, obviously accepting the role of peacemaker or at least buffer. "He's also my friend, and I expect you to treat him with courtesy."

Calla ignored him. "Is Maddy around?"

Jeb walked toward her. "She's visiting Margaret Eilers. She shouldn't be long. You can wait if you want."

Looking disappointed, Calla headed for the house, then apparently changed her mind. With her hand on the railing she scowled at Dennis. "I hope you're happy."

"Thrilled," he snapped back, although he had no idea what she was talking about. Not that *she* needed any excuse to start an argument.

"You finished up here?" Jeb asked, clearly wanting to usher Dennis on his way and thereby avoid a confrontation.

"Yeah," he muttered.

"Oh, Dennis is *more* than finished," Calla sneered.

Dennis shook his head. "What the hell is your problem?" he asked angrily. "Where do you get off talking to me like that?"

"I don't think right now is the time for this," Jeb muttered, glancing anxiously from one to the other.

Dennis knew Jeb was uncomfortable, but he'd had it with Calla. Had it with her gibes and her attitude. Had it with her altogether. If she wanted to be miserable, then fine, but leave him and Sarah out of her sick little world.

"If anything happens to my mother, you'll pay."

"You think I'd hurt *Sarah?*" he yelled. "Are you insane?"

"You got her pregnant, didn't you? She told me how much you wanted a family. Well, I hope you're happy when you have your precious son. If the pregnancy kills my mother, why should *you* care?"

Dennis saw red and would have started for her if Jeb hadn't spoken. "Don't be ridiculous, Calla," he said sharply.

"Why don't you go back and live with your father?" Dennis suggested. The months Calla had lived in Minneapolis had given him the only peace he'd had in years.

"Dennis!" Jeb looked at him as if stunned.

Calla went pale.

Knowing what had happened at Willie's, Dennis regretted the outburst. If not for his uncontrolled fear and his lack of sleep, he would never have said something so immature, something so worthy of Calla herself.

"I think it's time you both cooled your tempers," Jeb said, not hiding his distress at the exchange between them.

Dennis agreed. He needed to remember who was the adult here. "That last comment was uncalled for," he muttered. "I apologize."

"You're an ugly, cruel man, Dennis Urlacher," Calla shouted after him as he walked toward his truck.

"You might take a look in the mirror yourself," he shouted back, then leaped inside his cab and gunned the engine.

Margaret could no longer avoid a trip into town. She had an appointment in Grand Forks with the gynecologist, where she discovered her weight was down five pounds. Dr. Leggatt wasn't pleased with her, but seemed to sense that her weight loss had little to do with the pregnancy and everything to do with her state of mind. She left after the brief examination.

In no rush to return to the ranch, she went to Hassie's for a soda first. No one, other than Maddy, knew she was pregnant. However, she couldn't help wondering how many people in Buffalo Valley knew about Matt and Sheryl.

She hadn't told anyone. Couldn't. It was too mortifying, too humiliating. Married less than five months, and already she was sure she'd made a terrible mistake. Matt claimed his affair with Sheryl had taken place before the wedding.

That was supposed to make her feel better? Well, it didn't. He should have told her!

Maybe she was being unfair, but she couldn't help how she felt. He was right about one thing: they'd eventually have to deal with this, but just now Margaret was too caught up in her own disappointment, her doubts and fears. She hated the things she'd said to him yet she couldn't seem to stop herself from saying them, from thinking them.

Hassie greeted Margaret as warmly as always. "You look like you could use one of my sodas," the older woman said.

"That's why I'm here." Margaret slipped onto the stool and glanced out the window. People had begun to gather outside 3 OF A KIND. "What's going on at Buffalo Bob's?" she asked. She hadn't seen that big a crowd since the night of Bob and Merrily's wedding.

"You didn't hear?" Hassie asked, adding soda to chocolate ice cream.

"They're getting Axel back?" It seemed a shame that the boy had been taken away from them, and she sincerely hoped the court had seen fit to return him.

"Bob and Merrily are going through the adoption process, the same as anyone else. The state of California sent someone out to interview them and see the home." Hassie set the soda on the counter. "The social worker's there now. Been with them an hour or so."

"Why's the crowd milling around outside?" That seemed odd to Margaret.

"Moral support. People in Buffalo Valley have taken a real liking to Bob and Merrily. I remember the first time I met him. He called Buffalo Valley a dead-end kind of town. It made me mad, but you know, at the time he was right.''

"It wasn't dead-end enough to stop him from taking over the bar and grill, though, was it?''

"That's what's so humorous. He was thrilled, claimed he'd do whatever he could to help save the town, and by golly, he stuck to his word.''

"Are they going to be able to adopt Axel?''

Hassie thought that over for a moment. ''If there's such a thing as fairness in this world, then Axel will come back here, where he belongs.''

For the sake of the couple, Margaret hoped Hassie was right. Unfortunately her current mood was anything but optimistic. Tears blurred her vision, and she brushed them aside. She didn't know if her mixed-up emotions were due to her pregnancy or to her good-for-nothing husband. These days, she didn't need an excuse to cry; her tears were so near the surface. A sentimental television commercial could reduce her to a puddle of emotion in seconds.

"I wish them well,'' Margaret whispered as she sipped.

Hassie stared at her, eyes narrowing. ''Margaret Clemens Eilers, are you crying?''

Margaret's bottom lip started to tremble. She opened her mouth, ready to deny it, but decided that was useless. ''I'm pregnant.''

Hassie's face lit up with delight. ''Margaret, that's wonderful!''

"That's a matter of opinion,'' she muttered.

Hassie frowned in surprise. ''You don't want this baby?''

Somehow the question had never entered her mind. When she'd first suspected she was pregnant, she'd hidden the news from Matt, wanting the pregnancy confirmed before she told him. Every time she thought about the baby, she felt a happiness she'd never experienced before. And yet there was something missing, something crucial. She couldn't share this pregnancy with her husband. Matt and his girlfriend had robbed her of that joy.

"I want my baby," Margaret whispered, her voice faltering. Embarrassed by the tears, she used the back of her hand to dash them from her face. Eager to leave, she reached inside her pocket for cash.

"It's on the house," Hassie told her.

Any other time, Margaret would have insisted on paying. She regretted the stop in town now and knew she was only postponing the inevitable. Matt would be waiting for her when she returned to the ranch. Despite Margaret's instructions, Sadie was giving him information; she was convinced of it. He seemed to know she was going to the doctor's when she left and had asked her to give him an update on the pregnancy when she got home.

Sure enough, he met her when she climbed out of the truck.

"What did the doctor have to say?" he wanted to know.

She noticed the shadows beneath his eyes. So he wasn't sleeping well. Good. She wasn't, either.

"I'm fine. The baby's fine. Kindly leave me alone." She pushed past him and made her way toward the house.

"I'm wondering if you remember what you said the day we were married?" he called out after her.

"What I said?"

"Our wedding vows," he reminded her in clipped tones. "You promised to love me for better or for worse. Okay, so the worse part is here. Are you going to stand with me, Margaret?" His eyes pleaded for understanding and forgiveness.

The irony of his quoting their wedding vows was almost more than she could take. "I can't believe you'd have the audacity to mention our vows."

"I never broke them," he said, "not once."

Unable to stop herself, she snorted. "You never *meant* them! You want to quote vows at me, then include *love* and *honor*. Are you trying to convince me that you feel *anything* for me? You're only interested in my cattle and my land. I'm just a means to an end—that's all I ever was and that's all I am now. Admit it, Matt, if not to me, then to yourself."

"You're wrong, Margaret!"

Sadly she shook her head. "Are you now claiming you *did* love me? You expect me to believe you would've married me if I didn't have a dime to my name?"

He lowered his gaze. She had him there and he knew it.

"It didn't hurt that you inherited the ranch. I won't lie about that, but it wasn't the only reason." He hesitated and swallowed convulsively. "You were the first person who ever believed in me. I told you that before, and it's the truth. You had faith in me. I've never had anyone stick up for me the way you did. Never had anyone look past my faults and love me despite them. Not like you—not with such sweetness…such innocence."

"In other words, I was a naive idiot."

"I never meant to hurt you. If I could go back and change any of this I would."

Margaret couldn't look at him and not feel the urge to forgive—but she refused to do that. He'd hurt her too deeply. "You can't change the past."

He gripped his hat with both hands and boldly held her eyes. "You got what you wanted."

She frowned in confusion. "I wanted this kind of pain? I wanted this agony? Never in my life have I hurt more! It wasn't this bad when my father died, and now you're telling me it's what I *want?* You're crazy!"

"You wanted me, remember?"

Unfortunately she did remember, all too well.

"I'm no prize. You knew that when you married me."

"All I want..." she sobbed "...is for all this pain to go away."

"If I could make that happen, I would. But I can't." He moved toward her, then stopped when she tensed. "I've talked to Sheryl and her attorney. The baby's due the end of June and she'll be my responsibility."

"It's a girl?"

He nodded.

"You've spoken to Sheryl?" She couldn't keep the dejection out of her voice.

"It was while I was in the attorney's office, and it wasn't a friendly conversation. Mostly I let him do the talking...."

She swallowed the huge lump that filled her throat.

"You're right, I didn't love you when we married. I'm guilty of that crime, but I didn't marry you just for the ranch. I needed someone to believe in me, and even if it was only for these five months, all I can do is thank you.

I've learned to love you, Margaret. Heart and soul, I love you.''

She could feel herself being drawn toward him, being lured back into his arms. Despite her own intentions, she was affected by his sincerity. ''You love me,'' she repeated doubtfully. ''That's mighty convenient, isn't it?''

''Assume what you want, but it's the truth.''

Margaret needed to think, needed to sort through the pain and all the confused emotions. It was too easy to allow herself to be swayed.

Pressing her hands to the sides of her head, she closed her eyes. ''I can't think now.''

''Take all the time you need. I'm not going anywhere. When you're ready to talk, I'll be here.''

That was fair, and necessary. She nodded, turned her back on him and walked inside.

Fourteen

Sarah couldn't sit still. She paced the living room and glanced at the clock every other minute, waiting for Dennis to come home. She would have driven down to the service station and confronted him, but it was his day to make fuel deliveries. Briefly she considered waiting for him there. However, when she was this angry, she preferred to discuss the matter in private.

An hour later, the door off the kitchen swung open and Dennis came in, still wearing his grease-smeared coveralls. From the way he dragged his feet, she knew he'd had a long, hard day, but that didn't stop her. She had to know.

"Did you and Calla have an argument last week?" she demanded.

Dennis snapped his head back, as though her sharp words had caught him by surprise.

"Did you have it out with my daughter?" she asked again, with the same outraged intensity. The anger had been festering inside her since morning and wouldn't easily be quelled. Not until she'd heard from her own husband exactly what had happened.

Not responding, Dennis walked into the bathroom and proceeded to climb out of his coveralls.

"Don't pretend you don't know what I'm talking about," she cried, refusing to be ignored.

"I'm not." He turned on the shower and started to undress.

"Answer me, will you?" After waiting all afternoon to talk to him, she wasn't willing to be put off.

"We'll talk about this when I've had a chance to unwind." With that, he eased her out of the bathroom and shut the door.

Standing in the hallway, her arms crossed defiantly, Sarah blinked. He'd actually removed her from the room, then calmly closed the door in her face.

Not knowing what else to do, she returned to the kitchen and chopped green peppers and tomatoes for the dinner salad. By the time she'd finished, the vegetables looked pureed.

Ten minutes later, Dennis entered the kitchen, his hair damp from the shower. He wore a clean pair of jeans and a short-sleeved shirt, suitable for the unseasonably warm May weather.

"Are you ready to talk now?" she asked, doing her best to hold back her irritation.

"In a minute." He got himself a beer from the fridge, poured it into a glass. Then he sat down at the table. "All right," he finally said with a beleaguered sigh, "what do you want to know?"

"Did you or did you not have words with Calla?" She was incredulous that it'd taken nearly a week for news of the confrontation to get back to her.

Dennis nodded.

"You didn't say anything about it to me," she accused him, furious that he'd hidden this from her.

"I couldn't see the point. I knew it would upset you, and—"

"You're damn right I'm upset! I can't *believe* you'd do something like this." In all the years of their relationship, Sarah had never known Dennis to lose his temper. She couldn't imagine what had happened, what Calla had said or done that would evoke such a reaction from her husband. And she worried that this might further damage her own fractured relationship with her daughter.

"Did Calla tell you?" Dennis asked, his eyes narrowing.

"No!" Calla rarely shared anything with her, and dammit, that hurt. Now Dennis was excluding her, too, and that hurt even more.

"Jeb?"

"No, Maddy happened to mention it. But she didn't do it maliciously." Her sister-in-law didn't have an unkind bone in her body. The conversation had occurred earlier in the day, when Maddy had driven into town on some business concerning the grocery. She'd stopped at the quilt shop to say hello and innocently asked about Calla. Reading between the lines, Sarah soon understood that her daughter had visited the ranch the week before and been upset and shaken by a confrontation with Dennis. Apparently Calla had talked to Maddy about it at length.

"I suppose you want to hear my version?" Dennis asked in a tired voice.

"Of course I do!" Since Calla's return from Minneapolis, Sarah had slowly but surely been rebuilding their relationship, taking one small step at a time. In the space of a few minutes, her husband had ruined months of effort.

"She insulted me, and—"

"What did she say?" Sarah broke in, not allowing him to finish.

Dennis cupped the glass with both hands. "For starters, she asked Jeb what I was doing at the ranch."

Still pacing, arms folded, Sarah frowned, sure she'd misunderstood. "That was an insult?"

"I was standing right there. The least she could have done was address the question to me."

Sarah felt sick.

"Sit down, Sarah," he urged, pulling out a chair. "All this anger can't be good for the baby."

"Let me worry about the baby."

"It's my baby, too!" He took a deep breath. "Look, Sarah, I've stayed out of the situation with Calla because that's what you wanted. You insist on handling everything yourself, carrying the full load. I'm your husband—"

"Then start acting like one," she cried. She saw the hurt in his eyes, but ignored it. "Don't you realize how hard I've tried with Calla? Everything is so tentative with her.... Your little outburst might have destroyed everything I've worked so hard to build."

"Then so be it," Dennis shouted, shocking her by banging his fist on the table.

She leapt at the unexpected noise. "What's gotten into you?"

"Calla. You. Everything. I've stood silently by, put up with her bad moods and insults for years. I'm not having a teenager talk to me like I'm scum, nor will I allow her to insult my wife."

"She's my daughter—"

"I'm your husband."

"Don't you see—"

"All I see," Dennis said, rising to his feet, "is the two of us walking on eggshells in an effort to appease her. I'm fed up with it, fed up with watching what she does to you—the way you feel whenever she rejects you."

"I was the one who lied to her...I should have told her..."

"You were protecting her just like you are now. She doesn't need your protection anymore. Furthermore, she doesn't want it. She was seventeen last month and it's time she grew up. Time she accepted responsibility for her own life instead of blaming everyone else."

"But—"

"You're allowing the guilt you feel about your first marriage to affect our lives. I won't stand for it any longer."

Trembling, Sarah sank into the chair. "I can't believe you're saying these things. Don't you realize... Don't you understand?"

"I understand that you've placed me in an impossible position. If Calla can't treat me with the respect due another human being, then she's no longer welcome in my home."

"This is my home, too."

Dennis sadly shook his head. "I've told you the way I feel. How you respond is up to you, but if Calla's ever here when I come home, I guess that'll be my answer, won't it?"

"She's my *daughter*..." Sarah didn't know why it was so important to keep reminding him of that, especially when the girl had chosen to live elsewhere. Calla had repeatedly turned her back on Sarah. The situation just never seemed to get better, despite all her efforts, and now it was creating tension in her marriage.

Dennis reached for his beer, raised it to his lips, then put it down. ''I need to think,'' he said. ''I'm going out for a while.''

''You're leaving?''

He was already halfway out the door. ''Yeah,'' he said, ''I'm leaving.''

Sarah watched him go, then buried her face in her hands. The entire conversation had gone badly. She'd been angry and frustrated and she'd taken everything out on Dennis.

Sarah felt sick again, both emotionally and physically. She was trapped between the two people she loved most in this world. Calla had been rude and spiteful to Dennis all along, going out of her way to cause problems.

If that was her goal, then she'd succeeded.

Sarah acknowledged that her daughter had inflicted numerous cruelties on Dennis and that Dennis had never let her goad him into overt anger. Maybe it *was* time for some decisive action. Maybe Sarah had to stand up for her husband and say no to Calla.

Dennis didn't return for dinner. Because of the baby, Sarah forced herself to eat, but she could only stomach a few small bites. At ten, she turned out the lights and went to bed. After years of sleeping alone, she was surprised to discover that a bed could feel so empty.

Sleep was impossible. Shortly after midnight, when she heard the front door open and the floor creak, she tossed aside the covers and hurried into the dark living room.

''Dennis?''

"I'm here." He switched on a table lamp, casting the room in a muted glow.

She flew into his arms, hugging him. "I'm so sorry," she wept, "so sorry."

He nuzzled her neck, his hands in her hair. "I'm sorry, too. I'll try to be more patient with Calla." He breathed the words, as though it'd taken great effort to speak them.

"No—you're right. We can't let Calla behave this way. I won't let her come between us."

Dennis held her face tenderly between his hands and kissed her. "I love you, Sarah Urlacher."

"I love you, too," she said, and slid her arm around his waist. She led him toward the bedroom, knowing she'd be able to sleep now that she'd made peace with her husband.

"I'm supposed to do *what?*" Jeb demanded of Maddy as they drove into Buffalo Valley.

"We're having a meeting about the town park," Maddy reminded him patiently, although he was well aware of the purpose of this venture into town. "I told you about it last week, remember?" And the week before, as well. She'd quickly learned that her husband conveniently forgot things when it suited his purpose.

Jeb glanced at her and sighed expressively. "You know how I feel about meetings."

"Yes, I do," she said, and slipped her arm through his. Leaning her head against his shoulder, she reflected that his being part of this committee was no small thing. He'd agreed when she'd first mentioned it. Only later did he start muttering, and Maddy had the feeling it was mostly for show. Gage and Lindsay were also on the committee, along with Rachel and Heath Quantrill, and Joanie and Brandon Wyatt.

The weather was lovely and Maddy was convinced that, with a minimum of effort, they'd be able to get a group of volunteers together right away. She and Rachel Quantrill were spearheading the project. Everyone seemed to be waiting for someone else to do it. Maddy understood; people were busy with their own lives. Well, she, for one, was determined to see this park become a reality.

"I wouldn't do this for anyone in the world but you," Jeb muttered, his voice gruff.

"I know, honey, and I appreciate it."

"Is Dennis going to be there?"

Maddy shook her head. "Not that I know of."

"How come he gets out of this and I don't?"

"Would you kindly stop your complaining? If all goes well, by the end of the summer, we should have a real park."

He muttered something else, but she noticed he didn't complain again as they continued the hour-long drive into town.

Lindsay and Gage were the only people already at the vacant lot when they arrived. Gage was carrying his daughter, Joy, and Julianne automatically went into Jeb's arms when he removed her from the car seat. Not long from now, the girls would both be walking. It seemed impossible to Maddy that just a year ago she'd been pregnant. So many wonderful changes had come into her life since the move to Buffalo Valley.

Lindsay and Maddy immediately started chatting. Now that they were both married, they didn't have nearly as much time as they would have liked to maintain their friendship. They found themselves depending on phone calls and even e-mail; at least they could stay caught up on news.

Gage and Jeb had their heads together, too.

"Hmm. There's a sight you don't see every day," Hassie commented as she approached the small group.

"What?" Lindsay asked.

"Two men, holding their baby daughters on their hips. I gotta tell you, it does my old heart good to see those two married and settled down."

Maddy and Lindsay glanced at each other and shared a smile.

"Is everyone prepared to work hard to make this park happen?" Hassie asked loudly. "It isn't going to come together by itself, you know."

"Maddy," Jeb called.

She walked over to him and he handed her Julianne. "Gage says he can get the tractor out here to churn up the land and get the grass planted."

"You'd be willing to do that?"

Lindsay stepped next to her and elbowed Maddy's side. "Don't look a gift tractor in the mouth. He volunteered, didn't he?"

"I can set aside some time next week," Gage told her.

"Wonderful." Maddy beamed at him.

"Harvey Hendrickson from the hardware store volunteered wood for a couple of picnic tables," Hassie added.

"I could build those," Jeb chimed in.

Joanie and Brandon Wyatt arrived, followed by the

Quantrills, and Maddy updated them on what had been discussed.

"We need playground equipment," Hassie said next. "If families are going to come here for a picnic, they'll want something to keep the youngsters entertained."

"It wouldn't take much to put up a few swings, would it?" Maddy asked, looking around. "Swings would be nice."

Heath and Rachel nodded.

"One of those big timber play sets would be good, don't you think?" Rachel asked.

Maddy liked the idea, but knew they were expensive. She mentioned the price listed in a brochure she'd read and watched the enthusiasm of her committee wane.

"And that doesn't include assembly," Lindsay said.

Brandon Wyatt cleared his throat. "I never thought of myself as much of a woodworker, but I did a fairly decent job constructing the display shelves for the video store."

"You did a fabulous job," Rachel insisted.

Maddy had admired his workmanship, too, and said so.

Brandon flushed at their praise. "Well, if the town could come up with money for the materials, I could build a jungle gym for the park."

"Consider it done," Heath said. "You order whatever you need and send me the bill."

It was all Maddy could do to keep from clapping her hands. Then she noticed Hassie, who seemed to have something else to say.

"Hassie?"

"Listen," she began, "I know I'm older and I won't

have grandchildren living here to enjoy the park once it's completed.''

"That doesn't matter," Maddy assured her. "If you have a suggestion, we'd like to hear it."

A number of people nodded in agreement.

"Everyone here knows I lost my son in Vietnam. I'm not the only mother to lose a son in war. I want this town to remember that there were a number of fine young men from right here in Buffalo Valley who died for their country and the freedom we enjoy." She paused, and Maddy could tell by the way her throat worked that she was swallowing the tears brought on by painful memories of her only son's death.

"Would you like a memorial built to honor those who died in war?" Maddy asked, taking Hassie's hand and squeezing her fingers, letting her know she understood. "The First and Second World Wars, Korea, Vietnam?"

Hassie returned the squeeze, then reached inside her sweater pocket for a handkerchief and blew her nose. "That would please me very much. Now, I know a memorial's going to cost a lot of money, but I'm prepared to pay for it myself. I've got a few dollars set aside and I can't think of any better use for it."

"If you'd like a sculpture, what about having Kevin work up a few designs?" Gage asked. "He'd be honored if you asked him to submit a drawing for this memorial."

Hassie nodded. "Kevin would be my first choice."

Maddy and Lindsay smiled at each other again. It'd been Lindsay who'd encouraged Kevin Betts to pursue his love of art, and now his artistic skills would serve the town. There was something very satisfying in that.

* * *

Matt sat at the kitchen table and watched Sadie as she fussed about the kitchen. Strangely enough, the housekeeper had turned into the best ally he had. Although she didn't actually give him information about Margaret, she was kind enough to drop hints now and then. If it wasn't for Sadie, he wouldn't have any idea what his wife was thinking.

This latest tidbit, however, worried him.

"You want a refill on that coffee?" the housekeeper asked, nodding toward the ever-ready pot.

"Sure." Although he'd already drunk two cups, he didn't want to leave, and the coffee provided him with a convenient excuse to linger. Although God knew if Margaret caught him inside the house, there'd be hell to pay.

"She's not suffering from morning sickness, is she?" he asked for at least the third time. Sadie had already told him that Margaret didn't appear to be experiencing any discomfort as a result of the pregnancy.

"She's in good health—physically," Sadie told him and then scowled in his direction, letting him know that her *emotional* health was a different matter. As if he wasn't already aware of how much his wife was hurting. Dammit, he was hurting, too.

"You don't know why she drove into Grand Forks, then?" This was as bold as his questions had gotten. Right after breakfast, Margaret had left without a word. Sadie had told him it wasn't a doctor's appointment; those were marked on the office calendar. When Margaret hadn't returned by lunchtime, Matt figured something was up.

Sadie finished pouring his coffee. "I have my suspicions about where she went."

Matt did, too, and it bothered him plenty. Banished to the empty bunkhouse with nothing more than a radio to keep him occupied, Matt was left to his own devices once work was through for the day. Most nights he lay on his bed, staring up at the ceiling. He worried about Sheryl and Margaret and their babies, about his marriage and whether he had any chance of saving it.

Pastor Dawson had told him to fight for Margaret, and Matt had taken the advice to heart. If his wife assumed he was going to roll over and play dead, then she didn't know him nearly as well as she thought.

"You're *sure* she didn't have a doctor's appointment?" he asked again.

"Positive."

Matt's stomach churned. His biggest fear loomed before him. "She's seeing an attorney, isn't she?"

Sadie returned to the sink, where she peeled potatoes with the skill of many years. The brown skins curled away from the sharp blade in a perfect spiral, falling toward the sink. "I can't rightly say if she's with an attorney or not."

"But you said you have your suspicions."

"I do."

The sick feeling was back in the pit of his stomach.

The sound of a car door closing echoed through the kitchen. Margaret must be home.

Sadie and Matt exchanged looks. For an instant he toyed with the idea of sneaking out the laundry-room door, but just as quickly, he rejected the thought.

"Let me talk to her for a few minutes," Matt suggested.

"You telling me to leave this kitchen?" Sadie asked, fire flashing from her dark eyes.

"No," he said quickly. "I'm asking you to give me a few minutes alone with my wife."

Sadie hesitated, then dropped the potato in a pan of cold water. She dried her hands on her apron and walked out of the room. No sooner had she disappeared than Margaret entered the house.

Seeing Matt, she went rigid, eyes narrowed. "What are *you* doing here?" she spat.

"I want to talk to you."

She ignored him and rushed into the long hallway. Not easily dissuaded, Matt followed. Margaret headed for the bedroom and would have slammed the door if he hadn't stopped her by planting his foot in the way. They met face-to-face, their eyes blazing.

"I have nothing to say to you."

"Hear me out. Then if you want me to leave, I will."

She folded her arms and pretended to be bored. "Did Sadie let you in?"

"No."

"Liar."

"I let myself in, so don't blame Sadie."

Frowning, she pinched her lips together. "Say what you have to say."

"All right." He'd known this wouldn't be easy. Running his hand across the back of his neck, he decided to make his first volley an aggressive one. "I need to know where you were this afternoon. Because if you were seeing an attorney, there's something you have to understand."

"Where I was and who I saw are *my* business."

"Not anymore."

"Like hell, Matt Eilers! I don't owe you any explanations. I don't owe you anything."

"This isn't a matter of owing anyone. Fine, don't tell me and I'll just go ahead and speak my piece." After a deliberate pause, he said, "If you saw an attorney with the intention of filing for divorce, then you should know I plan to fight you every step of the way."

She glared at him, as if to say she welcomed the challenge.

"I admit the situation is unfortunate. You regret our marriage. I can appreciate that. But you were the one who chose to marry me and by God, we're going to stay married."

She blinked and looked away.

"I've got regrets, too," he continued. "A whole truckload of those. Unfortunately, there's not one damn thing I can do to change the circumstances now."

His words fell into the silent room. Matt wasn't sure what he'd expected, but not this...this utter lack of emotion. It was as though she'd completely closed him out.

"Are you finished?" she asked curtly.

"No," he surprised himself by saying. "You're my wife, dammit, and it's high time you started acting like it." He could tell his words had hit their mark when the fire leapt back into her eyes.

If looks could kill, there'd be a funeral in Buffalo Valley that night. "I beat the hell out of you once, Matt Eilers, and I have no compunction about doing it twice."

He nearly laughed out loud, which would have been a big mistake. "If it'll make you feel better, then you're welcome to try.'' She'd caught him off guard before, but she wouldn't again.

Instantly she pulled back her clenched fist, and swung at him, but Matt caught her fist with his open hand. Despite her outrage and anger, her struggle was futile.

''Did you have an appointment with an attorney?'' he demanded.

''Yes,'' she hissed back.

The admission so deflated and discouraged him, he released her hand and slumped against the bedroom door.

She could have slugged him then and he wouldn't have cared. He sincerely doubted he would've felt anything beyond the numbness that had taken hold of his heart. She wanted a divorce.

Breathing hard, Margaret stood in front of him. ''I didn't originally contact him about filing for divorce,'' she said after a long pause.

Puzzled, he chanced looking up. Her hands were braced against her hips, but the defensive stance was gone, replaced with a more guarded one.

She surprised him by suddenly moving into the room, sitting on the end of the bed, her back toward him. ''I did talk to an attorney. Divorce was one of the options he presented.''

Matt swallowed hard. ''That isn't what I want, Margaret.''

She snickered softly. ''At this point, I'm not overly concerned with your wishes.''

He suspected that was true.

''I needed to know what my legal rights are in regard to Sheryl and her...baby.''

"I talked to an attorney, too."

"I knew that," she said, sounding matter-of-fact. "But I wasn't interested in talking to the same attorney you had."

Rather than question her reasoning, he asked, "What did your attorney say?"

"Nothing that I didn't already know. We're financially and emotionally responsible for your...daughter. It'll mean you and Sheryl will have to develop a parenting plan. The child will be spending time here, vacations, holidays—for at least the next eighteen years. She'll be part of our lives."

"She's my responsibility, I'll—"

"Get real," Margaret snapped. "If we're married, she'll be in this house, eating, sleeping, calling you Daddy right along with our child. She's going to need your love—and mine."

As Margaret had just reminded him, he wasn't the only one involved in this. The child would be a constant reminder of his faults, of the pain he'd caused his wife. More than that, he was asking her to love his daughter. No wonder Margaret was feeling overwhelmed. So far, all he'd sought was her forgiveness, her acceptance. That had been paramount in his mind. Everything else—the ramifications of fatherhood and of Margaret being his child's stepmother—had escaped him.

"You're right."

She didn't respond. Her back was to him so he couldn't see her face, couldn't read her thoughts, couldn't gauge her feelings.

"Do you want out of the marriage?" he asked bluntly.

"I don't know yet."

"I said I'd fight for you, fight for our marriage, and I meant it." He exhaled sharply. "But if you really want out, then I'll abide by your wishes."

He stood up and started to walk away.

"Why the change of heart?" She seemed genuinely curious.

"It's asking too much of you... I wanted, needed, your forgiveness, but this goes beyond that. Way beyond..."

"Yes," she whispered brokenly, "it does."

With nothing more to say, Matt left the bedroom. Sadie was back at the sink peeling potatoes when he walked through the kitchen.

She glanced at him and then did a double take. "What happened?"

He shook his head, unable to answer.

"That bad?"

"That bad," he echoed.

Fifteen

Buffalo Bob replaced the telephone receiver, but continued to grip the phone. He needed to hold onto something. Anything.

Pain, followed by escalating anger, charged through him. He felt breathless, as though he'd been kicked in the gut. Not knowing what to do, he sank into the chair and waited for the shock to pass. He had to be in control of his own emotions before he could deal with Merrily's.

"Bob, I—" Merrily came into the office and stopped short when she saw the look on his face. In that instant she must have known. "What is it?" she asked, her voice small and fragile.

For the life of him, he couldn't answer her. Not yet.

"Bob?" she cried.

"That...that was Doug Alder," he whispered hoarsely.

"He heard about the adoption?"

Bob nodded and slowly got to his feet. "Sit down, sweetheart."

"Sit down? Does that mean you have something to tell me I don't want to hear? Is that what you're trying to say?" She clutched her stomach and lowered herself into the wooden chair. Her arms still clutched her middle as she stared up at him. Her eyes, her big beautiful eyes, were wide with fear.

''We knew when we applied to adopt Axel—''

''Just tell me!'' she shouted, tears already brimming, ready to spill down her pale cheeks.

Bob felt like sobbing himself. ''The judge decided on another couple as the adoptive parents for Axel. Two doctors who've been waiting five years to adopt a child. They're...good people.''

''And we're not?'' she sobbed. Leaning forward she started to rock gently.

''Neither one of them has been arrested on drug charges,'' he muttered, repeating what their attorney had told him. Bob had hoped and believed and trusted that he'd done the honorable thing when he contacted the authorities about Axel. He'd known the risks, but he'd been willing to take them because he'd truly thought that in time Axel would be returned to him and Merrily. They were his parents. The only family he knew. They loved the boy.

His wife was sobbing now. She covered her face with both hands and continued to rock with grief. Had he been able to, Bob would have reached out and comforted her, but his own pain was too great. He had nothing to give her, nothing to help her through this.

''It's all my fault,'' he whispered.

''Why did this happen?'' Merrily wailed. ''Why?'' she demanded again when he didn't answer.

''We each have a police record.''

''That was years ago—it shouldn't matter anymore. Is the court honestly going to hold a five-year-old drug arrest against me for the rest of my life?''

''There's more...Doug said we displayed a less than ideal home environment.'' He shook his head hopelessly.

"Less than ideal what?" Her voice echoed the outrage he'd felt when he'd first heard the words. "Did they say I wasn't a good enough mother? Is that it? That I didn't love Axel enough? Because I couldn't have loved him any more than I already do right now. Bob, Bob, what am I going to do without my baby?"

Bob had no answers or reassurances, as desperate as Merrily was to hear them. Apparently, the judge didn't feel that living above a bar was the proper environment for a child. Or that Bob had potential as a father. Or Merrily as a mother, despite her love, despite the fact that she'd saved Axel's life.

He shook his head again, unable and unwilling to repeat what was sure to bring her more pain. "We both loved him enough...."

"Then why?" Her sobs made the words almost indistinguishable.

Bob wished it was possible for him to cry, to vent his own bitterness and sense of loss. Instead he shoved all the emotion deep inside.

"Blame me," he told her.

Merrily stared at him, her face streaked with tears, her eyes imploring him to untangle the court's message. "You?"

"Remember how the caseworker examined the new plaster on the wall?" he asked. He didn't wait for Merrily to respond. "She asked me about it, and I made up some excuse."

"You lied?"

"Yes, dammit, I lied. I couldn't very well admit that I rammed my fist through the wall, could I? Only it didn't do any good. If anything, it hurt us. These people are trained observers, and she put two and two together fast enough, especially since I'd recently been in a cast and she saw that, too.''

''Oh, Bob.''

''In her report, she concluded that I'm susceptible to fits of anger.''

Merrily gasped. ''The only reason you punched the wall was because I'd run away.''

''It doesn't matter why I did it.'' He couldn't, wouldn't tell Merrily what else the report said. No need to rub salt into her wounds. In making his decision, the judge had also cited Merrily's tendency to run away when confronted with problems.

''What are we going to do?'' She sobbed. But he had nothing to suggest. He'd never felt so inadequate.

''The attorney said the judge told him the decision was a difficult one.'' As though that was supposed to make them feel better. It didn't. Nothing would.

Without another word, Merrily stood, and he watched as she wandered blindly out of his office, then drifted upstairs. He watched her mount the stairs, one by one, her steps slow and uncertain. She headed toward their living quarters and didn't look back.

Unable to deal with customers, Bob closed the bar and restaurant for the day and sealed himself inside his office. He sat dazed with shock and pain, unable to do more than stare at the wall. He didn't know how long he remained there before the sound of someone knocking invaded his grief.

Reluctantly he went to check, and discovered Hassie

standing outside the locked door, peering through the window.

"Let me in," she demanded.

"I'm closed."

"Well, open up. Folks are worried about you."

Bob frowned. How could people already know—then again, maybe they didn't. With no enthusiasm, he turned the lock and stepped away from the door.

Hassie didn't wait for an invitation. She hurried inside and closed up after herself. "This is about Axel, isn't it?"

Bob nodded, unable to meet her gaze. Eventually the town would discover the truth. He and Merrily couldn't hide the fact that their son, the boy they loved, had been given to a different family.

"The judge awarded him to another couple," Bob said, figuring that was explanation enough.

A look of sadness came over her, and she gave a deep sigh. "No wonder you've closed up shop. Where's Merrily?"

"Upstairs."

"Come on," Hassie said, and led him into the kitchen as if she were steering a child. "I remember what it was like when those two young men from the Army came to tell me my son was dead. I couldn't think, couldn't eat, could barely function for days. Now listen, you sit down here and I'm going to make us all a pot of tea."

"Tea?"

"I know it sounds ridiculous. You lost your son and I'm boiling water, but it will help. Trust me on this, there are few things more soothing to the spirit than a cup of tea."

As soon as the kettle whistled, she had the tea leaves steeping. "Stay here, I'm going to check on Merrily."

Grateful, he nodded. He hadn't meant to abandon his wife, but he couldn't help her, not when he was hurting so badly himself. His heart actually ached. The lump in his throat was so large, he found it difficult to swallow or breathe normally. The telephone conversation had hit him hard. Until that moment, he'd been living with expectation, with the hope and promise of joy. It felt as though a bomb had gone off, devastating their lives.

Reality was slowly sinking in. Axel would now look to another man and call him Daddy. The boy Bob loved, who'd found his way into Bob's heart, would belong to some other man, a stranger who had more to offer him than Bob did. A physician, a wealthy man who could give Axel material goods. Perhaps so, but no one—*no one*—would love Axel more than Bob and Merrily did. It wasn't possible. They'd risked everything for the boy; surely that must prove something. Surely the courts had taken into account the courage it'd required to step forward, to risk losing their son.

The gamble, the giant gamble, hadn't paid off.

It was a long time before Hassie came downstairs. Her eyes were red, and Bob knew she'd sat and wept with Merrily. Their friend had held and comforted Merrily when Bob couldn't.

Silently, she poured him a cup of tea. "There isn't any pain in this world worse than losing a child. I know this situation is different from mine. You aren't going to stand there and watch Axel being lowered into the ground, the way I did my boy. But the pain is the same."

"He might as well be dead. He's dead to Merrily and me."

"True enough. You had him for a short while and changed his life. You have a great deal to be proud of. You and Merrily gave that boy the love he desperately needed."

"Merrily—is she all right?"

"No," Hassie said as she set the steaming tea in front of him. "She needs you, but she won't ask."

He suspected his wife was waiting for a convenient moment to disappear. Come morning, he fully expected to wake and find her gone.

Bob sipped the sweetened tea. It was too hot and burned his throat, but he didn't care. He tried not to think, tried to put Axel out of his mind. And couldn't.

It wasn't supposed to happen like this. By all that was right, they should be Axel's adoptive parents. Instead he was financially crippled by attorneys' fees, his heart was damn near ripped from his chest and his wife was upstairs sobbing. But how could he give her peace when he hadn't found any himself?

"What am I going to do now?" he asked Hassie. She'd lived through this; she would know. "What happens next?"

"Pain, lots of pain, but eventually you and Merrily are going to release your son," she said.

"Release him?" This was a sick joke. They'd lost Axel five months ago, only they hadn't realized it until this morning. The boy would never be theirs again.

"Not from your heart," Hassie was quick to amend. "That would be impossible. Never from your heart."

* * *

Early Friday afternoon Maddy was at the grocery. She generally came in once a week to check on her store, although most of the everyday management was handled by Pete Mitchell.

This arrangement worked well with Jeb and Julianne, too, and gave her husband one afternoon a week to spend with their daughter. Jeb had proved to be a wonderful father. Maddy delighted in watching her husband with Julianne and the tenderness that suffused his face as he rocked her to sleep.

Maddy was just finishing up some paperwork in the small cramped office when she heard Margaret. Her loud voice carried all the way to the back of the store. ''I'm here to see Maddy,'' Margaret insisted gruffly.

On their most recent visit, Margaret had broken into tears and told Maddy about her husband fathering a child with Sheryl Decker. It'd nearly broken Maddy's heart to hear such pain. When she'd finished telling her story, Margaret had asked for advice. Sadly, Maddy didn't know what to tell her. She was disappointed in Matt, but the fact that he'd fathered a child didn't distress her nearly as much as the heartache he'd caused her friend.

''Margaret?'' Maddy came out of the room, not knowing what to expect. She discovered her friend barreling down the produce aisle with all the grace of a lumberjack on his way to the mess hall.

''Maddy,'' Margaret cried, ''I've been looking all over for you!''

''Didn't Jeb tell you where I was?''

''He did, but I thought you'd be home and—'' She

paused, dragged in a deep breath. "I need to talk.... Can you spare me a few minutes?"

"Of course." Maddy stepped aside to allow Margaret into the compact quarters.

She fell into the chair, looking pale and about as forlorn as Maddy could remember. Maddy sat down, too, and waited, certain Margaret would tear into her reason for coming. When she didn't, Maddy decided to prompt her.

"Did something happen?" she asked, deciding to take the direct approach.

Margaret put on a brave smile. "I... Matt moved out this morning."

Maddy was sure she'd misunderstood. "Moved out?"

Margaret nodded. She blinked a few times and Maddy knew she was struggling not to break into tears. "I didn't know who else to turn to for help," she blurted out.

"I, uh, take it this came as a shock?" Maddy didn't know what else to say.

Margaret shook her head, then nodded just as emphatically. "I didn't ask him to leave, if that's what you're thinking." She hesitated, and as though embarrassed to admit it, she said, "But it was what I wanted, and I made sure he knew it." She bit her lower lip. "He said he was going to fight for me, for our marriage, but apparently he didn't mean that any more than the other things he claimed."

"You wanted him out of your life, right?"

Margaret swayed, and Maddy felt a moment's alarm, especially considering the pregnancy. But Margaret rallied and took a deep breath. "Some days I wanted us to patch up our differences," she said, "and then I'd start thinking about him with that woman and I'd get so damn mad I wanted to scratch his eyes out.'' She shook her head wildly, as though to dislodge the mental image of her husband with Sheryl Decker.

''Did something trigger this?'' Maddy asked, hoping to shed light on the current situation. ''The fact that he left, I mean?''

Margaret looked down and nodded. ''I saw an attorney.''

''You did?''

''I wanted to know my rights. Not Matt's. Mine.''

''Okay, I understand.''

''Matt and I talked afterward and…and it didn't go well, but then nothing has since that paternity suit. You notice Sheryl Decker included me in that lawsuit? She wants everything she can get from me.… Maddy, if you'd read her demands, why, it'd make you sick to your stomach. That woman plans to use her baby like a…like a weapon against Matt and me.''

The picture was beginning to take shape in Maddy's mind.

''You know who's caught in the middle of this, don't you?'' Margaret continued. ''Matt's daughter. The situation's horrible.''

''Oh, Margaret.''

''And now he's gone. He did it for me,'' she whispered. ''He left to spare me any more grief.''

Maddy sensed that in talking it out, Margaret had been able to gain control of her feelings, and perhaps a measure of understanding.

"A divorce isn't what you want, is it?" she asked quietly.

"No." Margaret stood, her back straight, her shoulders square.

Maddy got to her feet, as well. "You love Matt, don't you?"

Margaret didn't so much as hesitate. "With all my heart." Then as if it was all more than she could handle, she slumped back in the chair.

"I remember when you first told me about loving Matt Eilers," Maddy reminded her, hoping the memory would somehow help her friend—bring her comfort and resolve. "Frankly, I took your declaration with a grain of salt. I assumed your feelings were basically a schoolgirl crush." Maddy sat down again so they could meet eye to eye. "Then you said something I won't forget. You told me you knew Matt was no saint, but you loved him, faults and all."

The merest hint of a smile touched Margaret's mouth as Maddy repeated those fateful words.

"I don't like what's happened—with Sheryl and her baby. I'm not sure I can accept there being another child in our lives."

Maddy's heart went out to her. The situation was painful and difficult.

"But I want to save this marriage," Margaret said forcefully. "My baby's going to need his father and...I need Matt, too."

Maddy knew it wasn't easy for Margaret to admit needing anyone or anything. Emotionally, Margaret Eilers was one of the strongest, most self-sufficient women Maddy had ever known. "So what are you going to do about it?" she asked.

Margaret's shoulders sagged. "I don't know where he moved—where he is. Oh, Maddy, all I want is for this pain to go away." She stopped and swallowed hard. "When I realized he'd left...I felt this burst of relief...and then almost immediately this horrible emptiness. Nothing means anything to me without my husband."

Confused and anxious—and pregnant. Margaret had every right to feel unsettled.

Joshua McKenna didn't have much confidence in his skills as a father. Both his children had grown up to be decent, hardworking adults, but he accepted none of the credit for that. Marjorie had seen to the rearing of Sarah and Jeb, and he'd done little more than pay the bills.

Sarah had been a rebellious teenager, just like Calla was these days. History seemed to repeat itself. Marjorie had sat up many a night worrying about her failings as a mother, the same way Sarah fretted over how she'd failed Calla.

Jeb had always been an intelligent child—and much easier on his parents than his sister had been. Even before the accident that cost him his leg, he'd been an intense, quiet man. Joshua had watched with amusement the changes in his son since he'd married Maddy. She was everything Joshua had hoped Jeb would have in a wife. If only Marjorie had lived long enough to see their son this happy.

After nearly twelve years, Joshua still missed his wife. He realized he hadn't appreciated her nearly as much as he should have. A sad but all-too-typical commentary on marriage, he supposed.

He poured himself a cup of coffee and then sat in the

recliner in front of the television, hardly thinking about dinner or what he'd eat. Probably something from the freezer. Sarah had lived with him for so many years that he'd grown accustomed to having someone else cook. He'd hoped Calla would see to his meals the way her mother had, but the girl was rarely home. If she ate, it was generally with friends.

Last Christmas when Calla asked if she could live with him, Joshua had welcomed the prospect. The house felt downright empty after Sarah had married Dennis and they moved into a place of their own. So he'd invited his granddaughter to move in. Calla needed a home and he needed the company.

These days Joshua wasn't so sure it was a good idea. According to Jeb, Dennis and Calla had exchanged words not long ago. Sarah had been upset about it. Joshua couldn't exactly miss the fact that something was seriously awry. Calla hadn't been herself for days but, like him, she kept her troubles to herself.

Joshua wasn't one to intrude; for that matter he seldom even offered advice. He wouldn't say anything now, except that he felt it was necessary. Someone had to step in, and since Calla lived with him, he was the only real choice.

The back door banged and Calla walked into the house. "Evening, Grandpa."

"Calla." He set his coffee aside. "Do you have a minute?"

"Ah...sure." She came into the living room, and Joshua reached for the remote control and turned off the television.

"Sit down," he ordered.

Calla complied and sat on the edge of the sofa, obviously eager for this to be over so she could make her escape.

"How long have you been living with me now?" he asked.

She shrugged. "Practically ever since I can remember."

"That's right. I've seen you grow into a beautiful young woman."

"Grandpa!"

His praise flustered her and she seemed ill-at-ease with it, but he ignored that.

"I've stood by and watched what's happened between you and your mother for a lot of years. For the most part, I've stayed out of it, but I'm beginning to believe that was a mistake."

Her face was now devoid of emotion. "If you don't mind, I'd rather not discuss my mother."

"I do mind," he countered flatly. "In fact, I mind quite a bit."

She folded her arms, signalling her resistance. Joshua didn't care; he fully intended to speak his piece whether she wanted to hear it or not. How she responded was entirely up to her.

"Even though you rarely heard from your father, you placed him on a pedestal. Your mother didn't say or do anything to enlighten you. Wisely, she understood that you loved Willie and needed your father—or an image of your father. But, in my opinion, she did more than shield you from the truth. She shielded you from the world."

"She shielded me from nothing!"

"That was because you chose to run away. Of your own free will, you went to live with Willie. How long did it take to have your eyes opened?" he asked.

Calla glanced toward the ceiling, but didn't answer.

"My guess is you got the message the first week you were with him. You ran away from him, too, remember? Still, it took you a total of six months to own up to the truth, to swallow your pride and move back to Buffalo Valley."

Her shoulders rose and fell with a deep sigh. "Is there a point to this conversation?" she asked.

"Oh, yes, there's a very big point."

"Good, because it's exceedingly boring."

Joshua pretended he hadn't heard that. "From what I understand, you and Dennis recently had an argument."

"He's got a big mouth."

"Dennis Urlacher?" Her comment was enough to make Joshua choke back a laugh. "I've never heard that description of Dennis before."

"Whatever."

"Whatever?" he repeated. It was a word that seemed to punctuate his granddaughter's conversation. An all-purpose response.

When she didn't speak again, he said, "I heard that Dennis stood up to you and demanded to be treated with respect."

"He's a jerk."

"The hell he is," Joshua said, unwilling to mince words. "You're the one who's been unreasonable. At every opportunity, you've mocked and ridiculed your mother."

"It's what she deserves after—"

"Your mother *deserves* your respect," he shouted. He could tell by the way she went wide-eyed that his booming voice had shocked her. Good, the girl needed a shock.

"Your mother has done nothing but love you. She's

loved you so much she's overprotected you,'' he continued. ''When I heard about your little fight with Dennis, I wanted to stand up and applaud him for having the courage to challenge your rude behavior.''

Calla's lips were tightly pinched, but she said nothing.

''Good for Dennis,'' he said again. ''Hell, I wish I'd had the courage to do it myself. You needed to be brought down a couple of pegs. It was time. Furthermore, I sincerely hope you listened.''

''Grandpa, I know you mean well, but—''

''No, you don't,'' he muttered. ''You think I don't know how anxious you are to get out of here. I expect when I'm finished, you'll leap out of that chair like a prize-winning bullfrog and make a dash for the door.''

Calla merely shook back her hair, then examined her nails, painted a sparkling silver.

''I don't care if you do make a fast escape, that's up to you, but young lady, I advise you to hear me out.''

Glancing at her watch, she asked. ''Is this going to take much longer?''

''It'll take as long as it takes.''

She sighed and fell back against the sofa cushion.

''When was the last time you saw your mother?'' he asked.

''A couple of weeks ago. I see her a lot,'' she added defiantly.

''Visit with her, do you?''

''I have. It isn't like I ignore her.''

Joshua knew Calla had sometimes visited her mother after school, but that'd happened mostly when Sarah was bedridden.

''You owe your mother respect—and you owe her more

than that. You think she did you so wrong, but have you ever stopped to consider all the sacrifices she made for you? I doubt it. Did you ever once stop to consider how much she loves you and how hard she's worked to make you happy, often at the price of her own happiness?''

The bored, martyred look was back.

Joshua gripped both sides of his chair and then slowly leaned forward. ''Calla Stern, listen to me. *Grow up.*'' The last two words were nearly shouted. ''You're seventeen, and it's well past time you appreciated your family.''

She blinked, looking stunned.

''If you want to inflict your moodiness on your mother, then my advice is to stay away.''

''Fine. No problem.''

''If you can't treat Dennis and your mother with respect, then you and I need to have a serious discussion.''

''About what?''

''Your living arrangements here,'' he said. ''Either I see a dramatic change in your behavior or I'm going to have to ask you to pack up and leave my home.''

Calla didn't say anything for several moments. ''Are you telling me you want me to move out? I—I won't graduate from high school until next month.''

''I didn't say you were being forced to move,'' he clarified. ''What I said was that if you continue to behave like an unreasonable and immature brat, perhaps you should look elsewhere for housing.''

Calla stared at him as though she had trouble taking in the words. ''You don't mean that.''

''Trust me, Calla, I do. Shape up or ship out.''

Sixteen

It'd been a week since Bob and Merrily had heard from the attorney. Every morning, Bob expected to find an empty space next to him in bed. Most days he woke before the clock radio went off. His first thought was of Merrily, wondering if she'd slipped away as she had so many times in the past.

The alarm sounded, and although he knew his wife was already awake, he gently patted her backside, and got out of bed. Some mornings it was all he could do not to ask if she intended to leave. Knowing was better than this damnable waiting. Somehow he couldn't do it, though.

They barely spoke these days. Bob buried his grief in work—cooking, cleaning, tending bar, remodeling and repairs. Only on rare occasions did he rent the hotel rooms, but with the approach of summer, this seemed a good time to spruce them up. He was repainting the rooms that needed it and freshening those that didn't.

Merrily, on the other hand, sank deeper and deeper into a pit of despair. Most every day now, she sat in front of the television, numbing her mind with soap operas and game shows. At night, she went into Axel's old room and sat on his bed, weeping silently. Bob tried to help her, but nothing he said seemed to penetrate the wall of pain.

Wednesday afternoon, Pastor Dawson stopped by. It

wasn't his first visit since they'd received the news from California, but it was the first time Merrily had been downstairs.

"I thought I'd come over to—"

He'd barely started to speak when Merrily flew across the room with more energy than Bob had seen from her in days. "Get out!" she roared.

The minister stared, apparently too stunned to react.

"Merrily!" Bob had never seen her behave like this.

"It's all your fault! We'd have Axel now if it wasn't for you."

If Bob was shocked by this unexpected show of life, it didn't compare to his horror when she raised her fists and actually attacked the minister, pounding his chest as hard as she could. Acting quickly, Bob wrapped his arms around her waist and pulled her away. She started to sob then, a heart-wrenching wail that came from deep inside her. The kind of sobs that relate an unspeakable agony. Bob turned her in his arms and held her, his own throat growing thick. Closing his eyes, he battled down his pain and dismay as he attempted to comfort his wife.

Merrily clung to him, hiding her face in his shoulder.

Pastor Dawson stood close by, his eyes filled with pity and understanding. "Is there anything I can do?" he asked.

Bob shook his head sadly. There was nothing anyone could do. Merrily's outburst had come suddenly and without provocation. Bob didn't know what to think. They'd both been dealing with their disappointment in different ways; his method was to immerse himself in work, hers to drown in lethargy and tears. He would never have anticipated this type of reaction from her. It left him completely baffled.

He led Merrily to their bedroom and was grateful to find the minister waiting when he returned downstairs.

"Obviously Merrily blames me for what happened."

Bob shifted uncomfortably. "She assumes you threatened to turn us in to the authorities. I let her think that because I knew she'd never agree to contact them voluntarily."

John Dawson reached out and gripped Bob's forearm. "We talked about that earlier. It's not a problem. You did what you had to." He paused. "You had a difficult choice to make and I believe you did the right thing."

"*Would* you have turned us in?" Bob demanded.

"Thankfully, I didn't have to make that decision." His gaze held Bob's. "In truth, I can't tell you what I would've done. I was deeply relieved when you suggested talking to that attorney Maddy recommended."

"At the time, I thought we did the right thing, too," Bob added with bitter insight. But he'd been wrong, and he'd suffer from that mistake for the rest of his life.

"You and Merrily aren't talking much?"

Bob shook his head. "It's too painful... I don't have anything left inside to give her."

The minister followed Bob into his private office and sat across from him. "You need each other now more than ever. Merrily needs you more than you realize and—"

"Yes, I know, but—"

"And you need her," Pastor Dawson finished. "You said you don't have anything to give her. I understand your feelings, but Bob, it's together that you'll get through these next few weeks. One day at a time. Sometimes one hour, even one minute at a time. You've got to help one another and look to God for the strength to carry on. Take all the love you have for Axel and give it to your wife.''

A lump filled Bob's throat, the same one that had appeared at inopportune moments all week. ''Merrily didn't mean to do what she did,'' he said hoarsely, feeling the necessity to apologize. ''Her anger is really with me.''

''I know. It's forgotten, so don't worry about it.''

They spoke a few minutes longer. ''I'll think about what you said,'' Bob promised as he walked the minister to the door.

They shook hands and once again Bob was grateful for the good friends he'd made in Buffalo Valley. The pastor wasn't the only one who'd shown him love and understanding. Hassie came by nearly every day, often with the flimsiest of excuses. Bob welcomed her company and her wisdom. She'd lived through a similar ordeal and spoke to his heart in ways that others couldn't.

After the minister left, Bob waited a few minutes, then headed upstairs. He found Merrily sitting in front of the television, staring sightlessly at the screen. Taking the remote control from her limp grasp, he muted the sound. She barely noticed.

''I'm...sorry,'' she whispered.

''I know.'' Bob knelt in front of her and took both her hands in his. ''We need to talk about Axel.''

Immediately fresh tears threatened to spill down her pale cheeks. ''No... I can't... Oh, Bob, I don't know what I'll do without my boy.''

"We're going to get through this, sweetheart. It'll always hurt, but you and I are going to deal with this."

Her smile was weak but present, and his heart filled with love for his wife. "Now, about Pastor Dawson."

She glanced away, embarrassed.

"The judge's decision had nothing to do with the minister. If you want to lay the blame at anyone's feet, you don't need to go any farther than this room."

"What do you mean?"

"Sweetheart," he said, leaning forward to gently brush the hair from her cheek. "We were the ones who screwed up our lives. Just try to put yourself in that judge's shoes. He had two couples—maybe more—to choose from. All of us good people, each couple wanting Axel. He didn't have anything to look at but the facts, written in black and white on a sheet of paper. Nothing that would prove to him how much we loved Axel. Nothing that would discount our mistakes. Before we got married, you told me there were things you'd done..."

Merrily squeezed her eyes shut and shook her head.

"I have my own list of sins, and it isn't any shorter than yours. We both made errors over the years. The judge couldn't ignore that."

Merrily looked down and her hair fell forward. "I know, but no one will love Axel more than us."

"No one," Bob agreed.

"It seems so unfair when we've both worked so hard to be better people and...and we are, but—"

"We *are* better," Bob said. "We've both grown, and part of that process is learning to accept responsibility for the past. The angry drifter who got arrested for possession of a controlled substance several years ago isn't me. Not anymore. I'm a husband and a business owner, a member of the town council and the school board. But, unfortunately, I do have a past, and I have to accept the consequences of the life I once lived.''

Merrily studied him for a long moment, then nodded. ''I do, too.'' Sliding forward, she wrapped her arms around his neck and hugged him. It was the most physical contact they'd had since Doug's phone call.

''I've needed you,'' Merrily told him, her voice trembling. ''I've felt so alone.''

''I've needed you, too.''

''Then why did you stay away? Why didn't you hold me when I wanted you so much?''

Bob buried his face in the curve of her neck. ''I was afraid.'' He could tell by the way her body tensed that she didn't understand. ''Afraid you'd vanish. Afraid I'd wake up and find you'd left me again. I was protecting myself.''

''But Bob—''

''Every time you walk away, something dies inside of me,'' he said, as he gently wiped the tears from her cheeks.

Merrily caught his hand and brought his fingers to her lips. ''You're right, you know, about accepting responsibility for my past. I played a role in the judge's decision, too. You never said, but the caseworker learned about my little habit of running away, didn't she? It couldn't have looked good as a qualification for being Axel's mother.''

''I don't think they knew,'' he lied, wanting to spare her.

''Hogwash,'' she said, shaking her head. ''The judge had to know. You say we have to take responsibility for ourselves. I'm doing that, so don't try to make excuses for me. I did run away, but it won't happen again.''

''You're sure?'' Bob hated how uncertain he sounded, but he needed her reassurance.

Merrily smiled and briefly kissed him. ''Very sure. I learned my lesson the last time.''

She'd never spoken of where she'd gone or how she'd lived while they were apart. Not knowing had plagued Bob, filled him with doubts and gnawing questions, but he'd never press her for details. ''Did someone hurt you?'' he demanded, anger tightening his chest.

''No.'' She was quick to correct him. ''I realized I couldn't leave you or Buffalo Valley. My heart is here. You're my home, this town and these people are a part of me. We *will* get through this. It won't be easy, but together we'll survive.''

May 30th

Dear Kevin,

Your letter arrived today and I'm thrilled you've got some great ideas for the war memorial. I think it's way cool that the town council contacted you about the project.

So you've got a summer job, working at the Chicago Art Institute. I have to admit I'm a bit disappointed you won't be coming home. We've been writing a couple of months now, and it'd be nice if we could sit down and talk face-to-face. Funny, when we were in school together, we didn't say more than a few words to each other. Now all I think about is seeing you and talking to you in person. I know you'll be home for the Fourth of July weekend, but that seems so far away. Actually, I was thinking about checking out Chicago—more on that later.

Believe it or not, I've got my choice of jobs. I'm working part-time at Joanie's video store, after school and on Saturday nights, but Rachel approached me about working full-time at a new day-care center after graduation. She offered to pay for the college courses I'd need in early childhood development. I'm thinking about it. Buffalo Bob's going to hire three people for the summer, and my mother's quilting business has grown to fifteen employees. When you're home, you'll be amazed by the changes here. More and more people are moving to Buffalo Valley. One of the nurses from the new medical clinic moved into town last week. There's only a couple of vacant houses now.

I recently had a bit of a run-in with my grandfather. As soon as I graduate, I'm moving out. You've got a wonderful family and I think it's great how all of you get along, but that's not the case with me. My mother's remarried and isn't interested in having me around and frankly, I wouldn't live with her and Dennis, anyway. Gramps has developed an attitude, so it doesn't look like I'll be living there much longer. I was thinking about asking my Uncle Jeb about moving in with him and Maddy, but they live so far out of town. I wouldn't like being an hour away from my friends. Anyway, I've come up with an alternative idea. Hassie Knight. I've always liked Hassie. Everyone loves Hassie. She's been around forever and she knows everyone and…well, you understand. I thought she might like the company. What do you think of my idea? Not that I intend to live with her long. Only until I've got enough money to check out Chicago. Maybe I could go to school there—do Early Childhood or whatever. Plus, I'd be able to see you!

I wonder if you know how grateful I am that we're friends. It's incredible to me that someone from Buffalo Valley actually escaped. I know, I know, you talk about moving back one day and maybe you will, but for right now you're living in one of the most exciting cities in the world, experiencing things the rest of us only dream about. Minneapolis didn't work out, but I wish I could leave Buffalo Valley. I don't feel really connected with anyone here anymore. Jessica's started dating Joe, and I feel like all my friends are pairing up.

I'd better go, I'm at work just now. It's time to close down and count out the till. I'm so glad you answered my letter right away.

Write again soon. Okay?

Love,
Calla

Calla mailed the letter on her way home from school Friday afternoon. As she stepped out of the post office, she saw Hassie Knight entering the pharmacy. Not hesitating, she headed across the street. No time like the present to approach Hassie with her idea.

Not wanting to be obvious, Calla strolled into the pharmacy and slid onto a stool at the fountain.

Hassie wore a big smile as she made her way behind the counter. "Come for one of my sodas, have you?"

"I sure have," Calla said, propping her chin on her hands. "I thought about these sodas more than once when I was living in Minneapolis."

"I'll bet one of my sodas wasn't the *only* thing you were thinking about while you were away."

Calla didn't answer; no need to let Hassie know that she'd probably be leaving town as soon as she was financially able. The older woman was such a staunch defender of the community, she wouldn't understand Calla's eagerness to leave. "Actually I came for more than a soda," she said.

Hassie handed her the soda, then walked around the counter and pulled up a stool. "What's on your mind?"

Calla figured it'd help to have some kind of subtle lead-in to the question she wanted to ask, but she couldn't come up with one. Might as well wade right in. "I guess you know I've been having trouble with my mother."

"I did hear something along those lines," Hassie admitted.

Calla took a sip of her soda and smiled, letting the older woman know how much she enjoyed it. A little flattery was never a bad idea, and besides, Hassie really did make fabulous sodas.

"I don't blame my mother," Calla added, wanting to sound adult and mature. "In some families, parents and children just don't see eye to eye."

"Is that true of you and your mother?"

"It seems to be." Calla released a small sigh, as though

she considered this entire situation unfortunate and one she deeply regretted.

"It's never too late, you know."

This wasn't the path Calla wanted the conversation to take. "My mother has a new life now. She's got her business and her marriage. She's happy with Dennis and they're starting a family. I don't fit into that picture, if you catch my drift."

Hassie shook her head, her expression impatient. "Fiddlesticks."

"It's true, Hassie. I love my mother, but I can't live with her."

"I imagine you're grateful for your grandfather, then." Hassie raised her eyebrows expectantly.

"Oh, yes. Gramps has been wonderful. I don't know where I'd be if it wasn't for him—but lately we seem to be having a bit of a problem, too."

"You're not getting along with your grandfather?" Hassie asked loudly. "Is that what you're saying?"

Calla forced herself to look sad and woebegone. Lowering her eyes, she whispered, "We recently had a bit of a falling out."

"You and Joshua?" Hassie made it sound like that wasn't possible. "I've known your grandfather a lot of years, and he's an absolute marvel at avoiding conflict. Hates it. In fact, he'll do just about anything to get out of it."

"He didn't have any trouble speaking his mind with me," Calla informed her, remembering all too well the bluntness of his words. She inhaled a deep breath. "Seeing that I don't get along with him or my mother," she said quickly, "I was giving serious thought to..." She hesitated, wondering if her announcement would sound too melodramatic.

"Serious thought to *what?*" Hassie asked.

Her chin came up. "Disowning my family." That idea had felt very satisfying when she'd first thought of it.

Hassie's eyes narrowed to thin slits. "You mean before they disown you?"

Calla felt that barb and would have returned an even sharper one of her own if she wasn't looking to Hassie for help. All right, in all likelihood she *wouldn't* disown her entire family. She'd probably stay in contact with Jeb and Maddy, not as relatives but as friends. Jeb was all right as uncles went and Maddy was terrific. Besides, Julianne was the only cousin she had and the sweetest baby ever.

"You don't think I should disown my family?" she asked.

"Hardly. As far as I can see, they've done nothing to deserve it."

Apparently Hassie wasn't privy to the things her mother had done, but Calla preferred to avoid discussing the sordid details of Sarah's affair with Dennis Urlacher. Nor did she wish to talk about her father's pathetic life. Both her parents disgusted her.

She reached for her soda and took a deep swallow. This conversation was more difficult than she'd bargained for. Clearly, she needed to approach it from a different angle. "Have you noticed how many people are moving into Buffalo Valley?" she asked in a determinedly casual tone.

Hassie's eyes brightened. "The way this town's coming back to life is a sight to behold, isn't it?"

"It's really cool."

Hassie laughed, and patted Calla's hand.

"You seem to be doing good business lately." She nodded at the cash, where Leta was ringing up purchase after purchase.

"Very good," Hassie agreed.

"I don't suppose you could use any extra help?" She made the question sound timid, as though she was afraid to ask.

"I thought you were working at the Wyatts' video store."

"Oh, I am, but...I was looking for more hours. Whatever you could give me." The job inquiry was meant to lead into the subject of living with Hassie. Just until she finished school and had enough money to move away.

She'd always heard that honesty was the best policy, and seeing what a mess she'd made of this, Calla decided the direct approach would probably work better. "Actually," she said, staring down at her soda, "I was thinking I could move in with you."

"You want to live with me?" Hassie sounded kind of skeptical.

"Not for long," she promised quickly. "Just until graduation. Perhaps a while longer... I wouldn't be a bother, really I wouldn't. We could help each other. I'd do the housework and the cooking, work in the store, and you'd be helping me out."

Her suggestion was followed by a lengthy silence.

"You don't think it's a good idea?" Calla asked, chancing a look in the older woman's direction.

"No. In fact, I think this is the worst idea I've heard in twenty years."

"Oh." Calla's voice fell. A simple *no* would do, she thought resentfully. "Why?"

"First of all, you've already got more places to live than four teenagers combined. I know for a fact that your mother would love to have you with her—"

"No way!" As if Calla would deign to live in the same house as Dennis Urlacher! Not in this lifetime.

"So I understand, which is a pity. Your mother and Dennis deserve better treatment than you're giving them. So does Joshua. I don't know what happened between you two, but if he confronted you, then my guess is you damn well needed it. I can't imagine anyone with less reason to disown her family! One day you'll look back and realize how foolish you've been. For your sake, I hope it's soon."

Calla felt the heat of indignation fill her face.

"My advice, and you did ask for it, is to step back a moment, think about what you have and thank God every day of your life that there are people who love you and care about you."

Calla blinked back the hurt. She'd expected Hassie to be an ally. Obviously she'd been wrong. Slapping some money on the counter, she turned and with an indignant tilt to her head, walked out of the pharmacy.

Margaret drew in a deep, calming breath and spoke gently to the laboring heifer who was about to deliver her calf. This was her first birth and the poor thing struggled with each contraction.

"It's all right, girl," Margaret said softly. "You're doing just fine. Soon you'll have a beautiful new baby."

Margaret worried about the heifer. The birth was taking longer than expected and the animal was weakening. Rolling up her sleeves, she slipped on the long plastic glove and inserted her arm into the birth canal to feel for the hooves. They were there, thankfully. At least the calf wasn't breech. She removed her arm, slipped off the glove and patted the heifer, crooning encouragement.

"Can I help?"

At the sound of Matt's voice, she swung her head around. He stood no more than five feet away. She stared, hardly able to believe that her imagination hadn't conjured him up. She hadn't seen him in over a week.

"Say something," he said next. He seemed to need some sign of the kind of reception she was willing to accord him.

The cow bawled with pain and Margaret glanced back at her. "Yeah—I could use some help," she said.

"You've got it." A moment later, he was on his knees at her side.

"We're going to need a rope," Margaret told him.

"You sure she's ready?"

"Check for yourself."

Matt quickly washed his hands, then rolled up his sleeve. Soon his arm was sheathed in the blue glove and he was elbow-deep inside the cow. She didn't take kindly to the intrusion and protested loudly, thrashing her legs until Matt withdrew his arm.

"Apparently I'm not as gentle as you," he muttered.

Margaret let the comment slide. She wasn't there to discuss who possessed the better technique. She wanted to know his thoughts on how the birth was progressing. "Well?" she demanded.

"I agree with you. She's ready. I feel the hooves and the nose. As soon as they show, we'll put the rope to use."

The birth proved to be even more difficult than Margaret had anticipated. Soon after the calf's hooves emerged, they looped the rope around the front legs. Down on her knees with Matt, Margaret tugged and pulled, employing every ounce of strength she had. By the time the calf slid free of his mother, Margaret's arms ached and her face burned with exertion.

She had just started to rise when the first cramp hit her. An involuntary yelp escaped and she doubled over, cradling her stomach.

"Margaret!" Right away Matt was there.

"I'm fine, I'm fine." She slumped onto a bale of hay until she could assess what was happening. It didn't take long to realize she'd strained a muscle.

"Is it the baby?"

"No," she said through gritted teeth. "I'm fine. Leave me alone."

"There's something wrong. You're pale as a ghost," Matt argued.

"I said I was fine," she fired back.

"You're in pain."

Now that was a laugh. The man who'd broken her heart was concerned because she had a stomach cramp.

"Dammit, Margaret, you can't be doing this kind of physical labor. Not when you're pregnant."

The man had his nerve. "I'll do whatever I damn well please!"

"You can be angry with me if you want, but I can't allow you to do anything that'll hurt our baby."

"Like I'd intentionally do such a thing." Did he think she was an idiot?

"You're too damn stubborn for your own good."

Margaret opened her mouth to argue, then stopped. It wasn't outrage she saw in Matt's eyes, but love and concern. He'd been gone a week, seven days in which she'd had time to consider her options. Time to decide what was important. Time to consider her future and that of her child.

"Be angry if you want," he said again, "but you can't do everything by yourself. You need me."

"The hell I do!" Her response was automatic, her voice sharp.

"Okay, you don't need me," he countered just as sharply. "I'm the one who needs you. Hear me out and if you want me to leave afterward, I will."

"All right."

He sat on a bale across from her. "I've been with quite a few women over the years. I'm not proud of this, and I don't think it comes as any surprise."

She'd known the kind of man he was when she married him, but she hadn't understood exactly what that meant. She hadn't realized that he couldn't completely escape his history—as Sheryl had proven.

"You married me because I had something to offer that those other women didn't—my land and the cattle," she threw out angrily. "And because I believed in you, or so you've said."

"Yes," he said, equally angry. "But dammit, Margaret, there's more. You got to me. You're the finest cattlewoman

I know. The finest rancher, period. No one's better at managing a herd than you, and I respect that. You're attractive and you're smart and you have character. Okay, so you're no beauty queen. I'm not interested in pretty, shallow girls—they're a dime a dozen. But there's only one you.''

The intensity of his words, his eyes, told her he spoke with sincerity.

''There's something else you should know. Every other woman I've ever loved, I've loved from below the waist, if you know what I mean. But I love *you* with every part of me—my heart, my mind, my body.''

''Oh, Matt,'' she whispered and slid off the bale of hay onto her knees. He knelt, too, facing her.

He reached for her and she all but fell into his arms. His mouth sought hers and they kissed with the desperation of two people who'd experienced despair…and renewal.

Their kisses were deep and long. The new calf mewled softly and his mother nuzzled her offspring while Margaret clung to her husband. When they broke apart, there were tears on her cheeks. Matt kissed them away, his tenderness profound. He'd said exactly what she'd been longing to hear.

''I wasn't sure you'd be back,'' she whispered brokenly.

''I wasn't, either, but I couldn't give up on us. I thought, I hoped, that if I went away for a few days, it'd give us both time to think.''

''I did think,'' Margaret told him. ''In fact, that's all I've been doing. Now it's time we talked.''

They checked on the cow and her calf, then washed up in the barn and headed toward the house.

Sadie met them at the back entrance, holding open the

screen door. "I've got iced tea and chocolate chip cookies waiting for you on the front porch."

The thoughtful gesture pleased Margaret. "I don't know what you did to win her over, but Sadie's certainly in your camp."

"You honestly don't?" He grinned. "All I ever did to win Sadie was show her how much I love you."

With their arms around each other, they walked through the house and to the front porch, settling in the two wicker chairs that rested there. Her father often used to sit in this very spot and Margaret liked to think he was with them now.

"I do love you," Matt told her again, "and our baby."

"I know," she said simply.

"If we reconcile, I feel I should warn you that it isn't going to be easy with Sheryl." He gave her a pained look. "My lawyer and I tried to talk sense into her, but it did no good."

"She wants to raise your daughter herself?"

He nodded. "I suggested adoption, but she made it very clear that she intends to eke every penny out of me that she possibly can. The child is a means of holding on to me—and punishing me. For leaving her, and I think, for loving you." Matt reached for her hand, entwining their fingers. "She assumed I'd divorce you and marry her. She figured the pregnancy would be the incentive—and she figured you for a source of cash." He threw back his head, eyes closed. "Not once did I even consider such a plan. I swear it."

She pressed her hand to his jaw. "I believe you."

He opened his eyes, looked her full in the face. "I don't

know if it's possible, but some day I'll make all of this up to you. Maybe I can't but I intend to try. God knows I don't deserve a second chance, but I'm asking for one, anyway.''

They were in each other's arms again. Margaret found it almost impossible to keep her hands off him. They hadn't slept together in months, not since she'd learned of Sheryl's pregnancy. He'd been the one to initiate her into the physical aspect of love, and in the process had created a need in her that only he could fill.

"We have a lot to overcome, but I love you, Matt. As long as you're one hundred percent committed to me and our marriage, we have a chance."

"One hundred percent."

They kissed until Margaret heard Sadie clearing her throat behind them.

"Yes, Sadie?" she asked, her voice a mere rasp.

Matt continued to kiss the side of her neck, his hands on her shoulders, his lips moist and eager.

"Mr. Eilers has a phone call."

"Mr. Eilers?" Matt repeated, sounding amused that Sadie would be so formal.

"Gage Sinclair has a question for you."

"I'll be right back," Matt told his wife.

He left and Sadie folded her arms. "Well? Are you two back together?"

Margaret nodded.

"Good." Her smile was brief but undeniably genuine. "This time don't be so quick to give up."

Margaret laughed. "I won't."

Seventeen

"Bob, what's taking you so long?" Merrily called out from the back storeroom. Her husband had worked frantically doing spring cleaning and repairs. Merrily had joined him, working equally long hours.

"Coming," he shouted brusquely from somewhere in the kitchen.

She sighed, waiting impatiently for him to move the fifty-pound flour sack so she could continue cleaning the shelves. The more involved she became in this physical labor, the better she understood why Bob had worked himself to a frazzle those first few weeks after receiving word about Axel. It did help; it distracted her and left her tired enough to sleep. And she found the resulting cleanliness and order deeply gratifying.

Now, a month since the judge's decision, Merrily was feeling a kind of contentment. The tears didn't come as readily or as often. Instead of focusing on her loss, which seemed overwhelming, she took an inventory of her blessings. At the top of her list was Robert Carr, her husband. He wasn't the best-looking man she'd ever seen—in fact, it would be a stretch to call him handsome—but he was everything she wanted in a husband. No one had ever loved her the way he did.

"All right, all right," he muttered, walking into the storeroom, a little breathless. "What do you want?"

"Hey, don't snap at me, Buffalo Man."

"I didn't snap. I happen to be busy."

"And I'm not?" She rolled her eyes. "Do you want me to move that flour myself?"

"Don't be ridiculous."

"That's what I thought."

Bob lifted the sack as though it weighed no more than a shoe box and plopped it down where she wanted. Merrily thanked him with a kiss on the cheek, then reached inside the soapy bucket for her cleaning rag.

"I've been thinking," she began as he picked up a second bag, this time of sugar.

"About what?" he grunted.

"Us," she said calmly. She waited until she had his full attention, then drew herself up straight and looked him in the eye. "Tell me, is there any reason we couldn't have a baby of our own?"

The fifty-pound bag of sugar dropped to the floor with a solid thump. It was a wonder the sack didn't burst wide open.

"What did you just say?" Bob asked.

Merrily frowned. "You heard me! I asked your opinion on us having a baby."

Bob stared at her, mouth gaping slightly.

"Is the idea that wild?" She wasn't accustomed to seeing her husband speechless.

Bob sank onto the sugar sack, shaking his head as though completely overwhelmed. He glanced up at her. "I...I suppose we could try."

Merrily wasn't pleased with his response. She'd assumed he'd welcome the suggestion. Be excited. Eager.

Happy. But he was none of that. Whirling around, she resumed her task, attempting to hide her disappointment.

"What's wrong?"

Snorting softly, she ran the wet rag along the empty shelf. "You might have shown a *little* enthusiasm."

Once more he seemed at a loss. He shrugged his shoulders.

"I thought...you'd like the idea," she muttered, uncertain of her own feelings now. Bob had taken the news about Axel as hard as she had, perhaps harder. While the child was with them, Bob had loved and cared for him, had considered him their son. He seemed such a natural father, she'd expected him to jump instantly at the possibility of having a baby.

"I do like the idea," Bob insisted.

"Well, I sure couldn't tell."

He continued to stare at her. "It just takes some getting used to, is all."

She didn't reply. What was there to say?

"You honestly want a baby?" he asked.

"Would I have suggested it if I didn't?"

"I...guess it wouldn't hurt."

Merrily forced herself to look past her disappointment at his lukewarm response. Clearly she'd taken her husband by surprise, but she sensed that something else was troubling him.

"You'd better tell me what's wrong," she said.

"Nothing," he said quickly, far too quickly. "If you're finished with me here, I've got my own work to do."

"Fine, be that way." It was hard not to let her hurt feelings show, but she managed by turning her back to him and scrubbed the shelf with enough vigor to remove half the paint.

"Dammit, Merrily, if you want a baby, then we'll have a baby."

"I want *you* to want a baby, too," she snapped back.

"I do!" he bellowed.

"Everything you've said and done tells me otherwise."

He started pacing, his movements brisk and erratic. "I'm afraid."

His words stunned her, and she turned to face him. "You're afraid? Of what?"

Bob was sitting now, and he gestured weakly as he spoke. "What if something happened? You could miscarry. There's a risk with any pregnancy... And babies are so vulnerable. What about illness? Or accidents? We lost Axel and dammit, Merrily, I don't know if I could bear to lose another child. I can't deal with that kind of pain again."

"I couldn't bear it, either," she agreed, reaching for his hands and clasping them between her own. "No one will take our baby away from us. We were good parents to Axel—no one faulted us there. We'll be good parents to our own child, too." Her voice tearful, she whispered, "The risk is just part of life. You have to take all the precautions you can, and then...you have to trust."

"You know what I think?" Bob asked. He stood up and wrapped his arms around her waist, pulling her against him. "I think you're the bravest woman I know. If you're willing to do this, then, what the hell, so am I."

"I'm throwing out my birth control pills today." She smiled widely, the tears gone.

Holding her close, Bob threw back his head and laughed. "You do that, sweetheart, and leave the rest to me."

Despite his bravado, Merrily knew that Bob still felt some uncertainty about committing himself to this project. If you could call a baby a "project." So for the rest of the day, she formed a plan of action to lure her husband into bed. By the time she was finished with him, any lingering fears would be gone.

That night, after a lengthy shower, Bob walked into their bedroom, wrapped in his thick robe. He took one look at her and came to an abrupt standstill.

Merrily stood posed beside the bed, smiling saucily. Crooking one finger, she urged him toward her.

"What have you got on under that?" he asked, his voice husky.

"That's for you to find out."

"Merrily, I had a long, hard day. I'm tired...."

"I promise to make the night a whole lot more pleasant." Untying the sash, she let the short silk robe fall open to expose her breasts and smooth, flat abdomen.

"Ah..."

"You still too tired, Buffalo Man?" she asked softly.

"I think I've just found a new surge of energy."

Merrily beamed him an enticing smile and held out her hand, but he still hesitated. "Hey, Buffalo Man," she pouted prettily, "how much of an invitation do you need, anyway?"

He chuckled as he swung her into his arms and carried her to their bed. With a gentleness that always amazed her in a man of his size, he placed her on top of the covers.

"So, you want a baby, do you?" he whispered, smiling down at her.

She nodded.

"Tonight seems the perfect time to try."

"That's what I thought, too."

"And if it doesn't work tonight, we'll just have to continue doing this until we succeed."

"Oh, I agree with that." She slid her arms around his neck.

"I hope I don't disappoint you..."

"Not a chance."

"And I hope that getting you pregnant doesn't turn out to be as easy as you think it'll be."

She giggled again, and kissed his jaw. He captured her lips with his own and they were soon so caught up in their lovemaking that the only sounds they made were soft panting sighs.

Matt loved his wife. He'd come to recognize it in the first months of their marriage, but the intensity of his love had deepened after their reconciliation. His admiration for Margaret's hard work and leadership grew. But just as much as he admired her ability to manage a ranch, he loved her compassion and her capacity for forgiveness.

"Did anyone ever tell you how good you look on a horse?" he called out as they rode toward the ranch after a long day moving the herd to its summer pasture. The size of the herd was more than they could handle alone and there were several ranch hands working with them for the season.

"If you're trying to tell me I'm beautiful, just say so," she called back.

"You're beautiful," he shouted. "You're a fine rider, Margaret Eilers. You ride like you're part of the horse."

"Yeah, but which part?"

Matt threw back his head and roared with laughter. This was what he enjoyed most about their marriage, this banter and easy camaraderie. Margaret was more than his wife; she was his friend. The best friend he'd ever had. He'd never felt lonely until he'd nearly lost her. Never understood what brought a man home to a woman every night. Not just sex or domestic comfort. It was *this*—companionship. Understanding. A shared life. He couldn't imagine living without her now. Pastor Dawson was right; he had to fight to save his marriage.

Dinner was waiting for them when they arrived at the house. Soon afterward Sadie left for the day, but not before she caught Matt's eye and winked. It was the housekeeper's way of letting him know she was pleased that the situation had been resolved.

Only, everything *wasn't* resolved, and wouldn't be until after Sheryl's daughter—his daughter—was born. Matt and Margaret didn't talk about Sheryl or her baby, but they hadn't forgotten the other woman, either. Her time was drawing close and Matt expected to hear from her any day. In recent weeks, his only contact with his former lover had been through her attorney.

"Did you read that article I gave you about the new worming medication?" Margaret asked as they sat down at the table.

Matt nodded, helping himself to chicken casserole and green beans. "I did and I think it might be a good idea to give it a try." He'd run the numbers and saw a substantial savings for them if the medication did all it claimed. He described his conclusions and Margaret listened intently. The conversation then drifted to one of the newly hired ranch hands. Margaret wasn't pleased with his performance and said as much. Matt agreed with her complaints.

"If he can't get more accomplished in a day, then he's pushing his luck with me," Margaret told him as she reached for a dinner roll.

Matt smiled. "They don't call you a tough broad for nothing."

Margaret slathered butter on the homemade roll. "You trying to get on my good side?"

"Aren't I already?"

She attempted to keep back a smile and failed.

Then the phone rang, and Margaret glanced at Matt. "You want to get it?"

What she was really asking, he realized, was whether he thought it might be Sheryl. He shrugged and reluctantly started to get up.

"No, wait," she said, stopping him. "Let the machine take it."

He sat down again, and they both strained to hear the voice at the other end of the line.

Sure enough, it was Sheryl.

Matt's appetite instantly vanished and his stomach cramped. His eyes met Margaret's and he saw that she was just as tense.

"You'd better pick up, don't you think?" she asked.

He shook his head. "I'll phone her back later."

Margaret nodded, but the mood of the evening changed. They hardly touched what remained of their dinner. Matt carried his plate to the kitchen, scraping his leftovers into the garbage, then set it in the sink. Margaret followed him and he poured them each a cup of coffee.

"Are you going to call her back?" Margaret pressed.

Matt sighed, knowing it would do no good to delay the inevitable. "I'd better, otherwise she'll phone again." One thing about Sheryl, she was tenacious.

Flustered, Margaret hurriedly rinsed the dishes and loaded them into the dishwasher with jerky movements. "Do you want me to leave?"

"No." Already his stomach felt as if he'd swallowed hot coals. Walking over to the phone, he punched out her number, then braced his back against the wall. Margaret stood across from him, by the sink, staring at the floor.

Sheryl answered on the second ring.

"You asked me to call," Matt said, wanting to sound civil but not over-friendly.

"I had the baby."

"Did you name her?"

"Hailey Faith."

The pain in his stomach intensified with the unfamiliar and unwelcome mixture of emotions. He had a daughter, and while a part of him experienced joy and pride, another part felt fear and anger. "That's a fine name," he said after an uncomfortable moment.

"I thought so, otherwise I wouldn't have named her that."

"Was anyone with you?"

"Lee Ann came to the hospital. I wanted to phone you, but she wouldn't let me. Probably a good thing, because you wouldn't have liked the things I said about you when the labor pains got bad.''

Matt couldn't keep from smiling at that. ''I don't doubt it.''

''Are you going to come see your daughter?'' Sheryl lowered her voice, her tone confidential.

''I'm sure I will.''

''When?''

Matt's gaze flickered toward Margaret. ''I'll get back to you.''

''Ah,'' Sheryl said, ''the little woman's listening in, is she?''

''It's not like that.''

Sheryl sighed expressively. ''I'd argue if I thought it would do any good.''

''As I said, I'll get back to you about when you can expect us.''

''Margaret's coming with you?'' Sheryl's voice rose with indignation.

''That decision belongs to my wife,'' Matt insisted.

''If she comes, she's an even bigger fool than I thought.''

He ignored her remark. ''I'll be in touch with you later.''

Like everything else, Sheryl accepted this information with ill grace. ''Don't you want to know about Hailey? One would think a child's father might ask when she was born and how much she weighed.''

''Of course I want to know.'' Hearing the news of her birth had been jolt enough, although he thought he was prepared. ''Tell me the rest.''

''She was born two days ago. She's a little thing, only

five pounds, six ounces. The doctor said if I'd quit smoking, she might have been bigger.''

Matt tensed, suppressing the anger he felt at her selfishness. ''Did you have a hard time?'' he asked instead.

''You think giving birth is easy, you should try it. It's like shoving a watermelon through a doughnut hole.''

Matt didn't know what to say.

''I have to tell you though,'' Sheryl continued, her harsh voice softening, ''she's beautiful.''

''I'm sure she is.''

''Is that a backhand way of telling me I'm beautiful?'' Sheryl coaxed.

The question pulled Matt up short. ''What do you mean?''

''You just said Hailey must be beautiful, and I asked if you were telling me I'm beautiful, too. I *am* her mother, you know.''

''I...didn't mean anything.''

Sheryl blew out an exaggerated sigh. ''I don't know why you have to be so damned difficult. Nothing has to change with us—it never did. You're the one who decided to stay with Miss Moneybags, but I can forget and forgive. We had a good thing going. If you're interested in continuing our arrangement—the way it was before—I'd be willing to consider it. You can have me *and* go home to your wife.''

''No, Sheryl, I'm not interested.'' He made sure his response was curt enough to get his message across.

''We'll see,'' Sheryl said after a short pause. ''You come visit your daughter, and in the meantime I'll put on my thinking cap.''

''What?''

She laughed softly. "I'm going to look for some inventive ways to detain you." She groaned at the ensuing silence. "Bring your wife if you wish, but it won't matter. I'm not making any secret of it, Matt, I want you back in my bed. You belong with me—and with your baby. Little Hailey needs her daddy," she whispered, and then before he could respond, she hung up.

"Well?" Margaret asked when he replaced the receiver.

"Hailey Faith—that's what she named her." Shaken by the encounter, Matt gathered Margaret in his arms. Sheryl had just demonstrated what he knew to be true: she was determined to do everything in her power to either have him or destroy him.

"What is it?" Margaret asked, tilting her head back to meet his gaze.

He didn't answer, not knowing how to explain his own heart. Hailey Faith was his daughter, and he didn't know how to reconcile his feelings for this newborn baby. How could he love his child and at the same time detest her mother?

"Matt." Margaret held his face between her hands.

He weighed the pros and cons of letting Margaret know about their conversation and decided to tell her. "Sheryl wants to continue our arrangement," he confessed, deciding it was better to clear the air than hide anything from his wife again.

"Is that what you want?"

Her question shocked him. "Not on your life!"

"Actually it'd be *your* life. If you'd answered yes, I swear you'd be unable to walk upright without terrible pain for months."

He laughed; Margaret's sense of humor was exactly what he needed just then. But only later did he fully appreciate her wisdom and her insight into what the future held for them and Hailey.

"I have a daughter."

"No," she corrected him gently, holding his gaze. "*We* have a daughter. Hailey Faith is part of my life, too. I'm going to love her, welcome her into our home, nurture her and make her part of our family."

Matt stared at the incredible woman he'd married and couldn't find the words to thank her. They'd lodged themselves deep in his throat.

"We have a daughter," she repeated.

"We," Matt agreed, and held his wife close.

The pains started early Thursday afternoon in the last week of June. At first Sarah didn't recognize what they were. She was seven and a half months along, just getting to the uncomfortable, awkward stage of pregnancy. The baby moved often, stretching and kicking. The ache low in her back was simply muscle pain, she decided. Dennis was continually after her about doing too much. She didn't agree, but to be on the safe side, she left work and immediately went home and fell asleep.

The pains woke her an hour later. Now there was no disguising it: she was in labor. The low back pain worked its way around her abdomen with growing intensity. Checking her watch, she realized the contractions were coming regular as clockwork, every five minutes.

Not wanting to alarm her husband, the first person she phoned was Dr. Leggatt. Unfortunately he was out of the office, but she was able to talk to his nurse, Mrs. Berghoff.

"I'm in labor," Sarah cried, doing her best to control the blinding sense of panic. "It's too soon... I'm afraid I'm going to lose my baby."

"Relax," the woman told her calmly. "I'm sure everything's going to be all right."

"You don't know that," Sarah cried, clinging to the telephone receiver until her fingers went numb.

"You're right, I don't, but I do know that panicking isn't good for you or for the baby. Is anyone with you?"

"No—my husband's gone for the day." Leave it to this baby to choose a day Dennis was delivering fuel.

"Is there anyone who can drive you to the hospital?"

"Yes...of course."

"Good, then leave your husband a message and get started."

"Without Dennis? But...I want him with me."

"Mrs. Urlacher, for your sake and the sake of your child, don't delay any longer. I'll alert the hospital and they'll be waiting for you. This hasn't been an easy pregnancy. Let's not do anything to jeopardize it now."

"All right, all right," Sarah agreed, fighting back the fear and hysteria. "I'll come right away."

Dennis was out of reach, but she did take time to contact two families along his route, asking them to let him know she'd left for the hospital. With her husband unavailable, the first people Sarah thought to contact were her brother and Maddy, but they were an hour from town. She couldn't wait. Her second choice was her father. Her hand shook as she punched out the phone number.

Only it wasn't her father who answered, but Calla.

"Where's Dad?" she demanded.

"Hello to you, too, Mother," Calla said, her voice dripping with sarcasm.

"I need your grandfather," Sarah cried, unwilling to engage in pettiness. There'd been too much of that between her and Calla in the last few weeks.

Something in Sarah's tone must have alerted her daughter. "What's wrong?"

"I'm in labor. I need your grandfather to drive me to the hospital in Grand Forks." Sarah's voice trembled with urgency. A labor pain came over her, worse than the others, and she moaned softly.

"All right, all right, don't panic," Calla cried, sounding close to it herself. "I'll get Gramps and send him right over."

"Calla, please..."

"Mom, don't worry, I've got everything under control."

Sarah desperately wanted to believe that, but her fears had intensified, as well as her pains.

Within minutes, the old battered pickup that belonged to her father pulled up in front of the house. Reaching for her overnight bag, Sarah started out the door, but it wasn't her father who rushed to meet her. Instead of Joshua McKenna, there stood Calla.

"Where's my dad?" Sarah asked.

"Playing poker in Devils Lake. You ready, or are we going to stand here and argue all afternoon?"

Sarah hesitated, then nodded. Calla had a driver's license, had been driving for years. Despite their differences, she knew her daughter would get her where she needed to go.

Taking Sarah's elbow, Calla carefully helped her inside

the truck, then raced around the front and climbed into the driver's seat. "Hold on," she instructed as she revved the engine and shifted into gear.

Sarah clicked the seat belt into place and closed her eyes as another labor pain seized her. An involuntary moan slipped through her lips.

"You're in pain?"

Sarah nodded. "It's too soon—oh, Calla, it isn't good for the baby to come this early."

"You're not going to lose my sister," her daughter muttered. "Not if I have anything to say about it." Then, apparently realizing what she'd said, she added, "A brother would be all right, too, but I'd prefer a little sister."

Sarah didn't have time to comment. Her full concentration went into breathing. As much as possible, she tried to give her body over to the contraction. Despite her efforts, all she could think about was her husband's inevitable panic when he got word of what was happening.

"Relax, Mom," Calla urged, gripping her hand. She squeezed Sarah's fingers.

"When did you get to be such an expert on labor and birth?" Sarah snapped.

"I'm not," Calla returned, ignoring her sarcasm. "That's just common sense."

The drive took forever. Twice Calla pulled over to the side of the road when Sarah cried out with the intensity of the contractions. They were coming hard and fast now, and it was all she could do to endure them.

"What can I do to help you?" Calla cried frantically.

Doubled over in agony, Sarah shook her head. "Nothing...nothing."

"Mom, let me do something!"

"Just drive," Sarah wailed, convinced that if it took much longer, the baby would be born in the front seat of the old truck. "Get me to the hospital."

Calla tore back onto the highway for the second time, spitting dirt and gravel as she did.

Sarah noticed that Calla's knuckles were as white and tense as her own.

By the time they arrived in Grand Forks, Sarah was weeping softly. She pressed her hands over her abdomen, afraid that with all the complications she'd already suffered, plus a premature birth, her baby didn't have a chance.

Tires squealing, Calla pulled the truck into a spot normally reserved for emergency vehicles. Slamming her hand on the horn to attract attention, she cut the engine, then leaped out of the truck and raced through the doors into the hospital emergency room.

Almost immediately an orderly hurried outside with Calla, wheeling a chair. He opened the door and helped Sarah down.

"Be careful!" her daughter yelled.

"I'm fine, I'm fine," Sarah insisted, but she wasn't.

"Did Dr. Leggatt's office phone?" Calla demanded as the orderly rolled Sarah into the hospital.

"I wouldn't know," the man responded.

"Well, find out!"

"Please," Sarah sobbed, and gripped the orderly's sleeve. "Please..."

Calla reached for her hand. "Mom, it's going to be all right."

"Why does everyone keep telling me that?" Sarah shouted. "My baby's six weeks early—"

"Mom...Mom." Calla knelt at her side by the admissions desk. The attendant was studying her computer and assembling pieces of papers, giving Sarah and Calla a few precious moments together. "Listen to me—"

"No, no. You don't know—"

"I know you love your baby and that the baby can feel your love."

"It didn't work with you, did it?" Sarah hated being so caustic, but she couldn't help herself.

To Sarah's shock, Calla's eyes filled with tears. "Actually it did." Her daughter's fingers tightened around her hand. "Despite everything I did—running away, being a real jerk—I always knew you loved me. I always knew I could turn to you for help. I've been acting like a spoiled brat for so long, I didn't know how to tell you I regret everything I've done."

Sarah stared at her daughter, certain her state of mind had conjured up those words.

"I love you, Mom," Calla whispered. "I love my little half brother or half sister, too."

"How...what happened?"

Calla brushed the back of her hand along the arch of her cheek, wiping away tears. "Does it matter?"

"No."

They hugged and Calla buried her face in her mother's shoulder. "Gramps and I had an argument about...things."

"You and my dad?" Joshua hadn't said a word. How typical of him.

"I was thinking of moving out."

"Where?"

Calla's laugh was ironic. "I thought Hassie would take me in, especially if I came to work for her."

"She wasn't keen on the idea, I assume?"

"That's putting it mildly," Calla said. "She didn't laugh in my face, but she might as well have."

The orderly waved a paper. "I have to take your mother now."

Calla nodded and stood. "I'll walk you to the elevator." Holding her mother's hand, Calla escorted her as far as the elevator.

"Say a prayer for me," Sarah cried when the big steel doors slid open.

The attendant pushed her inside and then reversed her position so that she faced Calla.

"Mom...Mom..."

Another contraction struck and Sarah was left gasping by the force of the pain. They were worse now, worse than anything she remembered. She was hardly aware of the short journey to the labor room.

"Mrs. Urlacher," Dr. Leggatt greeted her as soon as she was settled. "This is a surprise."

"I don't want to lose my baby," she sobbed.

"Good," the physician said. "I have no intention of losing either one of you."

"My husband..."

"Phoned the hospital," Dr. Leggatt told her. "Don't worry. He's on his way."

Eighteen

Matt took Margaret's suggestion that he visit Sheryl and the baby by himself as a sign of her love and trust.

"Are you sure?" he asked before he left the ranch. His arms were burdened with gifts, ones they'd purchased together for Hailey.

"Yes. For the first visit, at any rate."

Still he hesitated.

"Matt," she said, and laughed, easing him toward the door. "Hailey's your daughter. I want you to have some time with her on your own."

He understood and appreciated her reasons, but he wasn't entirely sure he wanted to do it this way. Today's visit was going to be difficult enough. If Margaret accompanied him, they'd present a united front, proving to Sheryl once and for all that there was no chance of a continuing relationship. Instead, Margaret ushered him out the door to make his own peace with his former lover.

The drive into Devils Lake seemed to require double the amount of time it normally did. His hands tightened around the steering wheel, and Matt acknowledged how nervous he was. Not about any confrontation with Sheryl; she didn't tempt him in the least. He wasn't even worrying about her lawsuit; somehow or other, that would all be settled. In analyzing his feelings he realized his uneasiness had to do with his newborn daughter. This child was the result of his own carelessness—and Sheryl's greed. Yet Hailey was blameless. During the pregnancy Matt had avoided thinking about the baby, avoided forming an emotional attachment. Deep down, all he'd wanted was the whole thing to go away. Not exactly a mature or realistic outlook.

From the day he'd heard about Hailey's birth, he could no longer block her from his life. He was about to meet the daughter he'd fathered, the daughter he was prepared to love—already loved. The realization terrified him.

He parked outside Sheryl's rental house and saw the drapes part as she peeked out the window. The front door was open long before he reached the porch steps.

"You're right on time," she said, holding the screen door for him.

Matt had to admit she looked good, despite having given birth only a week earlier. She'd evidently gone to a great deal of trouble with her appearance. Her hair and makeup were done to perfection. She wore tight slacks and a revealing halter top, her breasts almost spilling out.

She must have caught him looking, because she instantly commented. "Nothing fits right anymore." Cupping the underside of the bra top, she shrugged her shoulders, then jiggled her breasts so they threatened to spill out entirely.

Embarrassed, Matt glanced away and set down the packages. "I brought Hailey a few gifts."

"How sweet." She leaned forward and kissed his cheek.

Matt reacted as though she'd burned him.

Sheryl giggled. "No need to be afraid. I promise not to hurt you."

An immediate argument came to him, but he squelched it. From the moment Sheryl realized he wasn't going to divorce Margaret and marry her, she'd done everything she could to hurt him. She'd tried to destroy his marriage and his life. If she couldn't get him back, she was going to make him pay.

"Where's Hailey?" he asked.

"Asleep."

"I'd like to see her."

"Don't worry, you will," Sheryl said. She motioned for him to sit. "Make yourself comfortable and I'll get you a drink."

"I'm here to see my daughter," he insisted, refusing to take a seat.

"Oh, Matt," she said with an exaggerated sigh. "Am I such a threat? I promise if you sit down I'm not going to pounce on you, although I have to admit the thought is tempting." She walked over to the liquor cabinet and brought out a bottle of Irish whiskey.

"I said I don't want a drink."

She frowned at him over her shoulder. "You might not, but I do. Frankly, I need something to help me relax. I was up half the night with the baby. She's already showing signs of a temper. Can you imagine? You should see her lower lip quiver when she doesn't get what she wants."

Sheryl poured herself a drink, then went into the bedroom.

Matt sank down on the edge of the sofa, but immediately stood as she returned with the baby. His heart pounded so loud, it echoed in his ears. Automatically he held out his arms for his child; Sheryl placed Hailey there, then stepped back as he took his first look at his daughter.

She was a tiny thing, he noted, just like Sheryl had said—so small she almost fit in the palms of his two hands. Her hair was dark and there was a lot of it. She didn't look like him, but she didn't resemble Sheryl, either.

"Don't worry, she isn't going to break."

Matt sat down and carefully folded open the blanket, then bent to kiss her forehead.

"You wake her and you get to put her back to sleep," Sheryl told him, taking a large gulp of her drink.

"I'll do my best," he whispered, awed by the strength of his emotions. He'd dreaded this for months and knew now that he had nothing to be afraid of. His daughter was incredible, beautiful, perfect.

"Pretty, isn't she?" Sheryl asked proudly.

"Beautiful," Matt whispered, using his index finger to brush a soft wisp of hair from her small face. This was the child who'd caused him such grief, yet all he could feel in that moment was love.

"People say she looks a lot like me."

He grinned, unwilling to fall into that trap again. "Time will tell."

Sheryl moved close and perched on the edge of the coffee table across from him. She leaned forward, pretending to study Hailey. Matt knew what she was really doing, and that was offering him a look at her generous breasts. He centered his concentration on his daughter, counting her fingers and toes.

"You want me to open the gifts?" Sheryl asked, gesturing at the bags.

Matt had purposely left them unwrapped. They weren't gifts for Sheryl. Everything he'd purchased was for Hailey. "Margaret and I picked up a few things we thought you'd need."

"How nice," she responded, but sounded more perturbed than grateful.

Enthralled as he was with Hailey, Matt didn't watch as Sheryl inspected the baby outfits and supplies he'd brought.

"So cute," Sheryl said.

"She really is, isn't she?"

"I was talking about this dress," Sheryl told him.

Matt looked away from the baby. "Margaret picked it out."

"Margaret, Margaret, Margaret! Is she all you can talk about?"

At Sheryl's shrill voice, Hailey woke and started to fuss. Matt didn't know much about babies, but he gently bounced her in his arms. That didn't seem to help, so he placed her ever so carefully on his shoulder and patted her back.

"Answer me, dammit," Sheryl demanded.

With Hailey wailing in his ear and Sheryl haranguing him, it took Matt a minute to compose himself. "Margaret's my wife."

"You'd never have married her if it wasn't for me," Sheryl said furiously. "You weren't supposed to fall in love with her, you idiot. Why am I surprised? Why?" She stood and slapped her sides. "That woman's no woman. I can't *believe* you actually fell for her."

Again Matt resisted correcting her. Insisting that Margaret was more woman than Sheryl could ever be wouldn't improve the situation. As much as possible, he wanted to keep his relationship with Sheryl neutral, for Hailey's sake.

"You were supposed to marry *me,*" Sheryl shouted. "How could you do this?"

The baby wailed louder still, and nothing Matt did seemed to comfort her.

"I'm sorry," he said in an effort to appease Sheryl.

"Not sorry enough. What's going to happen to us?" She glared at him, her eyes spitting anger.

"I'll make regular child support payments and—"

"Not me and the baby," she interrupted. "You and me! Us."

"Sheryl," he said as gently as he could. "There *is* no us. I'm married to Margaret. All you and I share is Hailey. I was hoping we could both remain adult about this...I realize the situation's difficult, but—"

"You're damn straight it is."

"If you want to blame me, then go ahead. I accept full responsibility..."

"Of course I blame you," she yelled. "You're an idiot. Don't you get it, you could have had me *and* Margaret's money? We were good together."

Matt's heart sank. Sheryl simply didn't understand. More than that, she refused to understand. He loved his wife. Marrying Margaret was the smartest thing he'd ever done, and to his dying day, he'd be grateful that she chose to love him.

Sheryl started to sob and covered her face with both hands. "Now look what you've done."

"I'm sorry," he said again.

"Don't apologize. You're worthless, you know. Worthless."

He stood, still patting the baby's back. It was time he left. Sheryl was in danger of exploding and his own patience was limited. Visiting his daughter shouldn't include having insults hurtled at him, and he wondered if this would be the norm. He supposed he should get in touch with his attorney, see what they could figure out. What kind of agreement or—

"Make her stop crying!" Sheryl shouted.

Matt wrapped his arm protectively around the newborn and rocked her from side to side, hoping that would work.

"Shut up!" Sheryl screamed at the baby and placed her hands over her ears. Whirling around, she glared at Matt. "This is all your fault."

"Fine, it's my fault, but screaming at a baby isn't going to help."

"Get out of here," she said, pointing at the door. "I want you out of my home."

He hesitated. Clearly, Sheryl was distraught, but there was little he could do. He carried the baby to the bedroom and lovingly settled her inside the crib. It was hard to turn his back on his daughter, especially when she was crying like this, but he had no choice.

"Get out of my home." Sheryl had apparently regained some of her composure. Tears glittered in her eyes, and he could recognize another emotion there, one that sent chills racing down his backbone. Hate.

"Sheryl," he said, determined to try one last time. "I told you before—and I meant it—if you want to blame me, do. But if the day ever comes when you feel you can't deal with the stress of the baby, call me. Margaret and I will raise Hailey.''

''Now you want my daughter, too?''

''Only if she becomes too much for you.''

Sheryl crossed her arms and stared at him with hatred gleaming from her eyes. ''I'll rot in hell before I give you my child. Go home to your precious Margaret and may you both get what you so richly deserve.''

Calla paced the waiting area outside the emergency room. She hadn't seen her mother in over an hour and each attempt to glean information had met with failure. She tried to sit and calm herself, but that didn't work for more than a few minutes. When she couldn't stand it any longer she bolted to her feet again and continued to wear a path in the floor.

Worries crowded her mind. With those worries came regrets. The last thing Calla saw before the elevator doors slid shut was the look of pain on her mother's face, mingled with a terrible fear. Although Calla knew little about pregnancy and birth, she understood that seven and a half months was too early. A premature birth would probably cause complications, especially since the pregnancy had already been difficult.

Before they'd taken her mother away, Calla had spilled out her heart. She hadn't intended to feel a thing for this baby. Dennis's baby. But she did. During the time her mother had undergone bed rest, Calla had spent a number of afternoons with her. Sarah had let Calla touch her stomach to feel the baby's movements. At first she hadn't been able to detect anything. But later, when she had, she'd felt a sense of genuine excitement.

Just then the hospital door burst open and Dennis rushed inside. He looked like a man possessed as he raced to the admissions desk. "My wife's here. Her name is Sarah... Sarah Urlacher. She's having our baby."

"Just a minute, Mr. Urlacher."

The receptionist sounded so calm. She turned to her keyboard and typed in the name. "Your wife has been admitted."

"Can I see her?"

"It says here she's on the third floor but doesn't give a room number."

"I'll find her."

Calla didn't doubt that he would. Unwilling to be left behind, she followed him. Distraught as he was, Dennis didn't notice her until after he'd hit the elevator button for the second time.

He stared at her, and Calla shifted uncomfortably under his scrutiny. "I drove Mom here."

He nodded, but said nothing.

When the elevator arrived, they both stepped inside. It rose slowly to the third floor, and when the doors opened, Dennis virtually leaped out and ran to the nurses' station.

"I'm here to find out about my wife."

Hospital staff might not give Calla information, but they wouldn't ignore Dennis.

After asking Dennis a few pertinent questions, the woman glanced at Calla.

"I'm her daughter," Calla said.

"Mr. Urlacher, your wife's in surgery."

"Surgery?" The word exploded from Dennis.

"Dr. Leggatt will explain everything as soon as he's

finished. We have a small waiting area here.'' She nodded toward a few chairs grouped around a low table. ''It shouldn't be much longer now.''

Looking defeated and broken, Dennis slumped into a chair and leaned forward, his arms braced against his knees, hands dangling.

Calla found a chair as far away from him as possible. It would have helped had there been other people in the waiting area. There weren't. Every minute claimed more of Calla's composure. The longer they were required to wait, the more certain she was that something had gone wrong. She could see Dennis had reached the same conclusion. His face was tortured with the pain of not knowing.

''Can you tell me what happened?'' he finally asked, hurling the words as if he couldn't keep from asking.

''I...Mom phoned, telling me she needed a ride into Grand Forks.''

''She didn't fall or anything?''

Calla shook her head. ''I don't think so.''

''She didn't mention what brought on labor?''

''No, only that she was afraid of losing the baby.''

At this, Dennis ran his fingers through his hair and exhaled harshly. ''Did they tell you why the surgery's necessary?''

''No.''

He was silent again for several minutes, then started to pace, his movemnnts full of frantic compulsion. Past the table, around the chairs, back to the table, again and again. He didn't look at Calla and she didn't look at him. At least she tried not to, but soon found it impossible. Dennis loved her mother, loved his unborn child, too.

"She wanted to wait for you, but the nurse told her to get to the hospital right away," Calla told him.

Dennis stopped abruptly and glanced at Calla, as though surprised she'd spoken. He swallowed visibly, then said, "I'm thankful you were there."

Calla nodded, no less thankful.

"I realize there's no love lost between us," she said, and heaved in a deep breath, "but I can tell that you care about my mother."

"She's the only woman I've ever loved." He sank back into the chair.

"I don't hate you, you know."

He raised his head. From the expression on his face, she guessed he was sorely tempted to call her a liar.

"I don't hate you anymore," she amended.

Dennis waited for her to continue.

"I've been a...a jerk the last couple of years and, well, I guess I wanted my mother to love me more than she did you. What I did was create a tug of war between the two of us."

"Your mother loves you, Calla."

"I know, but that wasn't enough for me. I didn't want her to love anyone else. I understand now that I was asking the impossible." She squared her shoulders, and figured this was as good a time as any to make the necessary amends. "I've said and done things that I'm not proud of, and I was thinking...hoping...you might be willing to forgive me."

He studied her as though to gauge her sincerity.

"I wouldn't blame you if you decided not to, but I'm hoping that's not the case." She should've known Dennis wouldn't make this easy, but then why should he? She'd gone out of her way to make his life miserable for a very long time.

"You don't have to like me," she whispered.

"Why the change of heart?" he demanded.

"Why?" Calla wasn't entirely sure when it had come about. Sometime after she'd argued with Dennis. She'd been furious, looking for people to take her side against him. Since then, she'd had long talks with people she respected. Maddy and Jeb were two of the first. Although her aunt and uncle weren't overtly critical of her, Calla could see they felt she was in the wrong.

Her grandfather and Hassie were more inclined to state their unvarnished opinions, and neither felt any compunction about bruising her ego. Still, Calla had been able to shake off their warnings and admonitions. But Kevin's letter had reached her in a way no one else could. Although it hadn't seemed like that at first read, and although he hadn't said it in so many words, he'd told her to grow up. It was time she made peace with Dennis, his letter said, and the sooner she acknowledged her own contribution to the problems, the sooner she'd have her family back. Despite everything she claimed, Calla had missed her mother. She'd found their estrangement increasingly difficult.

"Why the change of heart?" Dennis repeated.

Calla told him, and when she finished she held out her hand for him to shake. Dennis looked at her and then slowly, cautiously, a smile appeared.

"Just get one thing straight," Calla said, feeling close to tears. "I'm not calling you Dad."

"You don't have to," he assured her.

They both stopped talking when Dr. Leggatt approached, his face solemn. Calla and Dennis met him halfway. Calla's heart thudded hard against her ribs.

"Congratulations, you have a son."

"A son," Dennis repeated, his voice barely audible. "What about Sarah? Is she all right? What about the baby? How is he?"

"Unfortunately by the time your wife got here, the baby was in distress and so was she. We did what we could to stop the labor, but couldn't. In the end we were forced to perform an emergency caesarean. No fear, your wife did beautifully."

"And the baby?" Dennis asked nervously.

"Small. Three pounds, ten ounces. Our main concern isn't so much his size as his lung development. We have him in the neonatal intensive care unit now. You'll be able to see him soon, but I don't want you to be alarmed by the tubes and needles."

"He'll be all right?"

"Every indication at this point says so."

Dennis grinned at Calla, who battled back tears, then watched as her stepfather hugged the physician.

"A son!" he cried. "I have a son."

"I wanted a sister," Calla muttered, trying to lighten the atmosphere.

"Your wife is anxious to see you both," Dr. Leggatt said, then led them to her room.

Sarah looked shockingly pale against the sheets. When she saw Dennis, she stretched out a hand, and her husband moved toward her. At another time, an earlier time, Calla might have resented seeing the love between them. Although she'd made her peace with Dennis, it still hurt to know there was someone else her mother loved, but Calla recognized that what Kevin had said was true. One day she'd marry, and leave her mother for her own life. She was wrong to begrudge Sarah happiness.

Her mother *was* happy, she realized. She stood in the background and waited.

"Calla," Sarah whispered, reaching toward her now.

"I'm here, Mom," she said. She stepped close to the bed.

"Thank you..." Sarah whispered.

"Hey, I got a brother out of the deal. That's not so bad."

"Not bad at all," Dennis said, placing a hand on Calla's shoulder.

Her mother noticed the change between Dennis and her right away. "You don't need to worry, Mom, Dennis and I are square now."

"Square?"

"Yeah, everything's going to be all right."

Tears sprang to Sarah's eyes. Dennis took her hand and pressed his lips to her palm. "We've reached an understanding," he said. "We both love you and little Josh. Who knows, before long we might even like each other."

Calla had the feeling it wouldn't take long at all.

Buffalo Bob walked over to Lily Quantrill Park and inspected the newly planted grass. The park remained roped off to prevent anyone from walking on the fresh green shoots, but that hadn't stopped folks from stopping and taking a gander. Bob was pleased.

Right now, the park revealed little of what the town

council had planned for the future. By next summer, there'd be play equipment for the kids, including swings and a slide. The Boy Scout troop that met at the church on Tuesday nights was building a huge sandbox, and there was talk of installing a wading pool in a year or two. Lily Quantrill would be proud of what they'd accomplished in such a short time. A park would draw the community together, and Bob suspected that was what she'd intended all along.

Feeling good about life in general, he wandered over to the post office to pick up the mail. Merrily was busy with her friends, who were holding a baby shower for Sarah Urlacher at the restaurant. Bob used the shower as an excuse to leave. He'd prefer not to get involved in a women's gathering, with gossip and giggling and lots of talk about diapers and such.

He was greeted by a few friends as he headed into the post office, where he collected a handful of envelopes. Included was a statement from the attorney, and a few flyers. He'd open the bill later. He shot the breeze with Joshua McKenna and talked motorcycles for the better part of an hour.

By the time he returned to 3 OF A KIND, the baby shower had ended and the last of Merrily's friends was leaving.

"Is it safe?" he teased. He liked claiming that these women's get-togethers were really "weanie roasts" where no man was safe.

"Anything in the mail?"

"A bill from the California law firm."

Merrily frowned. "I thought we paid them off last month?"

Come to think of it, she was right. Merrily disappeared into his office with the mail, and Bob went into the kitchen where the prep cook was getting ready for the dinner crowd. Within a few hours, Buffalo Bob's would be bustling.

"Bob."

Merrily's voice shook, and it frightened Bob. Not understanding, he found her still in his office, her face streaked with tears. Instead of explaining, she handed him a handwritten letter.

"The attorney forwarded this to us," she whispered.

Puzzled, Bob reached for it.

July 5th

Dear Friends,

Forgive me for not using your names, but I don't know them. However, I felt compelled to write to you. Our attorney has spoken with the lawyers who represented you, and he didn't think it'd be inappropriate for me to write this letter. I beg your forgiveness if it brings you any sadness, because that isn't my intention.

After that rather lengthy prelude, I'd like to introduce myself. My name is Jenny and my husband, Michael, and I are the couple who adopted Axel. We understand there were rather unusual circumstances that led to his adoption and were given only a brief history of his life when we applied with the state adoption agency. Axel's personal history left a great deal unexplained.

When we asked to speak to his foster mother, we learned that he'd only been with the family a few weeks. For several months before that, we were later told, Axel lived with you. The caseworker informed us you'd saved Axel's life. It's hard to imagine parents who would abuse their own child and actually be willing to sell him. The purpose of my letter is to thank you from the bottom of our hearts for saving Axel from what would certainly have been a horrible fate. I can't bear to think what might have happened to him if not for you.

Our son is the joy of our lives. We waited five years for him, and had almost lost hope of ever receiving a child. You cannot imagine our delight when we learned we'd been chosen to raise Axel. He's a bright, cheerful boy, full of love and happiness. Every day is an adventure for him.

One day, when he's better able to understand, my husband and I will tell him about the brave couple who risked so much to save him. We want him to know the story of how you nurtured and loved him when he needed it most. My husband and I will forever be grateful to you both. We wanted you to know we appreciated the loving care you gave our son.

He's adjusting well and thriving. Enclosed is a recent photo so you can see for yourselves how well he's doing.

Again we can't thank you enough.

Sincerely,
Jenny and Michael
Axel's family

Bob read the letter a second time and his throat clogged with emotion. "Look," Merrily whispered, and handed him a picture.

Bob examined the snapshot. At first all he felt was his own sense of loss. Anger filled his chest. How dared these people rip open a wound that had only half healed? How dared they invade his life, even with the best of intentions?

That feeling didn't last, however, and was quickly replaced by a stronger one. Gratitude. Two strangers had reached across the miles to offer him and Merrily a feeling of closure to a difficult time in their lives.

"He...he's grown so much," Merrily said.

Not trusting his voice, Bob nodded.

"The letter was very generous. An act of kindness."

"Yes," he agreed.

"I wonder if Axel..." She stopped midsentence and when he glanced over, expecting her to complete her thought, Merrily shook her head. "It doesn't matter anymore. He's happy...I can see it in his eyes. It isn't important if he remembers us. Not anymore."

Later that night, after the restaurant had closed, Bob read the letter yet again. The snapshot was missing, and he suspected Merrily had taken it. Axel had adjusted; the photo told him as much. The boy had a good, loving home with these people—Jenny and Michael—and was obviously doing well.

"Bob," his wife called from upstairs.

"I'll be right there," he called back. He refolded the letter and tucked it away. Despite everything, his heart was heavy as he climbed the stairs.

"Are you coming to bed soon?" Merrily asked, meeting him at the top.

"As soon as I shower."

"There's a surprise for you in the bathroom."

"A surprise?" In his present frame of mind, Bob wasn't especially interested in surprises.

"Don't you want to know what it is?" Merrily asked as she wrapped her arm around his waist.

"Then it wouldn't be a surprise, would it?"

"No. I guess you'd better look and then if you want, I'll explain."

Deciding to humor his wife, he entered the small bathroom and saw nothing out of the ordinary. "What?" he asked, wondering if this was her clever way of telling him about a blocked drain. Frankly, he could live without a plumbing problem right now. Come morning, he'd deal with it.

"See that stick?" Merrily asked, her eyes twinkling.

"What stick?" he asked, glancing about the room.

"The one on the counter."

Sure enough, there was a plastic stick on a bed of tissue. "What about it?"

"It's blue."

"And what does that mean?"

"That, my darling Buffalo Man, means we're pregnant." Her smile was filled with such joy it took Bob's breath away.

"Pregnant. But—" It was too much. Stunned and delighted by turns, he collapsed on the edge of the bathtub. "You're sure?"

"Positive, if that test can be trusted. Oh, Bob, Bob, we're going to have a baby!"

Bob closed his eyes and threw his arms around his wife. The pain they'd suffered over the loss of Axel had been replaced with the joyful promise of a child of their own.

This ebb and flow of life. Grief mingled with pain. The happy with the sad. Lost and then found. Five years earlier, he'd rolled into Buffalo Valley, never suspecting this dead-end town would end up being home. Yet here he was, a business leader, a husband and soon to be a father. Life didn't get much better than this.

Epilogue

Six months later

"Mom!" Calla burst through the door of Buffalo Valley Quilting Company, clutching a letter in her gloved hand. Beneath her thick coat and hat, all that was visible were her eyes, nose and mouth.

Sarah looked up from her designing board and was struck by the sheer joy she saw in her daughter. The sullen teenager who'd become a fixture over the last few years was gone, replaced by the daughter she'd desperately missed. Since Josh's birth six months earlier, a great deal had changed in Sarah's life. Her son thrived and was growing, making up for lost time. After nearly a month in the hospital, Josh had been released, and they were able to bring him home to a doting older sister and a father intent on spoiling him. Not to mention an adoring grandfather—his namesake—and an uncle, aunt and cousin. Soon afterward Calla graduated from high school and as a surprise Kevin Betts had arrived for the ceremony.

Kevin had become something of a celebrity in town. An inspiration to other young people. He was about to enter his third year of art school and had proved to all of them that it was possible to achieve one's dreams.

"What are you so excited about?" Sarah asked. Calla

was home for the Christmas holidays. After delaying a decision about continuing her education, she'd applied at the last minute to the community college in Grand Forks, with plans to transfer to the University of North Dakota in her Junior year.

"I got a letter from Kevin," Calla explained.

"You get letters from Kevin all the time." Sarah was pleased with the budding relationship between her daughter and Leta Betts's son. He was a positive influence on Calla, and they seemed to understand and appreciate each other.

"First off," Calla said, sounding breathless, "he sold another sculpture and he's really excited."

"Wonderful."

"You know what else he said?"

Sarah could only imagine.

"He suggested I might apply for law school after graduation."

Her daughter an attorney. "Well," Sarah murmured as she mulled over the idea, "you certainly have a gift for arguing any side of an issue."

"That's what Kevin said, too. I've never thought about being an attorney, but I bet it'd be really interesting work. I'm going to think about it."

"Good. Buffalo Valley could use a capable attorney."

"Mother, honestly," Calla said with a groan, "what makes you think I'd want to practice *here?* The whole world's just waiting to be explored. If I do take up law, it'll be a long time before I set up an office in *this* town."

"You have years before you need to make that decision," Sarah told her.

"I'm heading back to school now, so I just came to say goodbye."

Although Calla was often home on weekends, Sarah always hated it when she had to leave. She stood and hugged her daughter, savoring the renewed closeness they shared. Their relationship wasn't perfect, and there were still times when Calla tried her patience, but it was infinitely better than it had been.

"I'll phone next week," she promised.

"Good." Sarah enjoyed their long telephone conversations immensely.

"Kiss Josh goodbye for me."

"I will," Sarah said, walking her to the front door. The wind roared and the chill factor was well below zero—a typical North Dakota winter.

Calla paused as she rewrapped the muffler. "Love you, Mom."

"Love you, too."

Still her daughter hesitated. "I'm really proud of what you've done with your quilting business. One day, your quilts will be known all over the world."

Her daughter's faith in her did Sarah's heart good. "Thank you, sweetheart. I hope you're right."

"I am, Mom, just wait and see."

"How'd the knitting lesson go?" Buffalo Bob asked his wife when he returned from the town council meeting.

Merrily, six months pregnant, sat in the rocking chair in their small living room with a pair of knitting needles and a pattern. "This isn't as easy as it looks, you know."

Bob had to grin. Once again, Leta Betts had stepped

forward and volunteered to give free knitting lessons. Joanie Wyatt had sold Merrily the yarn and other necessary supplies, and before he knew it his wife was busily working on a blanket for the baby. But Merrily wasn't the only one preparing for the birth of their child.

Bob had completely refurbished the spare bedroom, converting it into a nursery. The ceiling had been repainted, the walls papered, the floor recarpeted. His kid had yet to be born and already he or she was being showered with love. Not a bad start.

Working on the nursery, he'd found it hard to suppress memories of Axel. Merrily's suggestion about having their own baby had been a good one, although at the time it'd shaken him. His wife's wisdom was an unexpected blessing, just like her love. These days, thoughts of Axel weren't as painful as they'd once been. The boy was happy with parents who loved him. He had a new life. Axel was a precious gift he'd been able to have for only a short time and Bob could more easily accept losing him now.

"How'd the council meeting go?" Merrily asked, her feet propped on the ottoman. The knitting needles were close to her face and the tip of her tongue appeared as she slipped a stitch from one needle to the other.

"Long," Bob said as he took the chair across from her. "There's a lot going on. It looks like Heath's going to move the corporate headquarters out of Grand Forks sooner than expected."

Merrily glanced up from her knitting. "Really?"

"The plan's in the works."

"I figured as much when he and Rachel announced they were going to build a home here in town."

The Quantrills' two-story brick house was big news. It was the first brand-new home built in Buffalo Valley in nearly thirty years. The first of many to come. It was inevitable with all the growth.

"We talked about the Summer Fest and a parade next July."

"A parade," Merrily repeated, sounding delighted. "What a great idea! Whose—no, don't tell me, let me guess. Hassie's idea, right?"

"Right. We've already chosen a grand marshal for the parade. Want to guess who?"

Merrily stopped knitting and her brow furrowed. "There are several ways that could go. Sarah's business is thriving, and with all the people she employs now, it would be a small way for the town to thank her."

"And there's always Heath, president of the bank and all," Bob pointed out.

Merrily shook her head. "Nah, Rachel wouldn't want her husband to get conceited, and as council president she might think that was a conflict of interest. It isn't, but I think Rachel would rather be on the safe side."

His wife was right again. Heath's name had come up and Rachel had mentioned that very thing.

"All right, tell me," Merrily said.

"Actually, we chose Lindsay Sinclair."

"The high-school teacher?"

Bob nodded. "You might not remember, but she was the one who started it all. She saved the town when she agreed to step in and take over classes after Eloise Patten died. The entire course of this community changed after her arrival. It seemed only fitting to thank her."

"Hassie's idea again?"

"Yeah," he said with a grin. "But we have a big surprise for Hassie, too. This summer we're dedicating the park. Kevin's doing the sculpture, of course—it's a bronze of rifles stacked against each other, to represent the fallen soldiers. There's going to be a plaque in memory of all the men from Buffalo Valley who died in the different wars. Hassie's son is listed there. She doesn't need to worry about people forgetting him or any of the other men."

"Does she know?" Merrily asked.

"She doesn't have a clue that Kevin's practically finished the sculpture. But there's going to be more than that. It's still a secret, though."

"Tell me, Bob. I promise I won't breathe a word."

He could trust his wife; Merrily was nothing if not discreet. "There'll be a flower garden in the park dedicated to Hassie. Not once did she lose faith in Buffalo Valley. She's been a source of inspiration to us all and we love her." Himself included. Hassie had been both friend and mentor.

"She'll be so pleased."

Bob leaned forward and kissed his wife's cheek. "I'd better get back to work."

"Yes, dear," Merrily murmured, and reached for her knitting.

Three-month-old David Bernard Eilers woke with a loud, lusty cry. Margaret automatically moved into the boy's bedroom and cradled him against her. "I'll bet you're hungry, aren't you?" she cooed softly. Small but strong, David kicked and thrashed about as she quickly changed his diaper. Margaret then sat in the rocking chair and freed her breast to nurse her son.

It wasn't long before Matt came. He paused when he saw her and his face softened with love.

Margaret smiled up at her husband and marveled at the changes a year had brought into her life. She'd set her sights on Matt Eilers, chosen him as her husband, convinced him to marry her. It wasn't a perfect marriage, but after a less-than-ideal beginning, she could guarantee it was a strong one. It had to be.

Now Margaret was not only a wife, but a mother twice over. Little Hailey often spent weekends with them. Their contact with Sheryl Decker was limited, which was best all the way around. The waitress was bitter and difficult, despite a determined effort from both Matt and Margaret to make the situation as tolerable as they could.

Matt claimed the chair across from Margaret. She could tell that something was troubling him.

"Problems?" No doubt they involved Sheryl.

"I got a call from her attorney this morning."

"Again?"

Matt nodded, frowning. "Only this time it isn't money Sheryl wants." Margaret knew he worried about his daughter. Margaret did, too, but they were helpless to do anything but love and support little Hailey.

"Sheryl wants to give us custody of Hailey. Apparently, someone called Child Protective Services on her. A neighbor, as far as I know."

Margaret's first reaction was to feel elated. Then her practical nature asserted itself. "She doesn't suspect *us*, does she?"

"Oh, no," he murmured. "Sheryl says she isn't cut out for this motherhood business."

What she really meant, Margaret thought, was that using Hailey as a means of controlling Matt hadn't worked. All her frustration and bitterness had been directed at the baby. While Margaret had never seen evidence of physical abuse, she feared Sheryl had often left her unattended. That was probably what had motivated her neighbor to call the authorities.

"She says she's willing to sign over all rights to us," Matt said.

This was what Matt and Margaret had wanted, what they'd prayed for almost from the first. "Matt, that's wonderful news!"

"I thought so, too, but I had to be sure two babies wasn't going to be too much for you."

"Matthew Eilers, have you ever known me to walk away from a challenge?"

"No," he admitted.

"I can do this and will do it, with a grateful heart. A year ago, I was alone. Now I'm blessed with a husband and two beautiful children."

"They're a handful. It's like having twins. I'll help in any way I can, but—"

"I love Hailey," Margaret insisted, and she did. In the beginning, she'd wondered how she'd feel about Sheryl's daughter, but soon realized that Hailey was her husband's daughter, too, and Margaret deeply loved Matt. Besides that, Hailey was simply Hailey. She was a person in her own right, an innocent child not to be held accountable for her parents' sins.

"Have I mentioned lately how much I love you?"

Margaret had to smile. Not a day passed that Matt didn't show his love for her in one way or another. A year earlier she'd vowed to love him, faults and all; she'd discovered that the alchemy of marriage had changed both of them, for the better.

Raising two children, less than three months apart in age, wasn't the way she'd expected to be introduced to motherhood, but she welcomed Hailey into her home and her heart.

"We can do this," Margaret assured him once more.

"I doubt there's anything we can't do," Matt said with a deep sigh.

"Together," Margaret added. She reached out her hand to Matt, who took it in his own, linking them.

Hand to hand.

Heart to heart.

Child to child.